RED RIVER

Forge Books by P. G. Nagle

Glorieta Pass
The Guns of Valverde
Galveston
Red River

RED
RIVER

P. G. Nagle

A TOM DOHERTY ASSOCIATES BOOK

NEW YORK

RED RIVER

Copyright © 2003 by P. G. Nagle

This book is printed on acid-free paper.

Maps by Chris Krohn

Edited by James Frenkel

A Forge Book
Published by Tom Doherty Associates, LLC
175 Fifth Avenue
New York, NY 10010

www.tor.com

Forge® is a registered trademark of Tom Doherty Associates, LLC.

Library of Congress Cataloging-in-Publication Data

Nagle, P. G.
    Red River / P. G. Nagle.—1st hardcover ed.
        p. cm.
    "A Tom Doherty Associates book."
    ISBN 0-765-30344-2
    1. Louisiana—History—Civil War, 1861-1865—Fiction.   2. Texas—History—Civil
War, 1861-1865—Fiction.   3. Galveston (Tex.)—Fiction.   I. Title.
PS3564.A354R43 2003
813'.54—dc21

                                                                    2003004832

First Edition: August 2003

Printed in the United States of America

0   9   8   7   6   5   4   3   2   1

In fond memory of
Joe Leeming

Acknowledgments

A great many people lent their advice, support, and expertise to the creation of this book. I would like to extend particular thanks to Dr. Glynne Couvillion, who allowed me access to the private letters of Captain F. O. Cornay, and gave me much insight into Creole culture. Thanks also to Morris Raphael for answering my questions about the Bayou Teche Campaign, as well as for his excellent book on the subject.

Grateful thanks go out to Nancy Varian Berberick, Doug Clark, Yvonne Coats, Edward T. Cotham, Jr., Ken and Marilyn Dusenberry, Sally Gwylan, Earl W. Hester, Bruce and Marsha Krohn, Chris Krohn, Alan Lattimore, Jane Lindskold, Louise Malone, Laura J. Mixon, James L. Moore, Scott Schermer, Joan Spicci, Rob Stauffer, and John Taylor. To my editor, James Frenkel, and my agent, Chris Lotts, thanks as well.

I received much kind assistance from Daniel Stoute at the Port Hudson State Historic Site and Iva Lee Printz at the Avoyelles Commission of Tourism. The Louisiana State Museum Historical Center provided access to its collection of F. O. Cornay's papers. The Louisiana State Penitentiary Museum was a rich source of information about the history of Angola and neighboring plantations.

Very special thanks to the providers of the following invaluable online resources:

Mrs. Mabel Battley and Professor Tom Klingler (Creole Wake Song)
http://www.tulane.edu/Tulane2.0/creole_wake.html

Cornell University's Making of America Project (Official Records of the War of the Rebellion)
http://library5.library.cornell.edu/moa/

NOAA Coast and Geodetic Survey Historic Map and Chart Collection (online access to historic maps and charts)
http://chartmaker.ncd.noaa.gov/csdl/map-coll.htm

8 ✦ ACKNOWLEDGMENTS

Thanks also to the Mansfield State Historic Site, the Patterson Visitor Center, the Artillery Company of New Mexico, the New Mexico Territorial Brass Band, the New Mexico Civil War Commemorative Congress, the various Louisianians who made two wandering New Mexicans welcome, and many others, especially the editors and authors of histories and diaries covering the war in Louisiana, without whose work the present volume would not have been possible.

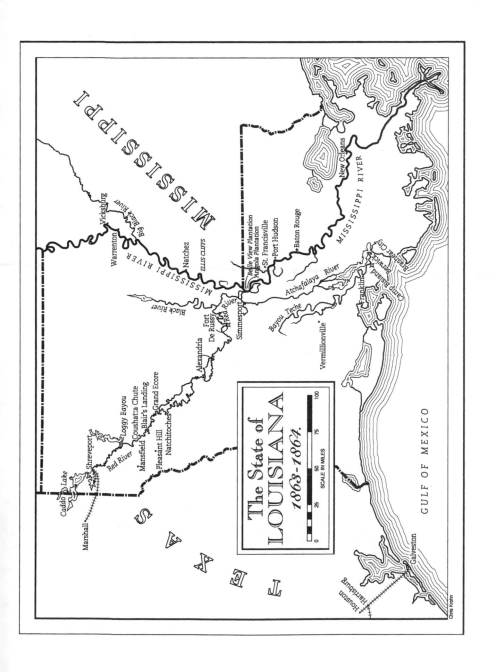

MISSISSIPPI

TEXAS

GULF OF MEXICO

Vicksburg
Warrenton
Big Black River
MISSISSIPPI RIVER
ELLIS CLIFFS
Natchez
Black River
Fort De Russy
Red River
Alexandria
Simmesport
Belle View Plantation
Angola Plantation
St. Francisville
Port Hudson
Baton Rouge
New Orleans
MISSISSIPPI RIVER
Atchafalaya River
Bayou Teche
Vermillionville
Franklin
Brashear City
Berwick
Camp Bisland
Loggy Eayou
Coushatta Chute
Blair's Landing
Grand Ecore
Mansfield
Pleasant Hill
Natchitoches
Red River
Shreveport
Caddo Lake
Marshall

Galveston
Houston
Harrisburg

The State of
LOUISIANA
1863–1864.

SCALE IN MILES

0   25   50   75   100

Chris Krohn

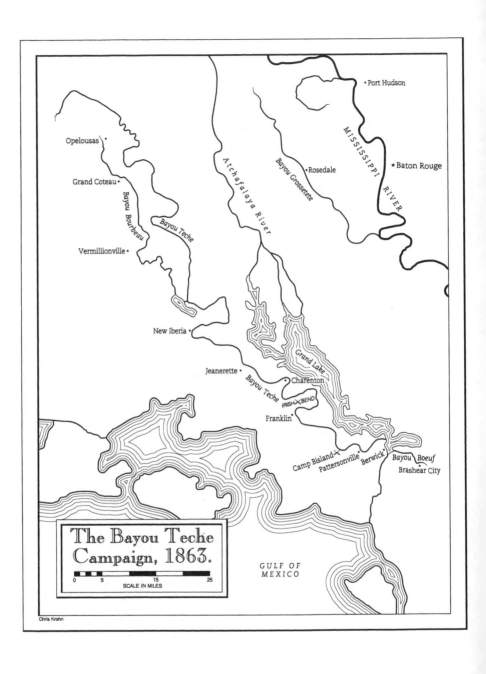

The Bayou Teche
Campaign, 1863.

0 · 5 · 15 · 25
SCALE IN MILES

Chris Krohn

• Port Hudson

MISSISSIPPI RIVER

Opelousas •

Grand Coteau •

Bayou Bourbeau

Bayou Teche

Vermillionville •

Atchafalaya River

Bayou Grossetete

• Rosedale

★ Baton Rouge

New Iberia •

Jeanerette •

Bayou Teche

Grand Lake

Charenton

IRISH BEND

Franklin •

Camp Bisland
Pattersonville •
Berwick •
Bayou Boeuf
Brashear City

GULF OF
MEXICO

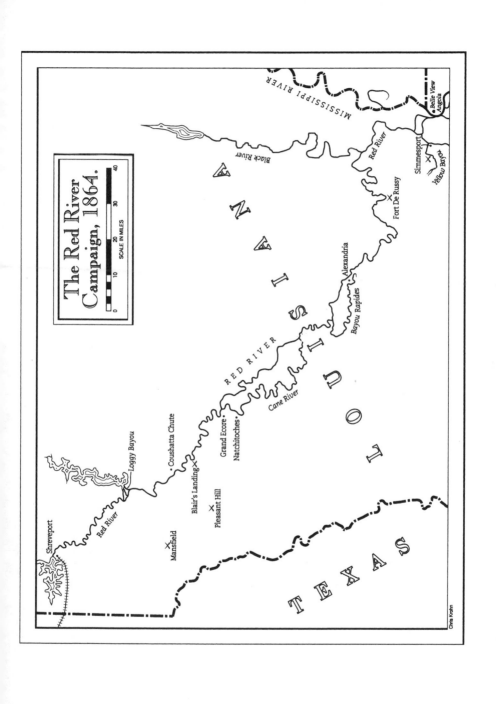

The Red River
Campaign, 1864.

SCALE IN MILES
0   10   20   30   40

LOUISIANA

TEXAS

MISSISSIPPI RIVER

Belle View
Angola

Red River

Simmesport
Yellow Bayou

Fort De Russy

Black River

Alexandria
Bayou Rapides

RED RIVER

Cane River

Grand Ecore
Natchitoches

Coushatta Chute

Loggy Bayou

Blair's Landing

Pleasant Hill

Mansfield

Red River

Shreveport

Chris Krohn

Whatever place my name is destined to occupy in the golden book of the Republic I expect to engrave it there with the point of my sword.

—Richard Taylor, Major-General, C.S.Army

1

. . . on the 1st instant I ordered Colonel Charles R. Ellet, in the
ram Queen of the West, *Captain Sutherland, commander, to*
run the batteries at Vicksburg and destroy the steamer City of
Vicksburg, *lying before that city.*
 —David D. Porter, Acting Rear-Admiral,
 U.S. Navy Commanding Mississippi Squadron

Nat Wheat glanced up from the cramped space between the wall and
the wheel in the *Queen of the West*'s pilot house, peering anxiously
toward the southeast where the sky over Vicksburg was lightening
with the coming dawn. He was sweating despite the February chill
that hung wisps of damp over the Mississippi River. Partly it was due
to the work, but mostly to the knowledge that this task had taken far
too long.

His gaze fell on Adams, the junior of his two mates, crouched in the
nearby corner waiting to assist. The negro was a good carpenter but
Nat was uncomfortable around him and just now he had no patience
to spare. "Step outside, Adams. There is not enough room here for
both of us."

Adams looked up, dark eyes meeting his gaze briefly, then without
a word picked up his toolbag and went out onto the hurricane deck.
Nat felt a stab of annoyance with himself—he had spoken rather
curtly, which Adams did not deserve—but there really was room only
for one to finish adjusting the wheel.

Nat was the *Queen*'s carpenter, and he and his mates had been
hard at work since 4:30 A.M. restoring the wheel to its proper place
after having moved it down behind the bulwarks the day before. Colonel Ellet had hoped the change would provide better protection for
the pilot, but when the ram had started forward toward Vicksburg in
the dark of early morning it had been discovered that the wheel

could no longer be handled with sufficient accuracy. Nat had tried to tell Ellet this would be the result, but the colonel had been adamant. Ellet was young—only nineteen, while Nat was twenty-four—and though his intentions were good he was sometimes impetuous and unwilling to listen to advice. It was a family trait, Nat thought with a grimace.

He checked the seating of the rudder cable on the pivot, then gripped one of the spindles and played the wheel back and forth a bit. Satisfied, he got to his feet and glanced toward the bench where the pilot, Mr. Long, sat reading a St. Louis newspaper. Nat took advantage of his inattention to grasp the wheel, enjoying for a moment the feel of the polished wooden spindles in his hands, the view of the river before him as he stood in the pilot's place, the place he wished was his. The growing dawn light to the east reminded him of his duty and he gave the wheel a final turn, then shouldered his toolbag and stepped out onto the deck. He noticed Adams sitting on one of the cotton bales that had recently been added to the hurricane deck to protect the pilot house and companionway from sharpshooters, but his attention was drawn to Colonel Ellet, who came quickly toward him.

"Well?" demanded the colonel.

Charles Rivers Ellet, trim and dashing in his high-collared coat and feathered hat, was the son of the man who had hired Nat. His father, Charles Ellet, had conceived the idea of a river fleet of rams, built it for the army, and led it to victory in the Battle of Memphis in the summer of 1862. This triumph, however, had cost him a shattered knee, and his refusal to have the leg amputated had cost him his life. Command of the ram fleet had fallen to his brother, Colonel Alfred Ellet, who on attaining a general's rank had in turn handed the fleet over to his nephew. All of the Ellets were contentious and stubborn, qualities that reminded Nat of his own father.

"Almost," he said to Ellet, and stepped to the side of the boat, looking down toward the main deck where his other mate, Sperry, was waiting. On Nat's signal Sperry went into the engine room to observe the movement of the rudder arm. Nat returned to the pilot house and slowly spun the wheel in either direction, judging the action to be right, then came out again.

Sperry reappeared on the deck below. "She's responding," he called. "She looks right!"

Nat turned to Ellet, who waited expectantly though he had surely heard Sperry's report. "She is ready, sir."

"Good." The colonel strode forward to the bow where Captain Sutherland stood gazing out over the river, and brought him back to the pilot house. Both went in, and a moment later Nat heard the bells for "ahead half," then the slow, muffled hiss and creak of the side-wheels beginning to turn. He felt the subtle shift underfoot as the *Queen* glided out into the current at last, heading for Vicksburg.

The Rebel city lay on the left bank just below a sharp bend in the Mississippi. Though the town was blocked from view by the wooded point around which the river turned, Nat knew there were batteries all over the cliffs poised to scour the river. At the feet of the bluffs lay the steamer *City of Vicksburg,* the *Queen's* first objective. Their orders were to ram the steamer at dock and sink her, then continue past the batteries to the lower Mississippi. Colonel Ellet's intent had been to run the batteries under cover of darkness, but moving the wheel had cost them that advantage. Nat wondered if the colonel had considered postponing the run. It appeared he had not.

Ellet came out of the pilot house and went down the companion-way. Nat should follow, he knew—an assembly had been ordered—but he wanted to stay a moment longer on deck. Glancing astern he gestured to Adams to precede him. When the negro had descended out of sight and he was alone on the deck, Nat looked up at the sun rising pale and yellow-gray through the mists that clung to the river.

The ram swept past the canal dug across the peninsula by General Grant's men in an attempt to bypass Vicksburg's batteries. It had never carried enough water for a fighting vessel, but Nat had tra-versed it in a skiff the previous summer to visit his brother Quincy, an acting master aboard the U.S.S. *Harriet Lane.* The *Lane* had then been stationed below Vicksburg while the *Queen* was above, but shortly afterward the *Lane* had departed for blockade duty in the Gulf. Today, the second of February, was one month and one day since the *Harriet Lane* had been captured at Galveston. Quincy was a prisoner of war.

Suddenly unable to bear the *Queen's* cautious progress, Nat turned and hurried down the companionway. The sound of Colonel Ellet's voice carried up from below. Nat followed it to the main deck, stop-ping on the bottom step and peering between the shoulders of the firemen and sailors crowding the deck.

First Master Thompson, one of the *Queen's* senior officers, glanced at him and smiled. "Hello, Chips," he whispered.

Nat smiled back, accepting the navy's customary nickname for the ship's carpenter. He joined Thompson and turned his attention to Colonel Ellet.

"We shall ram the *Vicksburg* under full steam," the colonel was saying. His gaze raked the assembly. "You are not to concern yourselves with rescuing her crew. When we strike her, you are all to shout out '*Harriet Lane*' as loud as you may."

A murmur of approval rumbled through the assembly. Nat's throat tightened as he thought of Quincy and the others who had served aboard the *Lane*. Her captain and executive officer had both been killed in the battle, and Quincy had been wounded.

"Sergeant Campbell?" Colonel Ellet continued.

"Here, sir," replied the gunner, raising a hand.

"You will shot the starboard gun with three turpentine balls."

"Yes, sir."

"Stand alert at your stations," said the colonel to the crew. "We shall be engaged within the hour. Dismissed."

Nat remained where he was as the men dispersed. Looking at Thompson, he raised an eyebrow. "The starboard gun?"

Thompson stepped nearer, speaking quietly. "Word from below is that the *Vicksburg* lies at the spot where the *Arkansas* was last summer."

Last summer, when the *Queen* had first run the Vicksburg batteries, and had struck at the Rebel ram *Arkansas* on her way down. Last summer, when old Colonel Ellet had lain dying, and when Nat had last seen his brother.

"We'll have to come at her across current, then?"

Thompson nodded. "And if it happens as it did before, we will be turned upstream."

Nat grimaced. Without the river's force behind her, the *Queen* had struck the *Arkansas* only a glancing blow instead of sinking her.

"That is why the colonel asked me to make the incendiary projectiles."

Thompson nodded, and Nat swallowed frustration. He wanted the *Vicksburg* destroyed, wanted it all out of proportion to his duty. He suspected Colonel Ellet felt the same.

The colonel, who had been speaking with the chief engineer, now came toward the companionway. Nat waited until he reached its foot, then said, "Thank you, sir—for the *Harriet Lane*."

The colonel paused and a sad, uncertain smile flicked across his face, revealing the youthfulness that his manner normally concealed.

"I cannot take credit for the idea," he said. "It was Admiral Porter's suggestion. A good one."

"Yes." Nat nodded, unable to say more.

"Be ready to make hasty repairs," Ellet added, resuming his air of authority. "We shall be under fire as soon as we round the point."

"Yes, sir." Nat resisted an impulse to apologize for the delay that had been none of his fault.

Colonel Ellet went up the companionway, and Thompson, nodding farewell to Nat, followed. Nat watched them go, then decided to visit the engine room to look at the rudder arm himself. Moving through the cramped space around the engines, he passed engineers and firemen all watchful and tense at their stations. He stayed long enough to assure himself that the rudder arm was indeed moving as it should, then returned to the companionway, uncomfortable in the closeness of the deck's confines. The *Queen*'s engines were on her deck, not down in her hold as on some of the gunboats. With her machinery protected only by the oaken bulwarks—not enough to stop a well-placed shot or shell from the heavy guns on shore—she was vulnerable. Damage to a drum or a pipe could fill the deck with steam, scalding anyone nearby in an eye's blink before it shot straight through the main cabin. Nat's stomach tensed at the thought. His Uncle Charlie had died as a result of such an accident.

Your uncle is dead, his father had said. Nat winced at the memory of the rage that had followed, and hastened up the companionway to the gun deck.

It was slightly safer here; should the boiler be hit he would have a few extra seconds before the steam reached him, possibly enough time to jump through a porthole and save himself. In theory. Not that it mattered. The Mississippi could kill just as thoroughly as an exploding boiler, and there were sharpshooters in the Rebel batteries if he happened not to drown.

Both 12-pounders already protruded forward out of the casemate, a crewman of each waiting with lanyard in hand. Sergeant Campbell glanced up as he arrived.

"Keep out of the way, Chips."

Nat nodded. "I will."

He took up a position by one of the narrow rectangular portholes on the starboard side, between the gun and the wheelhouse. Through the porthole he could see the sunlight beginning to touch the bare treetops on the peninsula. They were coming up fast on the point, the shore rushing past in a haze of gray leafless trees. A tingle crept over his scalp as the *Queen*'s bow passed the point and flew out into the swifter current at the river's narrowest part. A few seconds only of silence, then the discharge of a heavy gun sounded from the left bank. Nat's blood surged as the shot howled past overhead; high, but only just. The sound brought up memories of other fights, fire and blood, smoke and shouting. His pulse began to race.

The *Queen* proceeded around the point, crossing out into the current now, headed toward the left bank. Another gun fired from the shore batteries, and another—a muffled double thud as the round encountered compressed cotton, passed through, and fell spent on the deck above Nat's head. A breathless moment, a quick flurry of voices overhead; it was not a shell. Nat remained by the porthole, watching puffs of smoke rise from the shore, noting the location of the Confederate batteries. The port-side gun fired with a deafening thump, and its crew leapt to swab, load, and run out. It was mostly for show; what, after all, could two 12-pounders—one, at present, as the starboard gun had no target yet—do against the thirty or more guns on shore? It was defiance; it heartened the crew. The *Queen* was not a gunboat, she was a weapon in herself. Her bow, reinforced and filled solid with oak, could crush an enemy vessel's hull. Nat had seen it, had felt the shock underfoot, and wanted to feel it again.

He moved to the port side, keeping clear of the gun crew and covering his ears as he stood against the bulwark to stare out a porthole at the left bank. The first shore battery was behind them now, still pounding away. More guns awoke downstream. The pale cliffs lay in shadow, the sun just beginning to touch their edges with light. A puff of smoke from a clifftop; beyond it Nat spied a spire, then another. He was looking down the length of the city. His heart thumped as he strained to see the docks at the feet of the cliffs, but he could not make out the steamer.

A shell burst just off the port side, very nearly as loud as the 12-pounder's fire, making Nat flinch backward as fragments of iron ripped at the oak of the cabin. A flurry of general cursing gave way to cries of "There she lies!" Nat strained his eyes and found the dark shape of the *Vicksburg* by the shore, Rebel colors at her mast. The *Queen* was gathering speed, moving out into the main current, edging across the river as she made for the steamer. More guns fired; the 12-pounder answered, a single voice against dozens.

Nat found that he was clenching his teeth. With an effort he relaxed. He stared at the *Vicksburg* as if he could set her afire with his gaze, impatient for the attack.

The *Queen* angled across the current and seemed to bog, though her engines were driving her wheels as hard as they could. Rifle shots began to crack from the helpless Rebel boat; her steam was not up, she had no escape. Nat licked his lips, watching the span of water between the vessels shrink. The pilot was aiming just forward of the *Vicksburg*'s port wheelhouse, almost dead-on now; Nat could not have chosen a better spot himself. Despite past experience, he hoped and prayed that the blow would have enough force to crush her hull and sink her.

The rifle fire increased. The *Queen* slowed abruptly as she neared the shore, and the fast current caught her stern and began to swing it about, just as Colonel Ellet had expected. Nat looked over his shoulder, frowning in frustration. A horrific crash struck the bulwark ahead of him; splinters flew and a wave of sulphurous smoke enveloped him, then a mighty thud shook the deck. Turning, he saw the port gun dismounted, ruined, a man writhing beside it. A gaping hole in the bulwark revealed the *Vicksburg* mere yards away but at the wrong angle; the *Queen*'s bow was turned upstream, and struck with scarcely enough force to make Nat shift his balance. The steamer's hull gave, yes, and she heeled over toward her dock, but the damage would be minor. Nat glanced up at the starboard gun in time to see Sergeant Campbell give the lanyard a furious jerk. Fire belched from the muzzle; a dragon's breath playing over the *Vicksburg*.

"*Harriet Lane!*" cried Nat, rushing to the starboard side to watch the result of the incendiaries.

The gun crews took up the cry. "*Harriet Lane!*" they shouted again and again. Cheers filled the deck as flames leapt out aboard the steamer. The Rebel sharpshooters had stopped their popping and were scurrying about the steamer's deck.

"That's for you, Quincy," Nat murmured in the mayhem. He wondered if the *Queen* would come around again for another strike, to finish her off.

"Fire!" someone shrieked in panic.

Smoke began pouring in through the starboard portholes near the wheelhouse. Blinded and choking, Nat stumbled back, even as he realized the cotton on the deck above must have been set afire by the enemy's shell. More smoke came in from the shattered bulwarks forward; the cotton on the bow was alight as well, perhaps touched by the incendiary shells. The gun crews grabbed up their sponge buckets. Nat didn't stay to see more but ran aft to the companionway, clasping his toolbag.

The stairwell was filled with smoke. Nat held his breath, hand to the wall, gasping as he reached clear air on the upper deck. He glimpsed Thompson by the pilot house, heard shouts that he could not distinguish. Men were throwing buckets of water at the flaming cotton.

"No," cried Nat, coughing. "Cut 'em away!" He pulled his work knife out of his toolbag and attacked the ropes binding the bales by the starboard wheelhouse. A gust of smoke made him pause; he wiped the back of his hand across his streaming eyes and sawed on. Crewmen, river men, pulled their belt knives and joined him. A smoking bale tumbled over the side. The men cheered, then worked on.

Nat glanced up at the *Vicksburg*. The *Queen* was falling away from her, carried downstream by the current. The Rebel steamer's crew were dousing the fire. A wave of bitterness swept him as he saw she would survive, but at least they had struck a blow. He bent to the ropes, never looking up again, even as the Rebel batteries below Vicksburg took up their harassing fire.

Sunlight slanted through the gauze-curtained windows of the Capitol Hotel's breakfast parlor, accentuating the stark mourning clothes of Jamie Russell's two companions at table. He himself was in uniform— a Confederate artillery lieutenant's jacket and trousers that Mr. Lawford had insisted on buying for him, and which itched with new-wool stiffness. The cloth had come from the Huntsville penitentiary's mill, and the tailoring had been at the hands of the costly Houston expert who enjoyed Mr. Lawford's patronage.

Jamie glanced from his sister, Emma, to Mr. Lawford, who should have been their uncle and who had for months now behaved as though he were. Lawford's hair had been mostly black when they'd met last summer; now it was becoming a waving mane of silver, with only the side whiskers still dark. He had loved Aunt May with a silent passion, sheltered her from every breeze that threatened, spoiled her by catering to her extravagant whims, and failed to persuade her to marry him. If she had not fallen ill she might have yielded, but it was useless to ponder that now. She was gone, and having lost the object of his affections, Mr. Lawford had turned his lavish generosity upon her niece and nephew. Nothing would do for him but to whisk them away from battle-torn Galveston, lodge them in Houston's finest hotel, buy them their trappings of mourning and war, and hover protectively over them until Jamie, knowing Emma as he did, was silently impressed that she was able to refrain from shrieking at Mr. Lawford to leave her alone. The grief she had suffered over her fiancé's death last year had given her a new store of patience, perhaps, and all too clear an understanding of Mr. Lawford's pain.

Jamie looked at his sister, whose black bombazine gown was impeccably tailored, made by Aunt May's former dressmaker. She mourned as much for Martin as for May, though he had died nearly a year ago. Stephen Martin had been Jamie's captain, killed at Valverde, Jamie's first battle, far away in New Mexico. He swallowed at the memories—the horror of the carnage, of killing for the first time— and tried to shove them out of his thoughts.

Emma's dark hair was long enough now to be pulled back in smooth bands and pinned with a little jet comb that had been May's. She must have let Daisy dress it for her. Jamie knew his sister didn't care to be fussed about, but since inheriting May's two slaves she had tried to find things for them, Daisy in particular, to do.

She took a sip of coffee, then looked up at him. "Have you had any word about Dan?"

Jamie shook his head. "It's still too soon, I think." Their eldest brother's regiment, the 8th Texas Cavalry, better known as Terry's Rangers, had been engaged from the day after Christmas right through New Year's. While Jamie had been struggling against the Yankee navy in Galveston, Dan's regiment had spent a week of skirmishing in the rain culminating in two days of battle at Murfreesboro, Tennessee. Details of the battle were still filtering in—it was hard to communicate across the Mississippi—and though until today Jamie had been on detached duty at District Headquarters where the news would arrive first, he had not heard anything about the Rangers.

Emma set down her cup. "At least Matt bothered to let us know he wasn't killed at Fredericksburg. I swear it's the only letter we had from him all year."

No, Jamie thought, he also wrote to inform us he hadn't been killed at Sharpsburg, but as that was hardly a comforting reflection he kept it to himself. Emma also lapsed into silence. She had been rather quiet since New Year's. Jamie's heart inevitably quickened at the thought of the battle at Galveston—fresher in his memory than Valverde—and he sipped his own coffee to settle himself down. He could readily recall the huge guns on the Yankee ships hurling destruction into the city, the crackle of musketry around the wharf, the dead floating in the bay. It had been the worst of nights for Emma, too, caught in a city under bombardment while Aunt May lay dying after months of illness. Inside she grieved, Jamie knew, though she was tough as ever under the city-polish her visit with May had laid on her. In that respect, as in many others, she was May's opposite. May's grieving would have been an ecstacy of woe, with many vases of drooping white flowers and yard upon yard of black crape. Instead, Emma and Mr. Lawford had agreed upon a very simple funeral, followed by a quiet reception for May's many friends.

The friends had gone home days ago, May's affairs had been brought into order by Mr. Lawford, and Emma could at last return home to comfort Momma in her grief over the loss of her sister and her worry over Daniel's fate. Momma had not been able to face the journey to Houston, had dreaded being separated from Gabe, her youngest and only son still at home. Emma had stood in her place at the funeral, chief mourner by way of blood, though it was Mr. Lawford who was most deeply wounded by the loss.

Jamie finished the coffee in his cup—lukewarm, and far better than he'd ever get on campaign. Restoring cup to saucer with a small, strangely final click, he said, "I ought to be on my way. I have been absent from the battery far too long."

A shadow of disappointment crossed Emma's face, then she put on a smile. "Well, don't work Cocoa too hard. She's still thin."

Jamie smiled back. "I won't," he said. Emma couldn't help thinking like a rancher. Once she was home and back at work, she would be all right.

With a slowness born of reluctance to leave, he got to his feet, eyes straying to the luxuries of carpet, chandeliers, fine china and silver that he had never known before meeting May and Mr. Lawford. He would not see such comforts again for months, if ever. His place was in the field, and he found he was glad to be going back, though a certain dread attached to the prospect of another campaign.

Emma rose to give him a fierce hug, and Mr. Lawford stood up as well. Jamie shook the hand he offered.

"Thank you for escorting Emma home."

Mr. Lawford dismissed it with a shrug. "I was already going that way. I have some business to transact in Brownsville on behalf of the Hawklands."

Jamie tensed at the mention of the name, remembering with a start the last occasion on which he had seen the bewitching Mrs. Hawkland. It had been in this very hotel. A rush of memories, of the sort he could never discuss with his sister or even with Mr. Lawford, brought heat into his face. He glanced at the hotel's finery again, feeling suddenly awkward and out of place.

"You take care of yourself, son," said Mr. Lawford.

"Yes, do," Emma added briskly, "and hurry home."

Jamic couldn't agree to that. Who knew when he might get back to San Antonio? Maybe the next battle would be his last.

"I will write when I get to Louisiana." He caught Emma in one more hug, then let her go and left without looking back.

2

... the Red River ... flows southeast to the Mississippi through a broad, fertile valley, then occupied by a population of slave-owners engaged in the culture of cotton.
— Richard Taylor, Major-General, C.S. Army

Marie sensed daylight falling across her face and frowned, taking refuge in her feather pillow. She could not breathe through it, though, and she knew she must rise. Indulging in a sigh, she turned her head and opened her eyes.

"Lucinde?"

Her woman came forward from the tall French doors overlooking the gallery, where she had just pulled back the drapes. Winter sunlight, though feeble, assailed Marie's eyes and she blinked until Lucinde's form blocked it.

"Oui, Madame," said the slave in her deep, gentle voice. "Forgive my waking you. Monsieur is ready to leave."

Marie pulled herself up against the bank of pillows. "Yes, all right. Do you have my tea?"

Lucinde placed the delicate china cup and saucer into her hands almost as she asked. Marie sat forward while the slave adjusted the pillows for her comfort, and took the tea in small sips. She disliked the taste of the cannabis, but it had so reduced her sickness that she drank it faithfully every morning before leaving her bed, and sometimes in the evening if she felt unwell. She devoutly hoped that Dr. Montreuil was right, and that the sickness would soon diminish. It had been nearly four months, after all, though by Dr. Montreuil's reckoning it was closer to three. He, of course, did not know what Marie knew, and she would make certain it remained so.

"Ugh. No more."

Lucinde's hands—gentle, mahogany hands that had tended her all her life—reached for the cup, and had set it down and picked up her dressing gown by the time Marie threw aside the bedclothes and stepped into her slippers. Though she did not want to miss her husband's departure, she knew that to hurry would only make her nauseated, so she walked slowly to her dressing table. She sat on the brocade-cushioned stool and closed her eyes while Lucinde brushed out her hair. Always a comfort, Lucinde. She was the first slave Marie had ever owned, given to her when she was still in her cradle. There had never been a time when Lucinde's warm eyes and sweet voice had not been there to soothe her. Her smile, elusive and mysterious, was one of Marie's earliest memories.

"Will it rain today, Lucinde?"

"Damien says no. No rain all week."

"Good."

Clear weather would make her husband's journey easier. He was taking a hundred slaves to Dr. Montreuil's plantation on the Atchafalaya to assist with the construction of a new fort there, after which he would continue on to Houston to arrange for the sale of some cotton. Ordinarily Marie would have gone along, for she loved to travel, but Theodore was anxious for her health, and she had resigned herself to remaining at Rosehall on this occasion.

Lucinde finished pinning her hair and went to the wardrobe. Marie leaned toward her mirror and smoothed her fingertips across her forehead. No, it was not a line, only a shadow. She had lost none of her beauty as yet. How easy it was to worry over such trifles.

"Merci," she said as Lucinde draped a heavy cashmere shawl over her shoulders. The dark red, rust, and green paisley made her dressing gown of pale silk and lace seem ethereal. A glance at the full-length mirrors on the wardrobe doors—mirrors backed with diamond dust that glistened softly in the morning light—satisfied her that she looked well.

"I will be back up shortly to dress."

"Oui, Madame."

Lucinde opened the door for her. Marie smiled her thanks, and drawing the shawl close about her, crossed to the stairs. She descended carefully, a hand to the bannister, more because she knew her husband would be upset if she did not use it than out of any need. He was maniacally protective of her since he had learned of her delicate condition. Marie found this amusing but forbore to laugh at him. She knew how much this child meant to him; of course she knew. She had gone to great lengths to bear a child for him, precisely because she knew how ardently he desired it.

"God let it be a son and heir," she whispered as she did each morning.

The high-ceilinged hall was empty and a little chilly, with hazy sunlight spilling from the eastern windows at the back of the house onto the parquetry medallion of roses in the center of the floor. Marie hurried to the parlor and found Theodore standing by the front windows with a coffee cup in one hand, staring at some papers in the other, and tapping a booted toe against the thick Chinese carpet. She paused in the door, smiling as she gazed at her husband, who was possibly the richest man in Louisiana, certainly the richest in the county. Theodore Hawkland was kindness itself and always a gentleman, but he could also be ruthless in acquiring what he desired. It was what had made him choose to woo a Creole lady in the face of her family's disapproval, and it was what had fascinated her enough to leave their world in order to become his wife.

He looked up and saw her, his face lighting with a smile. "There you are, my blossom!"

She came toward him, took his cup away and put it on the sofa table, then nestled into his arm and laid her head on his shoulder. "Good morning, cher. I have not delayed your departure, I hope? I am sorry to have overslept."

"Nonsense. You need your rest."

The papers crackled as he embraced her. Marie looked up into his face, searching every familiar line. He was hearty, though many years her senior, and had the same fine shock of silver hair he had worn on their wedding day. Lately he tended to frown more. It was the war, she supposed. It was enough to wear any man down. She reached a hand up to stroke his cheek, wishing she could soothe away his worries.

Footsteps and the voice of the butler in the hall caused them to part. Marie moved to the sofa and sat down, reaching for the coffeepot, then looked up as Alphonse came to the door.

"Dr. Montreuil," the aged negro intoned with deep formality. He glanced at Marie, who nodded. The doctor was a friend, and had seen her in her dressing gown before. Alphonse ushered the visitor into the parlor.

Dr. Montreuil lived with his elderly mother on a plantation on the upper Atchafalaya, west of the Mississippi and some ten miles away. He was a young man, rather gaunt, with pale skin, black hair, and brooding dark eyes. He always dressed, rather dramatically, in ascetic Parisian black. Marie gave him a friendly nod.

"A cup of coffee, Doctor?"

"No thank you, Madame, and I recommend that you not drink any until you have breakfasted."

Marie took a triangle of toast from the plate on the coffee tray and nipped off a corner. "There. Breakfast."

She set the toast on her saucer and sipped her coffee, then added cream to the dark, rich brew. Theodore detested chicory and spared no expense to keep pure Brazilian coffee in the house. Marie had become accustomed to it, though she had grown up with chicory blend and did not mind its gentler flavor.

The doctor moved to the fireplace and poked at the coals, sending up a flurry of sparks. Theodore watched him, frowning slightly. "There is no harm in it, surely? She has never had much appetite for breakfast."

The doctor replaced the poker and stood up, brushing the knees of his black trousers. "Madame will find that her appetites are changing."

"Now, don't be cross," Marie said. "I have already drunk your excellent tea, and I will have only one cup of coffee." She bestowed a coaxing smile upon the doctor. Its immediate effect was evident in the flash of his eyes, quickly hidden. The doctor became interested in a porcelain shepherdess on the mantel; Marie busied herself with adding a lump of sugar to her cup.

Dr. Montreuil was so excitable; it would not do to appear too warm toward him. She enjoyed his admiration, certainly, but she was too fair-minded to wish to cause him pain. Also, he was useful to her, so she took care not to torment him. If he chose to torment himself, that was his own concern.

Theodore sat beside her and held out his cup to be filled. "You will heed the doctor's advice while I am gone, my love?"

"Of course, cher. Never fear, I shall be very good."

"I almost wish you had remained in New Orleans."

Marie set down the pot and retrieved her own cup. "It is overrun with Yankees. I will be much more at peace here."

"There are Yankees on the river as well."

"Yes, but they think of us as friends." Marie laid her hand over his. "You have taken care that they should, and so have I. I have our permit to show them. Perhaps I will even sell them some cotton."

He smiled. "We have a better use for the cotton."

"I know. May God prosper you on this journey, and bring you home safe."

His eyes softened as he gazed at her. Marie returned his smile, hoping to reassure him.

Dr. Montreuil cleared his throat and stepped toward the door. "I believe I will go down to the landing."

"I will be along shortly." Theodore raised his cup with an air of unconcern, but as soon as the doctor was gone he set it down, took Marie's cup away, and gathered her hands into his.

"Take care of yourself while I am gone."

"I will. Never fear, Dr. Montreuil will fuss over me as much as you could wish." Her smile did not erase the concern on his face, so she kissed him. "Hurry back to me," she whispered into his ear.

His grasp on her hands tightened. "I shall. And with luck, I shall not have to leave again for some time."

"Yes." She pulled away enough to smile up at him. "I hope Mr. Lawford will have completed the arrangements for our transaction. Please give him my best regards."

Mr. Lawford, who owned a carrier company and shares in several railroads, had labored for many weeks to arrange a transaction that would not only bring the Hawklands a large sum of money, but would secure arms for Confederate troops. If the deal succeeded, the cotton now lying baled at Belle View, Angola, and the Hawklands' other plantations would soon be on its way to Mexico and thence to France.

The mantel clock began to chime. Theodore glanced at it, looking annoyed. "I must go."

"I will see you to the door."

Alphonse stood waiting to open the front doors for his master. His presence precluded embraces, so Theodore merely kissed Marie's hands and pulled her shawl closer about her shoulders. "Go and dress, my love. You mustn't catch cold."

She stood on tiptoe to kiss his cheek. Alphonse, who had served her husband since Theodore's boyhood, was suitably blind and deaf to this display. He remained stone still, his gaze fixed toward some indeterminate point on the ceiling.

Marie stepped back, and as Theodore strode away the butler closed the doors, shutting out the chill breeze. She did not try to catch his eye, knowing that he felt it wrong to express any interest in the family's concerns. She also knew that he cared about them, however stiffly he behaved.

She hurried upstairs and crossed the upper hall to the windows overlooking the upstairs gallery. Her husband appeared from beneath the white railing, striding down the long avenue of crushed shell lined with bare rosebushes. Dr. Montreuil's tall, black-clad form was visible at the landing where the small steamer waited. The Mississippi flowed along, gray on this dull morning, with the brownish swirl of the Red River joining it from the far shore.

Marie crossed herself, praying for her husband's safety and success as she watched him board the boat. The steamer seemed to drift for a moment, then turned its nose upstream, its wheel churning the water as it fought its way across the Mississippi's current toward the mouth of the Red on its way to the Atchafalaya. She watched until it passed out of view, hidden by bare-branched trees. Only then did she let fall the gauze drapery, and slowly return to her bedchamber to dress.

Nat stepped back to run a critical glance over the repairs he and his mates had just completed, covering a large hole that a Rebel shell had made in the wall of the main cabin. It was not pretty, but it was sound.

The carpenters had worked long hours in the last couple of days and were still not finished with repairs. The Vicksburg guns had holed the *Queen*'s hull twice, but above the waterline, so those had been fairly easy to fix. A larger mess had been made by several rounds that had smashed into the main cabin. In all, the *Queen* had been struck twelve times as she ran the batteries. By good fortune, none of the damage was drastic.

"Time for a break," Nat said, starting toward the companionway.

Sperry needed no further invitation to follow him up to the hurricane deck. Nat was slightly annoyed that Adams came up as well, but he resolved to ignore the negro. He had become resigned to Adams, though he disliked him as he had the black laborers in his father's shipyard.

Adams, whose full name was George Washington Adams, had proved himself a first rate carpenter, and Nat had grudgingly accepted him as junior mate. It was an exalted position for a negro, but Nat had to admit he had earned it. He would not want to have had only Sperry's help, though privately he would have been glad to replace Adams with a white man. Recruits were too hard to come by, however; there were not even enough unskilled negroes to fill up a boat's crew, let alone white men. It was the same on every vessel on the river.

Coming out onto the deck, Nat paused to suck in a breath of bracing air. He was always more comfortable on deck than within the gunboat's bulkheads, and took every opportunity to go outside and look at his surroundings. Gazing at the river eased his soul, though it also reminded him that he had settled for being merely a carpenter. At the time, it had seemed the best way out of Cincinnati.

The *Queen* had been a towboat before the war, and Colonel Charles Ellet had commissioned her conversion to a ram in the shipyard owned by Nat's father, Nathaniel Wheat, Sr. Nat had worked on the project and by the time it was finished he had accepted Ellet's invitation to join the *Queen*'s crew, much to his father's displeasure. His choice had been influenced by his brother's promising navy career, his liking for Colonel Ellet, and his eagerness to escape the frustrations associated with being in his father's employ. He had not dared to ask Ellet to consider him as a pilot, for his only experience was one summer spent cubbing with Uncle Charlie on the steamer *Columbine,* and he feared Ellet would turn him down and leave him to rot in Wheat's Shipyard. His desire to get away from home had seemed more important then, but in the past year and a half he had become increasingly dissatisfied with his position. A pilot was what he wanted to be; what he had wanted for years. It was also the one career his father had expressly forbidden him to pursue.

The *Queen* glided down the Mississippi, winter's chill lending a sharpness to the breeze created by her motion. Nat glanced over his shoulder and saw that Sperry had made himself comfortable on the cotton-bale wall. A large gap remained on the starboard side where the fire had been, but the rest of the bales were still in place, a bit scorched here and there. Nat sat on one, stretching stiff muscles.

"Where are we, d'you think?" Sperry asked.

Nat peered at the shore, trying to spot a mark he recognized, but he had never learned the river below Natchez, and even that had been years ago. "Past the Red, anyway. Look at the water."

"Pshaw. How can you tell?"

"Don't you see the red tinge?"

Sperry shook his head. "Only in your eyes, friend."

"We are below the Red," Adams said from behind them.

Nat glanced up at the negro, who had seated himself a short distance away, then at Sperry, who turned a grimace into a sort of smile and leaned back on his elbows, staring at the sky. It would have been more companionable with only the two of them, Nat thought briefly, but he set the thought aside.

Adams nodded his head toward a small wharf on the left bank. "That there is Ratcliff Landing."

Nat took note of the mark, memorizing the landing's appearance, then looked at Adams. "You know these parts?"

Adams answered in a lowered voice. "Yes, sir. I was bred up at Angola Plantation, and worked at Belle View. My daddy bought his way free when I was ten and worked at Cairo until he could buy all the rest of us."

Adams seemed lost in thought, staring at the eastern shore. Nat followed his gaze and saw cotton fields beyond the fringe of trees, just visible from his vantage point on the hurricane deck; on a lower deck the shore would have hidden them from view. The low, scrubby brown bushes were mostly bare, but tufts of white clung here and there like errant snowflakes. There were no workers in sight.

"Hello, we've got company!" Sperry sat up.

Nat looked downstream and quickly got to his feet. A sidewheeler, about half the *Queen*'s size, was coming upriver toward them. As he traded a glance with Sperry she blew two short blasts on her whistle, signaling the *Queen* that she wished to pass her on the starboard side.

"She thinks we're Confederate," Nat said.

"She'll soon know better!"

Colonel Ellet came up the stairs, drawn no doubt by the sound of the whistle. He spared no more than a glance for the carpenters and strode to the pilot house. Nat heard the hiss of the wheels picking up speed and felt a surge as the *Queen* moved to intercept the other vessel. A moment later the steamer began to turn as well—toward the western shore. She had seen the *Queen*'s standard, perhaps, or was merely suspicious.

Sperry frowned. "She'll ground before we get to her."

Nat nodded agreement. He could now see the steamer's name— *A. W. Baker*—painted on her wheelhouse. He could also see a crowd on her hurricane deck. Taking out his pocket spyglass, he trained it on the *Baker* and saw a cluster of men, many in Confederate uniform, and a few ushering well-dressed women below.

"Ladies aboard her!" Nat passed the spyglass to Sperry.

"I don't see them."

"They've gone belowdecks. There, she's grounded!"

At first he thought the shock of running aground had knocked some of the soldiers from the bow. Men continued to fall into the water, though, swimming madly for the shore, scrambling up the swampy, overgrown bank even as the *Queen* bore down upon her captive. Nat reclaimed his glass and peered at the escaping men. They were Confederate army officers, he concluded, from the style and quality of their uniforms. In the few minutes it took the *Queen* to reach the *Baker* he counted more than two dozen who took to the water to escape capture. One was swept away downriver; Nat lost sight of him still struggling toward the shore.

A runner hastened below from the pilot house, and by the time the *Queen* had drawn alongside her prize a guard detail stood on the main deck, ready to board the captured vessel. Nat and the others watched them disappear into the *Baker*'s cabin. The official surrender would take place out of view.

Sperry stretched. "Well, that was amusing."

Nat picked up his toolbag. "Back to work, I suppose."

A splutter of shouting from the pilot house stayed them; Nat looked upriver and spied another steamer descending. This boat was larger than the *Baker* and waddled low in the river as if heavy laden.

Sperry swore in surprise. "Where did she spring from?"

"Must have come down the Red. We'd have seen her otherwise."

Nat shouldered his tools but stood watching as the *Queen* quickly disengaged from the *Baker* and turned upriver. He could not resist moving forward, though he took care to stay out of the way of the officers and runners who now came and went in a steady stream on the companionway. Between the funnels and the pilot house a crowd had collected into which he eased himself in time to see the bow gun fired in warning to the Rebel ship. She struck her colors at once, prompting a cheer aboard the *Queen*.

Sperry crowded up beside him. "Two prizes within an hour! Maybe we will get some decent prize money, eh?"

"How much?"

Nat turned to look at Adams, who had come up behind them. The negro's eyes were intensely bright; he seemed anxious.

"That depends on their cargo, and their condemned value," Nat told him. "Your share could be as little as twenty dollars, perhaps, or as much as two hundred or more. That is only a guess, of course."

Adams looked slightly disappointed, but nodded as he gazed at the captured vessels. Nat watched him, wondering why prize money mattered so much to a former slave who was earning a better salary than most men of his color.

Marie's solitary luncheon was interrupted by a commotion in the hall. Alphonse, glaring with indignation, stood in the dining room door and prevented Peter Shelton, the head overseer of the Hawklands' plantations, from entering. Marie looked up, somewhat offended, but also curious. Usually Mr. Shelton had the grace not to intrude upon her privacy, and came to Rosehall only when summoned by Theodore.

Shelton, a full head taller than the butler, his hair presently in disarray from the removal of his broad-brimmed hat, called past Alphonse, "Ma'am, I have to talk to you now!"

Marie finished sipping her broth and set down her spoon. "Let him in, Alphonse."

With displeasure marked by the rigidity of his jaw, Alphonse yielded the doorway. Mr. Shelton strode in without ceremony.

"There's a Yankee gunboat coming in at Belle View Landing."

"What? Where did it come from?" Marie put her napkin down beside her plate and stood up.

"From downriver. There are two steamers with it."

Marie hurried out to the hall and the windows that flanked the front door. Mr. Shelton followed and pulled back the drapes from one, giving her a view of the landing. There was indeed a large boat making its way slowly toward the shore, cotton bales lashed around its upper deck, the black snouts of two cannons protruding from rectangular portholes and another cannon on the prow, with a group of men standing by to fire it. Marie's glance darted to the two smaller vessels behind; neither was a military craft, and she saw with relief that neither was the boat her husband had taken. Indeed, she recognized them even before she could make out the names blazoned on their wheelhouses; they were the *A. W. Baker* and the *Moro*. She had seen both many times, carrying supplies from the Red River down to the troops holding Port Hudson. A Yankee flag now flew from the *Baker*'s stern. Marie frowned.

"Mr. Shelton, please tell the grooms to bring out the sulky. I am going down to speak with them."

Shelton looked at her sidelong. "The colonel wouldn't want—"

"Colonel Hawkland is not here. You may saddle a horse and escort me, but have that sulky to the door in five minutes, if you please." Marie turned without waiting for an answer and hastened upstairs for her cloak. She could not refrain from looking out her bedchamber's window at the three vessels. The big Yankee boat was no longer moving; it was too large to come to the landing, and was preparing to put a small boat into the water. The second steamer was approaching the shore as Lucinde came in.

"Lucinde, my cloak. Hurry, please."

Marie glanced at herself in the wardrobe mirrors as she pulled on a pair of kid driving gloves. The dull-green day dress she had on was not what she would have chosen to wear to greet visitors, but there was no time to change. Lucinde put her black velvet cloak about her shoulders and tucked her loose curls into a lacy cap, which she covered with a stylish black straw bonnet. Marie stayed only to let Lucinde tie the ribbons beneath her chin, then hurried downstairs.

The sulky was at the door with Old William, the most elderly horse on Belle View, between the shafts and the nearly equally elderly head groom on the tiny seat. Marie pressed her lips together but did not comment. Mr. Shelton waited beside the light vehicle, astride a chestnut gelding that stamped about restlessly. Marie got into the sulky, took up the reins and the long-tailed driving whip, and glanced at the boy standing by Old William's head.

"Let him go."

It took a snap of the whip over Old William's ears to wake him up, and another to move him to a trot. The sulky's wheels hissed over its white surface as she drove the half-mile sweep down to the river landing.

Marie could not help being happy to have visitors, *any* visitors. She had been out of the house very little in the past weeks, only for walks when the weather was pleasant. The breeze in her face, while a bit sharp, was refreshing, and the prospect of meeting even Yankee strangers was exhilarating. She slowed Old William to a walk to make the turn onto the levee road, and took the opportunity to speak to the overseer, who had kept as close to the sulky as the chestnut's temper would allow.

"Remember, Mr. Shelton. We want them to think of us as friends."

Shelton grunted. Ignoring his rudeness, Marie returned her attention to the landing where the second steamer, the smallest of the three vessels, had lowered its stage to the small dock. The little boat from the Yankee gunboat had launched, its crew laboring against the current as it made for the landing. Marie moved to descend.

"Wait, ma'am! Let me help you." Shelton dismounted and hastened to the sulky with the chestnut's reins in hand.

"Don't let that chestnut near William," she said sharply. "The creature likes to bite." She stowed the whip and allowed Shelton to help her out of the sulky. He looked annoyed, as if he disliked being reminded that she knew every horse on Belle View as well as he did.

The steamer was letting off passengers. Marie was surprised to see a number of ladies among them, looking annoyed as Yankee officers escorted them ashore.

"Good afternoon," she said. "What brings you to Belle View?"

The ladies all began speaking at once, but ceased as a plump, brisk woman stepped forward. "Our boat was captured, as you see. The Yankees are taking it up north, and since we do not care to go to Vicksburg, we asked to be set ashore here."

"Gracious," Marie said, glancing at each lady's face in turn. She did not wish to say more before the Yankees.

"We apologize for trespassing, ma'am," the lady continued. "We hope you will allow us to wait here until we can get passage back to our homes. I am Mrs. Captain Farrell."

"I am Mrs. Hawkland. I am afraid my husband is away, but you are welcome to wait here, of course." She included the civilian gentlemen who had disembarked in her welcome; they made slight bows of acknowledgment.

"Thank you kindly, ma'am," said Mrs. Farrell. The other ladies nodded and one shyly curtsied.

Marie turned and saw the overseer nearby, holding the gelding's reins. "Mr. Shelton, will you escort these ladies and gentlemen to the house, and ask Alphonse to serve them coffee? I will return presently."

Mr. Shelton's eyes narrowed slightly, but he made no objection. "Follow me." He turned and started up the drive.

Marie wondered briefly whether she should have sent for the carriage. It would have taken time, however, and more than one trip to drive them all to the house. Mrs. Farrell seemed equal to the walk, setting a brisk pace for the others. Marie watched them for a moment, the ladies in their hoops treading the great, white arc of the drive, the gentlemen offering their arms where their support might be welcome, altogether looking like guests coming to Rosehall for a party. It was some time since any sort of festivity had been held there, she thought wistfully. She was grateful for Mrs. Farrell's intrepidity, for she wanted to speak to the Yankees without the Southerners present.

By now a few men who looked rather less gentlemanly had also come off the boat. Marie sent them in pursuit of the others, recommending them to speak to Mr. Shelton. She glanced at the Yankees who had put them ashore. Only one officer remained overseeing the unloading of the civilians' luggage. It was the gunboat's launch, then, that bore the Yankee's representative. She stepped up to the end of the dock to await its arrival, drawing her cloak close against the river's chill.

3

We captured on her 5 captains, 2 lieutenants, and a number
of civilians, among them 7 or 8 ladies.... On reaching Red
River I stopped at a plantation to put ashore the ladies, who
did not wish to go any farther.
—Charles Rivers Ellet, Colonel, Commanding Ram Fleet

"That's her," Nat murmured, looking through his spyglass at the
woman standing on the landing. "It has to be."

"Eh?" Sperry asked him, blowing sawdust off a plug he was filing.

"Nothing." Nat put his glass in his pocket and reached for another
plug. Having gone back to work once all the excitement of capturing
two Rebel boats was over, they had finished repairing the major damage and were now filling in the holes made by rifle fire from the *Vicks-*
burg's sharpshooters. He glanced at the negro. "Adams, you're from
hereabouts, you said."

"That's right." Adams kept working.

"What house is that?"

Adams looked at him, then glanced out the porthole in a way that
suggested he hardly needed to confirm their location. "Rosehall," he
said. "Belle View Plantation. Colonel Hawkland's house."

Rosehall. Yes, that had been the name. Nat glanced out again at the
mansion with its huge white pillars and the long, wide drive that
Quincy had described in his letter. Quincy had been here last summer, and had written that it was the most elegant house he had ever
entered. Thanks to him, Nat knew that Rosehall's owner seemed
friendly and loyal, that the house was furnished without any regard to
expense, and that the front parlor boasted a full-length portrait of the
mistress of the house and all of Colonel Hawkland's plantations, the
lady Nat believed now stood at the dock awaiting Colonel Ellet's boat.

How he wished he were in that boat! He would gladly have pulled an oar for a chance at hearing their conversation. He was curious to make Mrs. Hawkland's acquaintance, but as it was unlikely that he would have any business ashore at Belle View, he resigned himself to glancing out of the porthole now and then and wondering what Colonel Ellet was saying to the lady of Rosehall.

"I sincerely regret the necessity of inconveniencing you, madam. Please extend my apologies to your husband when he returns."

Marie gazed at the young man before her, hoping her surprise did not show in her face. He had introduced himself as Colonel Ellet, and every Yankee present showed him unwavering deference. She smiled at him, watchful for his reaction.

"Thank you for explaining the situation, Colonel. I do not mind sheltering these people for a short while. Indeed, I am glad to know you are patrolling our river. But when did you come down? We knew nothing of your presence until now."

"We passed down quite early this morning. No doubt your household was asleep."

"No doubt," she agreed, thinking that in future the household would be more watchful. She drew a breath, making sure to keep her voice steady. "Has Vicksburg fallen, then?"

Colonel Ellet's gaze, already rather serious for a man so young, sharpened. "No. We succeeded in passing the batteries, however, and will hope for a speedy victory there."

Marie smiled. "And a return to commerce, I hope."

Colonel Ellet continued to gaze at her, his expression now thoughtful. Marie kept her face schooled into open pleasantness. If she could captivate him, so much the better. He was a handsome boy, with his arched brow and carefully trimmed mustache—paler than his hair and not yet filled in, but a passable mark of manhood. He was younger than she (he could be no more than twenty, and she would soon be twenty-five) but to gain his admiration could do no harm, and might even be useful.

"Have you cotton awaiting sale, ma'am?" he finally asked.

"Yes, indeed." Marie put as much enthusiasm as she could into her voice. "Would you like to purchase some? We have a permit from General Butler—"

"Not on this trip, I fear," Ellet said. "Perhaps we will send someone down from St. Louis to treat with you."

"He will be most welcome." She glanced down at her tightly

clasped hands and forced herself to relax them. "One mustn't complain, of course, but—oh, I shall be glad when this conflict is ended!"

"Indeed. Tell me, Mrs. Hawkland, do you see many vessels coming and going from the Old River?" He nodded toward the mouth of the Red on the far shore.

"Yes, quite often," she replied, feeling a little flutter at the memory of bidding Theodore farewell. "Sometimes they use our landing without even asking leave."

He met her gaze, then, and his own eyes seemed alight with righteousness. "I trust you will soon be free from such annoyance," he said.

She forced herself to smile yet more warmly. "Thank you, Colonel. I trust you are right."

An explosion rent the quiet air, making Marie start. She looked toward the gunboat, from which a puff of smoke rose.

"Do not be alarmed, ma'am," the young colonel hastened to say. "It is only a signal." He turned toward the gunboat, watching a man who had come out on the upper deck and was waving a flag. The message, whatever it was, was unnecessary; Marie could see smoke from beyond Turnbull's Island. A steamer was descending from the Red.

It was not Theodore's boat. She knew it could not be; he had gone down the Atchafalaya, yet still her pulse quickened.

"I must go," Colonel Ellet said, looking at her with earnest eyes. "Please return to your home at once, Mrs. Hawkland."

Marie gave him a tremulous smile that she had no need of feigning, and watched him hurry back to his boat. The gunboat was bringing up its steam, and the crew of the launch strained to row their colonel back to his vessel. Marie wanted to keep watching but she knew every man of her acquaintance, present or not, Yankee or Southron, would object. She hastened to the sulky and found that Old William appeared to have gone to sleep. She woke him and drove smartly to the house, slowing only to pass her unexpected guests. At the door the groom took charge of Old William and led him away.

Marie turned and saw that the new boat was now visible, smaller than the others; another supply ship. The Yankee gunboat was charging across the river toward it. Not wishing to watch the inevitable capture, she turned away and went into the house to prepare to receive her visitors.

Jamie blinked against the dimness of General Sibley's tent. "You sent for me, General?"

Sibley sat at his camp desk, frowning at a paper in his hand. A lantern's feeble light exaggerated the lines carved in his face and bled the color from his graying side whiskers. Jamie knew he was weary, and probably ill as well.

The general was at war with everyone. His brigade had no faith in him after their disastrous defeat in New Mexico; they wanted a new commander. Sibley had hoped to take them to Richmond or at least to Vicksburg, and instead was stuck here in Louisiana, lucky to have kept his command at all. After months defending himself for New Mexico he had only recently been authorized to relieve General Mouton of command at Rosedale, a tiny village on the railroad between Baton Rouge and Opelousas, held by a small Confederate force consisting only of the Valverde Battery—Jamie's unit—and three companies of cavalry.

"Ah, Russell. Good. Read this."

Sibley thrust the page at Jamie. Scrawled in haste and dated that morning, the dispatch was from an officer posted near the mouth of the Red River and warned that a Federal gunboat had appeared there, captured and placed prize crews on three boats, and proceeded up the Red. Jamie glanced up at the general.

"Take your section up there at once and try to recapture those boats. The *Gossamer* will carry you up to the Red. I'm sending one of Freret's cavalry companies along with you."

"Yes, sir." Jamie handed him the dispatch and turned to go. At the door he glanced back and saw Sibley removing the cork from a whiskey bottle. He turned away, hiding sadness and disgust.

Outside the afternoon was scarcely brighter than morning had been. It was a gray day, and Rosedale had a soggy air overall; recent rains had caused the bayou just to the east to flood, and the land was flat as could be, so everything was equally wet. Jamie glanced up at Live Oaks, the home of Mr. Dickinson who had graciously permitted the Valverde Battery to camp on one of his fallow fields. The gigantic old live oak out in front of the plantation house was the largest Jamie had ever seen. He strode past it on the muddy track lined with the wild rosebushes that gave the village its name, then jogged the rest of the way to the battery's camp. He found his tentmate, Lieutenant John Foster, the battery's chief of caissons, taking inventory of spare harnesses with the help of several privates, some from Jamie's section.

"Hey, John. I'm taking my section up to the Red."

A private holding an armful of leather glanced up. Jamie nodded to him.

"Willis, go tell Sergeants Schroeder and O'Niell we've got marching orders, then start rounding up the boys, double-quick."

Willis happily dumped his burden into an open chest and hurried off. Foster glared at Jamie over his spectacles. "Thanks. I was just wishing I could start over."

"Sorry," Jamie said, grinning. "Sibley's orders. We're off to catch boats."

"Hope you fall in the river." Foster pushed the spectacles up on his nose and flapped a hand in farewell before returning to his inventory.

Jamie hurried to the picket rope where the horses were tied. Cocoa tossed her head and whickered a greeting. He ran a hand along her flank—warm and soft, though a bit thin—and gave her a pat before ducking under the rope to fetch her saddle blanket.

"That's right, girl. We're going for a ride."

Cocoa wasn't that much to look at: a liver chestnut mare with a white star on her forehead, a little smaller than average and therefore suited to the ranch work she'd been bred for. She had been his from the moment she was born, and she was his chief consolation in the field. He had ridden her to New Mexico, lost her at Glorieta Pass, mourned all through the hellish retreat, and then by a stroke of luck taken her back from a Yankee Irishman in a skirmish in some godforsaken arroyo west of the Río Grande.

By the time Jamie had Cocoa saddled his section was beginning to assemble in the part of the field the battery used for drilling. The two cannon were ready: a 6-pound field gun and a 12-pound mountain howitzer, with the limbers that would haul them. This mismatched pair was not the usual complement of a field section, but they were special guns, trophy guns, guns men had bled over and died for and sweated to haul out of New Mexico. The names of the officers who had died in their capture were engraved on the tubes. Jamie couldn't have been more proud of them if they had been brand new rifled cannon.

The caissons that carried the spare ammunition chests were pulling into line as he arrived. The drivers were ahead of the game; most of the cannoneers were still finding their places in the column, shrugging into packs snatched up in haste. There were horses enough to haul the guns, but the battery never had been able to get enough to mount the men. At least they wouldn't have to march far, only to the Atchafalaya. From there the transport *Gossamer* would take them up to the Red River.

Jamie felt a flutter in his gut at the prospect of action. So far he had never commanded his guns in a fight. They were capable of killing many men at once; he had seen these very guns do so. Would that haunt him, he wondered, as the unknown Yankee he had killed with a shotgun at Valverde still haunted him? Perhaps he would find out today.

Evening was coming on by the time the *Queen* returned to the Mississippi. They had gone fifteen miles up the Red without encountering any more boats, and would have continued but for the fact that they were running short of coal. Nat and Sperry had come up to the hurricane deck after supper to watch the last of the sunset, a feeble, gray affair. By that time the *Queen* was making her way up the Mississippi at a painfully dawdling pace. The three prizes could not keep up with her normal speed. Their shapes were already distant and dim in the evening haze. Nat looked up at the early stars, remembering how Charlie had taught him their names.

There's a bright star shining for you, boy. You're a born pilot.

Nat's throat tightened all at once. He had loved Charlie—laughing Charlie, devil-may-care Charlie—who had taught him more about life in one carefree summer than he had ever learned from his father. He wondered if Wheat, Sr. knew it, and if that was what made him so hateful.

First Master Thompson came up the companionway and looked around until he spotted Nat. "Mr. Wheat, Colonel Ellet wants to see you in his quarters."

Nat looked up in surprise at Thompson's formality. He glanced at Sperry, then followed the officer below.

Oil lamps lit the cabin outside the colonel's quarters. Thompson knocked on the door, which was opened by Ellet himself.

"Thank you, Mr. Thompson," he said, and beckoned Nat inside.

The room was spare of furnishings and as tidy as the superabundance of correspondence on the desk would allow. The only things approaching ornaments were a framed daguerreotype of the colonel's late father on the wall and his plumed hat, embellished with the infantry bugle of the Mississippi Marine Brigade, hanging on a hook above the bed.

Ellet sat down behind the desk and waved Nat to a cane chair. "I want to thank you for helping with the incendiary charges we used against the *Vicksburg*. It seems to me that they were quite effective."

"Thank you, sir."

"I have had word that she was irreparably damaged in the fight. The Rebels have taken her machinery ashore."

Nat sat a little straighter. "Good news."

"Yes. Have you a good supply of turpentine remaining? Enough to spare more of it?"

"Yes," Nat said slowly. "How much more do you need?"

Ellet picked up a pencil from the desk and toyed with it briefly, then set it down with a snap. "Enough to ensure that the three boats we captured today burn."

Nat felt a moment's dismay. "Why?" he blurted.

"We cannot afford to wait for them. Our coal is too low."

Three perfectly good boats, Nat thought. Fifty tons of pork on the *Moro,* thirteen of flour on the *Berwick Bay,* plus sugar, molasses, cotton. All that potential prize money, burned and sunk. What a waste.

"The *Berwick* will be easiest," Ellet said. "That cotton will burn right enough." He gave a wry chuckle, and Nat glanced up to see him looking amused. Remembering their recent adventure with burning cotton, Nat gave a reluctant grin. Since Vicksburg the colonel had ordered that the bales be wetted down before going into action.

Nat tried to think of a way to avoid firing the boats, but there was none. To cast them adrift would be giving them back to the Rebels, whom the colonel wanted to deprive of the supplies as well as the transportation. They couldn't even save the supplies; the *Queen* was fully stocked except for coal, and crowded to boot, with the handful of officers taken prisoner from the *Baker.* Ellet was right. They would have to be burned.

"We can do it," he said, stifling a sigh.

"Good. I will send word to Captain Conner to recall the prize crews." He turned back to his desk, signaling dismissal.

Nat stood up and started toward the door, pausing to glance back at the young colonel, who seemed not quite so very young at the moment. "Good night, sir."

Ellet nodded once, not looking up. Nat pulled the door quietly closed behind him.

Jamie stood between his guns on the bow of the *Gossamer,* watching a skiff row toward them in the falling dark. The stamp and shuffle of confined horses sounded behind him. The cavalry company numbered only thirty, but they and the four teams of Jamie's section did a good job of filling the transport.

This waterway, the Old River, was the link that connected the Atchafalaya, the Red, and the Mississippi. Jamie didn't quite understand how they all came together, but he knew there was a large island in the middle and that Captain Freret's pickets were stationed on the west bank of the Mississippi below the confluence. Likely it was they who had sent the skiff. If not, there could be trouble in a minute.

When the skiff was in hailing distance, the *Gossamer*'s first mate, Edwards, called out a challenge. Sign and countersign were traded over the twilit waters, and the small craft came alongside the *Gossamer* and tied up to her. Two men in civilian dress got out. The newcomers spoke first with Edwards, then came over to Jamie. One of them stepped forward, his face barely visible in the shadow of his wide-brimmed hat, and reached out a hand.

"Russell? I'm Bill Freret." His handshake was firm but made no challenge. Jamie immediately liked him.

"Pleased to meet you, Captain. I've brought some of your men up."

"So I see. We'll land them back at Simmesport, if that's all right with you."

"What about the gunboat?"

"It came down again a little while ago and started up the Mississippi. I am afraid you have missed your chance to retake the boats. They are still in sight, if you want to have a look."

Jamie scowled, half frustrated, half relieved that there would not be a fight. "How close are we?"

For answer Freret gestured eastward, and Jamie saw that the *Gossamer* was about to enter a vast expanse of water—the Mississippi. He had never seen it. At first glance in the dark it seemed to go on forever.

Edwards gave hasty orders for the dousing of the *Gossamer*'s lights. The boat slid out into the great river and turned its nose upstream. This slowed its progress considerably; they seemed barely to be moving against the current.

"Are you going to put on more steam?" Jamie asked Edwards.

"Not for all your mother's jewels. If we blow any cinders in this dark, that goddamn gunboat'll come after us, too."

Jamie looked at the three captured boats strung out on the river, dark shapes that seemed small in comparison with a fourth, much larger vessel well above. "So close," he murmured.

Freret nodded. "Yes, but we're no match for that gunboat. She's got—Whitmore, how many guns did you say she's got?"

The other man who had come from the skiff stepped forward. He was tall, and before the lights had been put out Jamie had noticed that he wore a black suit and spectacles. "Five guns," he said. "I saw them myself."

Five guns, Jamie thought. It was a good thing he had arrived too late; his two cannon could not have done much against such a battery.

"You were aboard?" he asked Whitmore.

"I was on the *Baker* when she was captured. The gunboat came right up beside us." Whitmore turned to Edwards. "May I ask if you are the captain of this vessel, sir?"

"First mate. Captain's ill."

"I see. Well, sir, may I inquire whether you can take several passengers up to Alexandria? The *Baker* was to have brought us there."

"I'm all full of horses and army mules," Edwards said. "Got to take them back down to Simmesport, eh, Lieutenant?"

Whitmore spoke before Jamie could answer. "Then perhaps you could carry us there? I would not ask it, but there are several ladies among us, and they would prefer to find some shelter for the night. At the moment we are camped in the drawing room at Rosehall."

Jamie frowned. He had heard of Rosehall, hadn't he? He glanced toward Freret.

"It would be better for them not to be at Rosehall," the cavalry captain agreed. "The owner is away, as it happens."

"Then we should pick up the ladies," Jamie said.

Edwards chuckled. "Handful of ladies aboard? Won't that be a shame. Better tie up your boys, gentlemen, or there's like to be a riot." He laughed again at his jest, then added, "I'll go make them some room on the upper deck. How many altogether?"

Instead of answering, Whitmore shouted, "Fire!"

"Hsst!" Edwards clapped a hand over the man's mouth. The civilian pointed toward the boats upstream, and Jamie saw that one of them was indeed afire. He stared, helplessly watching as the flames climbed the steamboat's structure. Upriver, fire blossomed on the second, then the third boat.

Edwards hastened away, giving orders to retreat into the mouth of the Red River. He need not have bothered, for beyond the flames Jamie saw the gunboat speeding away. He, Freret, and Whitmore watched the abandoned boats become giant, floating bonfires. It was pretty, Jamie thought. Pretty and terribly sad. With a vicious pang, he remembered the loss of his wagon train at Glorieta Pass, that awful day nearly a year ago. It had felt like everything he had labored for was burning to ash and cinder before his eyes.

Once the *Gossamer* had withdrawn into the Red, Freret went out again in the skiff, and Jamie and the others waited on deck for his signal that the gunboat was out of sight. When it came, the *Gossamer*—still dark—crossed the Mississippi and glided up to the landing on the opposite bank as gently as a leaf drifting against the shore. Mr. Whitmore, waiting for the stages to be lowered, glanced over at Jamie.

"Thank you, sir, for rescuing our party."

Jamie smiled. "Hardly a rescue. Simmesport isn't near as nice as that." He nodded toward the great house set back from the river, its windows glowing with warm light. Above the front door a huge, round window of stained glass gleamed like a jewel.

"Then you may congratulate yourself on rescuing our hostess. No doubt she will be grateful to have her parlor to herself once more."

Jamie raised his brows. "I thought the owner was away."

"He is, but his wife is at home. A very gracious lady—"

"Go ahead, sir," said one of the men who had lowered one of the stages to the landing.

Whitmore stepped onto it. "We will not be long."

Jamie watched him go ashore and stride up a long, arching drive that glowed softly pale in the starlight. He stifled a sigh. It was inconvenient having to collect these stray civilians, but if it had been his own sister or mother who was stranded, he would have wanted the military to help. With that in mind he had vacated the small stateroom that had been made available to him in favor of the stranded ladies. It was only for an hour or so; Simmesport wasn't far. Perhaps the ladies would be pleasant company.

He laughed softly at himself. They were military wives according to Mr. Whitmore, and their husbands had either been captured or escaped into the river. They were unlikely to be in a pleasant mood.

A short time later Mr. Whitmore returned. "Our hostess has asked one of the officers to come up to the house. She wants a message carried to her husband, who is on the Atchafalaya."

"Why didn't she just give it to you to pass along?"

The civilian gave a slight shrug. "I do not know. Perhaps it involves some military activity—she mentioned the construction of a fort."

Jamie frowned. Freret had not returned, and he did not see the *Gossamer*'s mate. Very well; he could use a stroll.

"I will go."

The night air was brisk ashore, away from the closeness aboard the boat. On his way up the long drive he passed an open carriage filled with ladies and one distempered-looking gentleman on their way down to the boat.

The mansion was huge. The front porch had giant white pillars— so big he would only have been able to get his arms halfway around one—supporting a second storey that looked twenty feet high. A half dozen white-painted cane chairs did nothing to fill the porch. Windows flanked the tall double doors, and the stained-glass medallion above them glowed in tones of red, green, and blue—a large, open rose surrounded by bud-covered vines.

"Rosehall," he said to himself, frowning. He knew he had heard the place spoken of. Maybe one of Aunt May's friends in Galveston had mentioned it. No matter; he had an errand to discharge, the faster the better. It would be a long night before he had his section camped at Simmesport. Stepping up to the doors, he lifted the heavy brass knocker—rose-shaped—and gave three solid thumps.

The grizzled negro who opened the doors wore a black suit finer than anything Jamie had ever put on, and moved with a stiffness that came from being old or being over-inclined to grandness, Jamie couldn't tell which. Maybe it was both, he thought, as the slave fixed him with a critical glare.

"You are?"

"Lieutenant Russell. I am to take a message—"

"Very good, sah. This way."

The butler ushered him in, then proceeded down the main hall of the house. Jamie followed, suddenly conscious of his attire. The hall he was in could have swallowed the Russells' ranch house with room to spare. Its walls were adorned with pastoral murals. Huge, glistening chandeliers illuminated the room.

They passed an open doorway to a parlor occupied by murmuring civilians and miscellaneous items of luggage. Arriving at a closed door farther back in the hall, the butler knocked twice and then opened it. "The army officer is here, Madame."

Jamie moved forward as the butler made way for him. The room seemed to be a library; he saw plush velvet furnishings, bookshelves, and a writing desk at which a lady was seated, engaged in folding a paper. A fire glowing on the hearth drew his attention—he longed to kneel down before it—but the lady rose, waving her fresh-sealed note to cool the wax, and turned to him. Whatever she had been about to say died on her lips as her eyes widened in surprise. Equally surprised and a little alarmed, Jamie blurted the name that flashed into his mind.

"Mrs. Hawkland!"

4

Do you remember the paths where we met? Long, long ago, long, long ago.
— "Long, Long Ago," Thomas Haynes Bayly

Marie stood transfixed, gazing at a young man she had hoped never to see again. Her breeding came to her rescue and she managed to smile.

"Mr. Russell! What a surprise. I had thought you fixed in Texas." She glanced toward the door Alphonse had left open, hoping the butler had not heard even these innocent words.

Mr. Russell, who had paled at first, began to recover his composure. "No, ma'am," he said in a voice somewhat choked. "We are stationed in Louisiana now."

Marie fingered the note in her hands, trying to still her pounding heart, thinking furiously. She had not counted on being in the position of sending her one-time lover to carry a message to her husband. There was no help for it, however; to send him away empty-handed would only occasion remark. She thought she could trust him to be discreet—that was why she had chosen him to help her conceive a child in the first place, or at least partly why. His shy charm and youthful good looks, only slightly hardened by soldiering, had made the choice easy. She had counted on his remaining far away in Texas, though. She wanted no one to suspect what she had done for the sake of presenting her husband with a child and, she hoped, an heir.

"Forgive me, ma'am—I must not keep the boat waiting. Do you have your message ready?" He glanced at the note she held and a swallow moved the muscles of his throat, evoking memories of caressing that throat, touching the soft brown hair, gazing into hazel eyes alight with sudden passion. Even as the blood rushed to Marie's cheeks, relief flooded her; he would not betray her. He seemed as anxious as she that he should leave. While this hurt her pride a little, she knew it to be best, so she stepped toward him and handed him the note.

"My husband has gone down the Atchafalaya. He was to have spent tonight at Montreuil's Plantation, near Simmesport. Would you take this to him, if he has not already left there?"

The paper crinkled slightly as he took it. "I-I will. Good night, ma'am."

He said no more, but bowed and went out. Marie stood very still for a moment. Seeing Mr. Russell in her home had been rather a shock. She waited until she heard Alphonse's voice and the sound of the front doors closing, then took a deep breath before returning to her guests in the parlor.

The carriage returned, the last of the visitors were packed into it, and Marie had her home to herself once more. Feeling fatigued, she decided to retire, and went upstairs to her bedchamber. Stepping to the window she saw the carriage at the landing, its passengers getting into a small boat. The moon had risen now and she also saw, quite clearly, a solitary soldier walking down the drive. He paused at the landing and turned to look back toward the house, sending a pang of mixed fear and pleasure through her. She mastered the impulse to draw back, and stood watching as he walked up the stage onto the boat.

Lucinde came softly up beside her and moved to close the heavy drapes. "Let me get you ready for bed, Madame. Don't you watch those boats burn. You don't want to have nightmares."

"No," Marie agreed.

She left the window and allowed the slave to undress her. Now that the danger of discovery was past, she had leisure to roam through the memories that Russell's appearance had evoked. She smiled softly.

"I do not think I will have nightmares."

Jamie stood on the *Gossamer*'s main deck, brushing Cocoa with long, slow, deliberate strokes. Muffled voices sounded overhead as the civilians settled into their cramped quarters for the short trip to Simmesport. He ignored them and brushed the mare, watching the light from a nearby lantern glint off her soft coat. She hadn't really needed brushing, but it was soothing to both of them, and his troubled heart needed soothing.

Mrs. Hawkland. Why had he been so surprised? He knew she lived in Louisiana, but it was a big state after all. He had tried hard to forget about her—he didn't like the way she muddled his senses and confused all his feelings. Ever since that night in Houston he had been ashamed of his own weakness. He had let her seduce him; he had sinned and enjoyed it. While he wasn't particularly devout, he knew it was wrong. She had a husband, for God's sake.

A husband he would have to face. Jamie leaned his forehead against Cocoa's warm back. The letter in his pocket weighed on him, and would until he got it to Hawkland—Colonel Hawkland, no less, according to the direction on the letter. He had not known the man was a colonel. He knew almost nothing about him, really, except that he was rich enough to build a place like Rosehall, and keep his wife dressed in the finest fashions. Would he be able to look him in the eye?

"God."

He swallowed, wanting and not wanting to remember Houston, the Capitol Hotel, champagne, an unexpected kiss, the mad tangle that had followed. He had abandoned all his principles, caught off guard by the advances of a woman he had thought was a lady. No, she *was* a lady, still. In the eyes of the world she was, and who was he to say otherwise? She presided over that enormous mansion, and all her servants and all those civilians respected her. She had shown no sign of wanting to repeat their indiscretion, either, which was just as well, though strangely that annoyed him.

She had just used him for her personal pleasure, he supposed. She had been bored, perhaps. Maybe she made a hobby of debauching honest soldiers. Pity poor Colonel Hawkland.

"Stop it," he said aloud. Cocoa grunted and turned her head to look at him.

"Not you, girl."

He put away the brush and scratched between Cocoa's ears, causing her to half-lid her eyes in bliss. How he wished they were back at the ranch, out of this war and safe from complications like Mrs. Hawkland. Now he had to forget her all over again, and his body made it clear to him that it wouldn't be easy. The obvious source of relief didn't appeal to him; he avoided whores because he'd seen how the diseases they spread had decimated the ranks of Sibley's army when they entered New Mexico. Also, he didn't *want* to be a sinner, though he seemed to pile sin upon sin despite his best intentions.

Cocoa tossed her head; he'd stopped scratching. Jamie hugged her, then went back to grooming her. By the time they reached Simmesport her coat was gleaming, mane and tail were smooth and untangled, and her hooves were picked clean.

Jamie got his men into camp outside the town and spent the rest of the night trying to sleep. When the sun rose he abandoned the effort, got up and saddled the mare, then asked directions from a civilian who was much too cheerful and rode south along the levee that bordered the Atchafalaya.

A fort overlooking the levee was under construction on Dr. Montreuil's plantation, and Sibley had instructed Jamie to have a look at it while he was in the vicinity and advise the men building it on the placement of embrasures for cannon. This was where Mrs. Hawkland had said her husband would be. Jamie hoped he could deliver her message and get out of there quickly.

He reached the fort just as the sun made a misty bright spot on the gray horizon. It was nothing more than a half-built earthwork on a slight rise overlooking a bend in the Atchafalaya. The elevation was barely perceptible, but in this flat country every such advantage was to be exploited. Jamie frowned as he watched teams of slaves digging and moving the sticky, heavy mud. If he was stationed at Simmesport for any length of time, he feared it would be his fate to occupy this miserable little fort. He could picture moldering away here, his guns pointed out over the sleepy Atchafalaya, far from any real action and too close to Rosehall for comfort. Rejecting this dismal prospect, he dismounted and drew Cocoa's reins over her head.

About fifty yards away a small group of white men stood chatting beneath a stand of bare-limbed trees. Horses, saddled and bridled, waited along a fence underneath, nosing the ground at their feet for nibbles of dead grass. In the distance Jamie could now see a plantation house, not as well situated as Rosehall but nearly as grand.

Jamie led Cocoa toward the men along a narrow path that skirted the outside of the earthwork. The path was muddy around the edges, packed down toward the middle by many feet—many bare feet, he thought, glancing over at the laborers. Their pace was desultory, which didn't surprise him. Mud and gray skies were enough to dampen anyone's spirits.

The white men looked up as Jamie approached. Some were overseers, he decided, though two were better dressed and did not carry pistols thrust into their belts or shotguns over their arms. These might be owners, he thought. One was silver-haired, the other young and darkly handsome, dressed in black. Jamie lifted his hat as he joined them.

"Good morning. Can you tell me where I might find Dr. Montreuil?"

"I am Montreuil," said the younger gentleman.

Jamie breathed relief. Colonel Hawkland must be elsewhere. Maybe he would be able to leave the message with the doctor.

"How do you do, sir? I am Lieutenant Russell. General Sibley asked me to look in on the progress of the fort."

"Very good." Montreuil gestured toward the silver-haired gentleman. "This is Colonel Hawkland, who has lent some of his slaves for the work."

Jamie's heart tried to drop through his boots. He felt his mouth fall open and he quickly shut it. He had expected Hawkland to be a handsome, dashing officer—cavalry, probably—not a civilian of unremarkable stature who was sixty if he was a day. Could this really be the man on whom Mrs. Hawkland had bestowed her hand and heart?

A small smile began to curl the gentleman's mouth. Jamie coughed, and hastily reached into his jacket.

"I beg your pardon, sir. I have a message for you."

Hawkland accepted the note, looked at the writing and glanced sharply up at Jamie, then tore it open and quickly read it. "A Yankee gunboat has captured three of our boats on the Mississippi." He looked at Montreuil, who paled with alarm, then at Jamie.

"That is true," Jamie said. "I was sent to recapture the boats, but the Yankees burned them."

Hawkland frowned. "Pierre, I believe I must cut short my visit, and go on to Houston at once. You will look after the slaves?"

"Of course." Montreuil turned anxious eyes to Jamie. "And I hope this gallant officer and his men will protect the fort should the gunboat come this way?"

One of the overseers, a tall, rangy fellow with a shotgun over his shoulder, spoke up. "Don't you worry none about that gunboat. We can take care of 'em."

Jamie refrained from comparing the relative merits of shotguns and the five guns the boat was reported to carry. "We will guard you as long as we are stationed here," he told Montreuil, hoping privately that it would not be long at all.

Ten days after her first visit to the Red, the *Queen of the West* returned, bringing along a coal barge and a small tender, the *De Soto*. She had left these in the safety of the Old River while she made a sortie down the Atchafalaya, and was now on her way back to them.

Nat came out on the main deck after supper, pulling his coat tighter around himself against the evening's chill as he stepped onto the bow. A mist was stealing across the swampy flatlands. Some off-duty coal heavers were crouched on the deck aft of the bow gun, singing.

"I walk in the moonlight, I walk in the starlight,
To lay this body down.
I'll walk in the graveyard, I'll walk through the graveyard,
To lay this body down."

They kept their voices low, though the gunboat's presence was already well known to the locals. She had begun the day by capturing a Rebel wagon train near the Old River; her landing party had destroyed all twelve wagons and learned from their captives that the train had come from Simmesport. Colonel Ellet had paroled the privates and taken the officer in charge of the train aboard as a prisoner. At Simmesport the *Queen*'s crew found seventy barrels of government beef left on the shore by hastily departing Rebels. These they chopped open and rolled into the river. A landing party had gone out in pursuit of another wagon train but it had disappeared into the swamps, save for one ammunition wagon which the Queens had destroyed. In all, a satisfying day's work, though for Nat it had been idle.

Some of the officers had come down to listen to the music. Nat nodded a greeting to First Master Thompson. Captain Conner, who had taken over command of the *Queen* after running the Vicksburg batteries, stood nearby. Nat noticed Adams in the shadow of the bulwark, listening to the coal heavers sing.

"I go to the judgment in the evenin' of the day,
When I lay this body down,
And my soul and your soul will meet in the day,
When I lay this body down."

The crack of a pistol split the night. The group of singers evaporated; more shots came from the eastern shore. Nat stepped behind the bulwark's port side next to Adams, then risked a glance around its protection. The gunfire was sporadic, all small-arms fire, and seemed to come from atop the levee to the east. Nat couldn't make out the attackers. A ball sang past his head, making him duck back with pounding heart. Someone on the deck cried out in sudden agony, and a shout went up for the surgeon. Nat stayed where he was, listening until the gunfire ceased. He waited a few seconds longer, then stepped out, peering toward the levee.

Darkness, nothing more. The attackers, whoever they were, had fled. Nat noticed a low moaning, realized he'd been hearing it since the gunfire had stopped. He looked to starboard and saw a crowd on that side by the bulwark, where some poor beggar was lying on the deck. Nat took a step closer, trying to see who it was, but was brushed back as the surgeon hastened out of the cabin, shouting, "Give me room!"

The crowd opened to admit him, allowing Nat a view of the unfortunate casualty. He was shocked to see that it was Thompson, lying on the deck with his back arched in agony and his right leg bloodied at the knee. Captain Conner gripped his hands while the surgeon knelt beside him. At his touch Thompson's moan became a shriek, causing Nat to wince.

"Whiskey!" the surgeon demanded. "Who has whiskey?"

A half-dozen flasks were extended. The surgeon took the nearest and poured its contents down Thompson's throat without ceremony, pausing only to let the injured man breathe. Then he probed the knee, causing Thompson's voice to rise again, though less sharply now.

"Get him up to sick bay," the doctor commanded, standing up. "Quickly, now!"

Nat stood watching while four of the coal heavers lifted the officer, moving carefully in an effort not to jostle him. Thompson groaned piteously. The doctor came toward Nat, who stepped back to let him pass, but the surgeon stopped as Colonel Ellet came out on deck. The colonel took in Thompson's condition at a glance, and Nat saw his nostrils flare.

"Can you save the leg?" Ellet said roughly to the surgeon.

"I don't know. Let me get him inside before they begin shooting again."

Ellet made way, watching in silence while the injured man was carried in. Nat saw him look toward the levee, saw his brows snap into a frown.

"Captain Conner!"

"Sir?" The captain came forward, looking as shaken as Nat felt.

"We will anchor at the river's mouth and return here in the morning."

"Yes, sir."

Ellet glared toward the levee once more, then followed the surgeon inside. Conner traded a glance with Nat, then stepped to the starboard side to look at the bank. Nat's old habit made him do the same, marking the width and curve of the waterway, the presence of a dead tree atop the levee, the angle of the blurry moon. He would be able to find the spot again.

"I never saw the colonel so mad," Adams said from behind Nat, startling him.

"I have," Nat said quietly. "At Memphis. He was a medical orderly then."

"What happened then?"

Nat was surprised that Adams didn't know, but remembered that the negro had not been aboard the *Queen* at the time. Perhaps he had still been a slave.

"His father was shot. In the knee, as it happens. The wound eventually killed him."

"Oh." Adams looked toward the levee. "Guess they're going to be sorry, then."

Nat nodded. The cowards who had fired into the *Queen,* if they could be found, would be very sorry indeed come morning.

St. Valentine's day dawned gray and rainy, and Marie's spirits were low. She had risen but was reluctant to dress, and lay upon the chaise longue by the windows, still in her dressing gown, staring out over the gallery at the rainy river as she picked at the breakfast Lucinde had brought up on a tray.

She had been unable to stop thinking of Mr. Russell. At first she had enjoyed remembering their encounter, but she had begun to feel a gnawing doubt. What had the young Texan said to her husband? Could he be a danger after all?

Marie sat up suddenly, peering at the river. Through the haze of rain she had seen something—a small boat, she thought. She threw aside her shawl and stood, going to the French doors with quick, short steps. The glass fogged at her breath; she stepped aside to look through another pane. Yes, a boat was coming across the river.

"Lucinde?" Marie hurried to the bell rope beside her bed and tugged it sharply, then returned to the window.

A year ago, even a week ago, a boat on the river would have been no great cause for excitement. When the Yankee gunboat had returned three days previously, however, its crew had destroyed every small craft along the river including Theodore's favorite pleasure boat, which had happened to be at the landing.

Ten minutes later she was dressed and seated in the front parlor, watching the boat through the windows. Victor, the footman, came in and knelt beside the fireplace. He was a pretty boy with coffee-colored skin, and because of his good looks he had been chosen at an early age to serve in her husband's house. Marie had sometimes wondered if he was the result of Theodore's liaison with one of his slaves—she thought she saw a similarity about the eyes. How sad it would be if he might be Theodore's only real offspring.

Marie banished the uncomfortable thought and walked to the window, where she picked up the little glass her husband used for bird-watching and unfolded it, peering through the pane. There were two people in the boat besides the men at the oars; a man and what looked like an old woman. Both were muffled in cloaks, but Marie was fairly certain that the gentleman was Dr. Montreuil.

"Victor, when you have done with that go to the stables and tell them to send the closed carriage down to the landing. And ask Cook to prepare a tray with coffee and food for two guests. Something sustaining."

"Oui, Madame."

Marie stayed watching while the boat arrived at the landing and the carriage picked up its passengers to bring them to the house. When it reached the terrace she went into the hall. Alphonse opened the doors and the visitors came in, wet and dejected. Marie darted forward to the lady as Victor and Alphonse relieved them of sodden cloaks and hats.

"Madame Montreuil! You are soaked through! Come in at once and sit by the fire." She took the aged lady's hand in hers and guided her toward the parlor, glancing back at Dr. Montreuil, who looked more than usually pale. "What happened?"

He did not answer at once, and as Victor appeared with a tray of coffee, biscuits, and cold beef, she forbore to ask questions until she made her guests more comfortable. Madame Montreuil would take no food, and held her cup and saucer on her knee with trembling hands. Marie feared that something dreadful must have occurred. She glanced at Dr. Montreuil, who was watching his mother with a rather stunned look on his face.

"Madame, would you like to get out of those wet clothes?" Marie asked gently. "I think one of my nightgowns would fit you. My woman could help you, and you could rest for a while in the guest bedchamber until your gown may be dried."

Dr. Montreuil gave her a grateful look, then spoke to his mother. "Oui, Maman. You should rest."

Marie summoned Victor and sent him for Lucinde, then knelt before Madame Montreuil, who was staring blindly at the carpet. "You will feel better when you are warm and dry, Madame."

The old lady's eyes focused on Marie. "All gone," she said. "I would not have thought it could happen so fast." Her dark eyes filled with tears. Marie gently removed the cup from her hands and set it on the table, then took the lady's hands in hers. They were frail and very cold. The bony fingers clutched convulsively at Marie's.

Lucinde arrived, and Marie instructed her to attend Madame Montreuil. The slave gently assisted the old lady to rise, and when they were gone Marie looked expectantly at Dr. Montreuil.

"The gunboat has returned," he said.

"Yes. They destroyed my husband's favorite boat."

He gave a bitter laugh. "They destroyed my plantation."

Marie caught her breath. "What?"

"And those of my neighbors to either side. They burned every building."

She stared at him, horrified. "W-why?"

"Some of our overseers fired into the boat from the levee. The Yankees told us they wounded an officer. When they were unable to find the perpetrators, they set fire to every structure in the vicinity. The slaves have all run away. We have lost everything."

"Mon Dieu!"

Marie sank onto the sofa. Dr. Montreuil sat in a chair and dropped his head into his hands, his fingers clutching at the damp, disordered locks.

Are we next? Marie wondered. She was frightened, more frightened than she remembered ever feeling. She sat still, watching her neighbor's despair. When he was a little calmer, she refilled his coffee cup and offered it to him.

"What may I do to help you? You may stay with me for as long as you wish."

The doctor shook his head. "I will take my mother to New Orleans as soon we can get transportation. You should come with us. I know you have a house there. It will be safer for you."

"No." Marie shook her head. "My husband is expecting to find me here. The Yankees consider us their friends; they will not harm us."

"I hope you are right," said Dr. Montreuil. "They have ruined me."

Dusk was coming on as the *Queen* moved up the Red, though Nat found it hard to be certain whether the sun had set or not. The rain had gone to sleet and then to hail as the day wore on. Nat stood in the pilot house, assigned to support Mr. Garvey, the substitute pilot. Mr. Long had fallen ill, and though Nat had volunteered to take his place, Colonel Ellet had given the honor to Garvey, an assistant engineer who claimed to be familiar with the Red. Nat hoped it was true, for in this sort of weather the surface of the river was nearly unreadable. He remembered a day on the *Columbine* when it had poured like this, and Uncle Charlie had laughed when he asked if they were going to stop and wait for better weather.

Don't worry, boy. I could find my way through this stretch at midnight in a hurricane.

The *Queen* had begun the day with the capture of a small steamer, *Era No. 5,* along with 4500 bushels of corn, two lieutenants, and fourteen Rebel privates. The officers were under guard, the privates had been paroled and set ashore, and the *Era* was back with the coal barge while the *Queen* prowled farther up the Red. Nat was pleased with the capture. The presence of the barge gave him hope that this time they would be able to bring their prize safely home.

By contrast, the previous day had been depressing. Nat understood Ellet's anger, certainly—Thompson was a good fellow and he lay now in dreadful agony from the shattered knee—and it was only right that the *Queen* should respond to the attack. The retribution, however, had been grim. Nat, Sperry, and Adams had provided the two landing parties with turpentine and tar, then watched from the upper deck as flame after flame sprang up despite the drizzling rain. Large and small, mansion and shack, they had all gone alight, glowing dull orange through distance and haze. Adams, watching silently, had made Nat think of the unfortunates who had dwelt in the lesser buildings. Where would they shelter now? he wondered.

The remainder of that day had been spent coaling, a dirty, nasty business. Nat was not the only man aboard who was relieved it was over. Today had been better, and might end with yet more cause for celebration.

Mr. Garvey glanced over his shoulder with an unfriendly expression. Nat ignored it; he was there to be of assistance should Garvey require it. He would have preferred Long's company, as would Garvey, no doubt.

The *Queen* was approaching Gordon's Landing on the Red River, where the Rebels had made their slaves build a water battery they called Fort De Russy. Rumor had placed three large boats there, one of them reportedly the *Webb,* with which Quincy's ship had tangled the previous summer. Knowing the *Webb* was in the Red, Nat had recently reread Quincy's letter about the fight, and was tense with anticipation. The *Queen* was alone, Colonel Ellet having sent one of her two yawls to the *De Soto* with instructions for her to wait downstream. There had been some talk of waiting for the *Indianola,* another ram which was to run the Vicksburg batteries and join the *Queen* in patrolling the mouth of the Red, but Colonel Ellet was impatient. The *Queen* could capture three boats alone; she had done so on her previous visit. The only concern was the battery.

Nat could not see it yet—a sharp bend in the river hid both fort and landing—but he knew it was on the west bank and he couldn't help wishing Garvey would take the *Queen* farther toward the east. It was Garvey, though, who knew these waters and would be aware of any hidden snags, so Nat kept silent. As the *Queen* was approaching the bend, Colonel Ellet came into the pilot house, bringing Captain Conner with him.

"Slowly," Ellet told Garvey. "Just show our bow around the point. If they are too strong for us, we will retreat."

Mr. Garvey grunted and kept his eyes on the river. Nat strained his eyes in the failing light for any sign of movement on the shore. He noted thick, black smoke rising beyond the trees; the boats at the landing were firing up. The colonel and the captain must have seen it, must know that the *Queen's* approach had been noted.

Silent seconds passed. Nat scarcely dared to breathe. The point loomed nearer, the *Queen's* bow drew even with it, then a moment later cannon fire roared out from the shore. Twin tongues of orange flame and roiling smoke marked the hulking earthwork. At the same time, flames leapt up from some structure across the river, sending splinters of light dancing over the water. Against that light, the *Queen* would be easily visible to the Rebels, despite the rain. Nat glanced at Colonel Ellet, who was frowning, staring intently at the fort. Another gun fired, and another. Nat heard the shot strike the *Queen's* bulwarks.

"Back us out, Mr. Garvey," Ellet ordered.

Garvey turned the wheel, so quickly it surprised Nat, who had expected the pilot to back before turning. Before he could speak, he was thrown off balance by a grinding crunch as the *Queen* ran aground.

All was chaos, everyone shouting at once. Nat hastened out to go check on the damage. He ran for the companionway, down and down the rain-slick steps while more cannon shots struck the *Queen*. Emerging on the main deck, he hurried out to the bow and got down on his knees to look over the side. She was not far from the shore; Nat glanced up at the trees, and wondered how long it would be before the Rebels appeared.

"How bad is it?" a voice shouted above the din.

Nat looked up to see Adams beside him. "No damage I can see, but we're hard aground."

He glanced up toward the pilot house, wondering when the paddle wheels would be reversed; he had not heard them engage.

Something was wrong with the escape pipe, for it was not emitting steam. On the main deck, he saw Sperry making his way toward them through the crowd of firemen. Even as their eyes met an enemy shot crashed into the middle of the boat, followed by a huge explosion. Clouds of steam boiled out, enveloping the men on deck. Frozen with terror, Nat watched the wall of steam rush toward him. The next second someone bowled into him, knocking him overboard, and the cold river closed over his head.

5

It is to be regretted that the unfortunate illness of Mr. Scott Long, who piloted the Queen *past Vicksburg, rendered it necessary for me to trust the* Queen *to the management of Mr. Garvey.*
—Charles Rivers Ellet, Colonel, Commanding Ram Fleet

Nat thrust a hand above the water, felt the steam's heat but was not burned by it, and raised his head, gasping for air. A thick, hot cloud shrouded the *Queen,* so dense he could not see her length. Adams was treading water beside him. The negro had saved him from being scalded—had possibly saved his life.

Nat gazed at the wounded ram, fighting down panic. The steam had lessened, though it continued to hiss out of the main deck. That meant that the boilers had not exploded and were still functioning. Something else must have been hit—one of the pipes, probably the main steam pipe. It was not the catastrophe he had feared, but he was hesitant to return to the boat. Fear told him to stay away, to swim to the shore, but he knew that was folly. He would only be captured if he did so.

At last he summoned the courage to swim toward the *Queen,* and reached her in a few strokes. He scrabbled for a hold on the hull; he could hear shouting and someone back in the boiler area wailing, all muffled by the steam. It made him think of Charlie and he closed his eyes, shuddering as he clung to the hull.

A hand reached down and pulled at him, helped him scramble onto the deck. It was Sperry, still clutching his toolbag, his clothes clinging wetly, saturated by the steam. Nat smiled at him, weak with relief, and together they helped Adams aboard.

"Are you hurt?" Nat asked Sperry.

Sperry shook his head. "Got down in the hold in time. Most of us did."

A splash and shouting made the carpenters look up. Someone had put the yawl into the water over the port side. Nat could hear the men arguing, and glanced toward the shore. The Rebels must know the *Queen* was crippled. They would not be long in coming aboard.

Nat turned to his comrades. "We may have to burn her. Adams, go to the storeroom and bring up all the turpentine we have left."

Adams's brow wrinkled, but he nodded and turned to make his way into the dark, steam-filled interior. Nat started toward the group arguing over the yawl. It shoved off before he could reach the side, and he watched in mounting frustration as the boat, loaded with escaping men, drifted downstream.

"Damn you, Warner, now we're trapped!" shouted a man into the face of his neighbor.

"That boat should have been kept for the colonel!" Warner returned.

"Well, he ain't got it either, now, do he?"

Nat glanced up toward the pilot house, where he had last seen Colonel Ellet. All the *Queen*'s ports were dark. He turned back to the brangling men.

"Listen," Nat shouted. "Shut up a minute! Shut up!"

"You shut up, Chips!"

"Do you want to get away or not?"

That got the attention of the men nearest him. The noise fell enough for Nat's voice to be heard.

"We can use the cotton." He glanced at Sperry, who nodded and started for the cabin. "We'll go up and start cutting the bales free. You'll have to swim out to them, and you'd better be quick because the current is swift here. They'll carry you down to the *De Soto*."

"What about the colonel and the captain?" Warner said.

"I'll let them know. Be ready to jump, now."

Nat turned to follow Sperry, and took a deep breath before entering the interior of the boat. The cabin was still steamy—despite his fear the warmth felt good against his river-chilled flesh—and it was pitch dark inside. Night was falling fast.

The boilers, unstoked now for perhaps half an hour, were beginning to cool. Some poor bastard who had been scalded still moaned weakly in the darkness; murmuring voices told Nat he already had help, and he continued to the companionway, mounting the steps by feel with a hand to the wall. He groped his way down a darkened corridor filled with shattered furniture, toward voices coming from the sick bay.

One small candle was all the light in the room, and a glance told Nat that the portholes had been covered. Ellet and Conner were there with the surgeon, standing over First Master Thompson's bed. Thompson seemed delirious; he moved restlessly and muttered, but looked unaware of his surroundings.

"We will need a stretcher," the surgeon was saying. "We can take him down to the yawl—"

"Beg pardon, Doctor," Nat broke in, "but the yawl is gone."

Colonel Ellet turned to him, a frown shadowing his sharp features. "What?"

"Some of the men took it. I was too late to prevent them."

"Then we are trapped," Captain Conner said angrily.

"We are putting cotton bales into the river for the men to swim to," Nat said. "We can escape on them."

"I cannot take this man into the water," the surgeon said, indicating Thompson. He looked at the colonel. "I will stay."

"You'll be captured!" Ellet said.

The surgeon nodded in resignation. "At least I will be able to care for him."

Colonel Ellet grimaced, then said, "We will send the other yawl back from the *De Soto*. With luck you can still escape."

Nat frowned. He would have to tell Adams to leave off preparing to burn the *Queen,* but there was no time to go after him now; the cotton was more important. He looked up at Ellet. "If you will pardon me, sir, you ought to go down on the lower deck as soon as you may."

Colonel Ellet glared at him, but gave a curt nod. Nat went out and felt his way back to the companionway. He reached the upper deck to find that Sperry had lost no time; a bale toppled over the side as he emerged. It made a large splash, which was followed by the smaller splashes of men jumping in after it.

Nat took out his knife and started sawing at the ropes binding the next bale. It reminded him of the run past Vicksburg, cutting away burning cotton. That had seemed a disaster, but this was much worse. This time they were in danger of losing all.

A fit of shaking overcame him as he remembered the explosion of steam. If Adams had not pushed him into the water—if they had been inside, or up in the pilot house, where Charlie had been when the *Columbine* exploded—

"You all right, Nat?"

Nat looked up at Sperry, who was watching him. He swallowed and nodded, then laid his knife to the ropes. A hard knot formed in his gut. If only the *Indianola* had arrived before they had ventured up the Red. If only Garvey had not made the error that had grounded them.

"Damn it," he said softly, and slashed at the ropes with more vigor.

Jamie lifted the flap of his tent and ducked inside, grateful to be out of the rain. Foster, his tentmate, looked up from the task of sorting the battery's mail, which he had spread all over Jamie's cot.

"Almost finished," he said.

"Fine. What's for supper?"

"Salt beef, what else? Baker says he has a new way of mangling it."

Baker was the cook who served the officers' mess, and did a half-decent job with what little material he had. Salt beef meant nobody had caught anything interesting in the woods lately. What game there was in the immediate vicinity had apparently already been cleaned out, probably by Freret's fellows.

Jamie opened the door of the little stove in the corner and pushed the coals around with a stick to make room for another piece of wood. The stove put out enough heat to make the tent tolerably comfortable except on the wettest nights. He put a short, thick section of oak into the stove and watched the flames spring up yellow from the coals to lick at the bark. Green oak, and it smoked badly, but at least it burned. He shut the stove door and stood in front of it, letting it heat the backs of his thighs while he watched Foster carefully collect the stacks of mail and tuck them back in the bag.

The brigade was coming to Louisiana. They would be on the march soon if they had not already left Houston. Jamie looked forward to their arrival, not only because of the friends he would see again but because it meant they would finally be moving, doing something instead of waiting in stubbly fields whose owner was showing signs of wanting them gone so he could plant. It was the middle of February already. Rumors reached the camp daily about Federal attacks on Confederate vessels on Bayou Teche and elsewhere.

Foster shouldered the mailbag and strode to the door, shoving the tent flap back with one arm. "I'll be back soon."

"You forgot the captain's newspaper," Jamie said, picking up the folded paper from his cot.

"That's last week's. I already gave him the new one."

Jamie gave him a wave and sat down with the paper in hand, already scanning the headlines. News of any kind was scarce and always welcome. He had hoped for a letter from home or from one of his brothers, of course, but if there had been one Foster would have left it, so he had to settle for weeks-old news.

The front page was dominated by stories about the Yankee army under Burnside wallowing in Rappahanock mud and a debate in the Confederate Congress about Lincoln's proclamation emancipating the slaves in "states in rebellion against the United States." Turning the page, his eye was drawn to the now-familiar shape of long columns printed fine and his heart gave a heavy thump, as it always did when he saw the names of casualties. The list was titled "Battle of Murfreesboro, December 30, 1862–January 2, 1863." That was the fight Daniel's regiment had been in.

Jamie looked through the headings until he found the 8th Texas Cavalry. The list beneath was long; Terry's Rangers had taken a beating, it appeared. He read down the list of wounded, saw a few names that looked familiar but none who were close friends. The list of killed was shorter and Jamie read it in a hurry hoping to get it over with and get on, but he was stopped short by a single line that his eyes would not pass over.

Russell, Daniel, pvt Co. C.

That was all. It was too much, and not near enough.

Jamie stared at it a long while until finally his eyes fogged up so much he could no longer see the words and the paper slid from his numb fingers to the floor. He found he couldn't take a breath although he needed one badly. Finally he swallowed and inhaled raggedly and then the tears began to rain down his cheeks. He started wiping them away but wound up just rubbing them all over his face and finally leaning into his hands while tears poured out between his fingers.

Dan was dead. His brother was dead. The eldest, the leader, the level-headed one who kept them all out of trouble or got them out of it when they had ignored his advice. Gone. Gone forever.

God damn this war, was his last thought before he spiraled down into grief.

Nat woke with a start and put out his hands, barking a wrist on the wall of the *De Soto*'s tiny pilot house. Garvey stood at the wheel, spinning it back and forth in a peculiar fashion.

"What happened?" Nat said, blinking as he got to his feet. He should not have been sleeping, but exhaustion had got the better of him.

"This goddamn fog," Garvey said, turning and turning the wheel. "Brushed up against a bank. I think we've lost the rudder."

"No!" Nat stepped up to the wheel. "May I try it?"

Garvey shrugged and stepped aside. Nat took the wheel in his hands, and found that it played back and forth with an ominous lightness. He peered out at the river; he could barely see the water in front of the *De Soto*'s bow, but it was enough to tell him that Garvey was right. Moving the wheel brought no response from the steamer.

"Hell." He went out, pulling his wool coat closer against the chill.

Colonel Ellet came up the companionway as he was starting down, his face pale in the gloom. "What happened?" he demanded.

"Mr. Garvey says we brushed against a bank. The wheel isn't answering, we may have unshipped the rudder."

Colonel Ellet's mouth set into a grim line. He nodded Nat on his way and continued toward the pilot house.

Nat hurried down the short length of the boat, knowing there was little he could do. The *De Soto* was a small sidewheeler, less than half the *Queen*'s size, and her decks were now crowded with refugees from the *Queen* huddled together or sleeping wherever there was space to curl up. Nat had to pick his way carefully among them. It had taken more than an hour to collect them all. After the last cotton bale had been caught and its passengers rescued, the yawl had returned with the news that First Master Thompson could not be removed in time; he'd been left aboard the *Queen* along with the surgeon, one of the officers who had gone to rescue him, and a few others. The *Queen* had fallen into the Rebels' hands. Her damaged pipes would be replaced and the Confederates would put her to use against the navy. Nat swallowed the bitterness of that thought, and returned his attention to the *De Soto*.

"Did you see anything just now, when we scraped?" he asked the men grouped in the stern.

"No, but we heard a groan," said a fireman with wet hair plastered to his forehead.

Nat got on his knees and peered down at the murky water—a futile exercise, but he felt he had to do something. Guilt weighed on him; if only he hadn't fallen asleep! He might have seen the danger in time to warn Garvey. Shaking his head, he stood up. He wished to heaven that Mr. Long had not been ill. Long would never have made the clumsy mistakes Garvey was committing, running the *Queen* aground and now this. Frowning, Nat looked up toward the pilot house. It was just clumsiness, wasn't it?

Sperry came up to him, looking bedraggled after repeated dunkings. "It's gone," he confirmed. "She'll have to be beached for repairs."

Nat peered at the thick fog behind them. "When? Where? The Rebels won't wait while we fit a new rudder. They're out there. Maybe they'll catch us after all."

Sperry clapped a hand on his shoulder and squeezed. "You're tired, mate. Get some sleep, I'll go sit with the pilot."

"I couldn't sleep now." He glanced back up at the pilot house. "Thomas . . ."

"What?"

Nat grimaced. "I think our pilot bears watching," he said quietly.

"Old Garvey?"

Nat held up his hands. "It's just a feeling."

"You are tired!"

"Keep an eye out behind us. If you see any sign of the Rebels, come and give me the nod. Don't say anything in front of Garvey, all right?"

Sperry frowned. "All right. Don't do anything hasty."

Nat gave a nod, then started back to the hurricane deck. There wasn't much he could do, in any case, but now his imagination added new fears to his worries. What if Garvey laid on steam while the *De Soto* was rudderless? They might ground, even sink.

Nat wiped a hand over his face. Surely the engineers wouldn't obey such a ludicrous command. Except how would they know? The ship's safety was the pilot's responsibility, and his word was law.

Colonel Ellet was still in the pilot house, with Captain Conner beside him, when Nat returned. A stiff silence held. Garvey stood with lax hands on the wheel, Ellet beside him staring into the fog. Nat took up his seat on the narrow bench, listening to the night sounds of faint water slapping the hull mixed with the rustle and shuffle of uncomfortable men. The knot in his gut grew tighter by the minute as the *De Soto* drifted down the river. Now and then Garvey rang for one or the other of the sidewheels to be engaged, but only to swing the *De Soto* into the current. Nat's pocket watch, being waterlogged, had stopped, but he thought about two hours had passed when Ellet suddenly shifted and said, "There!"

Nat got up, peering out at the fog with eyes stinging from soreness. A low, hulking shape on the river caused him a stab of fear before he realized it was the coal barge lying near the shore. A moment later the *Era No. 5* appeared through the fog.

Relief so overwhelmed Nat he was dizzy for a moment. All the weariness of the long night rushed in on him, and he had to reach out a hand to the wall to steady himself.

"Drop anchor," Ellet said to Conner. "We will transfer to the *Era,* then scuttle this vessel and that barge."

Nat looked at Garvey, but the pilot merely shrugged, then seated himself on the bench and took a half-smoked cigar and a case of lucifers from his pocket. Unable to bear even the thought of a half-smoked, half-soaked cigar's aroma on an empty and gnawing stomach, Nat followed Colonel Ellet and the captain out. He caught up with Ellet on the companionway.

"May I have a word with you, Colonel?"

Ellet paused and glanced up with surprise. "What is it?" Nat hesitated, and the colonel said, "Come to my quarters."

Nat followed him to the tiny stateroom and waited while Colonel Ellet shut the door. He spoke quietly.

"Sir, I feel I must tell you that I begin to doubt Mr. Garvey's loyalty."

"You have reason?"

"It strikes me as odd that an experienced Red River pilot would ground the *Queen* and then lose the *De Soto*'s rudder all in a night."

Ellet frowned. "I do wish that Mr. Long had not fallen ill." He gazed at Nat, considering. "You will observe him," he said at last. "Report any thing unusual directly to me."

"Yes, sir."

Nat left the stateroom to return to the pilot house. He was glad now that he had been assigned there. He meant not to let Garvey out of his sight.

By the time the *Queen*'s crew had crammed themselves into the *Era No. 5* and Garvey had maneuvered her into the Mississippi, dawn was breaking. The river seemed much wider from the deck of the little sidewheeler, much less susceptible to the control of any one vessel. Nat grimaced, thinking of how cocksure they had been coming down here. Their glory had been fleeting indeed. The *Queen* with her broad beam, her bright guns, her powerful engines, was lost to them now. Far across the water on the opposite shore fog wreathed itself around the grounds of Belle View Plantation. Rosehall was a pale shadow amidst the shrouded trees on the hilltop, the carriageway a faint ribbon tethering it to the riverbank.

Nat remained in the *Era*'s tiny pilot house, sitting on the bench behind Garvey. The river was still thick with fog.

"Wish this pea soup would clear out," he said.

"Won't," Garvey said. "Not today."

"How can you be sure?"

"Because I know this river."

"Like you know the Red?" Nat muttered bitterly.

Garvey shot an angry glance back at him. "What the hell you mean by that, boy? I know the Red like the back of my goddamn hand!"

"Sure you do. That's why you grounded the *Queen*. That's why you lost the *De Soto*'s rudder." Nat felt anger growing in his chest. "You only got this post because the other fellow was sick as a dog. I could pilot this boat better than you."

"You? You little bastard, you couldn't pilot your finger up your own ass!"

Nat's anger flared. "You lost Colonel Ellet the *Queen* and the barge and our prize! If you knew the Red—"

"I *cubbed* on the Red, boy, with gentlemen who wouldn't give you and your little prick of a bluebelly colonel the time of day!"

Nat felt a tingle run down his spine. Garvey was disloyal! If he could get him to say such a thing again, in front of a witness perhaps—

He stood up, stepped to the wheel and put a hand on it, an insult to any pilot at his station. "You know the Red like you know a nun's fanny!"

"I know it a hell of a lot better than some goddamn pewling Yankee whelp from Cincinnati!" Garvey shouted, going red in the face. Nat sensed men out on the deck looking toward the pilot house, but Garvey seemed too angry to notice. "The day this river's free of the lot of you is the day I'll shout hallelujah! Get out of my pilot house! Get out!"

Without another word Nat turned and left, heading straight for Colonel Ellet's quarters. The door stood open, and Nat caught himself against the jamb.

"Sir, Garvey just made disloyal statements—"

The steamer suffered a jolt that nearly sent them sprawling. Shouts of protest went up from the men on the decks. The wheels continued for several turns, grinding through sand as the *Era* wallowed up onto a bar, ending at an awkward tilt with her bow out of water completely. Nat hurried out with Colonel Ellet close behind him, but he knew without looking that *Era* was hard aground.

Ellet snapped an order to Nat over his shoulder. "Send up a half-dozen armed men," he said. "I'm arresting the bastard!" Without waiting for answer he made straight for the pilot house.

"God dammit!" Nat muttered, and hurried to obey.

6

The best calculations are liable to be upset, and mine have been disarranged by the capture of the Queen of the West, *up Red River.*
—David D. Porter, Acting Rear-Admiral,
U.S. Navy Commanding Mississippi Squadron

Nat stood on the *Era*'s main deck, watching the water lap at the shoreline as she approached the river landing at Belle View. The fog had persisted all through the hours of labor it had taken to free her, through that night and the early morning. At dawn they had at last met the *Indianola* just below Natchez, coming down the Mississippi with two coal barges in tow. Colonel Ellet had gone aboard to confer with the ram's captain, Commander Brown, and had convinced him to go back down to the Red and have a try at destroying the battery at Fort De Russy, but a brush with the Rebel gunboat *Webb* had changed Brown's mind again. He would blockade the mouth of the Red with the *Indianola* instead of going up to DeRussy. Colonel Ellet, reportedly annoyed, had decided to take the *Era* back to Vicksburg. He wanted to clad her in cotton against a possible attack from shore batteries on the way up, hence they were back at Belle View and the mouth of the Red.

Night had fallen, with no sunset to speak of. Fog and darkness shrouded the plantation house from view, though Nat thought he could see the dim glow of a light from up on the hill. Adams stood beside him, silent and tense.

A figure stood waiting on the landing, a man wearing a wide-brimmed hat and a shapeless coat that hung baggy on his lanky frame. He came on board once the *Era* had landed, and a short time later disembarked again accompanied by Colonel Ellet, both striding up the wide carriageway toward the house.

73

Nat glanced at Adams, uncomfortable at the thought of what he owed to the negro. It annoyed him to be in Adams's debt, but he could at least show his gratitude.

"Thank you," he began roughly, but stopped. Adams seemed not to have heard him; his gaze did not move from the shore. Nat frowned, looking toward the big plantation house, wondering what was there that meant so much to Adams. "Belle View. That is where you grew up, right?"

Adams nodded, continuing to stare at the big house. Nat watched him a while, trying to decide if he was angry or homesick, or something else.

"I am going in to get some coffee," he said finally. With a swallow, he made himself add, "do you want some?"

Adams just shook his head. Fine, Nat thought. At least I tried. He turned and went inside the *Era*'s tiny cabin, glad to get out of the cold.

"Colonel Ellet, Madame."

Marie rose from the parlor sofa to greet her visitor. She had been surprised when Alphonse had told her Mr. Shelton was bringing Colonel Ellet to the house, for his vessel was not on the river, only another gunboat and the small steamer that had come to the landing. She had not ordered coffee, for she was angry with the colonel. It was he who had ordered the destruction of Montreuil's Plantation. Poor Dr. Montreuil and his mother had left for New Orleans only that morning.

She knew it was important that the Yankees continue to trust her. She therefore put on a smile as she greeted the colonel, who seemed less charming to her on this occasion than he had before, and offered him two fingers to shake.

"Good evening, Colonel Ellet. Would you care to sit down?"

Ellet, who looked weary, sank onto one of the velvet-covered chairs while Marie returned to the sofa. "Thank you, ma'am. I apologize for intruding upon you in your husband's absence, and at this unseasonable hour. The fact is that I am in need of your assistance."

Marie raised her brows. "I cannot imagine how I can assist you."

"I need cotton, ma'am. I believe you said you have some available for sale?"

She made herself smile, though she would rather have burned her cotton than sold it to him. "Why, yes. I had thought you were not interested in cotton."

"I need it to protect my vessel from the attacks of guerrillas."

"Is not your vessel well armored with oak?"

She saw Ellet swallow. "The *Queen of the West* is, yes. Unfortunately, she was captured by Rebels yesterday evening."

Marie felt a rush of glee, and to conceal it she bowed her head. "I am sorry to hear that, Colonel. You must be greatly distressed."

"We will get her back," he said in a tight voice. "That is not what I came to discuss with you. Can you sell me enough cotton to protect the *Era,* which is down at your landing?"

She rose and went to the window, pushing aside the heavy velvet drapes to look out at the boat, though she knew she had more cotton than any one vessel could carry. "How much do you think you will need?"

"A hundred seventy or eighty bales should be enough."

He had come to stand beside her. Marie glanced at him and saw a tinge of color rise on his cheek.

"I think we can spare that much."

"Thank you," he said, his eyes warming as he gazed at her. "I have not the funds by me, but I will give you a promissory note. The navy will pay."

Marie concealed her annoyance. "Of course. Please make yourself comfortable while I write you out a bill of sale."

"You need not trouble yourself—"

"It is no trouble. I often assist my husband with such matters."

If he thought she was fool enough to give him cotton without at least obtaining his signature on a bill of sale, he was mistaken. She was about to leave the room, but her breeding made her turn.

"Would you care for anything while you are waiting? Some brandy?"

He hesitated. "No, thank you, ma'am."

"Very well. I will not be long."

She left the parlor, abandoning her smile as she paused in the hall. She wished Theodore had been here to handle this transaction, but he was not, so she must decide on her own.

A hundred and eighty bales of cotton were worth eighteen thousand dollars or more on the open market. It was a considerable amount, but Colonel Ellet's goodwill might be worth it, even if she and her husband were never paid a cent. The more beholden the Yankees were to Belle View, the less likely they would be to burn it, or so she hoped. She would do it, then. She drew a breath and continued down the hall to the library.

Nat had obtained his coffee but had been unable to bear the close quarters inside the *Era*'s cabin, jammed full as it could hold with the

Queen's crew. He had come back on deck, and stood watching Adams watch the shore. The negro appeared not to have moved.

The second master came through the deck recruiting volunteers to move cotton. Adams stepped forward, and Nat caught his arm.

"What are you doing? That's grunt work!"

"I want to go ashore," Adams said quietly.

Nat frowned. "Why?"

Adams looked at him at last, a mulish stare that said ask no questions. Nat changed tactics. "All right. I'll go with you."

Adams's eyes lit with fury. "No. This is none of your business."

"I am your superior—"

"I do my duty for you, and what else I do is not your concern. You do not own me." Adams's voice remained low, but throbbed with anger.

Nat raised his hands, wondering why the negro was suddenly so angry. Adams glared at him briefly, and when he made no further objection the negro turned to join the volunteers. Nat watched him off the boat, then gulped the rest of his tepid coffee and left the cup on the deck as he followed Adams ashore.

He hung back in the crowd of men, working his way up slowly toward Adams. The fellow in the wide hat had returned to lead the sailors up a road that ran east from the levee. Tall trees formed an archway over it. With the night and the fog as thick as ever it was chill and dark beneath the branches, and the ruts were uneven enough to trip a man who wasn't paying attention to where he was going. After they had walked for a while Nat saw a light high in the air, off to the right of the road at some distance, dimmed by the fog. It looked ghostly, a will-o'-the-wisp high in the trees or a lantern hanging from the mast of some phantom ship, until Nat realized it must be an upper window in the house, Rosehall. They were much closer to it now. A couple of outbuildings were visible through the dimness under the trees. Nat observed Adams staring intently that way. A moment later the negro suddenly stepped off the road toward the outbuildings. Nat hesitated, then with a muttered oath he followed the negro into the woods.

The trees were mostly pecans, their giant, bare branches hung with Spanish moss, eerie in the foggy dark. Underfoot rotting nuts crunched and made walking hazardous. A low building loomed before him. There were no lights inside and he heard no sound, so he turned west toward a smaller structure where a dim light showed from the window. Nat approached it slowly and heard low voices from within. Smoke pumped from the building's chimney and the window was unshuttered and unglazed, though curtained with a scrap of cloth. Nat crouched beneath it and listened to the voices arguing.

"Won't be nothing but trouble you coming here," said a woman's voice. "You go on back where you came from."

"Not until I see Sarah," said Adams.

"She is none of your business now, cher. You leave her alone."

"She is my business and you know it. I'm going to marry her."

A soft crunch of a footstep startled Nat into ducking around the side of the building. He peered around the corner toward the sound and saw a figure resolve out of the haze—a woman, carrying a tray— coming from the direction of the house. Her face was shadowed by the cap she wore but Nat thought she must be a slave. What other servant would be walking outdoors at night in a winter fog?

The woman opened the door of the small building and went in. A moment later, even as Nat was returning to the window, she cried out in surprise.

"George!"

A jumble of voices followed, of which Nat could only distinguish the younger woman repeating "George, George!"

"Sarah, listen to me," Adams said loudly, silencing the others. "I'll come for you, I'm saving the money, you got to trust me and wait for me."

The girl started crying, and Nat began to feel uncomfortable about listening to what had suddenly become a very private conversation. He took a few steps away, back toward the road, then froze as he heard someone with a long, steady stride approaching from that direction. He stepped back to the window.

"Adams!" he called in a half-whisper. "Someone's coming! Get out here!"

For a moment the voices fell silent, then a hand pulled the curtain aside and Adams peered out. Beyond him Nat glimpsed two negro women in what looked to be a kitchen. One was the servant he had seen, whose face, now that he could see it, was young and sweet though just now it was tear-stained. The other was an older woman in a dark dress, probably the cook. The tray the younger slave had been carrying sat on a long wooden worktable along with a pile of potatoes.

Adams's eyes blazed as he saw Nat. "What are you doing here?"

"Adams, there is somebody coming—"

"Better hide, then." Adams let the cloth fall.

"Adams!"

The footsteps were getting closer. Nat doubted it was anyone from the boat; they would have carried a light in this darkness. Nat retreated into the shadows alongside the building and listened to Adams renewing his persuasions, albeit in a lower tone. The movement in the fog resolved into the baggy-coated man from the landing. He strode up to the kitchen without hesitation and walked straight in.

"Well, well," drawled a new voice. "Looks like a rat's got into your kitchen, Cookie. Want me to fetch up the hounds and run him off?"

"He were just leaving," said the older woman's voice.

"Were he? I saw you going up with them sailors to pick up that cotton, boy. Just like old times, hey? You must have missed it, that why you come back?"

Nat crept round to the window again. The cloth had fallen a little ajar and he could see a narrow strip of the room. He put out a cautious hand to push the curtain wider.

The man's back was to him. The other three stood in a line, the cook silent and unmoving, Adams defiant with the fire again in his eyes, and the girl, Sarah, looking fit to faint.

"We could arrange for you to enjoy some more of your old pastimes, Georgie."

"You can't touch me now," Adams said.

"No?"

The girl made a small, frightened sound as the white man took a step toward them. He seized her by the arm, and she let out a frightened protest.

"Maybe I'll just go for a little walk with Miz Sarah here."

"Let her be," Adams said, low and angry.

"Let her be?" The man laughed. "Why? She likes going out walking with me, don't you honey?"

"God damn you—" Adams began.

The taller man backhanded Adams with enough force to throw him against the wall. Nat flinched and dropped the curtain, then considered going in through the window, but the sound of bootheels coming toward the door and a whimper from the girl changed his mind. Instead he leapt up from his hiding place and made as if to enter the door. When it was pulled open before him, he put on a show of surprise as the man nearly collided with him.

"There you are," Nat said, fixing a commanding gaze on Sarah. "What's taking so long, girl? The colonel wants his coffee!"

The slave blinked at him, terrified and mute. The white man glared. "Who the hell are you?"

"I am here with Colonel Ellet," Nat told him, assuming a haughty tone as he squared his shoulders to make his uniform look more impressive. "Not that it is your concern. Shouldn't you be looking after the cotton?"

The man narrowed his eyes. Nat hoped the fellow had not seen him earlier. It was dark, and there had been plenty of white sailors besides himself going to help with the cotton.

Nat shifted his attention to the girl. "Well, don't stand there gaping, girl, fetch the coffee!"

"Just a minute," said the white man.

"What, is she your sweetheart?" Nat stared at him with contempt. "Well, come see her later. Colonel Ellet doesn't like to be kept waiting. Go on, girl, or I will speak to your mistress!"

Sarah shot a frightened glance at him as she stepped away from the white man, who let her go. She hurried into the kitchen. Nat looked in as she opened the door, and affected surprise as he saw Adams sprawled on the floor. The tall woman was dabbing at a cut on his cheek. Both looked up at Nat.

"Adams! What are you doing in there? Carousing again, are you? Get back to the boat before I put you on report."

Adams stared up at Nat, then his eyes flicked past him. Nat stepped into the kitchen and hauled Adams to his feet.

"Off with you. Next time the colonel will hear of it. Move!" Nat added a warning glare and a shove toward the door.

Adams looked over at Sarah, who had picked up her tray and stood holding it in shaking hands. He shot a glance at Nat and went out without a word. Nat looked at the cook who regarded him suspiciously but held her tongue.

"Hurry up with that coffee," Nat told her, and stepped out, shutting the door behind him.

He could hear Adams moving off toward the river. The white man was still standing outside the kitchen. Nat took a couple of steps toward the house, then turned to look at him. "Well? Have you no business to attend to?"

The man ignored this. "Nigger lover, are you?" he said, sneering.

"Less so than you, I would say," Nat said coldly. "She is not even pretty."

The other's eyes flashed, then narrowed once more. "You watch your back, Yankee boy. Don't come 'round here again."

"God forbid," Nat said, and turned away, striding toward the house. He counted twenty paces, his back prickling the whole while, before he dared glance back toward the kitchen. The man was still there.

Rosehall loomed over him, but with none of the charm Quincy had described. To Nat it seemed gloomy and threatening, a mass of brick and timber raised by slaves, served by slaves. In the little time he had been here, he had seen and heard more evil than he cared for. Hoping none of the household servants would notice him, he went up the steps into the shadow of the porch. A glance told him the white man was still watching. He had no choice but to open the door and go in.

Marie, stepping out of the library with the bill of sale in her hand, was astonished to see a stranger entering the house through the back door. He wore dark clothing like a navy man, though she saw no markings of office.

"Who are you?" she demanded. "Are you from the boat?"

The man jumped and looked at her with widening eyes. He hastily removed his cap, revealing fair, curling hair. She was reminded of someone—grasped at the fleeting memory, but was unable to retain it.

"I beg your pardon, ma'am. I was just . . . My name's Wheat, ma'am."

"Wheat?"

"Yes, I am from the *Queen*—the *Era,* I mean—"

Victor came out of the butler's pantry and looked from the intruder to Marie. "Madame?"

She stayed him with a gesture. "Wheat," she repeated, frowning. There was a connection, though it eluded her. She had no time to pursue it; Colonel Ellet was waiting.

One of the rear doors opened again and the downstairs maid came in, hastily shutting it behind her. When she turned and saw the intruder, she let out a startled cry.

"It is all right, Sarah," Marie said. "This man is just leaving."

Sarah ignored her; she was staring at the man who called himself Wheat with a peculiar intensity. "Thank you," she said to him hoarsely, then darted away into the pantry.

Marie turned startled eyes toward the sailor. Before she could demand an explanation he put up his hands in a placating gesture.

"I will go. Do you mind if I leave by the front door?"

Marie looked at him in gathering anger. "I think I would prefer you to explain how my maidservant knows you."

"She doesn't. I-I lost my way. Please forgive my disturbing you."

He turned and fairly ran toward the front doors. Marie gestured to Victor to see him out. She followed at a calmer pace, and by the time she reached the parlor Victor had closed the doors behind the trespasser.

Colonel Ellet rose as she came in. "Is there some trouble?"

Marie hesitated, then smiled. "I do not think so. A young man was just here who said he had lost his way. He gave his name as Wheat."

The colonel looked surprised. "That is my carpenter, ma'am. I do not know what could have brought him here."

"Perhaps he came ashore for a walk."

Colonel Ellet frowned and looked toward the window. Marie brought out her paper.

"Here is the bill of sale."

She placed it on the sofa table along with the pen and ink she had brought, and invited Colonel Ellet to sign it. After reading it over he did so, with a flourish, and added a notation.

"This may be presented for payment in St. Louis," he said. "Half the amount will be payable at once, the balance when hostilities have concluded."

Marie put on a smile she was far from feeling as the Yankee colonel rose and handed her the paper. She waved it gently to dry the ink, watching him. "Thank you kindly, sir. I am glad I could be of assistance to you."

Colonel Ellet bowed. "It is most fortunate that you had the cotton available. We would otherwise have had to confiscate it from some of your less loyal neighbors."

Marie held still briefly, then resumed waving the page, fanlike. "I cannot tell you how sorry I am that your vessel was captured," she said in a voice whose softness would have been a warning to those who knew her.

Colonel Ellet, not knowing her, mistook her meaning, and gave her a reassuring smile. "The *Indianola* will protect you. She remains here for now."

"And perhaps you will return presently?"

"That is my hope," Ellet said. "It will not be much longer until the river is completely free again."

"Thank you." Marie kept the smile in place and held out her hand.

Ellet bowed over it, glancing up at her as he straightened with an expression that told her his appreciation of her charms had not diminished. She slid her fingers from his grasp and went to the fireplace to pull the bell. Victor came to show the visitor out, and Marie remained by the fire until he was gone.

She looked at the paper in her hand. She might as well put it on the fire, for all the good it would do her. "St. Louis," she said to herself. As if she or Theodore would be going anywhere near the place.

She hoped her husband would not say that she had done wrong. Though burning the paper would have given her some small satisfaction, she instead returned to the library to put it away. It was better to have even an empty promise than nothing, she supposed. If she had not agreed to sell the cotton, the Yankees would simply have taken it. Perhaps this paper, signed by a prominent Yankee, would be useful at some time. She put it in a drawer of the desk along with the permit to sell cotton signed by General Butler, and the letter she had used to obtain it.

"Wheat!"

Snatching up the letter from the drawer, she stared at the signature: Quincy Wheat, Acting Master, U.S.N. Yes—the young officer who had been so obliging in New Orleans. He was not the man who had been here tonight, but perhaps they were somehow related. She glanced toward the front of the house, where she had last seen the intruder, trying to remember their peculiar conversation. Sarah's part in it occurred to her. Perhaps the girl could shed light on the identity of their interesting visitor. Shutting her useful Yankee papers in the desk, she left the library to seek out her parlor maid.

7

No more mistress' call for me/No more, no more,
No more mistress' call for me/Many thousand go.
—Negro Spiritual

Nat did not relax until he had set foot on the *Era* once more, at which time he let out a sigh of relief and leaned against the bulkhead. A moment later he laughed. He had seen Rosehall at last, and its beautiful mistress. Her eyes had indeed made him tremble, but not the way his brother would have expected. He would have to write to Quincy and compare notes.

His laughter faded. He could not write to Quincy. Quincy was a prisoner, incommunicado, somewhere in Texas. Swallowing a pang of heartache, he looked toward Rosehall.

She had known him, he realized. Or rather, she had known his name—but that was not possible. Mrs. Hawkland had not been at home when Quincy had visited Rosehall. His description of her beauty had been based on her portrait, not on firsthand knowledge. Frowning, Nat tried to think of an explanation. Could her husband have mentioned Quincy's name to her? But why would he do so, and why would it make enough of an impression that she would remember it?

He could not answer these questions. He was tired. With a pang of guilt he remembered his concern about Adams. He set out to search the boat for his mate, hoping Adams had not been foolish enough to return to the plantation.

"No, Madame. I don't know no Mr. Wheat."

"He was just here this evening. You thanked him."

"I never saw him before."

Sarah cast a scared glance at Marie and rubbed more vigorously at the spoon she was polishing. They stood in the butler's pantry, where

Marie had discovered the maid busy at a chore that was none of her duty, at a time of night when she should have been finishing her own work or in her bed, asleep. Marie restrained her impatience, and spoke gently.

"Very well, but why did you thank him?"

Sarah stopped polishing. The spoon slipped from her fingers to the table. "That Mr. Shelton . . ."

Marie looked at her sharply. "Has he been bothering you again?"

Sarah nodded. She picked up the spoon, then put it down.

Marie frowned. "I will ask Colonel Hawkland to speak to him."

"Monsieur is not here, Madame."

"When he returns I will ask him. Now put this away, Sarah. It is time you went to bed."

The girl's eyes flashed wide. "Please, Madame—please let me sleep in the house!" Her voice faded to an urgent whisper.

Marie gazed at her, surprised and angry, not at Sarah, but at Mr. Shelton for causing her to behave this way. She could hardly blame the girl for her fright. Theodore had reprimanded Shelton before, apparently without effect. Well, the overseer might spend all the time he liked in the general slave quarters, but she would not have him interfering with the house servants, and so she would tell him herself, if need be. A serving-maid who was likely to jump out of her skin at any moment was of no use to her whatsoever.

"You may not sleep in the house, Sarah," she said gently. "That is foolish."

"But, Madame—"

"Ask Cook if you may sleep with her tonight."

A little of the fright left the girl's dark eyes, but she looked toward the yard apprehensively. Marie concealed her annoyance. "Victor will walk you to the quarters. Will that do?"

"O-Oui, Madame."

Marie coaxed her into putting away the silver and coming out into the hall. There they met Lucinde coming in from the kitchen, carrying a tray with the cup of cocoa Marie customarily took before bed. Lucinde's sharp gaze went to the maid.

"Thank you, Lucinde," Marie said, taking the tray from her hands. "Will you take Sarah to Cook, please?"

"Oui, Madame," Lucinde said with a nod, forestalling the explanation Marie had been about to make. "Come with me, cher."

Marie watched them go out, her feelings mixed. She was glad not to have to trouble Victor, she was annoyed that it was necessary to have one of her servants escorted to her quarters, and she was curious to know how much Lucinde knew about the evening's unusual events. Trusting that Lucinde would soon enlighten her, she went upstairs to her bedchamber where she sat on the chaise longue in front of the fireplace, musing as she sipped her cocoa.

She had never found out from Sarah what the mysterious Mr. Wheat had done to earn her thanks; she had allowed herself to be diverted by the subject of Mr. Shelton. Perhaps Wheat had somehow protected the girl from Shelton's attentions? Or perhaps he was pursuing her himself. Marie pressed her lips together. She was not feeling so generous toward the Yankee navy that she cared to have them disporting themselves with her servants.

She could hear the rumble of wagons on the road—her own wagons, carrying cotton to the Yankee boat. It would take a few hours to move all the cotton, but she had reasonable hope the boat would be gone by morning, and that she might never meet Colonel Ellet again.

By the time Lucinde arrived, Marie had finished her cocoa. She stood up to be undressed. Not until Lucinde had put her gown away in the wardrobe, wrapped her in a nightgown and her velvet robe, and begged her to return to the chaise while she brushed out her hair did Marie's curiosity get the better of her.

"What happened with Sarah this evening?"

Lucinde brushed a few more strokes through Marie's glossy locks before answering. "George was here."

Marie sat up and turned to look at her. "Little George?"

"Oui, Madame. He come around looking for Sarah. Shelton near killed him out in the kitchen."

Little George had been Damien's assistant, helping with odd chores about the house and grounds, until his father had purchased his freedom a few years before. He and Sarah had been sweethearts. The girl had cried for days after he left, but Marie had thought that she had long since forgotten him.

"Where on earth did he spring from?"

Lucinde nodded her head toward the river. "From that boat."

"Is he still here?"

"No, Madame. He went back to the boat."

Marie turned to face the fire. "If he returns, he is not to speak to Sarah."

Lucinde was silent for a moment. "Oui, Madame."

The slave's gentle hands began to braid Marie's hair. She frowned, dissatisfied to leave the matter thus. "What does Little George want with Sarah?" she asked quietly. "Is it the same as what Shelton wants?"

"George want to marry her. Says he is saving the money to buy her free."

Marie pulled her robe closer about herself. "And does she want to marry him?"

"Oui."

So—she would perhaps have to replace the girl. It would be next to impossible to get a decent maid without traveling as far as New Orleans. If they used one of the field hands, a cotton puller, she would have to be trained for months before she could be trusted with housework. Marie rubbed her temple. Perhaps some of Dr. Montreuil's servants were still somewhere in the neighborhood. She supposed she could make inquiries at Simmesport, but what an annoyance it all was.

"Well, Sarah is not to speak to him," she repeated.

Lucinde finished braiding her hair and covered it with a lace-trimmed nightcap. Her silence made Marie glance up at her. The slave's dark eyes were full of undecipherable feeling. Marie stood up and faced her, speaking quietly but firmly.

"If George comes back, he must speak to Colonel Hawkland or myself first. Make that clear to Sarah, please."

The dark eyes glittered. "Oui, Madame. You will let him buy her free?"

"First he must scrape together the money," Marie said. "If he manages that, then we shall see."

Lucinde made no answer but seemed satisfied. Marie, who had her own opinion of how likely Little George was to obtain the price of Sarah's freedom, kept it to herself. She wondered how he had managed to get on the Yankee boat—signed on as a coal heaver, perhaps. Surely they didn't make enough money to purchase a skilled slave like Sarah. Theodore would demand eight hundred at least.

Yet another problem to lay before her husband when he returned. Deeply weary, Marie started toward her bed. Lucinde helped her into it and drew the lace curtains closed.

"Bon soir, Madame," said the slave. Through the lace Marie could see her smiling a little as she turned down the lamp and went out, softly closing the door behind her.

Nat made his way past the growing cotton bulkhead to the end of the main deck. He found Adams seated with his legs dangling off the stern, as if contemplating a swim in the murky Mississippi. The negro did not look up but his hand went to his face, touching the cut at the side of his mouth.

"Did he hurt your jaw?" Nat asked quietly as he sat down beside Adams.

"No," Adams said thickly. "Loosened up a tooth."

"Bit your tongue, too, eh? Lucky you didn't bite it in half."

"Uh-huh. Lucky."

They sat silent for a minute, listening to the water lap at the boat and the shore. Shoreline smells that would be thick and heavy in summer were muted by the cold. The fog lay like a blanket on the water, muffling sound and light.

Nat turned his head to look at Adams, though he couldn't read his face very well in the dark. "I see why you are so determined," he said. "She seems like a sweet girl."

"Thought you thought she wadn't even pretty."

Nat smiled. "Heard that, did you? I was just trying to get that fellow's goat. Who is he, by the way?"

"Shelton. Overseer." The two words throbbed with hate.

"Seems a bad man to cross."

Adams turned toward him, pulling one leg up onto the deck. "You did not have to step in like that."

Nat felt awkward all at once. He shrugged and looked out at the water. "I disliked that damned fellow striking my shipmate, and I disliked the way he was talking. I saw your gal get into the house before I left."

"Thank you." Adams sounded sincere and hopeless all at once.

Nat glanced back toward the house, then patted the *Era*'s deck beside him. "Maybe this old bucket will bring us some prize money." She was a prize, after all, though bought at severe cost; she was hardly worth a tenth of the *Queen,* and they had lost the *De Soto* as well. Not a very good showing for all their efforts.

"You think Colonel Ellet's going to get him another ram?" Adams asked, his injured tongue stumbling over the name.

"Probably. I half expected him to take over the *Indianola,* but I suppose he respects Commander Brown enough to let him be."

"Wants to bring a whole fleet down here and clean 'em out. One boat's not enough."

"I expect you are right. There is the little problem of getting the fleet past Vicksburg, though."

"Wonder where we gonna wind up."

Nat glanced at Adams. It had not occurred to him, but of course Adams was right—the *Queen*'s crew were bound to be reassigned. If the navy kept the *Era,* it would only be a tender or a transport at best. The carpenters would go to another fighting vessel.

Being a petty officer, Nat had the option to resign, though he had no intention of doing so. Adams was enlisted and would go where he was sent until his term of service was up, though if Nat requested it, he could probably have Adams assigned to him again as a carpenter's mate.

He glanced sidelong at Adams, surprised at himself for even considering it. The man made him uncomfortable; he had already involved himself more than he had intended in Adams's affairs. Adams had, though, done him a service aboard the *Queen.* The memory of the steam made him shiver.

He imagined what his father would say if he knew about his little escapade this evening, and couldn't help a grim smile. Father would be furious, and would no doubt read him a lecture on the dangers of associating in any way with men of color. Two years ago Nat would have agreed with him, too.

He looked at the negro beside him and could not help admiring his determination, against all odds, both to make something of himself and to win free his sweetheart. He resolved silently to do what he could to aid Adams in accomplishing his dreams. If that meant securing him a position as carpenter's mate, so be it. It would cost him little, and could possibly mean a great deal to Adams. Somewhat surprised at himself, Nat smiled into the darkness, feeling he had made a good decision.

Jamie's spirits, still low from the news of his brother's death, rose a bit as the battery trudged into Pattersonville behind Sibley's ambulance. The day was pleasant. Sunshine had dried up most of the mud, and the few white pillows of cloud spaced through a clear blue sky posed no immediate threat of rain. The village lay along Bayou Teche, a wide, slow-moving waterway whose rich green hue told of life teeming beneath its surface. The ground immediately adjacent to the bayou was high enough to support habitation and cultivation; about a mile out on either side it sank into swamps. Just about every patch of ground that wasn't swampland or planted in sugar was occupied by Confederate camps.

The Valverde Battery's arrival was hailed by old friends from the

4th, 5th, and 7th regiments of Texas Mounted Volunteers, this being the first time all of General Sibley's brigade were together since their return from New Mexico. Jamie had seen some of them during the fracas at Galveston, but that had been January, and it was now March. He had not realized how much he had missed his friends. He found himself peering at the faces of the men and officers the artillery column passed, nodding to those he knew, searching for those he knew best.

The column came to the 4th's camp; Jamie saw the colors hanging limp from their poles in front of the headquarters tent. He watched for a glimpse of his friend John Reily, who had transferred to his father Colonel Reily's staff, but it was Ellsberry Lane who emerged from the tent as the battery began to pass. Lane, the brigade's adjutant, leaped onto a large, shaggy-maned horse, rode up to the head of the column to exchange a few words with Captain Sayers, then fell back to ride with Jamie.

"Hola, compadre!" Lane grinned, his teeth flashing white beneath his mustache. "I see you have still got your mare."

"Hola yourself. Keep that plow horse away from her," Jamie said, smiling back as he reached across the saddle to shake hands.

"Don't worry. He looks like a brute, but he's smart, and pretty nimble for his size."

"Then he can write her a note if he cares to."

Lane laughed. "Wooster has saved you boys a big open field by the bayou for your park."

"The mosquitos will be grateful to him."

"Well, it is relatively dry." Lane paused while Jamie returned salutations from a handful of men in the camp, then added, "The boys missed you. You can expect a lot of visitors to admire the guns."

Jamie nodded. The battery's guns were all the brigade had to show for their efforts and sufferings in New Mexico. Men of the 4th and 5th regiments had hauled them by hand up and down the wretched arid canyons west of Fort Craig to bring them home. It was only natural that they should feel attached to their hard-won trophies. Jamie felt pretty attached to them himself.

The column came to an open field along Bayou Teche. Moss hung down over the dark water from trees along the bank, and wild flowers bloomed wherever they had not been trampled by the feet of hundreds of soldiers. Jamie caught a glimpse of a man fishing in the bayou, and for a second thought it was Daniel. His chest tightened up as he remembered that it could not be. Daniel was gone. He could not understand it yet, and still had to remind himself several times a day.

"James? You all right?"

He glanced up at Lane, who looked concerned. The tightness in Jamie's throat would not allow him to speak, so he nodded, blinking. For a minute the only sounds were the trudging of men and horses, the creak of wagons, the buzz of insects.

"Come have supper with us, once you have made camp," Lane said at last. "Colonel Reily has acquired a Creole cook. Sibley probably will not get hold of him before tomorrow."

Grateful, Jamie managed a smile. "Thanks."

Lane reached over and laid a hand on Jamie's shoulder, then squeezed and let go. Jamie watched his friend trot back toward the infantry camps, thinking it was good to be home. He laughed at himself softly. If home was the Sibley Brigade, he'd grown far more accustomed to army life than he'd ever expected.

Marie stood upon the gallery outside her bedchamber wrapped in a heavy shawl, watching cotton at last being loaded onto two large boats that would carry it up the Red River. Theodore had arrived home late the previous evening, bringing with him the boats and an unexpected guest, Mr. Lawford.

She had slept badly, and was unwell enough upon awakening to ask Lucinde for a cup of Dr. Montreuil's detestable tea, which had improved her constitution but not her mood. She had not yet welcomed the visitor, and was a little self-conscious about doing so. It had been through Mr. Lawford that she had met Lieutenant Russell, and though he had not been in Houston on the occasion of their liaison, she could not be certain he would not bring his young friend's name into conversation. She would have to be in command of herself, that was all. Reluctant to face him, she delayed, remaining on the gallery watching the boats.

Wagons passed back and forth on the road that bordered Belle View along the north, and dozens of slaves swarmed the landing, putting the cotton aboard the steamers as fast as they could. Fog had shrouded the river since dawn, lending an eerie grace to the movement of the figures on the landing. Marie gazed up the Mississippi, fearing to see another Yankee gunboat.

The *Indianola* had sat at anchor for a few days near Belle View, then started north again. Shortly afterward the *Webb* and the repaired *Queen of the West,* now flying Confederate colors, had pursued the

Yankee gunboat and captured her, though she had sunk and was later destroyed. That did not matter; the important result was that the river was open once more. There was no knowing how long it would remain so.

A soft sound drew her attention. She turned to see that Theodore had opened her bedroom door and stood peering in from the hall. Marie came in, closing the French doors behind her against the chill.

"I knocked," Theodore said.

"I did not hear. I was outside."

Draping her shawl over the chaise longue, she went to her husband and drew him into the room. He closed the hall door and gently embraced her, kissing her cheek.

"I came to see if you feel like joining us for luncheon. Lawford has been asking after you."

"How sweet. You could have just sent a message, cher."

"I wanted to see for myself whether you looked well enough."

Marie laughed and took a step away from him, turning around to display her lace-trimmed white morning dress. "And?"

"Ravishing, as always." Theodore smiled. "Perhaps you should put on something more sober for Lawford's sake. He is getting on in years, after all. You would not want to cause him undue excitement."

"Pooh," she said. Mr. Lawford was younger than Theodore, though it was true that he had seemed rather weary the last time she had seen him. That had been in Houston, months ago. He had told her then that his dear friend, Mrs. Asterly, was ill. She had died in January, and though Marie had sent him written condolences, she felt she should express them again in person.

"I will come down," she said. "Give me a few minutes to tidy myself."

"Shall I send Lucinde up to you?"

"No, but do let Alphonse know I am coming down. I had not decided, earlier."

He smiled. "I should warn you, I have been bragging to Lawford."

"About?"

"Your impending motherhood."

"Oh." Marie glanced down, feeling her cheeks color.

"I hope you do not mind."

"Of course not, Papa cher."

He laughed, kissed her tenderly, and left. Marie went to her wardrobe and selected a lace kerchief which she arranged about her shoulders and pinned with a pretty rose cameo Theodore had given her. Looking at herself in the mirrors on the wardrobe's doors, she thought she looked tired. That would not do. She must not allow herself to grow haggard.

Doubt suddenly assailed her. In giving her husband a child, was she sacrificing her youth? It would be worth it, if only the child was a son. Putting a hand to her belly, which was beginning to show a roundness, she wondered for perhaps the hundredth time if she had made a mistake in taking the steps she had to give her husband an heir. It was futile to argue with herself on that point, of course. She had decided long ago that a changeling would be better than no son at all.

She remembered Houston—the tension of waiting, the profound relief she had felt when she was certain she had conceived. She had confessed the sin (there, where the priest did not know her), done penance, and prayed hour upon hour for the child to be the blessing she hoped for. She could do no more, except to preserve her husband from the knowledge that would surely wound him.

She put on a smile and threw her shoulders back. That looked better. She nodded to her image in the mirror, and went downstairs to join the gentlemen, determined to maintain the bearing of a proud and happy planter's wife.

Nat looked out over Cairo, which was muddy and uninteresting, the streets in the vicinity of the river being occupied almost exclusively by warehouses. Nothing within view from the levee appeared the least bit attractive, a circumstance that only increased his general sense of dissatisfaction. He made his way to a boardinghouse to which he'd been referred, hired a room from the gruff proprietress, and leaving his traps there set out for fleet headquarters to report himself present and request a furlough.

The officers and crew of the *Queen* had scattered after disembarking from the *Era* below Vicksburg. Colonel Ellet had transferred to the ram *Switzerland,* leaving his crew to be absorbed into the depleted complements of other vessels and his officers to scramble for new appointments.

Adams had already been transferred to the *Benton* with a large contingent of the *Queen*'s former crew. Nat hoped that vessel would not be going down to the Red River; he feared that being near to Belle View might tempt Adams to sneak ashore again, and unless he himself found a berth on the *Benton,* he would not be at hand this time to get Adams out of a possible scrape.

While Ellet was away bolstering up the *Switzerland* with cotton for an expedition to recapture the *Queen,* General Sherman had ordered the *Era* stripped and scuttled, an act which had severely disheartened the *Queen's* crew. Captain Conner and several others had witnessed the destruction of their meager prize, and woe to anyone who had left personal property aboard. An army detachment had invaded her, snapping up everything, even removing her cabin-work for use as bivouac and tearing up some of the cotton bales—also a rightful prize of the *Queen's* crew—to make bedding for themselves. They had dismantled the *Era's* machinery and broken up her pipes, then towed her to the deepest part of the river and sunk her, leaving not a trace of her whereabouts to tempt the Rebels. This had so infuriated Colonel Ellet that it led to difficulties between himself, his uncle General Alfred Ellet of the Mississippi Marine Brigade, and Admiral Porter. General Ellet had defiantly sent two more rams to run the batteries in broad daylight, with the result that one was lost and the other disabled. Porter was reportedly enraged. The ram fleet was dissolving, and Nat feared Porter would do whatever he could to speed its demise.

It was in this morose condition that Nat, along with several of the *Queen's* officers, had caught a ride up to Cairo on a dispatch boat. The others had dispersed immediately upon disembarking, leaving him to his own devices. As he trudged along the muddy streets of the city he considered resigning and going home, but quickly rejected the thought. That would be to admit defeat, and he was not ready to do so. He wanted to avenge the capture of the *Queen,* and he was damned if he would give his father the pleasure of seeing him return home in dejection after the loss of his vessel. He would try for a transfer out of the ram fleet to the navy proper; perhaps that would change his luck. The thought of seeking a new carpenter's berth made him tired, though.

Fleet headquarters, located on a wharf boat moored at Cairo's docks, was bustling with constant comings and goings. Nat recognized one or two of the *Queen's* officers with whom he had lately traveled, but they were not close friends so he merely nodded to them in passing as he took his place in the queue awaiting the attention of a single, rather harried clerk, whose reddish eyebrows were nearly as bushy as his side whiskers. He took down Nat's name and lodging, nodding mutely when he identified himself with the *Queen*. Nat's carefully worded written request for furlough evoked a doubtful grunt.

"Can't promise anything. We are short of officers at present."

Nat nodded understanding. "Has there been any news of the *Harriet Lane*'s crew?"

One of the heavy eyebrows rose, and the clerk peered at Nat from beneath. "See that gentleman just leaving?" He nodded toward the door, where a slender, rather sallow looking man was going out. "That's the *Lane*'s surgeon. Penrose is the name."

Nat caught his breath. "Thank you!" He knew a moment's urge to shake the clerk's hand; instead he hastened after the surgeon, heart thudding with hope for news of his brother.

8

Tell me, tell me weary soldier from the rude and stirring wars,
Was my brother in the battle where you gained those noble
scars?
— "Was My Brother in the Battle?" Stephen Collins Foster

"Sir? Dr. Penrose?"

Nat caught up with the surgeon a few paces from the headquarters door. The man stopped and gazed at him, vague surprise in his tired eyes.

"I am Thomas Penrose."

"My name's Wheat, sir—Nat Wheat. I was hoping you could give me news of my brother Quincy."

"Oh, yes, Wheat." Dr. Penrose paused, looking Nat up and down. "Why, you are nothing like our Mr. Wheat!"

"He takes after my mother. Is he—is he well?"

"When I last saw him he was as well as can be expected for a man with a wound like his."

Nat's hope faltered. "Then he did not come up with you?"

Penrose shook his head. "He is still at Camp Grove. He has not yet been paroled."

Stifling disappointment, Nat nodded. At least Quincy was alive. "I see. Thank you." He started to turn away, then looked back at the surgeon. "May I buy you dinner, sir? I would be grateful for anything you could tell me of my brother. We have not heard from him since January."

Penrose smiled kindly. "Of course."

They repaired to Brown's Hotel, where the surgeon had engaged a room, and which laid an indifferent table but better, Nat suspected, than that of his own lodging. Over a meal of rather tough roast beef and boiled potatoes, Dr. Penrose favored Nat with his account of the *Harriet Lane*'s capture at Galveston. Upon learning that Nat had been serving on the *Queen of the West,* the surgeon informed him that since being paroled he had arrived at Port Hudson in company not only with most of the *Lane*'s crew and a handful of her officers, but also with the surgeon and twenty men from the *Queen* who were captured at Fort De Russy.

"It was rather an uncomfortable journey. We traveled a hundred miles across country on foot, and many of us were sick along the way, myself included. The others are at New Orleans, waiting to be exchanged, but Admiral Farragut sent me north in hopes that a better climate will improve my health."

Nat nodded, and filled the surgeon's glass from a pitcher of beer on the table. "Can you tell me why my brother was not paroled?"

"All of the acting masters were detained. I believe there was some concern that they had spent a good deal of time in the city of Galveston, and might be able to provide specific information about its defenses."

"Ah." This made sense, and explained why the family had not received any communication from Quincy. "Is his wound healed?"

"Pretty well. Dr. Cummings is looking after him—the 42nd Massachusetts's surgeon. He stayed behind to tend the few wounded who were not well enough to march with us."

Nat nodded, stifling a sigh. "Thank you."

"I am sorry it is not better news, but at least it is not bad."

"No, indeed. I am very grateful." He gazed at his plate, where a last slice of beef sat in a puddle of cold, greasy gravy. No longer hungry, he pushed it away. Glancing up, he noticed Dr. Penrose concealing a yawn. "I beg your pardon. You must be weary, and here I have been interrogating you without mercy."

Penrose smiled. "Not at all. It has been a pleasure to make your acquaintance. Your brother is a very good fellow. He was caterer of our Wardroom Mess, you know, and he always kept us well fed."

Nat couldn't help laughing. "Quincy? Quincy presided over the mess?"

"Quite competently. Is that a surprise?"

"Well, yes." Nat grinned. "He has always been something of a romantic. The sort who would rather pick a bouquet of wild flowers than think about what to have for supper."

"Rest assured, he has not changed. He was forever bringing me some little bloom he had picked up ashore and asking me to identify it. Why he thought I could escapes me."

Nat smiled. "You are a man of letters, sir. We mere sailors must always look to you for advice."

Penrose raised an eyebrow, and said only, "Hm."

Nat settled with the waiter and took grateful leave of Dr. Penrose, promising to look in on him before leaving Cairo. They parted in the hotel's lobby, the surgeon to seek his bed, Nat to walk through the fading light to his own lodging. He felt more cheerful than he had in some time, and looked forward to writing a letter to his parents informing them of what he had learned about Quincy. Though perhaps, he thought, smiling to himself, he would withhold the detail about catering to the mess. That tidbit might be useful later, when Quincy was restored to the bosom of his family and vulnerable to the sort of ribbing the brothers often dealt out to one another. He would have to make sure to raise the issue in the presence of Miss Renata Keller, whom they had both courted from time to time. Grinning to himself, Nat lengthened his stride as he made his way back to his boardinghouse.

"A little more wine, Jamie?" Colonel Reily smiled as he lifted the bottle from the table. The 4th's officers mess table was long, and at present it bore the wreckage of an excellent meal.

"Oh, no thank you, sir. Any more and I won't find my way back to camp." Jamie picked up the last bit of bread from his plate and ate it, then leaned back in his chair. The meal had been excellent, its centerpiece a dish of crawfish tails in an exotic sauce that had kindled a slow fire in the middle of Jamie's chest.

"We will make sure you get home all right," said John Reily, a glint of laughter in his eye as he looked down the table toward Captain Sayers. "Wouldn't want you to get in trouble with your commander."

Sayers affected to be deaf, going so far as to rub an imaginary itch in his ear. Both the Reilys laughed, and Jamie smiled but didn't answer. He had not had much to say over dinner, thinking of Daniel and how much he missed him. This was all right as the company consisted entirely of old friends. Colonel Reily, capable of great dignity, was at his ease presiding over the small party who were mostly members of his own staff. All had been together in New Mexico, and no other commonality was needed to establish them all in harmony.

Jamie liked the colonel, who had technically been his commander although as a quartermaster Jamie had been away from the regiment a great deal. Colonel Reily was a statesman and a true gentleman. He had been ambassador to Russia before the war, and during the campaign in New Mexico had served as an emissary to the governors of Chihuahua and Sonora.

John Reily, the colonel's son and present aide-de-camp, was something of a hothead. He had his father's high brow and clear, brilliant eyes, but rather less patience. He, Jamie, and Lane had been close friends in New Mexico, and that bond remained although lately their duties had often kept them apart.

"So, you have left Colonel Debray's service, Lieutenant Russell?" Colonel Reily said.

Jamie nodded. "It was only a temporary staff assignment. I had personal reasons for wanting to be near Galveston."

"Pity you could not have brought the battery with you," said John. "We could have used them."

"A pity indeed," Sayers said, glancing along the table at Jamie. "We would have much preferred a fight to marching to Monroe and back, though you seem not to have needed our assistance."

"We tried to get you," Jamie told him. "Magruder wanted the battery, but General Holmes blocked it."

"Well, General Holmes will no longer trouble us," said Colonel Reily, "and General Taylor seems to think General Smith will be a more helpful department commander."

"Have you talked with him much, sir?" Jamie asked. "General Taylor, I mean."

"Several times, since we arrived. He is intelligent and eloquent. This is his home country, and he is determined to deny it to the Yankees. I expect we shall do well under his command once we show him what we can do, though I fear he received rather a poor first impression of us."

"Oh?"

John Reily's eyes glinted sidelong at Jamie. "Caught a battalion officer dealing monte to some of his men, and gave him what-for. The general doesn't like our lack of discipline."

Lane gave a wry smile. "Perhaps the major should have refrained from inviting him to join the game."

What must Taylor think of General Sibley? Jamie wondered, but didn't voice the question. Sibley had been more than usually unwell of late, and had resorted to his customary medicine, whiskey. It made him querulous and unreliable; more than once in New Mexico Sibley had retired to his ambulance in the midst of a fight, leaving Colonel

Green, his second in command in Colonel Reily's absence, to manage as best he could.

As if summoned by Jamie's reflections, Green walked into the tent and was hailed by the company with a hearty welcome. He had rather a square face, with fair hair going grizzly and large eyes that looked to Jamie as if he'd had too little sleep. He gave a nod as the others made room for him at the table.

Tom Green was a bona fide hero. In his youth he had established himself as such at San Jacinto, and he had remained a fire-eater, the sort of commander who led his men with "Come on, boys," rather than "Go on." Though he drove them hard, his regiment, the 5th Texas, would follow him anywhere.

"We have eaten all the supper, I fear," Colonel Reily told Green, "but I can offer you some wine."

"Oh, no thank you," said Green. "I'm fed."

Jamie knew he preferred whiskey, though his reaction to it was the opposite to Sibley's. Green often fortified himself before battle—not from any want of courage, Jamie was sure—and the liquor made him even more reckless in the face of danger.

"I came to let you know the Federals are moving," Green continued. "We just heard Banks's army is marching on Brashear City."

Everyone paused for the space of a breath. "Then we will have a fight soon," said John.

Green nodded, his large eyes agleam. Like John, he looked forward to battle in a way Jamie could not. Jamie listened while the others discussed where the battle might fall. He didn't suppose it mattered that much—the country they were in was pretty much the same everywhere—Bayou Teche meandered through flat, swampy land. Listening to Green and Reily, he realized that things as minor as a narrowing of the bayou or how much dry land lay between swamps could make a significant difference in how a battle went, but not being a tactician himself, he wasn't able to imagine the possibilities very well.

The party broke up not long after Green's arrival. Getting to his feet, Jamie found that the wine's effects had begun to wear off, leaving him only a little sleepy. Colonel Reily came up to him, offering to shake hands.

"It was good to see you again, James. How is your family?"

Jamie felt a stab of grief, and had to swallow. "They are all right," he managed to say.

Reily's brows came together. "Your parents are well?"

Jamie nodded, then met the colonel's eyes and saw his concern. "My brother was killed."

"I am sorry," Reily said immediately. He laid a hand on Jamie's shoulder. "I will write to your father."

"Thanks," Jamie said, fighting back tears as Reily moved away. He glanced up and saw that Colonel Green stood nearby. Green threw an arm around him for a moment, and Jamie felt his wiry strength in his squeeze.

"We'll get some Yankees for him," the colonel said gruffly, and with a pat to Jamie's back, he moved on. Behind him, John and Lane stood looking dismayed.

"We didn't know," John said.

Jamie shrugged. "Hard to talk about."

"I am so sorry, James," said Lane. He glanced at John. "Let us walk you back to your camp."

"All right."

Jamie was glad to get away from the mess tent, out into the damp evening. John and Lane accompanied him silently at first. Once they were away from the 4th's encampment, walking down the rutted road that meandered along the bayou, Lane asked, "When was it?"

Under cover of darkness, Jamie could let the tears slide down his face. "Back in January, at Murfreesboro," he said. "Terry's Rangers got pretty cut up."

He told them what little he knew. He'd had one letter from home since learning the news, written by Emma on Momma's behalf. Momma wasn't doing well. First her sister's death, then Daniel's, had pretty much prostrated her, and Emma was now running the house as well as helping with the ranch. She reported that Daisy, one of two slaves left to her by Aunt May, was not fitting in very well. She had been a lady's maid and didn't know much about housework, so that Emma had to teach her practically everything. Rupert, the other slave, was doing better, and Emma predicted he would make a fine ranch hand once he got more used to riding.

"Maybe you could get a furlough," Lane said, interrupting Jamie's wandering thoughts.

"I doubt it. I just had one last fall."

"Well—special circumstances—"

"We will be all right," Jamie said, a little too sharply. They walked on for a minute in silence.

"Use it," said John, on Jamie's other side.

"What?"

"Use it. Use the anger. Throw it at the Yankees."

Jamie sighed. Maybe that would help, though the last thing he felt like at the moment was fighting.

"We'll be in it soon," John went on, "and you will be fighting your section for sure. Send that first volley out in Dan's honor."

Jamie let out a breath, then nodded in the darkness. "I will."

Afternoon sun slanted across the canebrakes beforc the Confederate line, turning the dry stalks pale gold. Skirmishers from the 5th Texas were out in the cane trying to tempt the Federals into a charge, a ploy that had been attempted more than once that day, but so far without success. Jamie stood beside Cocoa, watching scattered puffs of rifle smoke rising from the field and wondering why the cane had not been harvested. Had the plantation's owner gone to fight? Sent his slaves into Texas for safety? How would he feed his family this year, if he hadn't made sugar last fall?

The Confederate line was centered on Camp Bisland, at a bend of the Bayou Teche west of Pattersonville, and protected by some earthworks hastily constructed by negroes borrowed from nearby plantations. The Valverde Battery was positioned on the right with Green's 5th regiment and a battalion of the 2nd Texas under Lieutenant-Colonel Waller, all dismounted. Waller held the extreme right where a railroad ran along the edge of a swamp. To the battery's left, the center of the line was held by Louisiana troops and a couple of batteries, covering the ground up to the west bank of the Teche. On the bayou was a gunboat, the *Diana,* that Lieutenant Nettles's section of the Valverde Battery had helped capture from the Yankees a few days before. Nettles had been rewarded by being placed in command of the boat while Lieutenant Foster took charge of his section. On the east bank were more Louisianans, with Colonel Bagby's 7th Texas, also dismounted and still under strength with only three hundred men, holding the extreme left. The 4th Texas under Colonel Reily and the 2nd Louisiana Cavalry, a motley assemblage of Cajuns under Colonel Vincent, were in reserve. General Sibley commanded the forces west of the bayou; General Alfred Mouton, a gentlemanly Cajun planter whom Jamie had met briefly, commanded east of the water. In all, General Taylor's force of about four thousand had held this line for most of the day. Now with evening approaching, it began to look as if they would bivouac here for the night.

Jamie watched the skirmishers in the field, thinking how each battle he'd seen was different than the others. The cold despair, terror, and painful victory of Valverde was most immediate in his mind, followed closely by the devastating loss of the supply train at Glorieta. Galveston's hell of bombardment by the heavy guns of the Federal navy had been fearsome, but Jamie—on staff duty and distracted by worry for his family's safety—had not been as frightened there. Now, with prebattle tension heavy in the humid air over the narrow strip of land between swamp and bayou, he wondered how he would stand the coming onslaught.

His duty here was to direct his section's fire, if they ever began firing. He must also, somehow, inspire his platoons to fight, something he was not sure how to do. He remembered Colonel Green at Valverde, gathering volunteers for the desperate charge that had captured the battery and turned the tide of the battle in their favor. The colonel had ridden up and down the dry riverbed where disheartened troops were cowering, his bright eyes gleaming with whiskey-fired recklessness, offering a chance at glory that many of the men, Jamie included, had taken. General Sibley, meanwhile, had spent the duration of the battle in his ambulance, indisposed.

Jamie glanced westward to where Sibley stood with his staff, well behind the line. So far today the general had remained on the field, though Jamie would not have been surprised to hear of his retiring. Valverde was not the only battle the brigadier had missed.

"Here they come!" someone shouted.

Jamie's head snapped around and he saw the Federal line—no scatter of sharpshooters but a solid, dark blue inexorable wall—moving forward into the cane while Green's skirmishers fell back and scrambled over the works into shelter. His heart began beating faster and he looked at his watch, which showed just past four. Three, maybe three and a half hours to sunset. He mounted Cocoa and rode to where Captain Sayers and his staff stood some three dozen yards behind the battery. Lieutenant Hume, whose section was in the battery's center, was already there. As Jamie arrived, a courier galloped up to Sayers with orders from the chief of artillery.

"Major Brent's compliments, sir, and you are to commence firing when the skirmishers are all back to our lines."

Sayers, easy in the saddle of his big gray, acknowledged the message and watched the courier depart. Lieutenant Foster joined them, his face flushed with the excitement of his first field command of a section.

"Try to clear the ground immediately in your front, to begin with," Sayers told them. "Then keep an eye on the right—you especially, Russell. They may try to flank us. You will fire on my signal," he added, with a glance toward the battery's bugler who waited nearby with the color bearer. The battery's colors, the Confederate national flag embroidered with "Valverde" in gold letters, hung limp, moving only with the shifting of the bearer's horse. Jamie felt a flash of pride in the banner. The colors, like the battery, were as yet untried in battle. That was about to change.

The section commanders departed, Jamie turning Cocoa back toward his part of the line. He relayed Sayers's order to the sergeants who were the chiefs of his pieces. The cannoneers, who had been idle all day, now moved into action. Jamie watched and listened as they readied their pieces, the number four men stretching their lanyards, the gunners raising their hands to show they were ready to fire. He had placed the mountain howitzer, the battery's odd piece, on his left with the longer-range 6-pounder on the right. Glancing up, he saw the Federal line still advancing, half-hidden by the dead cane stalks, passing like a wave through a restless, pale sea. He coughed, his throat suddenly dry, and took a swallow from his canteen.

The bugle rang out over the field with the clear, descending notes of "Commence Firing." Jamie drew a breath as the first rounds flew toward the enemy line.

"For Daniel," he whispered.

The 6-pounder's round went high, the case shot exploding behind the enemy and spattering the cane with musket balls. The howitzer's went straight into the Federals in its front, causing that part of the line to waver. Jamie winced as he saw sudden gaps torn in the blue ranks by the round, yet the ranks continued to advance. He was killing again, he realized, the knowledge running cold down his arms. He saw the 6-pounder's gunner adjusting the elevation of his piece. Its next shot would be better placed.

Jamie found it best not to watch the Yankee line but to keep his attention on his men. Volleys of musketry from Green's regiment on his right joined the heavier sound of the guns, and the cannonade picked up all along the front. The next time he glanced up the enemy line had all but disappeared; the Yankees were taking shelter in the muddy drainage ditches that ran through the field. Jamie rode to Sergeant Schroeder, commanding the 6-pounder, and directed him to throw a couple of rounds at a ragged line of Yankees still advancing toward the right.

The field had largely been cleared in a very short time. Jamie felt a mixture of elation and relief, but it was short-lived. Within minutes, Federal artillery opened fire, and shells began to scream toward the Confederate line. The first one made Jamie flinch; Cocoa reacted by starting. He stroked her neck to calm her. Those were big rounds coming at them; the Yanks had 24-pounders all along their line, while Taylor had only two of these large guns positioned on the west bank of the bayou and a 30-pound Parrott on the *Diana*, all captured from the Federals.

Smoke hung hazy in the air while the sound of the guns intensified. Jamie glanced up at the cane field, but the Yankee infantry remained in the shelter of the ditches while shot and shell from both sides flew over their heads. He rode to each of his sergeants, shouting encouragement over the thunder of cannon-fire, urging them not to waste ordnance but to fire on clear targets, preferably the Yankee artillery. His chiefs of piece knew their business, and Jamie returned to his place between the two platoons, watching them fire round after round while the smoke fed an ever-thickening pall. Here and there a round fell into the cane, flinging up mud or scything through the standing stalks. A large shell buried itself in the ground to the right several yards behind Green's line, then burst, sending up a geyser of dirt, spectacular but harmless.

The sound of the guns on both sides became a continuous, endless, pounding roar unlike anything Jamie had ever heard. All the Fourth of July celebrations he'd seen, all the battles combined, did not come close to this ceaseless barrage. Even thinking was difficult in the numbing thunder; speaking was futile. When he had to address a subordinate, all he could do was shout directly into the man's ear. Battered by the noise and choked by the guns' pungent smoke, he began to feel they were sinking into hell.

Somehow a bugle's high notes cut through the din, and Jamie turned toward the sound, toward Sayers's HQ where the colors were just visible through the heavy haze. Frowning, he concentrated on hearing the bugle call and recognized it as the rising cadence of "Cease Firing." He rode to his sergeants to relay the command. One by one all the guns on the line fell silent, as did the Yankee guns, until quiet descended over the field, leaving a ringing in Jamie's ears. Looking at his watch, he was surprised to find they had been firing for an hour and a half.

He glanced over his platoons. Every man was in place; no casualties. The casualties were out in the cane field, wearing blue. It was dusk, he realized. The dimness was not just from the smoke hanging in the still air.

Hoofbeats sounded behind him; he turned to see Lieutenant Lane riding up to him along with a mounted private he didn't recognize. Jamie met his friend with a handshake, feeling a small stab of joy that Lane was unhurt.

"You are being taken off the line," Lane told him. "You are to take your section up to Charenton and report to Captain Cornay. Private Fontenot here is your guide."

Fontenot, short and wiry, wearing a butter-colored coat over dingy gray trousers, gave Jamie a salute that was none too crisp. Jamie doubted a guide was necessary to take him a few miles up the bayou road, but anything could happen and it was better to have someone by who knew the country.

"Does Captain Sayers know?" he asked Lane.

"I just spoke to him."

Jamie nodded. "Any news?"

Lane frowned and glanced eastward toward the bayou. "Federals are bringing a second force across Grand Lake to try and catch us from behind. That's why you're going up, to help hold them off. Watch out for yourself," Lane added, and rode off toward headquarters.

Jamie watched him out of sight, then looked at his guide, who waited with an air of long endurance. "Come along," Jamie told him, and went to his sergeants to order the ammunition chests replenished and the section formed in column of march.

Colonel Green, riding past on his way to HQ, saw the activity and came over to inquire about it. He raised an eyebrow when he heard about the Yankees on Grand Lake.

"Well, we will miss you tomorrow," Green said. "This was only the overture—the ball will begin in the morning."

Jamie nodded and gave a crooked smile. "Sorry I won't be there."

"You did good work, today, son," Green told him, and with a wave over his shoulder he rode off.

"How far to Charenton?" Jamie asked Fontenot.

The private shrugged. "Sixteen, seventeen mile. More if you follow the bayou."

Jamie hid a grimace. It would be a long night. He did not let his men pause to eat but set them in motion at once. As it turned out, Private Fontenot proved his usefulness by saving them several miles, cutting across sugar fields from Franklin to avoid a loop of the bayou he called Irish Bend. Still, it was late by the time the section reached Charenton.

Captain Cornay, a fair-haired Creole with sharp, blue eyes and a ready smile, accorded Jamie a brisk welcome. Cornay was commander of the St. Mary's Battery, named for the parish where it had been raised, which encompassed the part of the Teche where Taylor's army now grappled with the Federals.

"The Yankees are on transports out on the lake," Cornay told him in a low voice with a slight French accent. "We are to prevent them from landing. Let me take you to Colonel Vincent."

Jamie left his column waiting and followed Cornay through a camp of infantry and cavalry spread out along the west side of the bayou. They found Colonel Vincent talking with his staff in the shelter of a stand of cypress, the heavy-boled trees rising tall into the night, draped with long trails of moss. The colonel, also a native Louisianan, looked Jamie over with a heavy-lidded gaze.

"You will bring your section on out to Hudgins' Point," Colonel Vincent said. "I have a detachment of cavalry there. If the enemy show in force, do not wait for orders to fire. Drive them off if you can."

Glorified picket duty, Jamie thought, but kept it to himself. Finding that Colonel Vincent intended to accompany him and spend the night with his troopers, Jamie withheld judgment, though he could wish that a few more of Vincent's command had been placed across the bayou. He returned to his column and quietly rolled his guns across a wooden bridge. The road on this side of the bayou was bad, and in a short time he determined that he could not bring his guns anywhere near the point. Grand Lake's shore was too spongy; Jamie feared the carriage wheels would sink right into the ground. He brought the guns as close as he dared, posted a strong guard, and dismissed the rest of the men to eat and sleep as best they could manage on the damp ground. They could not have fires as the light would betray their presence to the enemy.

Jamie unsaddled Cocoa and found her some grass to nibble while he sat nearby at the base of a cypress tree, pulling some leftover cornbread out of his haversack. He had not had a bite since morning; had not wanted any, but he realized from his light-headedness as he dismounted that he needed to eat. He took a bite and chewed wearily, leaning his head against the smooth bark of the tree. He looked up through its looming, mossy branches, but the sky was overcast. No stars to comfort the weary men in their bivouac. There had been no time to extract the section's baggage from the battery wagons; they had brought along only one forage wagon with grain for the horses. Jamie wondered if the main force down at Bisland was sleeping on the battle line tonight.

Memories of the artillery barrage began to crowd in on him now that he was no longer moving, now that the long day was over. His first time fighting his section had not gone badly, though without question he had added to the number of deaths for which he was, at least in part, responsible. That he could no longer state the sum of his murders—not knowing exactly how many Yankees had fallen before his guns—was oddly comforting. Being a killer was part of his duty and yet he believed it was a sin; he still had not resolved this problem, but he kept it to himself. He had talked of it only once, with Lane, who assured him that all sane men felt as he did but that war was a necessary evil, used when no better tool was available. He could not see what had been accomplished by today's killing. Nothing, maybe.

A mosquito whined around his ear and he slapped at it. Crickets and cicadas droned. The night seemed strangely calm, but the air was still heavy and somewhere not far away Yankees were moving. He ought to get his blanket out, he supposed, but he was too tired to move.

An explosion jerked him awake into a pale gray fog. For a moment he thought he was dreaming, caught in some memory of the artillery duel back at Bisland. Then a shell shrieked overhead, slashing through the upper branches of the tree and sending shreds of moss drifting down on him. He was not dreaming. It was morning, and the Yankees were shelling the camp.

9

Shortly after daylight on the 13th the enemy commenced shelling at Hudgins' Point, and about two hours later I received intelligence from Colonel Vincent that the enemy had effected a landing at that point, and were advancing through the woods.
—F. O. Cornay, Captain, Commanding Saint Mary's Cannoneers

Jamie got stiffly to his feet and found his hat, then whistled for Cocoa. She appeared out of the fog and he hastened to saddle her and ride to his pickets. The men of his section were scrambling up, rubbing bleary eyes, feeling around for their gear. Shells continued to fall around them, appearing in weird orange flashes out of the dense fog on the lake.

The pickets stood in a nervous clump where he'd posted them. Closer to the shore Colonel Vincent's Louisiana cavalry were also rising. Jamie dismissed the pickets to their platoon and conferred with his sergeants, who had come up to him for orders.

"How many guns?" he asked them, peering into the fog.

"Four at least," Sergeant Schroeder said. "Parrotts, I think."

"Can you see their muzzle flashes?"

Sergeant O'Niell nodded. "Sometimes."

"Well, aim on that and send a few shells back at them. Try not to waste ammunition."

The sergeants hastened to get their platoons to their posts. Fog enveloped everything, making ghostly shadows of the men hurrying toward the pieces. It seemed to Jamie that the Yankees were increasing their fire. He glanced toward where the cavalry were now breaking camp, wondering if Vincent would bring more of his troops across the bayou to support the guns, or perhaps move them back into the woods, off the exposed point. He rode to the colonel's camp and found him issuing orders to his officers.

Vincent looked up at his approach. "Ah, Russell. Good. We are moving to Mrs. Porter's sugarhouse." He gestured southeast, back toward the bayou. Jamie peered that way but could not discern any building. "You will cover this point until all the cavalry are moving out, then bring your guns down after us."

"Yes, sir," Jamie said.

Colonel Vincent turned his attention to his captains, and Jamie returned to his section. They were firing as he had ordered, waiting for the Yankee guns to fire and aiming on their flashes, but there was no way to know the effect of their fire. Jamie kept an anxious eye on the cavalry as they mounted and rode slowly east. When they were finally all on the march, he ordered his men to limber up and they slipped away down the wretched muddy track through the woods, leaving the Federals shelling their ghosts.

As he rode, Jamie frowned back toward the lake. If they were to prevent the Yankees from landing, leaving this point did not seem the best way to accomplish it. He wished he knew more about Colonel Vincent, understood more about the larger picture. He would not be blamed for following orders, but he couldn't help remembering Sibley's moments of poor judgment in New Mexico and what they had cost: communication, supplies, transportation, horses. Lives, at the bottom of it.

A short distance down the road they came to a field where the cavalry had already formed a line. The sugarhouse was a large brick structure the size of a warehouse, with several chimneys, all cold this time of year. Jamie found Colonel Vincent standing by it, peering across the field to the woods beyond. His cavalry were ranged on the west side of the field, farthest from the lake.

"Place your guns here, on the right," Vincent told him. "Cornay is bringing his battery down from Charenton."

Jamie put his section into battery beside the sugarhouse as ordered, glad to hear they would be reinforced. The fog was beginning to lift, giving a clearer view of the field where well-tended rows of new cane were sprouting. Jamie's pulse jumped when he saw movement in the dark woods beyond, then he realized it must be pickets posted by Colonel Vincent. He ate a bit of cold meat from his rations and tried not to fret.

A short time later the welcome rumble of Captain Cornay's artillery approached on the road. Jamie was about to ride out to meet the captain, but sudden movement in the woods caught his eye. The pickets burst out of the cover, falling back across the field, running for the safety of their line and yelling about Yankee cavalry. Not waiting for orders, Jamie told his sergeants to load. He could hear the crunching of many hooves in the woods, could see movement under the trees. A line of Federal cavalry emerged, and Jamie greeted them with both guns.

Apparently the Yankees were surprised. They retreated to the shelter of the woods, then reformed. Jamie winced at the squealing of a wounded horse, glanced up trying to spot it and wishing he had a rifle, but that was no use. He told his sergeants to fire at will and tried to keep track of everything that was happening. Cornay's guns—two sections, Jamie saw—were hurrying into battery on the opposite corner of the field, to the left of Vincent's cavalry, who stood motionless. The Yankees came out of the woods once more but were driven back by Jamie's fire and did not appear again. After a few minutes, Jamie ordered his sergeants to cease firing and silence descended on the field. Overhead the last shreds of fog drifted gently past. The horse's screams had stopped. Jamie hoped it was dead.

Scouts sent forward by Colonel Vincent returned quickly, reporting the Federals had pulled back to the shore of the lake. There were a lot of them, and many more disembarking from their transports. The colonel ordered a retreat to the west side of the bayou, and sent couriers galloping for Camp Bisland.

As Jamie's section followed the cavalry across a nearby bridge, he caught Captain Cornay's eye. Cornay, whose guns were covering the retreat, did not seem happy. Jamie made up his mind to try to talk with the captain later on and see how much he knew about Colonel Vincent. He was lonely away from his own brigade, amidst Louisianans he had met less than a day before. All his previous field experience had been in the company of other Texans, men and commanders he knew. He felt isolated and adrift, and kept wondering what was happening back at Bisland.

After they had all crossed the bridge Cornay's men set it afire and the column proceeded down the road along the west side of Bayou Teche, toward Franklin. Cornay left his own guns in the rear of the column and came up to ride with Jamie at the head of the artillery. Jamie greeted him cordially. Now was not the time for discussing Colonel Vincent's virtues or lack thereof, but Cornay's worried look was not reassuring.

"Do you know how far we are going?" Jamie asked.

Cornay shook his head, lips pressed together in a thin line. "If we cannot hold Franklin they will have us trapped," he said in a low voice.

"Surely General Taylor would send reinforcements," Jamie suggested.

Cornay gave him a hard glance. "I mean they will have all Taylor's army trapped. There is only one road to New Iberia."

Jamie felt a sinking sensation in his belly. Were there that many Yankees against them? He looked down the road ahead. "That next bridge is already on fire."

Cornay followed his gaze and nodded. "Mrs. Porter's bridge. She had her overseer fire it after she got her household across."

Jamie's first thought—that Mrs. Porter owned a fine bit of property—was followed by the hope that she had somewhere safe to go. "You know this country pretty well," he said.

"I have surveyed much of it, and have also lived in Franklin. My family—" Cornay bit off whatever he was going to say next.

Jamie looked up at him sharply, remembering his own panic when Yankee ships captured Galveston while his sister and aunt were living there. Cornay's face was stony but his eyes showed his worry.

"I hope they are safe," Jamie said softly.

Small-arms fire began to pepper the air. Jamie glanced toward the bayou and saw rifle smoke beyond—some Yankees on the east bank near the bridge were exchanging compliments with Colonel Vincent's troopers. He pushed aside the ungenerous thought that it was about time the cavalry played their part, and gave his attention to a courier who was riding toward them.

The rider reined to a halt in front of Cornay and saluted. "Colonel Vincent desires you to open fire on the Federals."

The captain acknowledged the message and turned to Jamie, who at once said, "Where do you want me?"

Cornay gave him a small smile. "Beyond the bridge. I will take this side. Drive them off."

"We will."

The smile grew. Cornay nodded, then turned his horse aside and galloped down the column toward his own men.

Jamie ordered his guns into battery just past Mrs. Porter's burning bridge, had them load with case, and opened fire on the Yankees across the bayou. The first volley merely annoyed them; the second took casualties. Jamie cheered as a handful of Yankees fell, surprised at himself even as the cry left his throat. Sergeant O'Niell looked his way.

"Good shooting," Jamie shouted to him. "Keep it up."

He checked on Schroeder, then returned to his place between the guns. Cocoa snorted at the smell of the burning bridge, and stamped her feet restlessly. Jamie patted her neck. His own feelings were pretty confused but right now he didn't have time to think about it.

Cornay's guns were also firing across the bayou. The Yankees melted back into the woods, not interested in pursuing the issue, it seemed. In a few minutes Cornay's two sections fell silent, and when Jamie saw the captain riding toward him he ordered his sergeants to cease firing.

"That was well done," Cornay said, joining him. His bay horse muttered a greeting to Cocoa, who tossed her head.

"Thank you," Jamie said.

The captain appeared somewhat less troubled than previously after having given the Yankees some pepper. Jamie looked to where Colonel Vincent stood with his staff. The commander showed no sign of moving.

"Will you tell me about your battery?" Jamie asked Cornay. "When was it formed?"

The Louisianan smiled, glancing back toward his guns. "The St. Mary's Cannoneers. We mustered in Franklin in October of 'sixty-one. Our first duty was at Fort Jackson."

Fort Jackson was on the Mississippi below New Orleans, Jamie knew, and had fallen to the Federal navy the previous spring along with Fort St. Philip. Their loss had led to the capture of New Orleans, which had been a sad blow to the Confederacy.

"Were you there when the forts fell?"

Cornay nodded. "Every unit but ours mutinied. We were the only ones taken prisoner. Almost a year ago, now. Eventually we were exchanged, and came back to Franklin to refit as field artillery."

Having lost the heavy guns, Jamie thought privately. It must have been a terrible disappointment.

Cornay shifted in his saddle. "What about your Valverde Battery? I have heard the name, but do not know the history."

Jamie gave the captain a diffident smile. "We captured the guns from the Federals at the Battle of Valverde in New Mexico. They are our only trophies from that campaign. That's why we have not replaced the mountain howitzer—that and because we had no replacements."

"I wondered about that. The mountain howitzers are obsolete, are they not? I would like to have a look at yours."

"Do. You will see the names of some of the men who fell at Valverde engraved on it." Jamie fell silent, thinking of Martin and all the others who had died for the guns.

"You were there," Cornay said quietly.

Jamie glanced at him, then nodded and cleared his throat. "My first fight. The worst, too, so far."

The captain gazed at him silently for a moment, then looked out at the field. All was still, cavalry waiting in line of battle, cannoneers at their posts. The day was heating up, and insects whined in the heavy air.

"Show me your trophies," Cornay said, and moved to dismount.

Leaving their horses in the care of one of the artillery drivers, Jamie led Cornay forward to view the howitzer. He introduced Sergeant O'Niell and deferred Cornay's questions to him, giving O'Niell a chance to shine. The cannoneers were watchful, curious about the stranger. Cornay was a little more formal with them even than Captain Sayers usually was, but by the time they moved on to the 6-pounder Jamie sensed the Louisianan had won his men's silent approval.

A muffled report and a crash in the woods across the bayou interrupted his introduction of Sergeant Schroeder. All looked up, and Captain Cornay frowned.

"That is a fair distance off."

"They probably can't bring their guns through the woods," Jamie said. "I couldn't get mine out to the lake, and theirs are heavier."

Cornay nodded. "They will not trouble us much at that range."

Still, a few minutes later the captain received orders from Colonel Vincent to move the artillery down the road to the next bridge, and before long they were in column again and on the march. Cornay continued to ride with Jamie, telling him about the Teche country and General Taylor's pledge to defend it.

"Have you met the general?" Jamie asked.

Cornay nodded. "He is a quiet man, intelligent, and uncompromising. I prefer his sort to some who have more flash."

Jamie thought of Colonel Vincent and smiled. He could not help thinking of General Sibley as well.

They arrived at the bridge, which Cornay called Bethel's Bridge, to find it burning sluggishly. Soon new orders arrived from Colonel Vincent: they were to continue to Simon's Bridge and see that it, too, was destroyed. They had now traveled most of the way around the inside of Irish Bend. The farther east they marched, the more solemn Captain Cornay's mood became. Jamie watched him confer with the manager of Simon's plantation about sinking the bridge, and gladly contributed men to the effort, but could not think of anything to do or say that might raise Cornay's spirits. In truth, their situation looked increasingly grim. Jamie did not know exactly how far they had come, but it could not be much farther to Franklin.

Early in the afternoon the column was passing through dense woods when the sound of cavalry approaching reached them from the road ahead. The hope of reinforcements raised Jamie's spirits and he stood in his stirrups, straining to see the newcomers. The commander at the head of the column raised a hand to slow their advance, and Jamie found the style of the gesture familiar. He caught sight of the colors, confirming his hope.

"It's the 4th!" He turned to Cornay, grinning. "My old regiment. Colonel Reily."

"What sort of commander is Colonel Reily?" The sharpness of Cornay's eyes indicated it was not a casual question.

Jamie smiled. "Gallant, brave—well, you will see for yourself. I will ride ahead to meet him, if I may?"

He waited only for Cornay's nod before clicking to Cocoa for a trot. Her ears pricked and she responded willingly. Within moments Jamie was shaking hands with John Reily and the colonel.

"You must have galloped all the way here!" he said, turning Cocoa to walk beside the younger Reily's horse.

The colonel allowed no response to appear in his face, but John grimaced. "General Taylor was furious when he heard the Federals had been allowed to land," he told Jamie, "and he was already furious before that." He glanced at his father and continued. "Taylor gave orders for our line to attack at dawn, but Sibley decided to wait for the fog to clear. When Taylor found out he called the whole thing off, he was so angry, and then your couriers arrived. Couldn't you hold the Yanks off?"

"We could have, perhaps," Jamie said cautiously.

At that Colonel Reily raised an eyebrow, but merely asked, "Where is Colonel Vincent?"

"At the rear of the column," Jamie said. "That is Captain Cornay at the head."

"Can the captain provide me with a guide?"

"He would be a good one himself," Jamie said. "He is from around here."

"I will speak with him. Stay with the regiment, Captain," the colonel said to his son, and spurred up his weary horse.

Jamie rode back to the artillery column with Colonel Reily and introduced Captain Cornay. Reily immediately began asking questions about the lay of the vicinity, and Jamie found himself drawn into a discussion of how best to prevent the Federals from occupying the road to New Iberia. No one suggested soliciting Colonel Vincent's opinion.

"If it is at all feasible," Colonel Reily said, "I would propose distracting the Federals from the road by inviting them to attack us on ground of our own choosing."

Cornay brightened at once. "There is a large open field on the Bethel plantation. That is near the bridge we drove them from earlier," he added to Jamie.

"How far?" Reily asked.

"Less than two miles," Cornay said, "but we have burned Bethel's Bridge and sunk Simon's—those are the two nearest crossings. The next is down in Franklin."

"Can the sunken bridge be raised?"

Cornay thought for a moment. "Probably. Yes, I would think so."

"See to it, then. James, you'll go with him and render assistance, if you please."

"Yes, sir." Jamie glanced at Cornay, who was looking more hopeful.

"I will bring my regiment up behind you, and when you have repaired the bridge we will cross and possess your open field," Colonel Reily said. "I suppose I should have a word with Colonel Vincent as well," he added, and Jamie noticed a dark note come into his voice, unusual for Reily.

Jamie and Cornay started back to the Simon plantation. "I like your Colonel Reily," Cornay said.

Jamie smiled. "We all like him, too. He gives the best orations you ever heard—had all the citizens of San Antonio in a fever of patriotism when we left for New Mexico."

Cornay laughed. "Let me guess—he is a lawyer?"

"Aren't all colonels lawyers?" Jamie asked with feigned innocence.

The manager of Simon's plantation was happy to provide field hands with whose help the bridge was repaired in under an hour. Just as the work was finished, a mounted scout returned from the west in great haste and rode up to Cornay.

"The Yankees are repairing Bethel's Bridge," the man said, gasping for breath. "Some of their infantry is already across."

"How many?" Cornay demanded.

The scout wrinkled his brow. "Half a company? They can only cross in single file."

Cornay looked at Jamie. "Shall I go?" Jamie said.

"Yes. Drive them off. If there are too many get word back to me and I will send you another section."

Jamie was off on the words, ordering his cannoneers to ride on the gun carriages the short distance to the bridge. Before he reached it his column encountered a small file of Yankee infantry, who turned tail at once when they saw Jamie's artillery bearing down on them. He pursued them to the bridge, which he saw had only partly burned. Yankees had slaves swarming over what remained, trying to replace damaged timbers with newly hewn logs. More Yankees were at the structure beyond, which appeared to be another sugarhouse, and a Yankee battery stood in the opposite field. Jamie's heart began to pound as he saw how many enemy troops were massed on the far bank. Too dangerous to think about it; he turned Cocoa away and rode up to Schroeder.

"Put your gun there and open with case as quickly as you can," he said, gesturing to the right of the bridge. "Clear the bridge, then the structure, then shell their guns." He waited only to be certain Schroeder understood the orders, then rode to O'Niell and gave him similar instructions for the howitzer. Taking a deep breath, he clicked his tongue to Cocoa and trotted forward toward the bridge.

A minié ball whined past him, much too close. Puffs of smoke rose from a line of infantry across the bayou. The Yankees were in the field Cornay had mentioned, he realized. They had got to the ground first. It made him angry, but the first round from the 6-pounder went a way toward making up for it.

A few rounds of case were effective in clearing the bridge, and seemed to dismay a large group of Yankee infantry who took shelter behind the sugarhouse. The line of rifles in the field east of the bridge continued to fire on Jamie's battery, though, and he doubted it would be much longer before the battery began to shell him. He found himself reaching a hand to his hat to touch the star pin Emma had given him—had given Martin, rather, but it had been his since Valverde. His fingers found the smooth bit of metal, a small but significant comfort.

He checked on each of his sergeants, on his gunners, on his cannoneers, all performing just as they should. As he was riding back to position from the howitzer he heard a sudden strangled cry behind him, and turned to see a cannoneer fall at his post, blood spurting from his chest, the rammer he had been holding landing across his legs. O'Niell barked an order and another man caught up the rammer, taking the man's place. Jamie ordered two of his extra men to get the wounded cannoneer into the forage wagon, hoping the poor man would not bleed to death before they could get him to a surgeon. He sent a driver galloping back to Cornay with a report of the enemy force in his front: a battalion of infantry at least, and a full six-gun battery. He had done all his duty; there was no more for him to do but remain in his place and watch the conflict unfold.

10

Monday received information that, contrary to my instruc-
tions, Colonel Vincent had contented himself with placing a
small picket at Hudgins' and Charenton and encamped the
remainder of his command on the west bank of the Teche,
and that the enemy had succeeded in landing a large force at
Hudgins'.

— Richard Taylor, Major-General, C.S. Army

Smoke from Jamie's guns formed a growing haze over the bayou, blending with smoke from the Yankee rifles and now from their battery. Two sections had opened on him from the edge of the field, and he saw the third moving west past the sugarhouse. He would be taking fire from two directions once they were in place. He cast an anxious glance back down the road, but saw no reinforcements, no courier.

In addition to the shells and shot screaming toward his section, minié balls continued to annoy them like so many angry wasps, buzzing around them and occasionally stinging. He saw another of his cannoneers hit—a ball to the shoulder, splash of red on his gray jacket—bad enough to put him out of the fight; Jamie hoped no worse. The whine of the balls was constant, and it occurred to Jamie that the Yankee infantry might be making him a specific target. That idea—new to him—rattled him a bit, but he decided it was better to be angry about it than anything else. Noticing that the Yankee infantry had abandoned the sugarhouse, he ordered Sergeant Schroeder to concentrate on the line in the field, then rode to O'Niell.

"Load with case and fire on the cannoneers," he ordered, gesturing toward the Yankee section moving into place by the sugarhouse. "Don't let them get into battery."

O'Niell nodded and strode to his gunner. Jamie resumed his position, wondering whether he should retreat. Hard to think in all the chaos. If he stayed he might be overpowered and captured, might take a lot of casualties, too. If he left . . . the Yankees would cross the bridge and flank Reily, possibly catching him trying to get across the bayou. Jamie winced at the thought. No choice, then. He had to stay.

A piercing thud shook the ground before him. Cocoa's reaction was to flee sideways and he let her; they got a few yards away in the seconds before the shell burst, spattering them and the howitzer's crew with dirt. Cocoa neighed in frightened protest. Jamie leaned forward and spoke to her, stroking her neck, calling her a good girl. He glared at the Yankee sections in the field, certain the shell had been meant for him. They were loading more even as he watched—four guns with nothing to do but try to kill him and his men. Not a damn thing he could do except keep fighting back with what he had.

A report off to the right distracted him, then a shell sailed over the heads of the Yankees in the field, crashed through a corner of the sugarhouse and fell among the cannoneers beyond, bursting near one of the gun carriages. Jamie's heart leaped as he looked east and saw the St. Mary's Cannoneers deployed at the far end of the field, with some of Reily's cavalry forming a line behind them. A second round, this one of case shot, burst in the midst of the Yankee infantry, scattering musket balls and fragments of shell with deadly effect. Even as the bluecoats fell Jamie urged Cocoa to Sergeant Schroeder.

"Concentrate on the guns!" he shouted. He would leave the infantry to Cornay and Reily. Elation swelled in his chest, as vivid as the dread he had felt moments before.

Flanked, the Yankees abandoned the bridge and withdrew westward. In a few minutes they were gone from his front, though Jamie kept firing after them as long as they were in sight. Finally, wanting to keep hitting them but knowing it would accomplish nothing, he ordered his sergeants to cease firing. A wave of exhaustion and relief flowed through him, dizzying for a moment. Thank God, he thought. Thank God it is over.

Marie came into the hall with a basket laden with roses, which she relinquished into Alphonse's care as he greeted her. She kept one bloom back, twirling it beneath her nose and drinking in its perfume.

"Shall I arrange them, Madame?" asked the butler.

"No, I will. Just put them in the pantry, please. Thank you."

Untying the ribbons of her garden hat, she left it and her gloves on a rosewood coat stand in the front of the hall and strolled into the parlor. Her portrait above the mantel—slender and pert in her riding habit—caught her eye and she gave it a wry look, then sank down on the blue velvet sofa, permitting herself a sigh of pleasure. The child inside her kicked and she placed a hand on her belly, now showing a definite roundness.

She had spent the morning outdoors, walking the grounds of Belle View, visiting her gardens and the orchards, and even inspecting the kitchen. She felt well—extraordinarily well—but a bit restless. Clipping roses for the house made her feel useful. She had not done any gardening since the fall.

"Marie?"

Looking up, she saw Theodore standing in the doorway, panama hat in hand, gazing at her with a worried frown. She smiled and reached out a hand toward him. He left his hat on a chair along with his greatcoat of fine alpaca and came to sit beside her. She lifted the rose to his face, evoking a smile but not banishing the creases on his forehead.

"What is it?"

He captured her free hand and caressed it. "I have just learned of a battle."

Marie sat up straighter, which earned her another kick from the baby. "Where?"

"Down along the Teche. General Banks has marched a large army out of New Orleans. It is rumored he might come up the Atchafalaya."

This made her catch her breath, but she immediately recovered. "Rumors. They mean nothing."

"Cherie, I think I should take you to a place of greater safety."

"How can I be safer than I am in my own home?"

"My love—"

"With you to protect me?" She tickled his face with the rose until he restrained her, smiling.

"I am only human. I can protect you from brigands and villains, but not armies."

He was serious, she realized. She dropped her rose and reached up to touch his face. "Do you really think they will come here?"

"I do not know, but I had rather be too cautious than too sanguine." He caught her hand and kissed it. "Why don't I take you to visit your Tante Adèle? You have been saying you wished to see her, and it would be a change of scene for you before you are confined." He laid a hand on her abdomen, so tenderly she could not help but smile. She felt the baby move in response, and saw Theodore's face light with happiness.

"I would like to see my aunt," she agreed. "Shreveport is so far, though."

"Yes, my love. That is exactly why I suggest it."

Marie looked out of the window. It was true that she felt restless, but she was not certain a change of scene would cure her. "Let me think about it?"

"Of course. I am going across the river, but I should be back by the evening."

"Are you meeting Mr. Lawford?"

Theodore nodded. "I would like to get another shipment of cotton out, while the river is clear. He is trying to find us a boat."

"Bring him back for supper, but only if he deserves it."

This won her a smile. "How am I to decide that?"

"Ça se voit! He must get us a boat."

"A boat, of course. I will see to it. May I fetch you anything before I go?"

"A boat."

He laughed, which had been her object. Standing up, he bent to kiss her cheek. "You are remarkably single-minded, my love."

"When I know what I want."

"I believe you could manage our plantations without my assistance."

"I am certain I could, but we shall never know, shall we?" She put out her hands to be helped up, though she could have risen without it. He obliged her, then caught her about the waist, pressing her to him.

"Mon cher! The servants."

"I am not harming them." He kissed her throat.

"But I am supposed to be the guardian of their morals. And regardless, you must earn my caresses."

Theodore raised an eyebrow. Laughing, Marie twisted out of his grasp. "Bring me a boat," she said, and with an audacious smile left him to go and arrange the roses.

Jamie had supper with Colonel Reily and his staff again, this time seated on the ground behind the headquarters wagon, parked beneath a tree. Being removed from the immediate vicinity of the enemy, the men were allowed fires, and Jamie had helped build a large one for the HQ camp. He sat within reach of it now, tinkering with the logs from time to time, adjusting them with the aid of a long stick.

Captain Cornay and his two lieutenants, whom Reily had invited to share the meal, sat nearby. Cornay's chief of caissons, like Jamie's tent-mate Foster, was commanding a section in the absence of its first lieu-tenant, who was handling one of the captured 24-pounders back at Bisland. Jamie found the Louisiana men good company, if a bit edgy. They could hardly be blamed for that, he supposed, fighting in their home country.

The meal, being field rations, was quickly dispensed with. While Colonel Reily quietly talked over the day's events with Lieutenant-Colonel Hardeman and Major Hampton, John Reily came around the fire to join Jamie and Cornay.

"Miserable day, eh boys?"

Jamie nodded, and glanced at Cornay. The Federals, it turned out, had needed no invitation to attack Reily's small force. After Jamie and the others had driven them back from Bethel's Bridge the Yanks had managed to get across the bayou over Mrs. Porter's bridge, which had not completely burned. This forced Reily to return to the west side of the bayou, where he formed a defiant line of battle across the road. The Yankees drew up in line to face them, then darkness precluded hostilities. Reily, after consulting with Cornay about the immediate topography, reluctantly concluded they must withdraw below Franklin to ensure they would not be cut off from Taylor. The colonel had posted a strong picket on the road and moved the rest of his force four miles down to a plantation owned by a Mr. Carline. The pickets could not hold the road against an attack, but their token presence gave Reily a tenuous lifeline of escape.

The sound of a horse arriving interrupted Reily's conversation. All heads turned toward the newcomer, visible only as a shadow until he walked into the firelight.

"Lane!" Jamie and John said in chorus.

Lane glanced at them, then stepped up to Colonel Reily and handed him a paper. "From General Taylor," he said.

"Thank you, Lieutenant. I had not expected to see you riding courier."

"I volunteered. General Sibley's headquarters is not a happy place at present."

Colonel Reily gave a sympathetic nod and opened the dispatch. Lane came around the fire to join Jamie and John.

"Captain Cornay, may I introduce Lieutenant Ellsberry Lane?" said John with exaggerated formality.

Lane shot him a glance before shaking Cornay's hand. "My friends just call me Lane."

Cornay smiled. "For the same reason mine call me Cornay."

His two lieutenants laughed, and one of them supplied, "His Christian name is Florian."

"Oh, dear," Lane said, grinning.

"And his second name is Octave," added the chief of caissons with a grin.

Cornay threw him a dark look. "Enough. Save some of my secrets for the future; you might want to barter them."

"Octave. Does that mean you have seven brothers?" Lane asked, sitting down between Jamie and John, who made room for him. Jamie offered him some cornbread he'd saved out from the supper, which he accepted with a nod of thanks.

"No, it is a family name," Cornay said. "Never mind my concerns. What is the news? Were you engaged today after all?"

Lane swallowed a bite of cornbread. "Yes. The Yankees advanced at midday and kept at us till sunset. We held them off, but just barely. A shell burst in the *Diana*'s boiler."

Jamie sucked a sharp breath. "Nettles?"

"Oh, he was not aboard. He fell sick and had to turn command over to Semmes this morning." Lane's voice dropped. "Sayers was wounded, though."

Jamie winced, then glanced at Cornay. "My captain," he said, and looked back at Lane. "How badly?"

"Minié ball in the ankle," Lane said. "Got it when the Yanks charged our works. You'll be glad to know the Valverde Battery held them off, but Sayers is out of action. Cupples says he won't lose the foot, though." Lane paused to eat the last bite of his bread. "Colonel Bagby was wounded too—took a ball in the arm—but he stayed on the field until it was over."

Jamie sighed. It was not good news, but it could have been worse. With both Sayers and Nettles gone, Hume was in command of the Valverde Battery and Jamie was next in line, a thought he found disquieting.

"Do you happen to know anything of my third section?" asked Cornay. "Lieutenant Gordy?"

Lane frowned. "Gordy . . . yes. He is fine, though one of his guns was disabled. Took a shot through the axle tree and lost the elevating screw."

Cornay nodded. "Thank you."

"He will join you tomorrow. Maybe even tonight. The whole army is retreating."

The artillery officers all looked up at that. Jamie watched Cornay's brows snap into a frown.

"We are outnumbered," Lane explained. "They threw fourteen thousand men at us today, and they have more in reserve. Taylor's already got the wagons moving west."

"He will retreat to New Iberia?" Cornay asked.

"That is my understanding. Green is to be rearguard."

Cornay got to his feet without a word and slowly walked away. His lieutenants exchanged a glance, then rose as well.

"We had better turn in. Thank you for the news."

The Louisianans shook hands with Jamie and his friends, then followed their captain into the darkness. Lane looked at Jamie.

"Did I say something wrong?"

Jamie shook his head. "This is their home parish. Their families are here, or were. Some of them have gotten to safety."

"Oh."

"Poor devils," said John.

Jamie looked after them, nodding. He leaned his chin on his arms and stared into the fire, thinking of home and glad for once that it was far away.

The evening was well advanced when the steamer finally docked at Cincinnati. Nat was hungry, having run out of the bread and cheese he had purchased for the journey. His family would have dined hours ago, but he did not wish to waste one minute of his precious leave so he strode past the hotels and street vendors straight toward home, trusting he would be permitted to rummage the pantry.

The city looked strangely unfamiliar, though nothing he could see had changed substantially. He was viewing it with changed eyes, perhaps. Tidy flowerbeds, trimmed hedges, and cobbled streets had not been much in his experience of late.

Reaching Richmond Street, he turned the corner and saw his home aglow, windows open to the gentle evening air and gaslights illuminating the path to the front door. His parents were entertaining, then. Instinctively he hesitated at the gate, knowing his father would disapprove his presenting himself in company wearing a battered coat that had not been brushed in weeks; however, the thought of the scold his mother would give him if he tried to slip in the back door decided him. He would make up for the coat by explaining its recent adventures. Grinning, he strode up the path and took the steps two at a time.

Voices drifted out of the front parlor windows. He opened the door cautiously, not wanting to disturb the company. As he was closing it he heard footsteps in the hall, and glanced up to see his mother's housekeeper carrying a coffee tray.

"Oh!"

Nat put his portmanteau down beside the door. "Hallo, Biddy."

The housekeeper—a plump, kindly Irishwoman who had also been nanny to Nat and his brother—set her tray on the hall table and clasped him to her ample bosom. She smelled of cinnamon and sugar, sparking memories and making Nat's mouth water.

"Apple crisp?" he whispered. "My favorite!"

"Just out of the oven. Oh, will you look at you!" She smiled, holding his face between her hands.

"Shh," he said, laughing.

"I swear, you've grown three more inches," she said in a hushed voice.

"I'm twenty-four, sweetheart. I think I've done growing."

"Is that you, Biddy?" called his mother from the parlor.

Nat shrank against the wall and raised a finger to his lips. Biddy blinked, then nodded her understanding. "Yes, ma'am. I'm just after bringing the coffee."

"Well, come in, then. We are about to have music."

The housekeeper reached for the tray but paused and glanced up at Nat, eyes glinting mischief. She picked up the cream pitcher and thrust it into his hands, then lifted the tray and carried it past him into the parlor.

"Here we are, ma'am. Oh! If I haven't forgotten the cream. I'll be right back with it in a trice."

"All right. Come in quietly, please."

"Yes, ma'am. Quiet as a wee mouse."

The clink of china preceded Biddy's return to the hall. Nat kissed her cheek as she went by and got a roguish chuckle in return. He waited for the music to begin, sweet chords of a sentimental song played on his mother's piano. After the first few bars he stepped cautiously to the parlor door.

His parents were there, with their good friends the Kellers and the three youngest Keller children. The eldest, Michael, had enlisted when the war began and was now a captain off fighting somewhere in Virginia. Kenneth, the youngest at ten, and his twelve year old sister Lydia sat with their mother on the sofa in attitudes of polite stiffness. At the piano sat Renata, whom Nat and Quincy had both courted, looking even prettier than Nat remembered in a dress of pale green that set off her strawberry tresses. Though he could only see the curve of her cheek it was enough to set his heart astir, and as he stepped softly into the room she began to sing.

> *"Tell me, tell me, weary soldier*
> *from the rude and stirring wars,*
> *Was my brother in the battle*
> *where you gained those noble scars?*
> *He was ever brave and valiant, and I know he never fled,*
> *Was his name among the wounded or numbered with the dead?"*

Nat felt his chest constricting, and noticed the creamer was tipped sideways in his hand. He righted it just before it spilled, then swallowed and licked his lips, surprised at the strength of his feelings and at how powerfully Renata's sweet voice disturbed them.

> *"Was my brother in the battle when the tide of war ran high?*
> *You would know him in a thousand*
> *by his dark and dashing eye.*
> *Tell me, tell me, weary soldier, will he never come again?*
> *Did he suffer 'mid the wounded, or die among the slain?"*

"Nat!" cried a sharp young voice.

Nat's gaze shifted to the sofa, where Kenneth sat grinning at him as Renata's fingers faltered on the keyboard. Mrs. Keller began to hush her son, then looked up at Nat with surprise dawning on her face. A moment later pandemonium filled the room as everyone exclaimed and jumped up from their seats. Laughing, Nat set the creamer down on a side table and embraced his mother.

"Nat! Oh, my darling boy!"

"Don't cry, Mother."

"But I am so happy!" She laughed, and released him to dab at her eyes. He noticed more silver in her dark hair, more creases on her brow.

"You might have told us you were coming," said his father sternly.

"Well, I could have waited on your doorstep until you got my letter, I suppose. I left as soon as my leave was approved."

"How long can you stay?" his mother asked.

"Two weeks. I have to be back in Cairo on the thirtieth."

"Did you get in any fights?" demanded Kenneth at his elbow.

"Ah—yes, I was in a fight or two."

"How many Rebels did you kill?"

"Kenneth, please!" Mrs. Keller restrained her son with firm hands on his shoulders, then smiled up at Nat. "We are all so happy to see you."

"And I am happy to see all of you," he answered, smiling as he glanced around the room. His gaze caught on Renata, who had risen from the piano. She came forward, smiling shyly up at him, blue eyes alight, and Nat's heart felt as if it was trying to leave his chest.

"Welcome home," she said, giving him her hand.

Jamie jerked awake to the sound of drums playing the long roll nearby. He fumbled to get out his watch and squinted at it, barely able to make out that it was three o'clock. Staggering to his feet, he saw that his men were awakening to the battle call. It was drizzling. He put on his hat and was unrolling his overcoat when John Reily arrived, carrying a lantern.

"The Yankees are advancing on our pickets," he told Jamie, handing him a written order from Colonel Reily. "We are moving above Franklin."

Jamie gave a weary nod as he perused the orders in the light of John's lantern. They placed him at the right of the Confederate line, not far from where they had been the day before.

"General Taylor is here," John added. He grinned when Jamie looked up sharply, then strode off, swinging the lantern.

That final comment banished Jamie's sleepiness. If Taylor was present, he wanted his section in top form. He went to the picket rope where Cocoa stood awake with ears pricked at the activity. He brushed the moisture from her back and saddled her, then got his section in column and reported to Cornay.

The Creole captain seemed withdrawn, and placed Jamie in the rear of the column this time. Probably he wanted to talk with his own lieutenants, Jamie guessed. As he rode through the dark at the head of his section he thought about the rest of the Valverde Battery. They must be somewhere between Bisland and Franklin, part of the long retreating column. He wondered how Hume and Foster were holding up, and where Nettles and Sayers might be. An instinct from his quartermaster days stabbed him with concern for their welfare. In New Mexico, he had been forced to leave many of the wounded behind when the hellish retreat through the mountains had begun; he could see their gloomy faces, the yellow hospital flag whipping in the wind next to the sad little camp where he had left them to await capture by the Yankees. At least Colonel Canby, the Federal commander, had treated them kindly. Many—though not all—were back in the ranks today.

By daylight the Confederates had formed in a large open field inside Irish Bend. The right of the Confederate line rested on Bayou Teche, the left against an impassable canebrake through which a smaller bayou, which Cornay called Bayou Choupique, wound its soggy way. Before them was a dense stand of cypress, and beyond that another field—uncut cane, reminding Jamie of Bisland—was it just two days ago? The Yankees were beyond the cane field. Cornay had one of his sections in the road and one just to the right of it, with Jamie's section on his left beside Reily's regiment, who were now dismounted. A battalion of Louisiana troops, just arrived after marching all night from Avery Island, were deployed in the woodlands as skirmishers.

Jamie glanced to his left and saw Reily's colors nearby. The colonel and John were there, mounted, along with a man he did not recognize: bearded, not as tall as the Reilys and stockier, wearing a black greatcoat and sitting a large black horse with a calm air of command Jamie sensed even at a distance.

"General Taylor," said Cornay's voice nearby.

Jamie looked at Cornay, who had halted his bay beside Cocoa. Casting a glance toward his section, he was glad to see nothing amiss.

"There they are," Cornay said. "Bon chance, mon ami."

Jamie looked east and saw Federals advancing through the cane. His chest tightened as he thought of that first volley he had sent out in Daniel's name—how it had cut cane stalks and Yankees together—he was not altogether certain Daniel would have approved.

Cornay rode away to his section on the road, already moving up along with the skirmishers. In another minute the latter opened fire on the Yankees. Jamie was in the act of moving his section forward when a single gun flew past him on the road to join Cornay. Reaching the bottom of the cane field, Jamie put his guns into battery and opened fire, joining Cornay's guns and the infantry. Their combined efforts checked the enemy advance. The Yankees seemed disinclined to attack, and Jamie knew General Taylor wished only to hold them off while his main column escaped through Franklin, behind the Confederate line, on the cut-off road Fontenot had led him across.

A deep boom from beyond the cane field quickened Jamie's pulse; heavy artillery firing on them, too far for any of their guns to respond. Jamie concentrated his fire on the infantry and tried to ignore the large projectiles falling around his section.

A sudden crackle of rifles from the right drew his gaze—puffs of smoke from a line very close, a ditch across the road, not two hundred yards in front—firing on the St. Mary's Cannoneers. The Louisiana battery's fire fell off as the Yankee infantry poured a hellish rain of musketry into them. Someone screamed. Jamie hastened to shift his fire to the ditch, trying to stop the Yankee barrage. Some of the rifle fire reached his own men—one collapsed beside the howitzer—but the worst of it struck the St. Mary's. Jamie gasped to see Cornay's horse shot beneath him, but the captain was up again in seconds, onto a battery horse and riding past him toward Colonel Reily.

Jamie stood his ground, firing round after round. Cornay galloped past again, back to his suffering battery. Jamie had his men firing canister at the advancing Yankees, then all at once his own guns fell silent.

The Yankees were into his section, fighting hand to hand. He gasped and drew his pistol. Near him a cannoneer tried to fend off a huge infantryman with his rammer; the Yank bayonetted him. A sick flash of memory from Valverde made Jamie's gorge rise: blood and fire and chaos as he and dozens of others followed Colonel Green to capture the guns—these very guns—he must not lose them!

He fired at every bluecoat he saw until his bullets were gone, then drew his sword and bludgeoned away at any Yankee fool enough to come near him. He glanced to the right, but Cornay's guns were gone, vanished. Looking left, he saw the 4th massing to charge, Colonel Reily peering at the enemy through his glass, then slumping forward over his horse's neck.

Reily was hit! Jamie glimpsed John reaching toward his father, then a ball hissed past him, commanding his attention.

"Kill the bastards!" he shouted, wondering if his men could hear him. Pistols fired. Cocoa plunged and screamed amidst the grappling men, so panicked Jamie could barely stay on her. A Yankee put his hand on her reins and Jamie gave him the flat of his sword to his face.

He made up his mind to die rather than let the guns be taken from him, as McRae had done at Valverde.

The Yankees had captured Cornay's colors; he glimpsed a bluecoat running for safety with the prize. A roar to his left made him turn, full of dread, but it was the 4th, moving forward with a shout that grew into the Rebel yell as they flung themselves at the Yankee infantry. Relieved, Jamie kept hitting at the bluecoats, kept yelling encouragement to his men.

As quickly as they had attacked, the Yankees were gone. The 4th's charge sent them back to their own lines. Jamie found himself gulping for breath, hoarse from shouting. He urged his men back to their posts and while they were moving dared to peer toward the ground to his left, hoping and dreading to catch sight of the Reilys.

There they were—off their mounts—John kneeling beside the colonel who lay on his back in the field while the horses grazed nearby as if at a picnic instead of a battle. Jamie's raw throat constricted painfully.

A deep boom from the bayou to the right made him look up. A big gun; had to be the 30-pounder on the *Diana*—he had heard she was being repaired—firing into the field from the bank. He was grateful to tears, and felt ill at the same time.

A riderless horse galloped to the rear from the Confederate center. Jamie looked back to his guns, and seeing that the 4th had returned to their line he gave orders to resume firing.

There were more Yankees at the far side of the field—many more—too many. Soon they would charge again and that would be the end of it. Jamie called his sergeants to him, demanding in a cracked voice to know how much case shot they had left.

"Thirty rounds," Sergeant Schroeder told him.

O'Niell nodded. "About the same."

Jamie pressed his lips together and looked across the field at the mass of blue. "Tell me when you are down to ten apiece."

They went back to their work and Jamie watched, choking on smoke and grief. Reily hit—he could not believe it. He prayed the colonel was not badly wounded.

"Lieutenant!"

Jamie looked up to see General Mouton riding up to him; he recognized the Creole commander from a brief meeting on Sunday. He made a halfhearted attempt to straighten his shoulders.

"How many casualties have you taken?" Mouton shouted over the noise of Jamie's guns.

"Four," Jamie told him, glancing over his platoons to verify there were no more.

"Cornay was badly cut up. Can you cover our retreat?"

Jamie let go his breath. "Yes," he answered, deeply relieved that they were retreating.

"Good. We will fall back and take the cut-off road west. Do you know it?"

Jamie glanced over his left shoulder, toward the road that cut across Irish Bend. "Yes, sir."

"Continue firing until the main column is across the bridge over Bayou Choupique. Then you will retire to the bridge and cover it while the skirmishers cross."

"Yes, sir."

General Mouton rode on to the woods, collecting the Louisiana skirmishers. Jamie saw that the 4th was already filing away behind the screen of cypress trees. It meant they had done their job, that Taylor's army was safely on its way to New Iberia. Jamie gave a painful sob, caught off guard by the thought that this awful morning had been a success. He inhaled deeply, and when he felt more controlled went to his sergeants for reports.

He had seventy-four rounds of ammunition left, much of it solid shot. Of case shot he had only thirty rounds, of canister a dozen. It did not matter, he told himself. They were retreating, he was not likely to need the canister again. He tried to believe it, and ordered his sergeants to pace their fire so as to deter the Yankees while conserving the ammunition as much as possible. The *Diana* kept pounding the Federals from Bayou Teche, a comforting, regular boom.

Colonel Vincent rode past, a blood-soaked bandage around his neck, leaning on one of his aides to keep himself in the saddle. Jamie looked for the Reilys but did not see them; they must have already retreated to Franklin. At last a courier arrived from Mouton with orders for Jamie to fall back to the bridge. He limbered up his guns and started down to the cut-off road while the *Diana* continued to fire. Glancing back, he saw the skirmishers beginning to retire. It was nearly over.

Once his guns were out of the sloughy cane field they moved faster. He turned onto the cut-off road and urged his men forward. Ahead he saw smoke rising, and wondered if the army had abandoned some vehicle and burned it to keep it out of enemy hands. As he got closer to the fire he realized it was too big to be a wagon, then his gut sank. It was the bridge!

"O'Niell, ride to General Mouton and tell him—"

"Yes, sir!" O'Niell spurred away.

"On the double-quick, march!" Jamie shouted to his men. The drivers picked up a trot while the cannoneers ran beside the guns. Jamie halted them at the bridge and ordered them to throw water onto the flames. They waded into Bayou Choupique with sponge buckets, haversacks, whatever would hold water, and flung it at the bridge but it was no use—the structure was fully engulfed in flame. The supports were burning, and the fire was creeping up onto the bridge itself. Jamie called his men back.

Mouton, followed by Sergeant O'Niell, galloped up. The general's face was red with rage as he gazed at the bridge.

"Fils de putain!" Mouton looked at Jamie. "Get your section across at once!"

"The skirmishers—"

"Your guns are heaviest. Go!"

Mouton galloped away again, and Jamie turned to O'Niell and Schroeder, who had joined them. "Cover the ammunition chests with wet blankets. We are going across."

It took precious moments to carry out this precaution, but Jamie did not dare forego it. A stray spark or even too much heat could ignite the remaining ammunition and destroy bridge, guns, and men all together. He rode to the foot of the bridge and stared at the tunnel of flame.

"God," he muttered, "if I have any sway with you, please get my men through this." He dismounted and took off his coat. Beyond his section he could see the first of the skirmishers running toward them. The Yankees would not be far behind.

He draped his coat over Cocoa's head, covering her eyes. She whinnied a protest, but he knew she would trust him.

"Good girl." Drawing a deep breath, with Cocoa's reins tight in one hand and the other holding his coat over her head, Jamie started toward the flames.

11

With a force of at least 14,000 men in our front and this movement of the enemy in our rear in heavy force the situation of our little army, which at the commencement of the contest was less than 4,000, was most critical.
—Richard Taylor, Major-General, C.S. Army

Fire licked out at Jamie from the sides of the bridge, the flames making their own wind—choking hot—billowing smoke stinging his eyes. He went as fast as he dared to lead his frightened mare, crazily counting his paces because he was too terrified for any more complicated thought. Fifty to get halfway across, and now he heard the rumble of the first gun carriage behind him. His heart lurched at the thought of thirty-odd pounds of gunpowder coming within an arm's length of the flames.

Cocoa whinnied in fright and tried to toss her head, but he kept an iron grip on her and strode on, lungs aching with each breath of searing air, legs feeling as if they would slip out from under him as he hastened down the far side of the bridge, unable to see the bank for the smoke and the wavering heat. Suddenly he was through, stumbling on the muddy road, coughing cool, moist air. He forced himself to keep moving, out of the way of the guns and caissons behind him, off the road into a field of green, wonderful green. He stopped there and leaned against Cocoa, both of them trembling all over. Removing his coat from her head, he petted and praised her, then got into the saddle and turned to look at the bridge.

It looked even worse than it was. If he had not just been there himself he would have been horrified to see the skirmishers dashing into the fire. His 6-pounder had cleared the bridge; the howitzer was halfway across. Jamie rode to Sergeant Schroeder and told him in a croaking voice to unlimber his piece in the field and cover the retreat. The cannoneers looked dazed but they responded, coughing and wiping their sweating faces as they moved into position. Relieved drivers calmed their teams and got back in their saddles. Jamie moved among his men, congratulating them on crossing the bridge and urging them back into action.

Across the bayou General Mouton waited with his staff, their horses already hooded with coats and blankets. Jamie's heart swelled with admiration at Mouton's gallantry, for not until the last of the skirmishers was across the bridge did the general move onto it, by which time the timbers were beginning to fail. One crumbled and dropped into the bayou, hissing and throwing up a cloud of steam. Jamie's gaze was riveted as Mouton and his staff rushed over what was left of the bridge. When they were safe he drew a relieved breath and coughed, lungs still aching.

Mouton ordered Jamie's section to form in column and serve as rearguard. In a short while they caught up with the main column. Jamie saw Mouton ride forward to consult with Colonel Green, then after a brief conversation the general continued ahead, probably looking for Taylor. When he was assured that his section was in its place in the column, Jamie rode to Green as well. The colonel was frowning.

"Sir, have you seen Colonel Reily?"

Green's frown deepened. "He died on the field."

Stunned, Jamie blinked and swallowed, his dry throat protesting. *No,* he thought stupidly. *No.*

"Are your boys all right, son?" Colonel Green asked him in a strained voice.

Jamie nodded, batting at his stinging eyes. "S-someone set the bridge on fire before we got to it."

"I did."

Astonished, Jamie gaped at the colonel. Green's face was grim.

"I was ordered to. I was given to understand that everyone was across."

"Who gave you the order?" Jamie asked in disbelief.

"General Sibley."

Nat walked up the path to the Kellers' elegant town house, pausing before ringing the bell to cast an anxious glance at the sleeves of his newly brushed coat. Biddy had labored long on it, beating out the marks of its service which included the residue of several river-dunkings. He had other coats, but the cachet of a uniform—even one so plain as his—was not to be lightly dismissed. He had Quincy to compete with, after all.

Evans, the Kellers' negro butler, answered the door. "Good morning, Mr. Wheat."

"Good morning. I am here to take Miss Keller for a walk."

Evans nodded. "If you will step into the parlor, I will inform her that you have arrived."

Nat entered Mrs. Keller's fashionably appointed parlor, and to pass the time he examined the pictures on the wall. Most were familiar, but there were two new watercolors—one a pretty river scene, the other a rather fanciful painting of Liberty standing upon a vanquished snake—which he suspected were Renata's work. He found himself smiling at the Liberty, which looked a little like Renata herself.

"There you are!"

Renata smiled at him from the doorway, angelic in a pale blue dress trimmed with many rows of ruffled ribbon. Her face was framed by a straw bonnet adorned with more of the ribbon and a great profusion of lace, and she carried a small parasol.

"I hope I have not kept you waiting long," she said, coming into the room.

Nat smiled back. "Not long at all."

Mrs. Keller followed her daughter into the room. She was still a beauty, though beneath her stylish breakfast cap the golden hair was now fading to silver. Nat and Quincy had run loose in her home ever since he could remember, and had treated her as a second mother.

"Good morning, Mr. Wheat," she said. A sparkle of humor in her eye contrasted with her tone, and she extended a hand clad in a dainty lace mitten with slightly exaggerated formality.

Nat responded by stepping forward to bow deeply over the hand. "Good morning, Mrs. Keller. Thank you for permitting me to take your daughter out walking. I will bring her back safely in an hour's time."

"You need not hurry. If you are back by noon you may join us for dinner."

Nat's smile grew into a grin. "In that case, we will be back at twelve sharp."

"Oh! You see, Mother? It is your hospitality he is really after." Renata affected displeasure, with no greater success than her mother's attempt at formality. Her pout was certainly pretty, but the glance she cast up at Nat to gauge its effect quite destroyed any illusion of disdain. He chuckled.

"Blame my exposure to the military, Miss Keller. A soldier's creed is never to turn down the offer of a meal."

"But you are not a soldier, sir."

"No, thank heaven. Shall we go?"

Renata accepted his arm and, bidding farewell to her mother, accompanied Nat out of the house. He led her toward the river, where the partially built towers of the new suspension bridge stood looking rather forlorn, their potential strength unfulfilled, water swirling about their feet. The work had been stopped when the war began, as much out of fear the Confederates would use the bridge to invade the city as from lack of resources. Nat turned away, guiding Renata toward the green banks beyond the riverfront.

"Tell me about the places you have seen," she said.

"Well, I wrote to you about Vicksburg, what we could see of it. Truth is, we did not see much of any place except from on deck."

"Did you never go ashore?"

"Not much." A memory of Belle View came to mind. "I was ashore at a plantation, but it was in the evening."

"What was it like?"

Nat hesitated, remembering the encounter between Adams and the malicious overseer. "The house was most impressive. It is called Rosehall, and belongs to—"

"One Colonel Hawkland!" Renata turned bright eyes toward him. "Yes, your brother was there, too—he wrote to me about it and described the house. He was invited in with his captain, and was in raptures over the beauty of the place. He even sent me a rose from the garden, pressed in a letter."

Nat looked out at the river. "The roses were not blooming when I was there."

They walked in silence for a little, then she said, "Do you know what boat you will be on when you go back?"

"Not yet. I was offered an appointment as a paymaster's clerk, but I am better with carpentry than with figures."

"You are perfectly capable with figures; you are merely too impatient to sit down and do them. Remember how you used to offer me sweets to write out your arithmetic homework?"

Nat looked at her, grinning. "And you used to take them."

"Only once!" Her eyes flashed, then softened. "Father gave me such a scold, I did not dare to do it again."

"I wish my father had satisfied himself with scolding." His tone was more bitter than he had meant it to be.

She glanced up at him with swift concern. "You and he are still at outs?"

"Always."

"I am sorry. I wish it were not so."

Nat gazed at her, glad for her sympathy but unwilling to pursue the subject. She seemed to understand, for she looked away to watch a laden packet make its plodding way up the river.

"So, not a paymaster's clerk?"

"No. Probably another carpenter's berth." He found himself frowning as he said it aloud.

"Why not pursue what you really want?" she said softly. "Why not become a pilot?"

Nat's pulse jumped and he stopped walking to look at her. "What makes you think I want to be a pilot?"

She smiled. "Oh, perhaps because you never went a day in school without talking about it. You still want to, do you not?"

Yes.

He swallowed and looked at the river, uncomfortable with the strength of his feelings. "I would have to get a license. I do not have the training, and it would—" He shook his head, thinking of all the difficulties. "Besides, my father would never allow it."

Renata was silent. He glanced at her, and the expression of sympathy on her face made him feel ashamed. Perhaps he should have tried harder to get along with his father. She could not understand, though—her own father was kind, generous.

A chestnut tree shaded them, its spreading leaves dappling the sunlight, yellow to white to green. Nat peered at Renata in the shifting light. "The song you were singing when I came home last night was very beautiful."

Her eyes softened. "Thank you. I sing it quite often. Whenever I feel anxious about Michael, it makes me feel better. I don't know why—it is not a particularly cheerful song."

Nat nodded. "It made me think of Quincy, but it was more than that. It was that you were singing it, coming home to find you there— I was so moved—it is hard for me to describe. I cannot recall ever feeling like that before."

She gave a small smile, and looked shyly away. Gazing down at her face, Nat found his feelings overcoming his ability to form a sentence. She was so lovely, so sweet—her reddish gold curls framing creamy cheeks now becoming tinged with rose—he felt not only his heart but his body responding. When had his childhood friend grown into this Venus?

A burst of high-pitched laughter startled them. Turning, Nat saw two little girls chasing a butterfly along a hedge of flowering bushes, their watchful nanny in attendance. He offered Renata his arm again, and they strolled away from the children.

"May I ask you a personal question?"

She gave him a guarded look. "You may ask."

"Do you care more for Quincy than you do for me?"

It had caught her by surprise; she looked away. "I have always thought of you both as brothers," she said slowly.

"I do not wish you to think of me as a brother now."

"Oh." The word was barely above a whisper.

She slid her hand from his arm and moved away. Nat watched her walk a few steps toward the river. Perhaps he had just ruined any chance he might have had with her. If that were so, he prayed she would be kind and tell him so.

"You certainly are serious today. How unlike you, Nat."

"Perhaps I'll get over it," he said, half to himself.

"That would be a pity. I think I rather like you this way."

What did she mean by that? He waited, watching her toy with her parasol as she walked back toward him.

"Have you heard there is to be a charity ball on the Saturday after next?" she asked. "The Ladies League is raising money to send vegetables to the regiments in the field."

"No, I had not heard. Do you plan to attend?"

"I do not know." She peered up at him from beneath the brim of her bonnet, smiling. "It depends upon whether I receive an invitation."

Nat drew a breath. "May I have the honor of escorting you?"

"If you can get tickets."

"I will make it my business to acquire some."

She cast him a playful glance. "I heard they were selling like hotcakes."

"I will attend to it at once then," Nat said with mock gravity, feeling a little more sure of his ground. He made a formal bow and extended his arm once more, smiling. "Immediately after dinner."

"The ordnance wagon is here." Sergeant Schroeder looked haggard. Standing at Jamie's knee, he had to shout to be heard over the noise of the guns. "Shall I take my caisson back?"

"No, stay with your piece," Jamie told him. "I'll do it."

Schroeder nodded and hurried back to his position behind the 6-pounder, which was firing at a line of Federal skirmishers in the woods on the far side of a cane field. Jamie glanced over at the howitzer to make certain O'Niell needed no help before turning Cocoa toward Schroeder's caisson. Corporal Reese, who ordinarily commanded the caisson, was out of action with a chestful of shrapnel from a shell that had burst over the section earlier in the day and wounded five men, two severely. That had been two skirmishes ago—or was it three? Jamie had lost count of the times they had unlimbered. His section had joined the rearguard under Green's command, along with the 5th Texas and Waller's Battalion of the 2nd. They had been engaged off and on throughout the hot, miserable day, holding the enemy back while the rest of the army tried to gain a lead. Jamie's guns remained on or near the road while the cavalry would dismount and spread into the fields, woods, or occasionally swamps, on either side. All day they had either been fighting or marching with only the briefest of halts, scarcely long enough to catch their breath, never enough to cook rations. The only thing Jamie had eaten was a chunk torn from a loaf of bread that a townswoman, weeping tears of gratitude, had handed him at the roadside as they passed through Jeanerette. He had been almost too tired to thank her, almost too tired to eat, and had given most of the loaf to Schroeder and O'Niell who had shared it with their gunners. His cannoneers had also received gifts of food from civilians along the way, for which he was unspeakably grateful. Otherwise they might well have dropped by now.

Jamie ordered the caisson's drivers to follow him to the ordnance wagon that had been sent back down the column to replenish his nearly exhausted supply. He found it parked beneath a spreading oak, and entered the shade with a small sigh of relief. Dismounting, he left Cocoa with one of the drivers and went to help fill the ammunition chests on the caisson, making sure the rounds were in good condition and properly packed, wondering in the back of his mind whether Corporal Reese would recover to resume this duty, or whether he would have to choose a replacement. Such thoughts were a constant trouble to him; he had no rest from them, no peace.

"Lieutenant?"

Jamie looked up at the mounted man who had come up behind him: dark coat draping over muscular thighs; dark eyes in a stern, mustached face he had seen but did not place at once. It took him a moment to remember Captain Cornay pointing the man out to him that morning, a century ago.

"General Taylor." Jamie was too weary to be much surprised, but he made an effort to straighten his shoulders.

"How are your men holding up?"

Jamie glanced back toward his guns. "Fairly well, sir. They are getting a bit tired."

"I know you have had a difficult day." The general's eyes flashed beneath frowning brows as he glanced eastward, likely thinking of the fiasco with the bridge. "If you can continue for the rest of today, I will arrange for you to be relieved tomorrow."

Jamie felt a flood of gratitude, so strong it surprised him. He managed to smile. "Thank you, sir. We can finish the day."

Taylor gave him a nod, still frowning. "You are aware that Colonel Green was not at fault—"

"I know, sir. I trust Colonel Green. We are old friends."

The general nodded again, a small smile of approval flicking across his face. "Carry on, then."

Jamie watched the general ride away toward where Green and his staff stood beneath a clump of trees at the edge of the field. The 5th were plying their rifles from the cover, such as it was, of the drainage ditches that crisscrossed the cane. Most of them were muddy from head to foot by now. Wiping sweat from his eyes, Jamie gave silent thanks that he was not in the infantry and returned to the task at hand.

When the chests were full he returned the caisson to its place and ordered O'Niell to send his own caisson back to be filled. By the time this was done he received orders from Green to limber up again and move. He still had two chests that needed filling, but the other six should last him for the rest of the day. He squinted at the sweltering sun, trying to guess the time. He put it at four o'clock, then checked his watch and found it was almost five. His men had been up since half past three that morning, and in action or marching since dawn.

Jamie squeezed his eyes shut. He did not want to begin thinking over the events of this day; he could not bear it, not now. He clung to his duty, giving it all of his flagging energy, watching over his section as they limbered up once more and followed in the wake of the army. He began to see stragglers—men heading off across the fields, alone or in small groups—Louisianans, going to their homes. Jamie supposed he could understand their reasons for leaving the column, but felt angry just the same. He was glad to note that none of Cornay's men were among the deserters. They seemed mostly to be from Colonel Vincent's command or from the Yellow Jackets.

Twice more Colonel Green deployed the rearguard to fire on the pursuing Federals, the second time after sunset. When Jamie got orders to move on again he began to wonder if the march would ever end. It was beginning to assume something of the nightmarish character of the retreat from New Mexico, though at least here there was no concern about water. He looked over his platoons and asked his sergeants to report on their condition, though he could see for himself that the men were exhausted. When Schroeder and O'Niell gave him the numbers he grimaced. Five men dead and twelve wounded since morning, and six horses killed. His strength was trickling away. If he lost many more horses, he might have to put Cocoa in harness.

"Just a little longer," he told the sergeants. "General Taylor is going to relieve us tomorrow. Tell the boys." He hoped the news would give his men the strength to continue, and prayed that the general would be true to his word.

At last, long after dark had fallen, Colonel Green sent orders to halt for the night. The men threw themselves down where they stood, too exhausted to cook or to eat. Only the drivers stayed up, hobbling on saddle-sore legs to feed and water their teams before collapsing. Jamie dismounted gingerly, his own legs raw from far too many hours in the saddle. He saw to Cocoa's needs himself, letting her drink until the edge was off her thirst, then taking her to a patch of grass at the edge of a field where he sat down to watch her graze for a while. There was no moon, but the stars gave just enough light for him to see that this field was planted in something other than sugar. Yams, maybe. They grew yams around here, didn't they?

"Lieutenant Russell? Wake up, sir, please?"

Jamie started, panicked for a moment until he remembered where he was. He sat up and cast an anxious glance around for Cocoa, saw her silhouette against the paler darkness, grazing peacefully nearby.

"Sergeant Schroeder," he said, rubbing his eyes. "What time is it?"

"Almost five," Schroeder told him. "Our relief is here."

Jamie got stiffly to his feet and followed Schroeder to where a broad-shouldered lieutenant waited, holding his horse's reins. On the road beyond him Jamie saw two guns—long ones—with their crews ready to move forward.

"Winchester, Pelican Battery," said the section's commander in a

Louisiana drawl as he extended a gauntleted hand. "I am here to relieve you."

Jamie shook hands. "Are those rifles?"

Winchester glanced at his guns and nodded. "Three-inchers. They'll give the Yanks something to think about." He reached into his coat and produced a folded page torn from a pocket notebook. "Colonel Green asked me to hand you this."

"Thanks." Jamie squinted at the page but could not read it. He bade farewell to Lieutenant Winchester and gave orders for his section to form in column, then found a lantern and read Green's note, which confirmed his relief and ordered him to proceed forward along the column to rejoin his battery. They were miles ahead. Lord knew when he would reach them, but at least he was through fighting for now.

That thought raised a surge of emotion; Jamie coughed, unwilling to yield to it. He took a deep breath and found an idea to grapple onto, that of locating John Reily, also somewhere ahead in the long, strung-out column. He wanted to talk to John. Must do that first, then he would think about the rest of it.

He roused his men and marched them a mile, halting at an empty field to give them an hour to cook and eat. Starting forward again in the predawn, they passed units still camped or rather sprawled wherever they had halted the night before. His weary men made no complaint; they were moving away from the enemy and that was enough. Jamie walked for a mile or so leading Cocoa, trying to shake the aches and the sleepiness out of himself. By dawn he was finally awake and the troops they were passing were getting up, lighting fires, filling the air with the smells of coffee and bacon. He mounted, wincing, and rode back to check on his men. O'Niell reported one man had collapsed and been loaded on a limber, the rest were holding together.

Jamie nodded. "Come and tell me if any more fall out."

"Yes, sir."

Riding back to the head of his section, Jamie began to doubt if he would reach the battery today. Once the army was marching he would not be able to change his position in the column. He searched the bedraggled troops he passed for a familiar face, a familiar flag. The section came up behind some cavalry forming in the road and Jamie was about to order his men to halt, then to his surprise the horsemen moved aside, letting him pass, cheering as he reached them. He knew the faces, he realized, though he was too stupidly tired to remember the names. It was the 4th, and there was Lieutenant-Colonel Hardeman, now in command, raising his hat as the cavalry cheered Jamie's section on. With Hardeman was John Reily, his face fixed in frowning grief, sitting like a statue in the saddle.

"Lead them on, Sergeant," Jamie told Schroeder, and turned Cocoa out of the column. He rode toward Reily, who caught sight of him now and nudged his bay forward. They met on the verge, reaching across their horses' necks to clasp hands.

"John, I am so sorry," Jamie said in a strangled voice.

Reily's face crumpled. All of a sudden Jamie thought of Daniel and the two of them sat frozen, hands gripped tight and tears streaming down both their faces while their horses quietly grazed in the peach-colored sunrise.

12

Colonel Reily, of the 4th Texas Regiment Mounted Volunteers, who fell in the battle of Franklin, was a gallant and chivalrous soldier, whose loss I deeply regret.
—Richard Taylor, Major-General, C.S. Army

"I still cannot believe it," John Reily said. "I cannot believe he is gone."

Jamie turned his head to glance at his friend, who had come to walk with him at the head of his section. They had been marching since dawn, and were leading their horses in order to spare them in the high heat of the day. John's brow was furrowed but he seemed more stunned than aggrieved. The grief and the anger would come later, Jamie knew. He was still struggling with them himself.

The road had dried and was beginning to go dusty, and the barren blue-white sky offered no promise of relief. Jamie could feel a blister developing on one heel. The muffled sound of the rearguard still skirmishing behind them told him there would be few halts again today. When he glanced back at his men, their faces were set in expressions of grim endurance.

At least they were now reunited with the rest of the Valverde Battery, which was just ahead of the 4th in the column of retreat. Foster and Hume had welcomed Jamie warmly, though both their faces showed the strain of the last few days. The rest of the battery had been badly cut up on Tuesday—the day Captain Sayers was wounded—while Jamie had been helping to destroy bridges. His losses since then had brought his section to a condition more or less equal to theirs. Foster was worst off in loss of horses; in a tight moment he had been forced to abandon one of his guns, but some Dutch boys from Company C of the 4th had found it and hauled it off by hand, unwilling to see their hard-won trophy left behind.

"I keep wondering how I will tell my mother," John said.

Jamie thought of the painful time he had spent composing a letter to his sister when Martin had died. There was no easy way to convey such terrible news. He had chosen to be direct, though judging by Emma's reaction that might not have been the best approach. He refrained from offering advice to John, who must know better than he how to address Mrs. Reily. Instead he asked gently, "Do you want to tell me about it?"

John's frown deepened. "There is not much to tell—it happened so fast. One moment he was reconnoitering the enemy line . . ."

John stared unseeing at the road ahead for a while, reliving the battle, perhaps. The instant in which Colonel Reily had been shot was etched in Jamie's own memory—a glimpse of the colonel slumped over his horse's neck—never to be forgotten. It would stay with him, joining other such pictures of horror frozen in his mind like a gallery of grim cartes-de-visite, preserved not by his will but by his inability to escape the memories.

"I have to take him home now," John said in a bewildered voice. "I do not know what to do. Will you help me, James?" He turned haggard eyes toward Jamie.

"Yes. Of course."

Of course he would help. He had been a quartermaster, he knew what to do about coffins and transportation. New Iberia was too small and would soon be overwhelmed by the army, but it would not be difficult to find a coffin maker in one of the larger towns. He swallowed the lump that rose in his throat at the thought of Colonel Reily, grand old Reily, lying in a coffin draped in black.

At least John and his family had a body to mourn over, he reflected, and immediately felt shame and frustration both at the terrible thought. He kept it to himself, and wondered silently where Daniel had ended up. Someday he would find out. He would talk to any of Terry's Rangers he could find, learn what had happened, where Dan was buried—if he'd been buried. Maybe they'd had to leave him on the field. Maybe he was in some mass grave somewhere in Tennessee, like the ones they had dug at Valverde and in which Jamie had placed Stephen Martin's corpse. Maybe Jamie would never find Daniel. Even if he was very, very lucky and did find the place, it would not happen soon. Not for months, years maybe. Not until this war was over.

Marie gazed out toward the river from the shade of Rosehall's downstairs gallery, where she sat in a white wicker chair crocheting a cap for the baby to come. Afternoon sun was beginning to encroach on the colonnade, dappled beams slipping through the boughs of the old oak northwest of the house, which had been preserved by Colonel Hawkland during Rosehall's construction for the sake of its shade in summer.

Lucinde sat at the gallery's edge in this mixed light, her long limbs dangling over the side, white cotton skirts draping all but her feet which were clad in sandals of woven grass. Her head, wrapped in a turban made from a bright-red and violet cast-off silk scarf Marie had given her, was bowed over the neck of a guitar. She strummed it with long, dark fingers, gentle music for a sleepy afternoon.

Down at the river landing a small, somewhat run-down steamer was being laden with cotton. The sight gave Marie warm satisfaction, though she could have wished for a larger vessel. That Theodore had managed to obtain any vessel was near to a miracle however, and indeed she was grateful. Boats were getting harder to come by as the Yankee vessels prowled the river more and more.

Theodore shook hands with the boat's captain, taking leave. When she saw him start toward his horse Marie picked up a silver bell from the table beside her and rang it. The music paused as Lucinde raised her head at the sound, but a moment later resumed.

Slow footsteps approached, not Alphonse's stately pace but the lighter tread of the downstairs maid. Marie, staring at her work so as not to lose count of her stitches, said, "Bring out the lemonade now, Sarah."

"Oui, Madame," said the girl in a hoarse voice.

Marie glanced up, but the maid had already turned away and started toward the door. She moved listlessly, but in this heat that was not surprising. Returning her attention to the soft yarn in her fingers, Marie hastened to finish a row. She completed it just as Theodore reached the house, the rhythmic thudding of his horse's hooves on the crushed shell of the drive jumbling to a halt as he reined in.

Marie set her work aside and stood up to welcome him, waiting in the shade. Theodore fed a lump of sugar to his horse and left the animal in the care of a stable boy, then turned to her with a smile and mounted the steps to the gallery.

"Well? Do we prosper?" Marie asked, presenting her cheek to be kissed.

"We prosper. I have promised the captain a bonus if he gets back from Shreveport in time to take up another load."

"Not too large a bonus, I hope," said Marie, resuming her seat.

Theodore sat in a chair on the opposite side of the little table and removed his hat, fanning himself with it. "Have no fear for our profits. Lawford says he can sell as much as we send him at a handsome gain."

"Good." Marie smiled and picked up her crocheting. "Do you believe the river will still be open when the boat returns?"

"Who can say? It costs us nothing if it is not."

"I would be happy if I never saw another of those horrid gunboats."

"I hope you never do, my love." Theodore looked up at the maid's return. "Lemonade? How delightful!"

Marie smiled. "I thought you might enjoy a glass of something cool. Put it on the table, here, Sarah."

The maid bent down with the tray, on which the heavy pitcher suddenly slid, tipping tray and all toward Marie's lap. She gasped as cold lemonade spilled across her hands, crocheting, and dress. A glass struck the wooden porch and shattered. Everyone stood at once, all exclaiming.

"Marie, are you all right? Clumsy wretch!"

"Sarah! What is the matter with you?" Marie cried at the same time.

Sarah began to weep, babbling in between wailing sobs. Marie grabbed the slave's chin and wrenched it up, hoping a stern gaze would put an end to the girl's hysteria.

The guitar's strings intoned a troubled discord as Lucinde thrust it aside. "Madame—"

"Sacre Dieu! What is this?"

The girl's face was swollen with bruises, one eye nearly shut. Marie swallowed a sudden mouthful of bile.

"Good God!" Theodore said.

Marie released the girl, who hung her head, uttering great, rasping sobs. "S-s-sorry, Madame," she choked out.

"Never mind that. Who did this to you?"

The slave made no answer, but stood weeping piteously. Marie looked at Lucinde as she stepped up behind the girl.

"Madame . . ."

"Take her away," Marie said. "Clean her up and put her to bed—"

"Oh, no—no—" Sarah cried, showing eyes wide with fright.

"Ask Damien to watch over her," Marie added quickly. "Is he on the grounds?"

Lucinde nodded. "In the workshop. I will fetch him."

"Will that do?" Marie said to Sarah, who made no answer but grew calmer, hanging her head again. "Go along, then," Marie told her gently. "Lucinde, when you have settled her I would like a word with you."

"Oui, Madame."

Lucinde took the girl by the shoulders and gently moved her toward the door. Theodore took out his pocket handkerchief and rubbed at Marie's sticky hands. Neither spoke until the two slaves had gone into the house.

Marie drew a breath. "Mon cher, I must ask you to speak to Mr. Shelton again."

"You believe it was he?"

"He is the only one who has ever bothered that girl."

Theodore frowned. "It could have been one of the slaves."

"Damien would have dealt with a slave." Marie reached down to pick up her crocheting. Glass fell from the sodden yarn, tinkling on the porch.

"Be careful, my love. Never mind that, it is ruined."

Marie let the half-finished cap fall. Her dress might well be ruined also. She should go upstairs and change it. She looked at Theodore, who met her gaze with one of equal concern.

"I really do not wish to leave home just now," she said. "Not with things as they are."

"I will speak to Shelton," Theodore told her. "This will not happen again."

"I sincerely hope not," Marie said.

The footman appeared with a bucket and mop, ending their tête-à-tête. Marie stepped out of his way. "Thank you, Victor. When you have finished, please bring in the guitar."

Victor nodded, kneeling to pick up the broken glass. He dropped it piece by piece onto the silver tray.

"I am going in to change," Marie told her husband. "Shall I have Alphonse bring you out more lemonade?"

"No, no. I will be in the library."

"All right." She reached toward him but stopped herself, holding her hands in the air. Blowing him a kiss instead, she managed a light-hearted smile though her humor was far from easy as she went in.

In her bedchamber Marie stripped off her dress and petticoats, filled her wash basin with cool water from the pitcher and bathed her hands and arms, then changed her drawers for a clean pair. Her corset, laced loosely over the swell of her abdomen, had mostly escaped the lemonade and was soiled only in a small spot on one corner, not enough to make it worth the effort of changing. She was dabbing at it with a damp handkerchief when Lucinde came in and closed the door softly behind her.

"Madame—"

"Ah, bien. Bring me a fresh dress, please. The lightest you can find." Marie stepped into the clean skirt she had taken out and draped a fresh petticoat over it while Lucinde went to the wardrobe and returned with a loose-fitting robe of white muslin trimmed with lavender ribbons. Marie did not speak again until Lucinde had tied the last bow of the jacket front, partly because she did not wish to speak harshly and so must master her temper. At last, as she accepted a clean kerchief from her woman, she felt composed enough to address her.

"Why did you not tell me of this trouble, Lucinde?"

Lucinde looked down. "Je regrette, Madame. The girl begged me not to."

Marie pressed her lips together as she tucked the kerchief and her amber rosary into her pocket. "Did she think us blind?"

"She is very frightened, Madame. I can maybe believe that she has been threatened."

Marie directed a sharp glance at Lucinde, who returned her gaze steadily. This Shelton was more trouble than he was worth, she thought, but she knew Theodore would be hard pressed to replace him. There were the overseers of the separate plantations, but most of them were friends of Shelton's; if he were dismissed they might all leave in protest.

"I have asked my husband to speak to Mr. Shelton."

"With respect, Madame, I think Mr. Shelton does not listen to Monsieur about Sarah."

"I do not know what more I can do. If I sold her away she might not fare any better."

"Take her with you."

Marie looked up. Lucinde's face, usually unreadable, was tight with concern, her eyes burning intently. "Take her with you to Shreveport. She can wait on you and I will stay here."

"She is not a lady's maid!"

"She can learn. I will teach her before you go. Please, Madame. I ask you, please."

Marie could not recall Lucinde having ever asked anything of her before. She gazed at her, wondering how much her dark eyes had seen that she had never shared with her mistress.

"Perhaps," Marie said slowly. "I will consider it."

"Thank you, Madame."

Lucinde cast her eyes down and stood silent, returned to her customary tranquility. Marie sighed. She did not want to take the girl to Shreveport. It would mean discomfort, inconvenience. No one could care for her needs as well as Lucinde.

"She is sleeping?"

Lucinde's eyes met hers briefly, and she shook her head. "Resting."

"Very well. You may go."

Marie waited until she heard the door softly close, then opened the French doors onto the upper gallery. A wave of moist heat washed over her as she stepped out. The boat, heavy with cotton, was just leaving the landing. She watched it steam across the river to the mouth of the Red, turn up it, and slowly vanish behind the trees. Its smoke trail was visible for some minutes, moving north and west, the way she herself would shortly travel. The Yankee boats were present on the river more and more, and this brief respite from their hovering presence could not last. If they could get one more load of cotton out, bien, but what then? There might not be another time when the river was free. Vicksburg was all that was keeping the Yankees to the north in check. What if it fell? How then would they sell their cotton and sugar? Would they be forced to sell it to the Yankees?

All her life she had made difficult choices, often against the conventional wisdom of family, church, or society. Always her view had been to better her position, to improve life for herself, then for her husband, and now for her growing family. There had always been cost, though she tried not to engender cost to others. There had always been risk, but risk was necessary if one was to reach high. She had married outside her Creole culture, which had upset her family even more than the disparity in age between herself and Theodore. By marrying thus, however, she (and by association, her family) had attained greater prosperity than would have been brought by any match she could foresee for herself among her own people. She had brought with her a full understanding of how a successful plantation was run, for among the Creoles women were managers and owners of plantations as often as men. Together she and Theodore had increased their prosperity, until they now owned five plantations here along the river and a handsome townhouse in New Orleans, in addition to Theodore's properties in Tennessee. Difficult choices had been made all along the way, but God must have approved, for they had been greatly blessed. Until the war began, each year's profit had exceeded that of the year before.

Marie felt a sudden restlessness. She had been at home for so long, feeling unwell and delicate, but she now felt perfectly strong. It would be good to travel while she could. Once the child came such movements would be much more difficult, and the Yankees would soon return to restrict traffic upon the river.

She would take Sarah with her. Her grandmother would have said she was spoiling the slave, and perhaps she was, but she could not bring herself to ignore the girl's distress nor the urgent request of her oldest servant. Her world was changing in many ways, some of which she did not like. Perhaps this small kindness would be a credit to her in heaven's view.

Jamie stood with John Reily in a mortician's workroom in Vermillionville, where the exhausted army had stopped for a few hours' rest. An oil lamp was suspended from the ceiling over a long table upon which rested a hastily assembled coffin. Jamie could smell the sawdust from the fresh carpentry. The box was of pine, with black cloth tacked over it. They had not the time to wait for paint to dry. The lead lining was more important, as the coffin would have a long way to travel.

Inside this humble casket lay the remains of Colonel James Reily, founder and commander of the 4th Texas Mounted Volunteers. He wore the uniform he had died in, one side of the gray coat stained dark with blood; there had not been time to retrieve his baggage and get a different suit of clothes. John had said he did not care. He stood now, holding one of his father's cold hands in his, shedding silent tears.

Jamie looked away, resisting the emotions brought forward by the scene. Instead he thought about his section, who along with one of Cornay's were standing guard over the town's main bridge. Beyond it, General Banks's army was slowly falling behind Taylor's fleeing Confederates, delayed by the Yankee soldiers' wanton looting along the Teche. By even the most conservative reports, Banks was allowing his army to ransack every community and dwelling in its path. Hideous stories were circulating. Jamie wondered what Captain Cornay and his men must be feeling.

At last he heard John draw a ragged breath and let it out with a sigh. Jamie looked up to see his friend step back from the coffin and nod to the mortician, who carefully set the lid in place and began to nail it shut. After a minute, Jamie touched John's sleeve. John met his gaze, nodded again, and started toward the door.

"I will bring a wagon in the morning," Jamie said to the mortician, then followed John out.

Outside the air was cool, the night sky clear and spattered with stars. Jamie walked with John toward the 4th's camp.

"Thank you," John said.

"You are welcome."

"I have another favor to ask of you."

Jamie looked at him, waiting. There was no moon, but starlight was enough for him to see the pain in Reily's face.

"Come with me as far as Shreveport."

"I—"

"You are better than I at arranging for transportation and such things, and I do not feel able . . ."

Jamie put a hand on Reily's shoulder. "All right. Yes. I will ask Colonel Green's permission."

It was General Green now, though Jamie was not yet used to that. General Taylor, in his fury over the fiasco at Franklin, had removed Sibley from command and sworn to court-martial him. Giving Sibley the ignominious chore of commanding the baggage train, Taylor had promoted Green to command the brigade in his stead. The change pleased nearly everyone. Sibley was not only responsible for the ill-timed destruction of the bridge at Franklin, but as Jamie had later learned, he had on the same day made another blunder that resulted in the capture of the steamer *Cornie,* carrying all of the sick and wounded from Camp Bisland.

Green would make a good brigadier. He was forthright and fearless. His own regiment, the 5th, would follow him to hell and back, and the rest of the brigade would no doubt do the same. He got along with General Taylor, too.

With two such commanders, Jamie thought the army would do well. Since meeting General Taylor his respect for the commander had steadily increased. Taylor seemed always to be in the thick of things, yet he also showed great ability in handling his army, planning even the smallest details so that troops, supplies, wagons, and so on were all where they should be at the right time, assuming no outside interference such as Sibley's creative interpretation of orders. Even though most soldiers took it for granted, Jamie knew it was no small feat to manage an army so skillfully. The only pity was that he had to manage them in retreat, but at least that was better than capture.

"When do we march, do you know?" John asked.

"Tomorrow, I think. After the men have had a night's sleep." Jamie glanced sidelong at his friend, trying to read his shadowed face. "You should get some sleep as well."

John did not answer, and Jamie suspected he knew what his friend was thinking. It was hard to sleep when all you could think of was a loved one whose face you would never see again.

Familiar smells swept over Nat as he walked through Wheat's Shipyard: old rotting wood, newly sawn lumber, turpentine, tar, paint—sparking memories with each shift of the breeze. His father led him between stacks of lumber and huge coils of cable, up the steps to his office where they paused on the small, railed porch from which it was Mr. Wheat's custom to observe the progress of his contracts.

The yard was busier than Nat had ever seen it. Two boats were in dry dock, their structures swarming with workmen, piles of iron plates waiting to be applied to the sloping wooden sides being built to enclose their decks. When Nat had left two years before, his father had just bid on a new contract to convert riverboats into tinclads for the navy. Since then two had launched from Wheat's Yard, three more were under contract, and new contracts were bidding even now.

"New design?" Nat asked, gesturing toward the boats.

His father nodded. "Yes."

"I hope they will have improved ventilation belowdecks."

"Most of the changes are to the armoring. Of course, if you were to take charge of refitting them, you might be as careful as you chose with the ventilation."

Nat glanced at his father, whose fair complexion had taken on a permanent ruddiness from years laboring out of doors. Wheat, Sr., had hair a shade more pale than his elder son's, bleached lighter still by the sun, and straight rather than curling. His blue eyes had a reddened, watery look about the lower lids, and Nat could see tiny blood vessels along the sharp cheekbones, crossed by long wrinkles at the corners of the eyes. It occurred to Nat that he might grow to look somewhat like this himself one day. The thought made him uncomfortable.

He smiled, and attempted a joke. "You would have to retire if I built them. There is no room for another job."

"I am contemplating making an offer to Steadman," his father replied.

Nat's eyes widened and he glanced toward Steadman's Warehouse, which stood next by the shipyard. Profits must be considerable if Father was thinking of offering to buy the property. It would double their working space, if Steadman could be induced to sell.

"It depends upon you, of course," his father added.

Nat looked up at him, surprised. "On me?"

"My hands are full with this." His long arm swept out toward the two boats building in the yard. "I cannot expand without help."

"Mr. Young—"

"Young is an excellent foreman, but he has no head for business. What I need is a partner." He turned to look squarely at Nat, something he rarely did. Nat felt the skin at the back of his neck tighten.

"I am prepared to offer you a junior partnership. One-third interest in the shipyard, effective immediately upon your resignation from the service."

Nat bit his lip and looked away, out over the yard. He had not expected such an offer from his father.

"What do you say, then? Shall we make it Wheat and Son?"

The warmth sounded strange in his father's voice. Nat turned and saw him smiling, an unusual occurrence when his mother was not near.

"Let me think about it, please."

The smile faded, replaced by an expression of affront. His father had expected him to fall on his knees, perhaps. Nat felt uneasy, and thought he should attempt to explain.

"I have an obligation to my country. I swore an oath—"

His father snorted. "Bullfeathers. You are not some common sailor enlisted for the bounty. A man in your position may resign whenever he pleases."

"It is not so simple as that." Nat clamped down on his anger and tried for a lighter tone. "Would you have me turn my back on Quincy?"

"Do you imagine your returning to service will help him in the slightest way?" His father was frowning now, a much more familiar expression, and speaking in an exasperated voice that took Nat back to a hundred past disputes. Still, he could not help trying to make his father understand.

"I want to avenge his capture. I want to avenge the loss of the *Queen*—"

"Vengeance! What an idiotic reason to risk your life!"

"And I want to serve my country!" Nat's temper flashed; he gave up trying to control it. "Father, do you even care what this war is about? Or do you only care for your profits?"

"Profit *is* what this war is about!" his father roared. "Deceive yourself with patriotic sentiments if you wish, but it is *commerce* that drives this conflict." He pounded his fist on the railing with the words. "Commerce initiated it, and commerce will finish it!"

He paused, his face deep red. Nat sensed the scrutiny of some of the workers in the shipyard. He glanced toward where Young, the foreman, stood, and saw him just turning away.

Apparently his father had noticed as well, for with some effort he moderated his tone. "I understand your wish to contribute, but consider where your skills may be best employed. Any fellow who is decent with hammer and nails can be a ship's carpenter—"

"There is a little more to it than that."

"—but would it not be a greater contribution to build the finest warships on the water?"

Nat swallowed, furious and chagrined, knowing that there was at least some truth in what his father said but wanting to go against him out of pure resentment. Slowly, carefully, he replied, "I would like some time to think about it."

The elder Wheat's eyes narrowed. "There are a hundred young men of talent in this city who would leap at the chance I am offering you." Nat could hear the suppressed rage in his father's voice.

"Why don't you hire one of them, then?" Nat said, a little unsteadily.

"Because they are not my sons!"

It was said in a tone of accusation. Stung, Nat replied without thinking.

"Oh, this offer is made out of love, is it?"

Their eyes met and held, glaring. Nat felt the queasiness of anger mixed with the helplessness that had always accompanied quarrels with his father. It need not, though—it need not. He was a man grown, he could make his own choices, and he was damned if he would be bullied into anything.

A vein was standing out in his father's temple; Nat could see it throbbing with his pulse. After a long, dreadful silence his face relaxed into a mirthless smile. "Think about it then, but do not think too long. Steadman is retiring. If I do not buy him out, someone else will, and quickly."

He went into the office, pulling the door shut behind him with a snap. Nat closed his eyes and drew a deep breath, then turned around to lean against the porch railing and look out over the activity in the shipyard.

At first glance one might think it chaotic, but it was systematic chaos and Nat understood it. He could watch the foreman directing his underlings, see how they in turn controlled the crews, bringing order and progress out of the myriad forces at work in the yard. He could see coming problems before they manifested—materials blocked from access by other stacks of supplies, tools needed in more than one place at once. He would be good at this, he knew. He had already done it every summer since 'fifty-five, and full-time for four years before he had joined up.

And why had he joined up? Partly for the reasons he had just expressed, and partly to get away from this place. If he accepted his father's really quite generous offer he would be trapped for good.

Nat watched a small altercation break out between two crew chiefs—a dispute over the tools, as he had foreseen. It was as if the poison that had passed between him and his father had drifted out across the yard and afflicted the workers. Mr. Young dropped what he was doing and hastened over to resolve the problem. The solution he adapted did not surprise Nat in the least: the tools went to the crew that was made up of white men. The other crew, mostly negroes, would have to wait until the whites had finished with them. It was a solution Nat's father would have implemented.

Perhaps, he thought, I could improve things here. See that the negroes were treated a little more fairly.

Remembering Adams, who was really quite capable and intelligent, Nat wondered where he was. He wondered how many of the men on the crew now standing idle in the yard were as clever as Adams. Had anyone ever bothered to find out?

Commerce. Was it really commerce at the bottom of it all? Nat had an uncomfortable suspicion that his father was right. Take away all the rhetoric, the idealistic speeches, the patriotic fervor on both sides, and what you had was a dispute over the commercial future of the Southern states. With their "peculiar institution" intact, they would prosper and grow. Without it, their sun was already setting.

Nat leaned his elbows on the rail and rested his chin against laced fingers, gnawing absently on a knuckle. If I accept this partnership, he thought, I will never have to worry about money again. I can live where I wish, do as I please. Take a wife and start a family.

With a rush of feeling that almost made him wince, he realized that he very much wanted a wife—if she were Renata. The thought of touching her, kissing her, made him feel hot; the thought of anyone else doing so drove him wild with jealousy.

Slowly he straightened, clasping the railing at arm's length. Renata changed the complexion of the question. If he were to propose marriage to her as junior partner in his father's shipyard, he thought she might very well accept him. He could offer her not only a secure home but a generous income; her prosperity would be equal at least to what she now enjoyed in her father's house.

If, on the other hand, he returned to the navy, he might be able to support a wife on his carpenter's pay but certainly not in style or perhaps even in comfort. The choice seemed clear. If he wanted to marry Renata, he should go into the office behind him and accept his father's offer.

Or perhaps try for the pilot house. Pilots earned far better pay than carpenters.

Nat raised his eyes to the river, the gray-brown Ohio, flowing lazily around the bend as it cupped Cincinnati in its cold embrace. He saw it as but a small strand in the wider web of water that glistened across the continent. A handful of boats bobbing on that vast web were part of the struggle to bring an end to the war, and with that tiny fleet lay his present path. What his father had said was true; he was not obligated to see it out, he could resign without dishonor. He would be richly rewarded for doing so. The only trouble was, he did not wish to.

A choice of wars, that was all he really had. Return to the greater war and risk death for what his father had dismissed as mere patriotic sentiment, or stay in Cincinnati and submit to the continual paternal skirmishing that might well eat his soul out of him. Could Renata's love preserve him, or would his father's animosity sour that as well?

Slowly he walked down the steps and through the yard, speaking to no one, meeting no one's eye. He left the riverfront, walking at random through the city, hoping to stumble upon an answer.

13

Ah! may the red rose live alway,
To smile upon earth and sky!
Why should the beautiful ever weep?
Why should the beautiful die?
   —"Ah! May the Red Rose Live Alway!" Stephen Collins Foster

"The launch is here, my love."

Marie came out of the music room, where she had been checking that her harp was properly covered. "Has our luggage been put aboard?"

Theodore smiled indulgently. "Yes. We await only your pleasure."

"All I need is my cloak." She started toward the stairs, but he caught her hand, detaining her.

"Let me fetch it down for you."

"Very well," she said, humoring him. He dropped a kiss on the hand and hastened up the stairs.

Left alone in the hall, Marie felt a sudden pang of homesickness—absurd when standing in the middle of her home. She gazed at the pastoral scenes on the hand-painted wallpaper Theodore had imported from France, at the parquetry medallion of roses inlaid to the polished floor of yellow heart pine, at the rose window of similar design through which muted sunlight sent jewels of colored light to scatter like soft petals about the hall. Theodore had teased her so about that rose window—saying she wanted to live in a cathedral, not a house—but he had commissioned it for her all the same, even though the design of the house had to be altered to accommodate it. She stepped into its light, letting the reds, blues, and greens wash over her, turning her fawn carriage dress into a harlequin's robe. Stretching out her hands to either side toward the parlor and the music room, she sought to gather the essence of her home to her that she might carry it along on her journey. At Theodore's tread on the stairs she let her arms fall.

"Here you are, my love." He proffered the cloak folded over his arm. "Do you wish to wear it?"

"Not yet. When we are on the water."

"I will carry it, then." He caught her to him, letting a hand rest on her large belly.

"He is sleeping," she said. "He sleeps more now."

"Not so much room to dance about in any longer, eh, little man?" Theodore said, addressing her belly.

Marie tucked her hand into Theodore's arm as he led her toward the front doors. She paused on the threshold, turning anxious eyes up to him.

"Promise me you will come for me in a month's time."

One silvery eyebrow rose. "How can I make such a promise? Who knows what the situation will be on the river?"

"I want to have our child at home."

Theodore's face softened. "Even if I have to smuggle you past Yankee gunboats?"

"They will let us by." She smiled. "I do mean it, cher. Please bring me home again in time."

"Well—when did Montreuil say you should expect to lie in? Middle of July?"

Marie glanced down at her hands, pale gloves against the blue of his coat. "Wasn't it earlier than that? And I will not wish to travel so close to my time. Please come for me before the end of May."

"We shall see. If it is safe I promise I will fetch you home. All right?"

"C'est bien." Marie smiled, knowing further urging would be unproductive, and not wishing to annoy her husband just as they began this journey. She let him lead her down the steps and hand her into the carriage for the short ride down to the landing.

Sarah waited in the carriage, sitting stiffly with her back to the driver, dark hands clutching Marie's jewel box which rested on her knees. Marie smiled at her as she settled into the opposite seat, but the maid was too nervous to respond. Her face looked almost normal again, though Marie could still see a darker blotch near one eye.

As Theodore climbed in beside her Marie looked out of her window and saw Lucinde standing by the carriage. She reached up to offer a tiny bundle of white cloth tied with red yarn.

"For you, Madame. To keep you safe in your travels."

"Thank you, Lucinde."

The carriage started to move, and Lucinde stepped back. Marie smiled at her, waving until the vehicle turned toward the river and she could no longer see the house. Leaning back in her seat, she looked at the little packet in her palm. How kind of Lucinde to make her a gris-gris. She thought she detected a faint smell of sweet herbs, and wondered what Lucinde had put into the charm, though she knew it was probably better not to ask. She tucked it into her pocket and glanced at Theodore, who was watching her.

"It does no harm, cher."

He raised a hand. "Who am I to question unseen powers?"

Marie smiled. "Some would say it is sacrilegious."

"I heard no mention of God or Christ. I believe Lucinde and I have the same thing in mind. She makes a charm, I whisk you away to Shreveport."

The carriage ride, even at the gentle pace set by the driver, did not take long. Marie gazed out at her rosebushes, their blooms fading now as the heat increased. Indeed, she saw few new buds, and hardly any blossoms that were not already blown. She repressed a wish for her pruning shears, and leaned against Theodore's arm.

At the landing he assisted her to step down from the carriage, and she turned to look back toward Rosehall. The white drive, the white columns of the house gleamed in the sunlight. She could not shake the desire to run back, to stay at home. Odd, for she always enjoyed traveling, but this time her heart did not wish to leave.

Theodore draped her cloak about her shoulders, and she thanked him with a smile. Taking his arm, she walked to the landing where a slender steam launch waited to carry them across the Mississippi and down to Simmesport where they would board a riverboat for Shreveport. The journey would take three days.

Theodore assisted her into the launch, the middle part of which was covered by an awning. As Marie's eyes adjusted to the shade she gasped. Just behind the funnel was a beautiful bower. Several large urns filled with armfuls of roses and lilies framed a couch draped by a soft rug and scattered with rose petals, quite incongruous in the small, sleek launch. The scent of the flowers was heady in the warm air.

Marie turned to her husband, whose eyes were agleam. "Madman," she said fondly.

His smile broadened as he tenderly guided her to the seat. "I knew you were sad to be leaving, so I thought we could bring a part of the garden with us, at least."

"And a bit of the parlor, I see."

She sat down, inviting him to join her. He did so, first extracting a rose from an urn and placing it in her hands. The launch rocked a little; Marie glanced behind her to see the maid sitting down amid the luggage, hot sun gleaming off her dark skin. Marie felt sudden pity for the girl, frightened as she yet was, unsure of herself. She suspected Lucinde's hurried coaching had only served to make her nervous.

"Sarah?"

The slave looked up, wide-eyed. Marie summoned her with a wave of her hand. Slowly, unsteadily, the girl rose and came toward the couch, holding the jewel box before her.

"There is room for you here in the shade," Marie said kindly. She gestured with the rose toward a space between two urns.

Sarah cast a scared glance at Theodore, who was not attending. He knew better than to interfere in Marie's domestic management. She nodded encouragement to the girl, who tucked herself into the small corner, looking shyly at the flowers all around her.

"Thank you, Madame," she said, barely above a whisper.

Marie smiled and tossed the rose to her. It landed in her lap atop the jewel box, where the girl stared at it for a moment. Cautiously picking it up, she sniffed at the bloom, then gave Marie a hesitant smile.

The launch cast off and moved out into the current, engine thrumming. Marie faced forward, leaning against the arm Theodore had thrown across the back of the couch, and watched Rosehall as long as she could until the boat turned and slowly chugged its way across the Mississippi.

Alexandria's streets were in pandemonium, and Jamie could not help but be glad to be leaving the city. He glanced at John as they left their overnight lodging and walked toward the river. John looked calm enough, though rather tired. It was now ten days since Colonel Reily had been killed, and John's shock had worn off during the long and exhausting march to this place. The army was in camp a few miles to the south, resting for the next move, which looked not to be long away.

General Kirby Smith, the departmental commander, was in the process of removing his headquarters to Shreveport, an act which Alexandria's citizens recognized as presaging the army's imminent withdrawal. Many were preparing to follow Smith's example and had obstructed the city's streets with vehicles of every description, loading them with furniture, household goods, and merchandise. An air of suppressed panic prevailed in the town.

Jamie had secured passage westward for himself and John Reily on a big sidewheel steamer belonging to the army, the *New Falls City*. The boat had arrived late the previous evening at Alexandria's landing and was already crowded, mostly with soldiers and refugees. John's rank and his father's prestige had resulted in his and Jamie's being given the last available stateroom, a circumstance for which Jamie was silently thankful. Though the boat was no longer a commercial craft, it was pleasantly appointed, and a room to themselves would, he thought, offer John a refuge from the crowds should he desire it.

Wagons heaped with all manner of cargo jammed the streets, making it difficult for Jamie and John to walk down to the landing. When they finally reached it Jamie paused to get his first good look at the Red River. It was certainly red, like the soil all around these parts, which was richly productive of cotton, sugar, indigo, and grain. Had he been the quartermaster in charge of this retreat, he would have taken steps to carry as much of this abundance with him as possible when he left, and destroyed the rest so that the enemy could not make use of it.

He and John worked their way through the crowd to the stages and boarded the steamer. A steward guided them to a stateroom on the upper deck, which he called the boiler deck. The deck had a wide covered promenade, still adorned with riverboat gingerbread, though Jamie could see where the trim had been knocked about a bit and needed a lick of paint. Cane chairs were scattered along the deck before the ornate railing, inviting the privileged passengers to take their leisure and admire the view. Some of their fellow travelers were already strolling about or standing at the railing watching the activity on shore.

Just now that view was busier than Jamie cared for. He turned his attention instead to the stateroom, which afforded less space than the wall tent he shared with John Foster. He set his valise inside and watched John slump onto a narrow bed.

"I am going down to the cargo deck," Jamie said.

John looked up. "To make sure Father made it aboard?" He nodded, one corner of his mouth twisting up in a wry smile. "A good notion. It would not do to leave him behind."

"Anything I can bring you?"

"No. Thank you—perhaps I will take a turn around the deck."

"All right. I will be back soon."

Passing from the airy upper deck down the stairs to the main deck was like descending to a different world. Here, cargo took up most of the space that was not occupied by the steamer's machinery, the remainder being crammed with poor refugees and a couple of companies of infantry. Red-faced engineers strode back and forth shouting, roustabouts strained to pack cargo into every available space, and the steerage passengers crammed themselves wherever they could fit in between the boxes, barrels, and crates. Jamie found two broken down farm hands making a couch of Colonel Reily's coffin, and ordered a couple of privates to help him shift it to another location where it would not be so casually used. Satisfied, he returned to the cooler and infinitely less crowded upper deck, fully sensible of his good fortune in residing there instead of on the main deck.

He found the stateroom empty and strolled along the promenade, looking for John. The steamer's whistle blew a warning, its deep tones echoing back from the brick and stone walls of Alexandria's buildings. On the deck a few yards ahead Jamie saw General Taylor standing with an attractive lady and four children, two girls and two little boys. His first impulse was to greet the general but he held back, realizing the moment was precious and private. The lady, Mrs. Taylor he assumed, smiled cheerfully as if she were going on holiday instead of fleeing an invading army. Jamie was moved by her bravery and support of her husband; he remembered hearing that their home and plantation near New Orleans had long since been overrun by the Yankees. He watched the general hug each of the children before leaving them. Once the farewells were made, Taylor strode swiftly toward the steps and down them to the stages. Only when he was ashore again did he turn to look back at his family, who stood waving at him from the railing.

The steamer's whistle sounded, long and loud, a last call to those still on shore. Jamie saw the deckhands raising the stages, and a few moments later the boat began to move. He glanced down at General Taylor standing silent on the dock amidst the bustle and fever of the crowd, one hand raised in farewell. How bitter to be parting from his family after what must have been the shortest of visits, sending them away to safety while he remained to continue the struggle against the overwhelming numerical superiority of Banks's army. With a pang for his own loved ones back in Texas, Jamie looked away, not wishing to intrude further on the general's privacy. He began walking along the rail away from the Taylors, looking for John. He gave a nod to an older gentleman who was approaching and was surprised when the man's face lit with a smile.

"Lieutenant Russell!"

Jamie knew he should recognize the gentleman, and at the same time he felt a sense of unease. Distracted, he shook the hand offered him while trying to jog his memory.

"What a pleasure to see you again," the gentleman was saying. "My wife is just here—I know she will want to greet you—Marie? See who I've found!"

Jamie followed the gentleman's gaze toward a stateroom from which a lady had just emerged. Her back was turned, but upon hearing her name she glanced over her shoulder and Jamie's heart lurched. It was Mrs. Hawkland.

Of course, the gentleman was Colonel Hawkland. Furious with himself for not recognizing him in time to escape, Jamie tried to school his features into a disinterested smile while he watched Mrs. Hawkland stroll toward them. He thought he had seen an instant's alarm in her eyes at first, but now she wore a pleasant expression and offered him a gloved hand to shake.

"What a charming surprise."

The words echoed away in Jamie's mind, fading before the realization of what he was seeing. Beneath their joined hands the roundness of Mrs. Hawkland's body gave unmistakable evidence that she was carrying a child.

14

One morning, one morning, one morning in May
I spied a young couple all on the highway
And one was a lady so bright and so fair
And the other was a soldier, a brave volunteer
　　　　　—"The Nightingale," Traditional

Is it mine?

Jamie struggled free of a storm of memories and hasty calculations, knowing he must say something, anything but what he was thinking, to the Hawklands. He released Mrs. Hawkland's hand and managed to form an unexceptionable thought. "Indeed, ah—quite a surprise."

Colonel Hawkland beamed. "You must sit with us at dinner, and tell us all about your recent campaign."

"Oh, no, I—that is, I am not traveling alone—"

Hawkland's brows rose. "Well, we are only two. If your party is not very large we might occupy a single table."

"It isn't that, it—" Jamie realized he was staring at Mrs. Hawkland's belly and forced himself to look at the colonel. "You see, my friend is—recently bereaved."

"Oh, how sad," Mrs. Hawkland said. "You will wish to remain quiet, perhaps."

"Yes, I think . . ."

Jamie saw John coming toward them, and for an instant wished he could hide or just disappear, but it was too late. John had spotted them, and seeing Jamie looking his way he came forward to join them.

Resigned, Jamie turned to the Hawklands. "May I introduce my friend, Captain John Reily? Colonel and Mrs. Hawkland." He watched John bow to Mrs. Hawkland and shake the hand offered by her husband.

"How do you do?" Hawkland said, his voice kind and gentle. "We were just expressing the hope that your party might join us at dinner."

165

"That is very kind," John said with a valiant smile. "Some company would do us good, I think." He looked at Jamie, who pinned on a smile which he hoped would hide his dismay and glanced at Mrs. Hawkland. She seemed absorbed in straightening the lace of her sleeve.

"Well, that is settled, then." Hawkland drew an ornate watch from his pocket. "We shall look forward to meeting you in the cabin in—dear me, just an hour's time. We had better take our promenade while we may. Good morning, gentlemen." He put away the watch and offered an arm to Mrs. Hawkland, who bestowed a fetching smile on Jamie and John before turning away.

"Good morning," John said, bowing again.

Jamie watched the Hawklands stroll down the deck until he realized he should not stare after them so. He wrenched his gaze away and turned toward the river, stepping to the rail and clasping it with both hands, needing to steady himself. The boat was just navigating the falls, as they were called, though they were really just rapids. It was to the falls that Alexandria owed its existence; early shipping up the Red River would often stop short of the hazard, and the riverport town had quickly grown prosperous.

Jamie glanced back toward Alexandria, which was already well behind. He was trapped on this boat with the Hawklands for the next two days, until they reached Shreveport.

Is it mine?

It couldn't be. A single encounter, and too long ago, wasn't it? Ridiculous even to think of it, but he could not keep himself from calculating the time that had passed.

October. It had happened in early October, just after Galveston had been occupied by the Federals, and it was now late in April. A little over six months.

Oh, God.

A stray memory of her words the next morning returned to him: *Would you be surprised if I told you I don't usually do this?*

"They seem a pleasant couple," John said, joining him at the rail. "How do you know them?"

Jamie drew a breath and chose his words carefully. He would not lie to John, but he did not wish to tell him all the truth. "Colonel Hawkland owns a plantation on the Mississippi, opposite the mouth of the Red. I met him earlier this spring when I was up that way on picket."

"Ah." John leaned out into the cool breeze created by the boat's movement and inhaled deeply, the lines that recent days had worn into his face relaxing. He turned to Jamie with a smile. "Mrs. Hawkland is very charming."

Jamie nodded, swallowing. "Yes."

"I do not know when I last dined with a lady. Certainly not since we came to Louisiana. It will be a pleasant distraction, for which I have you to thank." John smiled. "I am most grateful to you, James, for all you have done."

Jamie shrugged it off. "Forget it. I was glad to help."

"You found Father all right below, I presume?"

"Yes. Not in a very good place, though. I had him moved to a spot with a better view."

John laughed softly, the first laugh Jamie had heard him utter since Franklin. The darkness seemed to be lifting from him a little, for which Jamie could only be glad.

"Would you care to take a turn around the deck?" John asked. "I have been around it once, but if you wish to join the promenade—"

"No, I believe I have had enough exercise," Jamie told him, pushing away from the rail. "Think I will have a look at the cabin."

He started toward the double-doors that gave into the steamer's interior. Inside there would be less chance of meeting the Hawklands again. There would also be a bar, most likely, and despite the early hour Jamie felt he could use a drink.

"Hand me my fan, Sarah." Marie stood up from the dressing table and stepped back to view her appearance as best she could in its mirror. Her dress, a simple straw-colored sacque gown of lightest silk, fell loosely from her shoulders to drape over her hooped skirt, minimizing the conspicuousness of her condition, not that it much mattered. Mr. Russell had clearly noticed; she was only glad he had kept his wits together enough to talk of other things. It was extremely unfortunate that he should have boarded this vessel, but there was no mending that now. Getting through dinner would be the greatest difficulty; after that she believed she would be able to evade him.

She had tidied her hair herself, knowing she could do it faster than Sarah in the short time she had to prepare. How much more soothing Lucinde's presence would have been—but it was folly to indulge in such reflections.

Sarah brought her a delicate fan of blond Chantilly lace. The girl held it as if afraid she would break it.

"No, no, the ivory fan. It is too hot for lace."

Marie saw Sarah wince before scurrying back to the half-unpacked trunk, and pressed her lips together. She had not spoken harshly—a bit sharply, perhaps. Really the girl was too tiresome. She picked up her reticule from the dressing table and, glancing at herself in the mirror, saw that she was frowning. That would not do; she schooled her features into calmness, then added a pleasant smile. Confidence would carry her through this. It must.

A gentle knock fell upon the door. "Are you ready, my love? They have rung the bell."

"Almost, cher. Un moment."

Sarah was still rummaging through the trunk. Marie only hoped she would not damage anything. Her gaze fell upon her traveling dress, hanging from a hook on the wall. On impulse she stepped to it and slid her hand into the pocket of its skirt. Her fingers closed around the little gris-gris, which she withdrew and slipped into the pocket of the dress she was wearing. Absurd, but it made her feel better.

"There it is," she said, crossing to the bed and picking the ivory fan out of the jumble of scarves and gloves that Sarah had made.

The girl's shoulders drooped. "Sorry, Madame."

"Never mind," Marie said as gently as she could. "We shall be at dinner for at least an hour, so you will have time to sort all this out." She smiled, but Sarah was not looking, and Marie was not in the mood to cajole her. She turned away, drew a deep breath to calm herself, and opened the door into the parlor.

The room, ordinarily a stateroom, had been arranged with chairs and a chaise longue to form a small but comfortable private parlor connecting her stateroom with Theodore's. He had caused the urns of flowers from the launch to be placed there, hence the heady scent of roses met her as she entered.

Theodore rose smiling from his chair. "Ah, radiant as the sun!"

"If by that you mean that I am glowing, I am not surprised. It is unspeakably hot in these rooms."

"My poor love. The cabin will be cooler, I trust."

He offered his arm and led her through the interior door into the main cabin, which ran the entire length of the boat. Double-doors at the head of the staircase were open to the breeze, which set in motion the crystals of chandeliers hung from the ceiling's carved and white-painted beams. Sunlight filtered down through high stained-glass windows, and a thick, if somewhat worn, carpet of red and gold was a comfort to

Marie's tired feet. Beneath the chandeliers a long line of tables had been set out, draped in white linens and laid for dinner. Colored waiters moved among them with covered plates that gave off tantalizing aromas. Marie became aware that she was quite hungry.

She glanced at the passengers who were already seated but did not see Mr. Russell and his friend among them. Theodore spoke with the headwaiter, who led them toward a table set for four. Before they reached it a young boy, scampering through the room, collided with Theodore's legs and went sprawling.

"Ho, there!" Theodore knelt to help the child to his feet, steadying him with gentle hands. "Careful, lad! Some of us old folk are fragile."

The boy, who was no more than six, blinked at Theodore in confusion as if trying to figure out how he had come to be on the floor. A pretty, dark-haired woman hurried up to them and caught the child in her arms.

"Zack! Que faites-toi? You must apologize, petit!"

"I am sorry, Maman."

"To the gentleman, not to me." She kissed his cheek, then stood up and with her hands on his shoulders gently nudged him toward Theodore, who was still on one knee. The boy made a gallant little bow.

"I beg your pardon, sir."

"I grant it you, sir." Theodore bowed as well, and offered a hand which the child gravely shook.

"I do hope you were not hurt," said his mother as Theodore got to his feet.

"No, no. Happy to meet such an energetic fellow." Theodore smiled down at the boy now clinging shyly to his mother's skirts, then glanced at Marie. "We are hoping to have just such a little scamp ourselves before long."

The lady's face lit with a smile, and her dark, liquid eyes danced as she turned to Marie. "Are you indeed? Accept my felicitations."

Marie smiled back, warming to this fellow Creole. "Thank you. I hope he is half as handsome as your little boy."

The lady laughed. "For your sake I hope he is half as troublesome, and no more." She gazed fondly down at her son, smoothing his hair.

"You look familiar to me," Marie said. "Have I seen you in New Orleans, perhaps?"

"Perhaps. Our home is near there." The lady's smile grew wistful.

"We have a house in Rue de Chartres. I am Mrs. Hawkland, and this is my husband."

"How do you do? I am Mrs. Taylor," the lady replied, shaking hands. "This is my son Zachary."

"Zachary Taylor?" Theodore's brows rose. "Is he related to the late president?"

"His grandson," said Mrs. Taylor.

"Well, well! I am honored to make your acquaintance, young Mr. Taylor." Theodore bowed again. "And yours as well, ma'am."

"Thank you. You are very kind. I believe you were on your way to a table when Zack intruded upon you, so we will not delay you any longer."

"Perhaps we will meet again later," Marie said.

"I would enjoy that," Mrs. Taylor said, her merry smile breaking out. "Allons, Zack."

Marie watched her thread her way between tables, leading Zack by the hand. The headwaiter, who had stood by all the while, now cleared his throat.

"If Madame and Monsieur will be comfortable at this table?"

Theodore handed him a coin. "Yes, this will do nicely. Thank you."

Marie stepped toward a chair, but paused as she saw Mr. Russell and his friend approaching. She drew a long breath and put on a friendly smile.

"Welcome, gentlemen," said Theodore as he pulled out her chair. "Please, make yourselves comfortable."

Greetings were duly exchanged and all were seated, Mr. Russell taking the chair opposite Marie's, his friend—Captain Reily, she remembered—on her right. The party were soon provided with cool drinks and a platter of oysters on ice. Marie declined to take a glass of champagne—regretfully, for she was very fond of it, but she wanted to keep her wits about her—and instead accepted iced lemonade adorned with a sprig of fresh mint. When the waiter offered to pour champagne for Mr. Russell she saw his eyes flick to the bottle, then to herself. A second later he looked away, quietly declining, but the glance had been enough to remind her of another occasion on which the two of them had partaken of oysters and champagne. Marie felt a blush rising to her cheeks, which annoyed her. She reached for her lemonade and took a deep sip.

A silence fell, into which Marie's instincts of hospitality prompted her to speak. She turned to Captain Reily, whom she judged to be about her own age, handsome in a long-boned way, with firm features and a high forehead.

"You came aboard at Alexandria, I believe?" More than believing, she was quite certain of it; however it made an innocuous subject of conversation.

It was Mr. Russell who answered. "Yes, as did Mrs. Taylor. We noticed you talking with her just now. Are you well acquainted?"

Marie set down her glass. "No, we have just met."

"Introduced by that young rascal of hers," Theodore added, chuckling. "He nearly knocked me over. Do you know the family?"

Mr. Russell shook his head. "I saw General Taylor saying good-bye to them. That is how I knew who they were."

Theodore turned to him with an expression of interest. "She is General Taylor's wife? Now that she did not mention. I wonder that a Creole lady should be so reticent!" He cast Marie a teasing glance which she chose to ignore, then continued. "She is certainly a handsome creature. How many children has she?"

"I saw two boys and two girls," Mr. Russell replied.

"A fine young family. We should like to have at least as many, eh, my dear?"

Marie met her husband's happy gaze and found that her mouth had gone dry. She managed to smile, then looked at her plate, picking up her oyster fork and toying with it, not daring to glance at Mr. Russell.

"Are you shy as well, today?" Theodore said. "Well, you must pardon me for boasting. We are soon to welcome our first child."

"Congratulations," said Captain Reily after the slightest of pauses.

"Yes," added Mr. Russell, his voice sounding a bit tight. Marie looked up, but he was helping himself to an oyster.

"Thank you." Theodore smiled delightedly and raised his glass to Marie.

She wracked her brain for a safer topic, fighting to overcome an alarming numbness. She was rescued by the appearance of the waiter with their next course—turtle soup, served with a small glass of sherry on the side. Marie tipped hers into her bowl and, glancing up, saw Mr. Russell watching her. He made haste to follow her example.

"This boat is quite grand," Captain Reily said, looking up at the ceiling. "It is almost a pity it was taken out of trade. The last time I saw anything so ornate was in St. Petersburg."

"You have been to Russia?" Marie asked, grasping onto the subject.

He smiled. "Very briefly. My father was appointed consul there several years ago, but the climate did not agree with him and we left before he had assumed his post."

"Does your father travel a great deal?" Marie asked. His hesitation made her look up from stirring her soup, and she saw that his smile had vanished.

"He did, yes," the captain said quietly.

Marie set down her spoon. "Forgive me—is it for him you are in mourning?"

He met her gaze—clear eyes beneath a troubled brow—and nodded. Marie felt her heart go out to him.

"I am sorry."

"Please accept our condolences," Theodore said.

"Thank you." Captain Reily was staring down at his plate; he roused himself, and made an effort to smile at Marie. "Please do not let my troubles spoil your dinner. I am most grateful for your kindness in inviting us to join you. Do you travel all the way to Shreveport?"

Marie smiled back, taking up the topic. "Yes, I am going to visit an aunt who lives there."

Reily looked from her to Theodore, who added, "I will return home after escorting her there. I do not wish to leave my plantations unattended."

Marie saw a glance pass between the two soldiers. Theodore must have seen it, too, for he went on.

"We believe the Yankees will not trouble us. We have tried to maintain a neutral relationship with them in order to protect our holdings. We even sold them a little cotton this spring."

Marie took a mouthful of soup, which tasted sour. She pushed the plate away. Mr. Russell knew quite well that she was far from neutral. When they had met she had been arranging for his friend Mr. Lawford to sell her cotton to France. She wondered if he had told Captain Reily.

One more subject to avoid. Marie was beginning to regret that she had agreed to this dinner. She took out the ivory fan and began to ply it while she sought yet again for a safe conversation. "I do not know when I have been so warm. Does the weather get this sultry in Texas?"

Nat was invited to dine at the Keller home before the charity ball, an opportunity of which he took full advantage. By the time the meal was ended he had already wheedled three dances from Renata: the first and last on her card, which he claimed as his due for securing the tickets, and the promise of an extra.

Renata smiled as the family rose from the table. "I must go and change my dress. I will not make us late, I promise!"

Nat followed her out of the room in hopes of snatching a moment with her alone, but was foiled by Mr. Keller who joined him in the hall. "May I offer you a whiskey while you wait?" His mustache broadened in a smile. "It may be some little while, you know."

Nat glanced up the stairs, where Renata was just disappearing. "A small one, perhaps."

"Come into my study."

Mr. Keller, whose flaming hair still fringed a shining bald pate, had come to Cincinnati a penniless immigrant and founded a whiskey distributorship which had made him rich. A man of few pretensions, he enjoyed lavishing money on his family, and his house on Pearl Street was acknowledged to be among the best in the city. He now led Nat into a handsome room with a rich oriental carpet and shelves filled with knickknacks and books along all the walls. A modest desk occupied one corner of the room, but it was obvious that the two stuffed leather chairs before the fireplace were much more often in use. Mr. Keller invited Nat to sit in one of these and poured him a scant finger of whiskey in a cut crystal glass.

"We have all enjoyed your company very much these past two weeks, Nat." Mr. Keller settled into the second chair with a comfortable sigh and sipped at his own whiskey. "We count ourselves fortunate that you have been able to spend so much of your leave with us."

Nat glanced up at Renata's father, wondering if he meant to criticize. It was true that he had spent as much time as he could manage in Renata's company, but he had also paid visits to a number of old friends and had spent many hours with his mother, usually when his father was from home.

"Thank you," he said, "though it is I who am fortunate in your welcome. When I am in this house I sometimes feel as though I had only been away for a day or two."

"Instead of for over a year," Mr. Keller observed. "Tell me, do you intend to make the navy your career?"

Nat took a sip of whiskey. "No," he said slowly, "I mean only to serve for the duration."

Mr. Keller gave an approving nod. "That's good."

Nat wondered what had prompted the question, but Mr. Keller did not elaborate. They enjoyed their whiskey in silence for a few minutes, then Mr. Keller set down his glass on a small table that stood between the two chairs.

"Well, my boy, do you have anything you wish to say to me?"

Surprised in the act of finishing his whiskey, Nat coughed. Mr. Keller smiled indulgently.

"Not the moment? No matter, lad. Dora and I have seen what's in the wind, and if we had disapproved, you would have heard so by now." He chuckled, evidently pleased with himself. Nat set his glass down on the table, searching for something polite and noncommittal to say, but the sound of footsteps on the stairs put an end to their repose. Mr. Keller stood up. "Here they come. You have a pleasant evening, lad, and be sure to bring her home by the stroke of midnight."

"Yes, sir. Thank you—thank you for the whiskey."

"Ah, you're welcome, my boy. Come now, we must not miss the grand entrance!"

They went into the hall. Mrs. Keller, just descending, joined her husband and with a proud smile gazed up toward the landing. Nat turned his attention that way as well and saw Renata gliding slowly down the stairs, seeming almost to float. He smiled, thinking how unlike his impetuous friend this was; she who was changeable as quicksilver. This display was for his benefit, and he enjoyed it with deep appreciation.

Her ball gown was of white crape with three deep flounces of needle-lace and pale green velvet ribbons, over a skirt so large it took up the full width of the stairs. Well aware of his duty, Nat stepped forward as Renata arrived in the hall, and swept her a bow.

"You look enchanting, Miss Keller," he said with formality.

She smiled up at him in amusement and made a small curtsey. "Thank you, Mr. Wheat."

Mrs. Keller came forward and kissed them both. "Have a wonderful evening, my dears. Enjoy yourselves."

Amidst farewells and reminders to return promptly, Nat escorted Renata out of the house and down to the street, where waited the hack he had hired for the occasion. He helped her in, retrieved from the driver a small bundle of damp moss he had left in the man's keeping, then joined her in the carriage. Once the horse was in motion he produced from the moss a posy of lilies of the valley and forget-me-nots surrounding a single red rose.

"For you, Miss Keller." He presented the small bouquet with a flourish.

Renata raised the flowers to her face to inhale their fragrance. "How lovely. Thank you," She glanced up at him, eyes twinkling.

Nat smiled back. "I am delighted they please you. Thank you for accompanying me this evening."

"Red, white, and blue. Are you expressing your patriotism, Mr. Wheat?"

"I am ever patriotic, Miss Keller, but the flowers are intended rather to express my sentiments."

It was too dim in the carriage for him to tell, but he thought she might have blushed. She did fall quiet, and kept the posy to her face. Nat, with the florist's assistance, had chosen the flowers quite deliberately for their meanings: lily of the valley stood for renewed happiness, forget-me-not as its name implied, and the red rose's significance was obvious. He had taken a risk including it, but now was the time for risks, if he was going to take them.

Renata lowered the posy. "I am so glad you were able to secure tickets for the ball. You never told me if you had trouble doing so."

"Any effort is worthwhile for an evening in your company. Especially as this may be my last evening in Cincinnati."

"Your last? You have not mentioned that before." Nat thought—hoped?—that he heard a hint of dismay in her voice.

"I have not been absolutely certain about it." His hand went to his breast pocket where his ticket resided, and he frowned slightly to himself. "If I am to return to Cairo by the expiration of my leave, I must board a steamer tomorrow."

"If?"

Nat drew a deep breath. This was his moment to speak of his hopes for the future, yet he hesitated. "My father wishes me to stay. He has offered me a partnership."

"Nat!" Renata clapped her hands, letting the flowers fall in her lap. "Oh, congratulations—this is wonderful news!"

"I have not yet accepted."

"Whyever not? Of course, everyone has always assumed you would inherit the shipyard, but—"

"It is never safe to make assumptions where my father is concerned." His tone of voice was too hard; he knew it, but could not make light of this subject. Perhaps he should let it pass. He had no wish to spoil Renata's pleasure.

"Oh, Nat," she said quietly. "I wish you could be reconciled with him. I am so sorry for you, and when I think of how kind my own father is—"

"I do not want your pity." Nat winced even as the words left his mouth. As a declaration of his affection, which he had intended this private ride to be, it was not going well. He glanced out the window and saw that they were nearing Franklin Street. His time was running out. He turned back to Renata.

"If I asked you to marry me, what would you say?"

"Nathaniel Wheat! You know very well no self-respecting young lady would answer a question phrased in that way."

She had been leaning toward him, and now she leaned back against the cushioned seat. Her hand still lay on the seat beside her, though; Nat touched it, and when she did not pull it away, gently took it in both of his.

"I only want your help in deciding whether or not to stay. Because I think I could bear to work at the shipyard if I could come home to you, instead of being trapped with him at his house."

"You need not be trapped," she said softly. "You could live on your own."

"Then I would be trapped with myself." Nat gave a rueful smile. "I would want someone to comfort me, I think."

"I can think of a dozen girls who would be happy to oblige you, Mr. Wheat." Her tone was much lighter, an attempt at levity, though he thought her voice pitched a little too high.

"I don't want just any girl. You know that, Renata."

Renata held quite still, her small hand resting in his. After a moment she spoke in her natural voice. "What are you trying to say, Nat?"

"I am saying—"

The hack came to a stop and the driver at once jumped down, calling, "Here we are, sir!"

Nat released Renata's hand just as the man opened the door. Red-gold sunset spilled into the vehicle, illuminating her face with a sudden clarity that made Nat catch his breath. She was looking at him, her lips curved in a smile, eyes alight with laughter at the awkward moment. He climbed out of the hack and took a deep breath of cool air, then offered to help her down.

There was no more opportunity to speak privately, for many other vehicles were arriving and depositing their passengers at the curb to make their way up the walk to Woodward Hall. The building, a new one that Nat had not seen since it was finished, had been erected on the campus of the high school that he, Quincy, and Renata had all attended. Its entrance bore a large banner proclaiming the Ladies League Charity Ball; its interior had been adorned with patriotic bunting and garlands of spring flowers, and was lit with enough candles to necessitate opening at least some of the windows to the cool spring evening.

Nat led Renata through the opening march, proud to have her beside him, speaking lightly of trivialities and laughing together as old friends. At the end of the dance he regretfully relinquished her to her next partner, and turned to seek out his own. He spied her standing close to the orchestra with some other young ladies and went to make his bow.

"Good evening, Miss Koch. I believe this is my dance?"

Miss Koch, a shy brunette, smiled gratefully and cast her friends an exultant glance which almost set Nat to laughing as he led her onto the floor. He knew Miss Koch better as Sallie, the younger sister of a schoolmate. He remembered her not so long ago chasing frogs by the river with a gaggle of girls all in muddied pinafores. She had bloomed into quite a pretty young thing. He swept her into a schottische and did his best to amuse her, but whether from shyness or uncertainty about the steps she conversed rather poorly, and Nat caught himself watching for a glimpse of Renata.

His next partner was rather too talkative, though she too was charming. All his partners were charming. He found himself in great demand, and not only because of his uniform. Gentlemen of any age and occupation were in short supply, and Nat soon underwent the novel experience of being asked to dance by a lady. As his card was already filled he could decline with a clear conscience, thinking it strange to what extremes hard times could push people.

This war was changing the very breath and pulse of society. The Cincinnati to which he had returned was different than that he had left; he had sensed it in the stark discussions of news in saloons or at dinner tables after the ladies had departed, in the thoughtful silences wherein he sometimes found his mother—a lady who never used to be still or to dwell upon what she could not change—and this evening in the hectic, brittle laughter of ladies determined to be gay without reference to tomorrow.

At ten o'clock a light supper was served in an adjoining hall. As Renata's escort, Nat claimed the right to lead her in, to the great disappointment of three sparks in whose company he found her. She accepted his arm with a smile and raised her posy to her face, eyes laughing at him over the flowers.

"Nat! Hey, sailor, over here!"

Nat turned to see Vernon Koch beckoning to him from a table where he was seated with his little sister. Nat glanced at Renata, who nodded.

"Yes, I think we should join them. It may be our only chance at a table. Doesn't little Sallie look pretty!"

Sallie's smile lingered on Nat for a moment, then she welcomed Renata. Her brother, who had the same dark hair and fair skin, stood up to offer Renata a chair.

"Thank you," Vernon said. "I did not want to leave Sallie here alone while I fetched us some supper. It looks like a mad crush over at the buffet table."

Nat looked at Renata. "Shall I bring you something?"

"Yes, please. Lemonade, and some ham if there is any."

"Ham in Porkopolis? Who ever heard of such a thing?"

Sallie looked shocked. "Papa never lets us say 'Porkopolis'!"

"He doesn't want his children demeaning his packing-house," Vernon explained. "Marry some rich fellow, Sal, and you can say Porkopolis all you like."

Nat grinned and set off with Vernon to brave the supper crowd. He glanced over his shoulder and saw Renata and Sallie already talking, heads bent together over their dance cards.

"Thank you for dancing with Sal, Nat," Vernon said. "I hope it wasn't too awkward."

"Not at all. She dances charmingly. Some rich fellow will snap her up before you know it."

Vernon broke into a proud grin. "Actually, my father has already turned one not-so-rich fellow down."

"Oh? I hope Sallie was not brokenhearted."

"Lord, no. She has never really lost her heart. Though I think she could lose it to you, if you tried."

Nat noted the edge of warning in his voice, and gave him a sidelong glance. "Well, I won't. No offense to Sallie."

"Of course not. She is only sixteen, after all."

They reached the buffet and piled plates with shaved ham, canapes, and dainty little tea cakes, then carried them back to the ladies and fought their way to the drinks table for punch and lemonade. By the time all four were at last seated around their small table, Sallie and Renata appeared to have become fast friends. Sallie looked up at Nat, all trace of shyness gone, and said, "Have you heard that Meg Schiff married Tom Litton?"

Nat folded a paper-thin slice of ham in quarters with his fork. "I thought she was engaged to Marcus Gunter."

"She was! That is what makes it so dreadful. Ever since Marcus went to war Tom has been making up to her." Sallie's eyes were wide with delight at the scandal. "Poor Marcus does not even know of it yet. While he is off fighting for our country, she has jilted him for that no-good stay-at-home!"

Something twisted in Nat's chest. He swallowed the ham, which had suddenly lost its flavor, and glanced at Renata.

"I do not think it quite fair to call Tom a no-good," Renata said, setting down a cake she had just picked up.

Sallie gave a small shrug. "Well, he *is* a stay-at-home. His father paid three hundred dollars so Tom would not have to fight." She looked at Nat. "I think it is the duty of every patriotic girl to save her affections for our soldiers."

"And our sailors, one presumes," Vernon added. "Thank you, Sal, for consigning me to eternal bachelorhood."

"That is different! Papa needs your help at the packing-house."

"Perhaps Mr. Gunter needs Tom's help as well," Renata said.

"All he does is sell books! Anyone can do that."

"Anyone who docs not aspire to win the affections of a patriotic girl," Vernon added. "Enough, Sal. Save your affections for whomever you wish, but do not be hard on poor Tom."

Renata picked up a dance card from the center of the table. "I see that you are engaged for all of the waltzes, Sallie. Has your brother been teaching you the steps?"

Sallie launched into raptures over her first ever two public waltzes, which had occurred during the first half of the ball. Nat had lost his appetite, and sipped at his punch while the others finished their supper and chattered about the evening. Vernon consumed all his ham, then eyed Nat's plate. Nat pushed it over to him. He answered the occasional question put to him, but otherwise watched Renata and thought without enthusiasm about the waltzes to come which he must dance with other ladies.

The orchestra played a brief fanfare, signaling the recommencement of the dancing. Renata raised her head at the sound, and turned to Nat.

"There is to be an extra first. Would you like it to be yours?"

Nat stood up at once. "Ridiculous question. Will you excuse us, Miss Koch? Mr. Koch?"

He led Renata into the ballroom, where to his silent delight the orchestra began to play a waltz. As yet the floor was not crowded, so with one hand at her waist and the other gently clasping her fingers, he twirled Renata in breathless sweeps around the room. She responded nimbly, trusting in him to lead her, smiling up at him in a way that made him feel giddy. Other couples joined the dance, and Nat had to reduce their wild pace.

Renata looked up at him. "Mr. Wheat, do you remember that intolerable question you asked me earlier?"

"Yes. Must I beg your pardon?"

"No. Tell me what you would do if I said yes."

Nat's heart skipped. He drew her a little closer to avoid colliding with another couple twirling by. "Do? I would fall at your feet—"

"No, I mean what would you do about the navy. Would you go back?"

There was no humor in her expression; she was quite serious. Nat licked his lips. "What would you wish me to do?"

"We are not discussing my wishes, we are discussing yours."

"But they depend upon yours."

"Then what would you do if I did not exist?"

Nat gazed at her in surprise, then glanced away to mind their progress through the growing crowd of waltzing couples. Before he could consider her question Renata spoke again.

"It is so warm in this room. Would you mind very much if we stepped out onto the front lawn for a breath of air?"

Nat fairly sighed with relief. "Not at all."

He waltzed her to the side of the floor, then offered his arm, on which she lightly laid her hand. As he led her from the hall he noticed his heart was beating pretty quickly, and not entirely because of the dance.

Outside the air was cool and the sky aglitter with stars. Renata started across the lawn toward an ancient willow that had stood there as long as Nat could remember.

"Shall I fetch your shawl? Your father will be angry with me if you catch a chill."

Without stopping, she called back to him. "No, thank you. I am not cold."

Nat caught up with her as she reached the willow. She drew aside the curtain of its leaves with one hand as if to go inside, but then let it fall. In younger days they had played within that magical tent, but they were no longer children.

She turned to face him, lamplight from the street casting shadows across her face. "Have you thought about my question? If I were not here tonight, if you had danced with everyone else and had to decide whether to leave tomorrow, what would you do? Would you go back?"

Nat swallowed. He wanted to lie, but knew she would know it. "Yes. I would."

"I thought so."

"But, Renata, that doesn't matter. You *are* here." He caught her hand and kissed it. "Do you want me to stay?"

"No. I want your heart to be free of any yearning for what you might have accomplished. I want you to become a pilot."

Stunned, he could only stare at her. She looked very serious, the laughter gone from her face.

"If you and your father cannot resolve your differences," she continued, "then you may as well do what your heart really longs for. I do not wish to be your solace from a life in service to him. You would hate it, and so would I. If you choose to step away from him, though, I will stand by you."

"Renata—"

She took a step toward him and laid her free hand on his shoulder, as if to waltz again here on the lawn. "I will wait for you," she said into his ear, her breath tickling his neck. His heart thumped painfully, and it was all he could do to refrain from wrapping his arms around her.

"I cannot ask that of you." His voice came out hoarse, and he swallowed again. "I might not come back."

She looked up at him. "Oh, yes you will come back, Nat Wheat!" Her whisper was so fierce he could not help smiling.

"Yes, ma'am."

Renata lifted her chin. "Besides, I am a patriotic girl, and I reserve my affections for whom I wish."

Aware that his smile was fast becoming a foolish grin, Nat got rid of it by leaning forward to kiss her. For one sweet moment she was still, then she pulled away.

"I believe Mrs. Quillen is watching us from the steps," she said in a small voice.

Nat glanced toward the hall, shielding Renata with his body, and saw that she was right. Mrs. Quillen, one of the Ladies League organizers, stood on the top step of Woodward Hall, lazily plying her fan.

"We had better go back in, then. Are you ready?"

She blinked, and said inconsequentially, "I left my flowers in the supper room."

"I will fetch you some more." Nat felt rather wild. "How many dozens of roses would you like?"

Roused to a smile, she looked up at him. "I only want the one you gave me tonight."

"Shall we go find it, then? If Vernon has not eaten it."

She laughed, a sound that went straight to the top of his head. This time when he offered his arm, she slid her hand into the crook of his elbow. Nat led her back toward the lights of the hall, so happy he was ready to dance with every woman in the room, for he knew that when the last dance came—and if fate was kind to him, forever afterward—Renata would be his.

15

Here I am where I must be,
Go where I would, I can not
                    —"Katy Cruel," Traditional

The evening was quiet, although Jamie could hear music drifting out from the cabin where a brass band—a pretty good one—was playing. He leaned on the railing, gazing out over the water at the dark shapes of cottonwood and pine rising above the riverbanks. Somewhere overhead the moon must be shining, for it lit the moving ripples of the river with glints of silver.

Dinner had been awkward but not disastrous, and when it was finally over he had felt profound relief. Hawkland appeared unsuspicious, and John was too preoccupied to notice more than Jamie's ill mood. Pleading exhaustion, Jamie had collapsed in their stateroom and fitfully slept the daylight away, with the result that he was now wide awake and yet unrested.

Some time tonight they would reach Natchitoches, then another day's travel would bring them to Shreveport. He could avoid Mrs. Hawkland for that short amount of time. Everything would be all right. He would never see her again.

Jamie closed his eyes. Here, alone on deck in the quiet and comforting dark, he allowed himself to understand the small, nagging feeling he'd avoided admitting until now. A part of him, a tiny part he had long kept subdued, *wanted* to see her again.

Memories arose that he'd tried so hard to banish, of a friendly meal that had suddenly become much more than friendly, shock and surprise that had vanished under the onslaught of passion. He could still smell the spilled champagne and the heady scent of her perfume. He swallowed, then opened his eyes and took a deep gulp of night air.

He should not let himself think about it. It had been wrong. To lie with another man's wife—and not just once, either, but all night long—was a terrible sin. It was one of the worst things he had ever done, and he had regretted it from the moment it began, but had been too weak to stop himself.

Which was worse, he wondered—adultery or murder? Not that it mattered, for he was guilty of both. Murder on a battlefield was sanctioned, but to him it was still murder. How had he come here in a few short months? How had he strayed so far from what he'd meant to be?

Two years ago he had thought himself destined for a rancher, helping his father grow the Russell family's fortune. He had believed that good Christian men and women joined together only under the sanction of matrimony, and that killing another human was unquestionably wrong. Maybe he still believed those things, though he had seen and done much to the contrary since then. Seen others act to the contrary as well, many of them without the slightest remorse. He wasn't sure why such things bothered him so much, when many another soldier felt no shame about all kinds of beastly behavior.

Someone moaned, somewhere—a muffled sound, a hidden woe. Jamie gave a soft laugh, in sympathy with the unknown sufferer. It was possible to be surrounded by luxury and still be miserable as hell.

Marie sat up in bed, listening. She heard music, but that was not what had roused her. Was Theodore awake? He had been tired, and gone early to bed in his own stateroom, which she had not minded as she was feeling rather drained herself.

There—again. A groaning.

"Theodore?"

She reached for the lamp burning low on the night table and turned up the flame, blinking against the brightness. Throwing back the sheet, she glanced around for her wrapper but did not see it— the stupid girl did not know to put it out for her—no matter. She snatched up her shawl, threw it around her shoulders and picked up the lamp, then opened the door into the parlor.

The maid was standing outside Theodore's door as if listening, the cot on which she had been sleeping in disarray. As Marie came forward the girl cast a frightened look at her, then jumped aside. Marie knocked softly at Theodore's door.

"Theodore?"

She heard movement, a sliding of cloth as though he was getting up, then a rush of muffled thuds sounding very like a fall. She pulled open the door and saw her husband lying on the floor, tangled in his own bedsheet.

"Theo! Oh, cher!"

Thrusting the lamp into the slave's hands, Marie knelt beside him and lifted his head. His face was burning hot; he gave no sign of recognition. Her concern grew to alarm.

"Sarah, help me get him back into his bed."

Sarah's eyes grew wide. "Madame, you cannot lift him. You must not try."

"We can both lift him."

"No, no, let me do it! Let me."

The girl swiftly turned to place the lamp on the night table, then knelt and pulled Theodore's arm around her neck, trying to raise him. He was too heavy for her to move, slip of a thing that she was.

"Let me help you—"

"No!" Sarah's face wore an expression Marie had not seen there before, one of certainty, one almost of defiance. "I will get help," she said, getting to her feet. Without waiting, she strode to the parlor's outside door.

Marie struggled to stand. "Not that way—Sarah—"

A sound from Theodore drew her attention. She thought he had spoken, but he did not answer her, seemed not to know her voice. Panic rose up from her gut to squeeze at her heart. She cradled his head in her lap, crooning endearments, smoothing his sweat-dampened hair.

Footsteps returning; Marie glanced up to see Sarah come back in from the deck with a man, some hapless passenger. "Sarah, you should not have troubled this gentleman. Go into the main cabin and find a steward or . . ."

As the lamplight fell on the man's face she saw it was Mr. Russell. He stepped forward to the door of Theodore's room.

"What happened?"

Marie tried to swallow the lump in her throat. "My husband is ill. Do you think you could lift him into the bed?"

He nodded, and held out a hand to her. Reluctantly, she shifted Theodore from her lap and accepted Mr. Russell's assistance to rise, then stood aside while he went into the narrow stateroom. He hauled Theodore up seemingly with little effort and got him back onto the bed, then peered at him closely and felt his neck.

"He's burning with fever. He needs a doctor."

Marie felt a small shock as the soldier's eyes met hers. Her mind would not function; she seemed numb, almost stupid.

"Is there a doctor aboard?" she asked, as if he would know any better than she.

"I will find out."

He stepped out of the room, passing close to her on his way to the parlor's inner door. He paused there to glance back at her, then went out into the main cabin.

Marie stared at the closed door for a moment. Part of her mind tried to calculate dangers, risks—what to say, what not to say. That part was drowning, though; washing away under waves of fear. She returned to Theodore's room and carefully sat beside him on the bed, taking his hand into hers. It was dry and hot, so hot. She felt her throat closing, tears threatening. She frowned, staring at her husband's reddened face. She did not wish to cry at this time.

Sarah came in carrying a basin of water and a handful of handkerchiefs. Marie had been dimly aware of her moving about, but was nevertheless surprised to see her make these preparations. The girl seemed to have lost all her hesitation.

"Excuse, Madame."

"I will do it," Marie began, but Sarah shook her head.

"This I know how to do."

Too distraught to argue, Marie yielded her place and watched the slave dampen a kerchief and gently bathe Theodore's face. After a moment she thought of her own bedraggled condition, hair all mussed and in nothing but her nightgown and shawl.

"I should dress. No, I don't need your help. Please continue. Call me if . . . call me."

Sarah looked up at her and nodded. Marie tried to smile her thanks.

She went to her own stateroom, able to think clearly about this small task at least. It made her feel somewhat better to be doing something. She put on her sacque dress again as it was easy to get into, and stepped into the parlor to check on Theodore. He seemed a bit easier; the cool water must be soothing him. Marie returned to her stateroom, took out her brush and comb, and with fingers shaking only slightly, began to tidy her hair.

"Is there a doctor on the boat?"

The steward grimaced. "There is, but he is occupied."

Jamie frowned. "How many are ill?"

The man's eyes were wary. He stepped to a counter in the office area of the cabin and reached for paper and a pencil. "If you will give me the number of your stateroom, I'll ask Dr. Bower to come to you as soon as he is free."

"It's Hawkland. I don't know the number."

The steward consulted a large, leather-bound register. "They are in thirty-two through thirty-six. I will give him the message."

"Thank you." Jamie watched him finish writing. "Did the doctor say anything about what it might be?"

The man cast a wary glance up at him. "I couldn't say."

"Did he mention anything at all?"

The steward straightened, regarding Jamie for a moment. When he spoke it was in a very low tone. "Nothing is definite, but I heard him speak of scarlet fever."

Jamie's heart sank. "Thank you," he said in a parched voice.

He turned away and walked slowly back to the Hawklands' suite. The band had stopped playing. Footsteps hurried toward him; he glanced up as a lady brushed past, not Mrs. Hawkland. Someone else in distress, someone else with a loved one fallen ill. He did not know much about scarlet fever, but he did know it was deadly and it spread like wildfire. This beautiful boat had become a floating nightmare.

Jamie paused outside the Hawklands' door, trying to think how to break the unwelcome news. He was not very good at that, but it had to be done. No inspiration came to him. Giving up, he knocked softly. "It's me, Russell."

Mrs. Hawkland opened the door, dressed and alert, her pretty brow creased with worry. She stepped back to let him inside.

"Is there no doctor?"

"There is, but he is seeing someone else. He will come as soon as he can."

Her frown deepened. "What is it?"

"A fever," Jamie told her.

"Of course, but he has had the fever before, and it was not like this—"

"Scarlet fever." Her eyes widened, and Jamie hastened to add, "Possibly. Not for certain."

She turned toward her husband's room, stepped to the door. Jamie moved to block the way.

"Don't go in."

"What? How dare you!" Her eyes blazed.

"Think of your child!"

She gasped, as if he had slapped her. Jamie swallowed, scarcely believing what he had just said. He watched a storm of emotions cross her face, ending in grief. She looked past him, and now he moved aside; he had no right to deny her, but she did not go in. She stood in the doorway instead, stricken, staring. Her chin began to tremble; she bit her lip to stop it.

"Should I go?" Jamie said in a low voice.

"Yes, please," she whispered.

He moved toward the door. "I'm in room twenty-four, if you need me."

She gave a single nod. Jamie turned away and put his hand on the crystal doorknob.

"Thank you for your help."

Her voice sounded strangled. Jamie glanced back at her, feeling a rush of pity, but she was not looking at him. She was standing silent watch over her beloved, proud and beautiful in her grief. He gazed at her for a moment, wondering if anyone would ever stand vigil for him thus. At last he turned the knob and softly left the room.

"Madame? Please, Madame?"

Marie started awake, confused to find herself sleeping in a wing chair until she remembered that she had placed it before the door of Theodore's room so as to be able to watch him. The doctor, when he had come, had confirmed scarlet fever, confirmed that she should not go into the room. Sarah was thus become indispensable, and Marie had to admire the girl's courage. Looking up at her now, she saw not the slightest trace of fear in her dark eyes.

"What is it?" Marie said, still hazy with sleep. It was dark yet, and heaven knew what was the hour.

"Madame, he is calling for you."

That was not surprising; he had called for her off and on all night. It tormented her not to go to him but she had spoken to him from the doorway, though often it seemed as if he did not hear her. Why Sarah had wakened her now she did not know, but she stood up, putting aside her shawl which had been tucked up around her shoulders. Her hair had long since come undone, and she had pulled out the pins and let it fall loose, not caring how she looked.

The lamp on Theodore's night table burned at half-height, enough to light the room with a gentle glow. Marie peered toward the bed, and dared to take a step into the room.

"Theodore?"

"Cherie." His voice was weak, and he looked frightful. The rash had spread all over his neck and chest; his face was bright red except about the mouth where it was pale. Marie had to force herself to smile.

"Do you feel a little better, love?"

"Tired. I just wanted to look at you."

Sarah, who had retreated to a stool in the corner by the night table, reached to turn up the lamp. Theodore's eyes glittered strangely bright as he gazed at Marie, smiling.

She tried for a jest. "Do not look too closely. I have not been at my dressing table in many hours."

"You have never looked more beautiful," he said softly. "I want to remember you this way."

Misliking the sound of this, she took another step toward him. He raised a feeble hand.

"No, love. You mustn't come in."

"I so want to hold you," she told him, gripping her hands together instead. "I am saving up kisses for you. There are over a hundred now."

He smiled. "We will share them another time."

"Only you must hurry and get well, because I cannot hold them all inside." Her eyes began to sting; she blinked, refusing the tears.

"You are strong. I think you are the strongest woman I know."

Marie managed a laugh. "Only because you never met Mamere."

"I wish I had met your grandmother. You make her sound so terrifying."

"She was."

He leaned his head back against the pillow. Marie saw that his breathing was shallow. His eyelids drooped.

"Could you eat a little bit, cher?" she asked. "Some broth?"

"No. I just want to sleep now. Will you sing to me?"

Sing? She could scarcely think. She cudgeled her exhausted brain, and began to sing the first song that came to her.

"Au clair de la lune, mon ami Pierrot,
Prête-moi ta plume, pour écrire un mot..."

A child's song, a nonsense song. She continued, watching Theodore's eyes close, his breathing slow a little. She felt so small and frightened, standing in the doorway singing to her poor, tortured love. She finished the song and waited.

"Theodore?"

He sighed, and did not answer. Asleep again.

She glanced at Sarah, still in the corner. The maid gave a silent nod, a faint smile on her lips, and turned down the lamp once more.

Marie returned to her chair and sat straight up so as not to fall asleep. She watched and waited, prayed. A deep stillness filled the rooms. The boat seemed to have stopped moving; she had not noticed when. Earlier in the night she had heard weeping from somewhere, a child crying, but all was silent now.

Gradually light crept into the rooms, glowing through the gauze curtains on the outside doors. It was morning, then. She did not move. Her eyes ached with weariness, but she would not close them. She watched her husband, praying for him to get well, to rise up and embrace her. Watched every breath rise and fall in his chest, until at last it fell with one deep sigh, and rose no more.

"Theodore?"

All was still. She stared, willing him to breathe again.

"Mon cher? Theodore?"

Sarah woke at the shrillness of her voice, gave her a startled glance, then moved to the bed. Marie held her fist to her mouth as the tears began to fall, as she watched the slave girl touch the beloved face that she must not touch, feel the throat for a flicker of life, fold his hands together on his chest.

No. No.

She closed her eyes, feeling a shriek rise within her but she would not give it voice. It would bring intruders, and she wanted no one. Words and touches would only torment her further. She would grieve alone.

Jamie and John sat sipping coffee over a breakfast neither of them particularly wanted. Daylight poured down from the cabin's high windows, dappling the carpet and glinting from china and crystal on many empty tables. A few other parties were present but most of the passengers were in their own rooms, either sick, attending the sick, or afraid to venture out. Jamie had tried to speak with the doctor but had only managed a brief conversation with his harried assistant, who informed him that both of Mrs. Taylor's little boys had come down with the fever but was unable to enlighten him about the Hawklands.

"Perhaps you should check on them," John suggested.

"I don't want to be a nuisance. I don't know them that well."

"You are not afraid, are you?"

Jamie looked up at his friend. "Afraid of fever? No." Afraid of other things—perhaps. He stared into his coffee cup, swirling a few grounds in the bottom.

"Is that her?" John said.

Jamie looked up to see Mrs. Hawkland walking along the aisle of the cabin toward the front of the boat. She wore a cloak, which was a bit odd in this warm weather, though perhaps she had put it on to cover her dress which he recognized as the same she had been wearing when he last saw her. He looked at John.

"Will you excuse me?"

John put down his cup. "I will come with you."

They abandoned their breakfast and followed Mrs. Hawkland forward, catching up with her at the office where she was speaking with one of the stewards. She appeared calm, but Jamie could see the strain in her face.

"I wish to return to Simmesport," she was saying. "Will the boat be going back there?"

The steward shook his head. "No, ma'am. I doubt you will find any boats going downriver now."

"But I must get my husband home."

"I am sorry, ma'am."

She stared at the man as if she could not comprehend him. "I have to get home," she repeated.

"I cannot help you."

Jamie stepped forward. "Excuse me—Mrs. Hawkland?"

She looked at him with hollow, haunted eyes and swiftly cast her gaze down, as if to collect herself. A small frown, as if she suffered from headache, had settled on her brow.

"May I be of any help?" Jamie asked.

"I have to go back." Her voice was hoarse, a half-choked whisper.

Jamie exchanged a glance with John, who looked grave. A cold feeling settled in his gut. Mrs. Hawkland's cloak was black, he realized. Was that why she had donned it?

John offered Mrs. Hawkland his arm. "Come and sit down, ma'am," he said gently. "Perhaps we can find a way to help." She hesitated, then laid her hand on his arm and allowed him to lead her back toward the cabin.

Jamie stayed behind and caught the steward's eye. "How long until we leave Natchitoches?"

The steward glanced up at a clock on the wall, which read just past eight. "A little under an hour."

Nodding his thanks, Jamie followed the others to a table near the front of the cabin. The doors at the head of the grand staircase were open to the morning air, and through them Jamie glimpsed buildings on the hillside beyond. John drew out a chair for Mrs. Hawkland, and was sitting down opposite to her as Jamie joined them.

"My husband is dead," she said, staring blindly at the space above the table.

Jamie drew a sharp breath, even as he saw John wince. Mrs. Hawkland must have seen it too, for she looked at him.

"I have to take him home."

"Are you sure you would not rather go on to Shreveport?" John said gently. "Things are pretty uncertain below at this time."

"There is no one to look after our plantations. I must go back." Her voice was absolute as she said this, then she seemed to lose some of her strength. "Is it true no boat will go down the river?"

"I expect so. General Banks is marching this way." John looked troubled. "If you are quite determined, James can help you. He was a quartermaster. He can find whatever you need."

Mrs. Hawkland drew herself up slightly. "I have no wish to trouble you with my concerns."

She did not look at Jamie; it was John who turned expectant eyes his way. Jamie felt as if he was being backed into a corner. He stood up, unable to keep still.

"I will go ashore and try to find you some transportation."

Her shoulders slumped a little, as if defeated. John caught Jamie's eye and gave a nod of approval.

"I will stay with her," he said.

Jamie turned toward the open doors, already planning. Less than an hour to find transport for a lady, her maid, baggage, and a corpse.

"Wait."

He turned and saw Mrs. Hawkland reaching into her reticule. From it she withdrew a stocking-purse heavy with coin. She held it out to him, at last raising her eyes to his.

"You will need this. Take it, please," she added when he hesitated.

Jamie's hand came up and closed around the money, far more than he would need, he was certain. She was trusting, but perhaps she didn't care about money. It could not buy her what she wanted most. She gazed at him, sorrow etched into her weary face, which even yet was lovely.

"Better have your maid pack your things." The words came out rough; Jamie swallowed.

"She is already doing so." Mrs. Hawkland's gaze drifted downward, then she looked at him again. "Thank you," she whispered.

As if released from a spell, Jamie turned away, slipping the purse into his pocket. He felt an irrational urge to run, which he solaced by taking the stairs two at a time and striding out briskly once he reached the landing.

Natchitoches seemed asleep compared with Alexandria's state when he had left it, though when he looked closely at the few people moving about on the landing he saw that their expressions were rather serious, some urgent. Two men were loading furniture from a cart onto a neat little steam yacht that would have suited perfectly, but Jamie did not bother to approach them; it was clear they were headed up the river, and from their grim faces there would be no persuading them otherwise. He glanced up toward the bluff above the landing where a row of shops built of brick with fancy ironwork invited commerce. He would venture up there later if there was time, to look for a casket-maker, but transportation was the foremost problem.

A boat was his first choice; to journey by land would be slower and far more cumbersome, especially with General Smith's wagon train coming in the opposite direction. The roads would be jammed. He cast an eye over the boats tied up at the landing as he walked along the riverfront, dismissing anything not powered with steam. If Mrs. Hawkland insisted on risking a voyage down to the Mississippi, it would be best to hire as speedy a vessel as he could find.

He paused as a swell of distress washed though him. Mrs. Hawkland was widowed. Why should that trouble him? He scarcely knew her, certainly did not love her. He was sorry for her, but he owed her nothing. He was helping her because it was the right thing to do, the gentlemanly thing. Despite all the wretched things he had done, he clung to the idea that he was a gentleman, an honorable man.

No time for this. Shoving his feelings aside, he stepped up to a shallow boat with a funnel not much taller than himself amidships and a lean-to covering the rear half of the deck.

"Hello? Anyone on board?"

A grizzled man with leathery skin emerged and peered at him. "What can I do for you, soldier?"

"I'm looking to hire a boat down to the Mississippi."

The man gave a great guffaw. "Might as well ask for the moon, boy! Ain't you heard them Yankees is comin'?" He disappeared back into the lean-to without waiting for an answer.

Jamie got much the same response from every boatman he approached. As he neared the end of the landing he began to reconsider asking the furniture men. He glanced behind him to see their yacht just pulling away from the landing, starting upstream. Frowning after them, he let out a sigh.

He looked at the next boat, one he had planned to pass over. A fishing boat, bigger than he needed and badly in want of some paint; he could just make out the name, *Ellie Mae,* in peeling letters on the bow. It did have a steam engine, though—a strong one, if the stout funnel was any indicator. On the deck a large negro sat mending a net. Jamie was about to ask where his master was, then changed his mind.

"This your boat?"

The man nodded without looking up. "How much you offering?"

Taken aback, Jamie hesitated. The man raised his head and met his gaze squarely.

"Heard you talking to Smitty. He won't never go down where the Yankees may come. I might, though. If the money's good."

"The money's good," Jamie said. "Twenty dollars, in gold." He saw the man start to sneer and added, "And twenty more when you get there."

The fisherman gazed at him. "I dunno. Get caught by the Yankees, they might take my boat away. Then what I do?"

"Fifty dollars, then," Jamie said, hoping Mrs. Hawkland would not be angry. It was more than half what he made in a month.

"Who be in the party?"

"A lady and her maid. And her deceased husband." Jamie sensed the man would not take well to any surprises.

"He in a box?"

"He will be."

The man looked at the net in his hands, finished tying off a knot. "Fifty dollar. Down to the Mississippi, then where?"

"To a plantation, right across the river."

"What plantation?" The man's face was suddenly hard.

"Belle View."

"Oh. Belle View."

Jamie was relieved to see the negro's features relax. Clearly he held some grudge, but it appeared not to be against the Hawklands. The man dropped his net to the deck and stood up, coming to the side of the boat. He was even larger than Jamie had thought, a great bull of a fellow.

The negro crossed his arms over his massive chest. "Tell you what. It take three days to get down there, three to come back. I do it for ten dollar a day."

Sixty dollars. Jamie glanced past him to the two other boats at the landing—neither of them much better looking—and remembered all the rebuffs he'd received. Time was getting on, too, and he still had to find a coffin.

"Can you start this morning?"

The man nodded. "Soon as I get wooded up. Take an hour or so."

"All right." Jamie produced a ten-dollar piece from his pocket, where he'd put a few of Mrs. Hawkland's coins. He showed it to the man, watching for a glint of greed, a hint that he might take the money and run. He saw no such sign, and his confidence grew. "You get fifteen more when they board, the rest at Belle View."

"They bring they own food, and I don't haul no baggage."

"Done. I will have the bags delivered."

Jamie gave him the coin and offered a hand, which the fellow shook with a grip that hinted at the power of his arms.

"You can expect the baggage this half-hour."

"I ain't goin' nowhere." The negro returned to his net.

Feeling relieved if not exactly jubilant, Jamie hurried up the hill and into a general store where he ordered a box of food to be delivered to the *Ellie Mae* for Mrs. Hawkland—crackers, cheese, pickles, and so-on, not the dainty fare she was used to, but enough to live on for three days—along with two gallon jugs of lemonade. The merchant directed him to an undertaker in the town, who offered him his choice of a plain pine box or one that was on display in the front parlor of his establishment, covered with fine black cloth and ornamented with a cross tricked out in silver nails. Jamie thought of Mrs. Hawkland and her evident adoration of her husband, and paid rather too much for the better coffin. The undertaker agreed to deliver it to the packet immediately, and accepted an additional dollar to transfer the coffin and Mrs. Hawkland's baggage to the fishing boat.

Jamie checked his watch. Ten minutes to nine. He hurried back to the riverfront, running the last part of the way down the hill and across the landing. The boat was already getting up steam; great puffs of smoke rose out of the funnels, and as he started up the stairs the whistle blew a warning, making him jump. He went straight to the office.

"Mrs. Hawkland and her maid will be disembarking here."

The steward's brows rose. "They'd better do it quick, then."

Jamie held down a flash of temper. "She will be taking the body of her husband ashore," he said in a low, tight voice. "He died last night of scarlet fever. Perhaps the captain will not mind accommodating her by a few minutes."

The man paled. "I am terribly sorry. Please tell Mrs. Hawkland we will—that is, I will speak to the captain. I am sure he will not mind a short delay."

"Thank you."

Jamie left the office, and was about to start through the cabin when he noticed a small commotion on the stairs. He recognized the undertaker talking with one of the waiters, and hurried to join them. Two men—sons of the undertaker, by their long limbs and dour expressions—stood patiently at the foot of the staircase bearing the coffin.

"Thank you," Jamie said to the waiter. "They are expected." The waiter turned away, looking relieved, and Jamie shook the undertaker's hand. "Thank you for coming so promptly. The suite is this way."

He led them along the promenade, not wishing to create an uproar by parading a coffin through the cabin. Even so, a woman gave a muffled shriek into her handkerchief and collapsed into a deck chair as they passed. A man in her company moved to comfort her, so Jamie could safely ignore her, thinking in passing that Mrs. Hawkland had a great deal more fortitude. At the outer door of the Hawklands' suite, he paused, then gently knocked.

"Mrs. Hawkland? It's Lieutenant Russell."

John opened the door. Jamie could hear the maid moving about in the next room, and saw Mrs. Hawkland sitting erect in a chair, still in her dark cloak, to which she had added a hat and gloves. She was gazing at something in her hands—a rosary, he thought—and looked calm, if rather pale and worn.

"I have made the arrangements," he told her. "There is not much time."

Mrs. Hawkland rose slowly, supporting herself on the arms of the chair, the weight of her belly hindering her somewhat but not enough for her to accept the assistance silently offered by John. She came to the door and blanched when she saw the coffin waiting outside, then lifted her chin and met Jamie's gaze.

"Thank you," she said. "How very kind you are."

He stepped in and directed the undertakers to Colonel Hawkland's room. The parlor was cluttered with baggage and urns of fading roses, leaving little room to spare. Jamie thought of suggesting that Mrs. Hawkland might prefer to wait out on the promenade, but a glance at her face changed his mind. She watched in intent silence as the undertakers opened the coffin and carefully placed Hawkland's body within. As they were about to replace the lid, she cried, "Wait!"

Catching up an armful of roses from one of the urns, she carried them to the coffin and scattered them over her husband's chest. She turned back for more, her calmness gone, raw grief upon her face. Jamie caught John's eye and they moved as one to help her, bringing every vase and jar of flowers forward and watching as she cast them by handfuls into the coffin, until the body was covered with a blanket of roses. Only Hawkland's face remained visible, and this she reached toward when all the urns were emptied. She drew back briefly, then touched his cheek with great tenderness, murmuring something in French. When at last she stepped away and signaled the undertakers to close the lid, Jamie saw a tear glistening on her cheek, the first he had ever seen her shed.

Now she allowed John to lead her out onto the deck. Jamie stayed behind to speak with the undertakers about the baggage. He glanced into the other room—that which had been Mrs. Hawkland's—and found her maid just closing up a trunk. Seeing everything in train, he joined Mrs. Hawkland and John outside where they stood at the railing, gazing at Natchitoches.

Jamie took Mrs. Hawkland's purse from his pocket. "Ma'am?"

She gazed dully at it for a moment, then accepted it. "Thank you."

"You will be traveling on a fishing boat, the *Ellie Mae*. It will not be very comfortable, I'm afraid."

"That does not matter."

"The owner asked for sixty dollars. I gave him ten, and I have fifteen more for him when you are aboard. He will expect the rest at Belle View."

Mrs. Hawkland frowned at the purse in her hand, as if trying to comprehend. "I am sorry," she said in a broken voice. "How much should I give him?"

"I think you should let James worry about that," John said gently. He looked up and met Jamie's startled gaze. "He can escort you."

Jamie opened his mouth to protest, but John forestalled him. "You have done all you can for me," he said with a sad smile. "I will explain to General Green."

"I cannot inconvenience you so," Mrs. Hawkland said, giving Jamie a fleeting glance. "Not after everything—after everything . . ." Her face began to crumple.

"I will go," Jamie said, a little alarmed at what she might say, but forgetting his misgivings in the desire to stave off her pain. "I will see you home."

16

Farewell sweet mother,
Weep not, weep not now for me
— "Farewell Sweet Mother," Stephen Collins Foster

Nat looked around his bedroom, checking to be certain he had not left anything he needed behind. The room was filled with the artifacts of his youth—a flute he had whittled, a favorite ball, a prize cup from a sculling race he and Quincy had won—childhood treasures, some that had lost their meaning, others that still struck notes of fond memory. He had not missed a single one of them in the time he had been away. He could walk out of this room today without regret, and never return again.

He picked up his dance card from the charity ball. This memento he would keep. Tucking it into his pocket, he glanced once more about the room, then closed his portmanteau and carried it out, down the hall and down the stairs, to set it by the front door before going in to breakfast.

The drapes had been thrown back from the tall windows of the dining room, and morning light glowed through the gauze curtains beneath. His mother was there before him, seated at the foot of the table, charming in a lace-trimmed robe and morning cap. She looked up from pouring coffee as Nat entered. "Good morning! How was the ball?"

"Delightful, of course." Nat took the chair to her right and offered his cup to be filled.

"Is that all you have to say?" She put down the pot, and when he reached for it, moved it away. "No, you must tell me all about it. I want to hear everything!"

Nat smiled to himself. She would not hear quite everything, not from him, at any rate. Perhaps someday Renata would tell her what he would not.

"Let me see. All the ladies were beautiful, there were not enough tables for supper, and not enough cakes—"

"No, no, you go too fast! What did Renata wear?"

"Well, a dress. White, I think, with some pale green about it, and a lot of lace."

"An unedifying description, but I will let it pass. Did she look lovely in it?"

"Certainly. She was the most beautiful lady in the room."

His mother smiled. "Ah, that is better. You really thought her the most beautiful?"

"Of course. It was my duty as her escort to think so. May I have some coffee, now?"

She pressed her lips together, but her eyes laughed. "Impossible boy." She picked up the coffeepot.

"Thank you. The orchestra was in fine form, by the way."

"They have been quite good this season."

"Sallie Koch has grown up to be a pretty little thing."

His mother tilted her head, watching him. "As pretty as Renata?"

Nat sipped his coffee, considering. "Not yet. Maybe in a few more years, after Renata starts having passels of brats."

Her cup struck its saucer with a sharp click. "Nat, that is an abominable thing to say!"

"Is it? Even if I have every hope they will be my brats?"

At that his mother's eyes grew very bright. She laid a hand on his wrist. "Have you proposed to her?"

He could no longer keep from smiling. Putting down his cup, he turned to her, all joking aside. "No, but we have an understanding." He took her hand in his, smoothing the lace of her cuff. "I did not want to bind her to a promise when I am going away again. She said she would wait for me, though. What is it?"

His mother had looked unhappy for a moment, but now she smiled with delight. "Nothing, dear. How wonderful. I have always hoped one of you would make her my daughter."

"Always? Since before we were born?"

"Since just after."

He glanced down at the table, his smile fading a bit. "Do you think Quincy will mind very much?"

"Oh—how can I say? I know he is fond of her."

"Am I a rat, Mama?"

She squeezed his hand. "No. Of course not."

Biddy came in with a tray, ending private conversation for the moment. Nat picked up his coffee cup, sipping pensively while the housekeeper laid steaming plates of eggs and bacon before them and put a basket of hot biscuits in the middle of the table. He took one of these and began to spread it with apricot jam. Neither he nor his mother spoke again until Biddy left.

His mother set down her fork and touched her napkin to her lips. "You know, Nat, your father and I have been hoping you might remain at home."

The look she directed toward him was rather less casual than her tone. Nat didn't like it when that little worried frown came into her face. He put down his knife.

"Have you heard what is being said of Meg Schiff and Tom Litton?" he asked.

"Oh. Well, yes, that was rather the talk of the town for a while."

"I never want people to speak that way of Renata."

"But surely they would not! You have done your part. No one can call you a shirker."

Nat frowned. "I do not wish to tell my children that my contribution to the war was to lose three boats in succession."

"You did not lose the third! It was taken from you by the army."

"Still."

"And their loss was not your responsibility."

Nat tore his half-biscuit in half again, then dropped the pieces to his plate. "I have not accomplished much. Certainly not when compared with Quincy."

"He lost a ship, too," she said softly.

"Yes, and took a wound and was made prisoner defending it. He will be quite the hero when he comes home." He looked up at his mother with a rueful smile. "I cannot be outshone by my little brother, Mama."

"Nat, that is foolish and you know it."

He sighed, and took her hand again. "I am not explaining very well. I *want* to go back. I—"

His father entered the room at that moment. Nat straightened as his mother withdrew her hand.

"What is the meaning of this?" his father demanded, holding Nat's portmanteau aloft.

Nat sat back in his chair. "It generally signifies travel," he replied, trying for a lightness he did not feel.

"None of your nonsense, if you please." His father put the portmanteau down and came to the table, leaning his fists upon it as he glared at Nat. "I thought you agreed to consider my offer."

Nat held his gaze. "I have considered it. I have decided to finish out the war."

Fists left the table and slammed down again, causing all the china to chitter. From the corner of his eye Nat saw his mother flinch.

"Leave us, Mrs. Wheat," said his father.

"She has not finished her breakfast."

"I said leave us."

Nat's temper flared. "Whatever you have to say to me, she has a right to hear it!"

The look on his father's face was awful, but before the storm could break his mother stood up. "I am going," she said, smiling an apology to Nat as she pushed in her chair. Thwarted, he stared at his uneaten breakfast while she left the room.

"I had not thought a son of mine could be so ungrateful," his father said when the door had closed behind her.

Nat swallowed, trying to speak calmly. "Father, I am extremely conscious of your generosity—"

"You have a peculiar way of showing it."

"I would be honored to accept your offer when the war is over."

"I need you *now*!"

Nat winced at the shout and looked up at his father's wrathful face. "I am sorry," he said, holding his ground.

Mr. Wheat began to pace the room, frowning. "If you must know, I have already made an offer to Steadman. I intend to buy him out. Do you not see that I must have help at once?"

"You had better hire someone, then."

His father stopped and stared at him across the table. "Is that what you wish? When you return from your quixotic heroics, to find a stranger in your place?"

"Of course not, but I understand that you will do what you must to keep the shipyard going. Just as I hope you will understand—"

"No! No, I do not understand why you will not oblige me in this, and secure your own fortune. I can think of no reason to justify it."

Nat drew a careful breath. "I appreciate your concern for my welfare, but I am a grown man now. You must let me take the risks that may make my character as well as my fortune." He met his father's gaze, saw puzzlement in the cold blue eyes. "You took such risks yourself, when you first came here and founded your business. I can hardly do better than to emulate you."

Wheat, Sr. stared at him in seeming amazement. Nat, aware that his next words might sever him from his family forever, nevertheless felt he owed his father the truth.

"I am going back to Cairo, and I am going to request training as a pilot."

His father's face went white beneath the sunburn. "That again! I thought you were over such nonsense."

"The navy is short of pilots. It is an excellent opportunity—"

His father hurled a coffee cup against the wall, smashing it in a hundred fragments. "No son of mine will waste his life in that manner!"

Trembling, Nat got to his feet. "Charlie's life was not wasted."

The blue eyes flashed. "Much you know about it. He took advantage of every opportunity to debase himself. Gambling and carousing his way up and down the river. He was eternally in debt, or didn't you know that?"

Nat had not known, but it made sense. He wanted to say that at least Charlie had been loved—he'd had friends all along the river and on every boat that plied the Mississippi from St. Louis to the sea, whereas the only friendships Father had were those established and maintained by his mother. Despite his anger he could not bring himself to say such a hurtful thing. Instead he said, "What did Charlie tell you to say to me when he died?"

Wheat, Sr.'s eyes hardened to the pale blue of sunlight glinting on polished steel. "Nothing."

Nat had asked the question before, and received the same answer. He knew it was untrue. He glared at his father for a moment, then walked to the door and picked up his portmanteau.

"I will disown you," his father threatened in a low, angry voice. "It will all go to Quincy."

Nat's stomach twisted. He had expected this, and responded as steadily as he could. "Very well. I daresay he is more deserving than I."

That appeared to surprise the old man, for he stood staring as Nat walked past him. He was halfway down the hall when his father shouted after him.

"You will not have a penny! You will never set foot in this house again!"

Nat kept walking. He reached for the front door and found that his fingers were shaking.

"Nat?" His mother's voice was just above a whisper. He turned to her, smiling crookedly as she came out of the parlor and caught his free hand in hers.

"*You* won't disown me, will you, Mama?" he said quietly.

"Of course not. He doesn't really mean it, you know."

"Oh, I think perhaps he does."

"Give him time, darling. He loves you, truly he does."

Nat shook his head, unable to believe it. The hall clock struck the half hour, and he glanced at it.

"I am late. I will write to you."

"Be careful."

"Of course. Good-bye, Mama." He kissed her cheek and gazed at her a moment, trying to memorize her pretty, anxious face. He blamed his father for every tiny line, every silver hair. Mustering a smile for her, he opened the door and hurried out.

The walk to the riverfront settled his feelings somewhat, though he could not be entirely easy. He had behaved rather well, he thought, in declining to lash back at his father.

The transport on which he had obtained passage was loading a crop of new army recruits. Nat decided to wait until they were aboard before attempting to board himself. He stood watching their eager, laughing faces, and thought of his own first departure from the Queen City. These fellows had no real notion to what they were going.

"Mr. Wheat! Did you really think you were going to leave without bidding me farewell?"

Nat turned, a smile springing to his face as he saw Renata approaching, dressed in her Sunday best. He caught the hand she held out to him.

"I had assumed you would be in church."

"I convinced my mother that after last night's exertions I would be better able to attend to the sermon at the late service. We are just on our way to it now."

Nat glanced past her to where Mrs. Keller stood admiring the wares of a pie-seller. She looked up and gave him a serene nod. He wished he could escort them to church, but there was not enough time. He would attend whatever prayer service was held on the transport.

"Thank you for coming," he said, turning to Renata. "My spirits needed a lift. I just had a battle with my father," he added as her delicate brows rose in question.

"Oh, dear. Over the shipyard?"

Nat nodded. "He did not want me to leave."

"No one *wants* you to leave, silly." She smiled up at him, and Nat felt a strong desire to kiss her as he had done beside the willow tree and again, several times, in the hack taking her home from the ball.

"Too late now," he said, his voice rasping a little.

Renata raised her other hand and offered him a flat, rectangular package wrapped in cloth. "You said you wanted a picture."

"Yes, but I meant a carte-de-visite. I thought you were going to have one made."

"Well, I will, but in the meantime I did not want you to go away empty-handed."

"Thank you." Nat accepted the package and fingered the cloth, feeling the frame underneath. "I may be coming back empty-handed," he added, his throat tightening. He met her questioning look, and shrugged. "The old man threatened to disown me."

She gave an indignant gasp. "He could not mean it!"

"We shall see. Anyway, I wanted you to know. I will not be angry if you change your mind."

"Mr. Wheat, I am surprised at you. After your behavior last night I hope you know I expect you to do the only honorable thing!"

Nat couldn't help grinning. "Damaged your reputation, have I?"

"You know what a gossip Mrs. Quillen can be."

"I am a dastard, then, certainly, to abandon you thus."

Her eyes glinted with laughter, then softened. "Come home safe."

"If I possibly can."

"And write to me."

"The moment I get a berth."

She stood gazing at him, her bosom rising slightly with each breath. Nat glimpsed Mrs. Keller moving closer.

"You had better go. You do not want to be late for church."

"You should go too, shouldn't you?" Renata nodded toward the transport, and Nat saw that the soldiers were all aboard.

"Yes." He did not want to let go of her hand. He squeezed it, then bowed to kiss it. "Farewell, Miss Keller." He let her go, picked up his bag, took two steps backward, then made himself turn away.

"Good luck, Nat," she called after him.

It was all he could do not to go running back. He raised the picture she had given him and waggled it in salute, then tucked it under his arm and took out his ticket. The transport launched as soon as he was aboard; only then did he dare to look back, supposing Renata would have gone but he was wrong. There she stood, with her mother on the edge of the landing. He waved; they both waved back. Some of the recruits, seeing this, responded by hallooing and waving to Renata.

"Stupid," Nat heard one of them say to another. "She isn't waving at you!"

"Why not? I'm a hero, ain't I?"

Nat smiled, and walked past them to the stern of the boat. He stood gazing aft long after he had lost sight of Renata. Finally, when even the landing was out of view beyond the bend, he remembered the picture and unwrapped it. It was one he had seen in the Kellers' parlor, of Liberty vanquishing a snake. Renata had added an inscription in the corner; he laughed aloud as he read it: "From your Patriotic Girl."

Theodore was dead. Marie could not quite believe it even now, with his coffin resting below the deck of the dismal fishing boat in which she now traveled. His absence left her feeling as if she might fall at any moment, without his familiar support. She was used to considering herself capable and independent; she felt neither now that she was in fact alone.

The engine thrummed as smoke trailed from the funnel, smearing the sky behind them between the wall of trees on either shore. Marie stared numbly at the rusty colored water sliding past, waiting to be home again, trying not to think or feel anything until then. Once she was home it would be safe to fall to pieces, a little bit at least. It was not safe now.

Perhaps she would sicken and die as well. Perhaps the fever would take all of them, even the poor boatman.

"Madame?"

Sarah's dark hands held out a plate of food. Marie closed her eyes, shaking her head.

"Please, Madame, try and eat a little. For the bébé."

She looked up at the maid's face, which wore a new air of assurance. The crisis had given her confidence, it seemed. Marie accepted the plate, which she set upon her knees while she removed her gloves. Sarah went away again.

She looked at the food: a slice of cheese, soft bread, a pickle, dried apples, all on a tin plate. Never in her life had she eaten from a tin plate. She tore a corner off the bread and chewed it, almost gagging at first, but she managed to eat it, and to put another, smaller piece into her mouth. She must eat to sustain her child, the child Theodore had wanted so, the child she had risked so much to get. All for nought, now. All for nought.

Her throat began to close; she swallowed painfully and put the plate aside. Sarah came back with a pottery cup filled with tepid lemonade. Marie sipped it, then drank more deeply as her thirst awoke. She handed the empty cup back to the slave.

"Thank you."

"More?"

"Not now."

The girl set the cup down beside the plate and reached for Marie's cloak. "Let me take this, Madame. Too warm for this."

Marie relinquished the cloak, reluctant to give up its shelter but the girl was right, she felt much cooler without it. She was surprised at how much; she had simply not noticed the heat, she supposed. Sarah opened a parasol that had been in the luggage packed for Shreveport and placed it in Marie's hands. She must have found it when she was packing that morning. Had it only been that morning?

"Thank you, Sarah." Marie managed to smile up at her from the shade of the parasol.

The girl smiled back, then left, carrying the cloak. How fortunate that Sarah was along, Marie thought. How uncomfortable she would have been without her. How ironic, considering the very different opinion she had held when they had left Rosehall.

She closed her eyes, remembering the launch filled with roses. Tears threatened, but she took a choppy breath and willed them away. Think of something else.

The child within her kicked, protesting her distress, perhaps. She wrapped an arm around it, cuddling it. This would occupy her. She would give all her thought to the child, and perhaps the pain would be less. Theodore's heir. She wondered, did he know now? Could he see from heaven what she had done, and did he understand?

"Forgive me, cher," she whispered.

Time passed. She grew weary and lay down on a makeshift bed of baggage over which Sarah had spread her cloak. The girl laid a shawl over her; really it was quite touching how attentive she had become. She sat beside Marie, shading her face with the parasol while the day wore on.

Marie drifted, not really sleeping, sifting through the memories of her marriage and treasuring up all the happiest ones. Seven years' worth, for they had wed when she was eighteen, and she would be twenty-five in a short while. Her family had looked gloomy at her wedding, but she and Theodore had not cared a bit, and had danced the night away. She thought of herself in his arms, waltzing through a golden evening, soaring with happiness. He leaned close, whispering into her ear. *I understand.*

Marie blinked, opening her eyes a little at Theodore, whom she could see through her lashes sitting nearby, holding a rose in one hand. *I understand.*

With a sharp breath she rose onto her elbow, wide awake now. Theodore was not there; of course he was not, but she could not rid herself of the feeling that he had been.

She sat up. It was late, for the sun was riding low, straight behind them just now. The shawl had slipped, and she caught at it, pulling it around her shoulders as she looked about her. The negro boatman was in his usual place, piloting them down the Red. Sarah was sitting beside him and they appeared to be talking. Marie was surprised, for the girl was not usually friendly with strangers.

She turned around, searching for the parasol. She found it with its handle wedged between two pieces of baggage, shading the spot where she had lain. Beyond it she saw the soldier sitting in the stern of the boat, staring back up the river. Mr. Russell, her—no, not her lover, but the father of her child. He had not spoken to her since they came aboard. Indeed, she had scarcely seen him, except when he had taken off his coat—she remembered that coat, a worn gray uniform with two gold bars on the collar and a damaged sleeve mended with rough stitches—and gone to help the boatman bring on fuel at the woodyard. She knew very little about his character, really, except that he had been discreet and forbearing and, recently, extraordinarily kind. He was a good man, she must conclude.

Marie got to her feet, stretching the stiffness from her back, and made her way carefully to join Mr. Russell. He hastened to stand up at her approach.

"I believe I have not properly thanked you," she said, surprised at the weakness of her voice. Her strength, both of body and of spirit, seemed unreliable at present. She held the parasol upright, clutching the handle with both hands for fear she might drop it.

"No need," he said roughly, looking out at the water.

"Indeed, I am most sincerely grateful."

He turned his head to gaze at her; a look she could not read. After a moment he glanced away. "Do you wish to spend the night ashore in Alexandria? You would be more comfortable in a—in a hotel."

"Would that not slow us down?"

He shrugged. "A bit."

"Then no. I want to be home as soon as possible."

After a pause, he asked, "Is there anything you would like me to fetch you from the city?"

Marie frowned. Thinking was such an effort. "I do not believe so."

"All right. Let me know if you change your mind."

"I will."

Marie gazed out at the water. So calming, running water. She never tired of looking at it, one of the reasons she had wanted her home within sight of the river. The light on the water, especially now, late in the day, was magical.

She became aware of Mr. Russell's gaze, and looked up at him. He glanced away; it was not her face he had been watching. Her hand moved to her belly, a protective gesture. She knew, though, that it was unnecessary. If Mr. Russell had meant to do her any harm, he would have done it long since.

"Yes," she said softly, almost a whisper.

His head came up; he half turned to face her, eyes sharp with question. Marie swallowed.

"I have seen that you are wondering," she said in a low voice, meant only for his ears. "Yes, it is."

17

Jamie's stomach did a slow flip. He had suspected, now he knew—unless she was lying, of course. She had lied to the Yankees, he remembered. She had admitted that at their very first meeting.

He looked out at the river, trying to decide what to think about it, what to say. All through the past day and more he had agonized about whether her child could be his, but now that he had an answer, he felt no more settled.

Mrs. Hawkland spoke again, barely above a whisper. "My husband was unable to father children. I paid his doctor not to tell him."

Jamie was surprised by a stab of anger on Hawkland's behalf. He felt his hands clenching into fists, and made himself flatten them against his thighs.

"He so wanted an heir," she said in a mournful whisper.

Jamie swallowed. "So you arranged for him to have one."

"Yes. I wanted to please him. I never meant that you should know." She paused, then added, "Perhaps we could go on as if you did not."

Jamie gave a gasp of incredulous laughter. "You think I can just forget about it?" He faced her, and the sight of her drawn features cooled his anger.

"I believed you would," she said quietly, not meeting his eyes. "I also believed we would not meet again. I—regret that it has not been so."

She put a hand to her cheek. Jamie watched her, his own feelings so tangled he could not even begin to articulate them.

"I have misjudged you, I see," she said, her voice very faint. "I do apologize."

She swayed, and Jamie reached out in alarm to steady her. He helped her down onto the food box he had been using as a seat, and squatted beside her, watching her. If this was artifice, she did it very well. He knew she was capable of deception, but his instinct was that she was sincere in this case. Of course, he had trusted her before.

He grimaced, angry with himself. When had he become so cynical?

"Forgive me," she said. "If you wish to disembark at Alexandria, I will understand."

Jamie drew a breath. "I am a man of my word, Mrs. Hawkland, and I have given my word to escort you home."

She looked at him, her dark eyes beautiful despite grief and weariness. "Thank you."

A smile trembled about her lips. Jamie felt a dangerous tug at his heart and looked away out at the river, westward, toward home. In silence they watched the sun sink into the trees through a hazy yellow sky. After a few minutes Mrs. Hawkland moved to rise. Jamie stood up to help her, then watched her return to the place they had made for her, a tiny makeshift shelter of baggage. Not much protection for a wounded dove.

What should he do? Offer to wed her? She did not need the protection of his name, and he had little else to give. Her own home far exceeded anything he would ever be able to provide. If he made such an offer, she might think he desired her wealth. In any case, she was too recently bereaved, which was just as well, for the idea of speaking to her about the subject made him uncomfortable.

He had not thought of marriage other than as some distant future possibility. He had only just come of age this year, though he had friends who were already married and starting their own families. He enjoyed the company of ladies, but had never met one who had struck him as a likely partner.

No, that was not quite true. There had been one lady who had intrigued him, and whom he had admired more than most. He smiled, remembering Miss Howland, who had nursed him out of a fever in Santa Fe. Her kindness, and that of their mutual hostess, Mrs. Canby, the Federal commander's wife, had touched him deeply. The two ladies had set aside politics and cared for a dozen or more wounded Confederates after the battle at Glorieta, just over a year ago. It seemed a decade.

Miss Howland would never touch him, though. Not in a hundred years. She was a Yankee through and through. Jamie laughed softly, wondering where she was now. Perhaps she had found her way back to Boston.

No, he had not thought of marriage, and did not really want to think of it yet. He was fighting a war, and that was hard enough without having to consider the consequences to others. Surely Mrs. Hawkland would understand that. She did not need him, or want him, probably. She had got what she wanted from him long ago.

Jamie swallowed, hating the bitterness he felt. She had used him, and besides the guilt he had suffered she had hurt his pride, but whether she deserved his anger or not it would only do harm to express it. The best thing to do would be to try to forget it.

He got up, suddenly restless. There was nowhere to go, however. He stood watching the daylight fade into dusk, thinking of the army and wishing he was with them, working to mend his battered section instead of riding this lonely boat down toward the Mississippi. From where he stood, military problems seemed much easier to solve.

Nat sat on a battered sofa in the transport's pilot house, watching an old friend of his uncle's, Lester Blount, guide the boat down the Ohio. Nat had taken to spending his waking hours here, for although Mr. Blount had ten years on him his company was more agreeable than that of the recruits. They had discussed everything from the philosophy of the present war to which river port tavern offered the best beer at the best price.

"What vessel are you serving on?" Blount asked him, keeping his eyes on the river ahead. "You never mentioned it."

Nat cracked open a peanut and dropped the shells into a spittoon already piled high. "I am in between assignments."

"*Mound City*'s carpenter got wounded when they ran the Vicksburg batteries, or so I heard. You might inquire."

"Rather not serve on an ironclad, but thank you, I will ask."

Nat got up to stand beside him, bringing a handful of peanuts with him. Blount held out his hand for one, and Nat obliged him.

"I am thinking of trying my hand at piloting."

"Ah-hah!" Blount grinned at him. "You would do well. You were pretty sharp-eyed, back when you were cubbing with your uncle. Learned the Mississippi fair as any could wish."

Pleased, Nat shrugged. "Only down to Natchez, and that was nine years ago. I will have to learn it all over again."

"Not the same as starting from scratch."

They stood in silence a while, Nat watching the river out of habit, noticing each small adjustment Blount made to the wheel and judging for himself why he'd done it. He was comfortable here. He enjoyed this. It brought back fond memories.

"Sad when old Charlie died," Blount said. "But he always did say he would die on the river."

Nat swallowed. *Maybe so will I.*

"You were not there, were you? In 'fifty-five?" When the *Columbine* exploded, he meant, but could not say it.

Blount understood, and shook his head. "Louisville? No, I was down at Baton Rouge. Heard about it through the grapevine."

Nat nodded. Charlie's friends on the river had sent letters. Wheat, Sr. had ripped them all up.

"He always used to say there was a bright star shining for me," Nat said softly.

"I expect there is, lad." Blount smiled, then returned to watching the river.

"Hey, Reb."

Jamie looked around at Cooper, the fisherman, who had not shown much inclination to talk except with Mrs. Hawkland's maid. The negro beckoned to him from his place at the rudder. Jamie got up and went toward him, glancing at Mrs. Hawkland as he passed. She was resting just now, napping in the afternoon heat. Three days on the *Ellie Mae* had told on her a bit but she was holding herself together, which was all that was to be expected. Her dress was disheveled but her hair was freshly arranged. He had watched covertly as her maid brushed it out each morning.

The maid got up and went to her mistress, leaving Jamie her seat. He took it and gave Cooper an inquiring look.

"See that boat there?" the negro said.

Jamie squinted and could just see a small craft coming toward them up the river under steam. "Yes."

"Looks a lot like one I seen down here when the Yankees was here before."

Jamie frowned and cupped his hands around his eyes, wishing he had his field glasses. The boat was too far away to discern the dress of its occupants other than that it was dark, but the flag flying from its stern looked like the U.S. colors.

"I'm thinking you might want to get below afore they get close," Cooper said.

A cold wave went through Jamie's gut. He grimaced in frustration; they were so near the Mississippi, almost there and now this little boat had to appear in their path. If there were Yankees on the big river they might very well have sent a patrol to scout up the Red.

He looked at Cooper. The negro's gaze was steady and unemotional, as always. Jamie wondered if the man could be setting him up somehow, but the easiest way to do that, if it was indeed a Yankee boat, would have been to leave him in ignorance of the fact. He glanced at the vessel again and nodded, getting up to open the hatch that led to the hold. He went into it, choking a bit on the smell of old fish, and left the hatch ajar, unable to bring himself to sit in darkness with the stink and with Hawkland's coffin. Also, he wanted to hear whatever might pass between Cooper and the men on the boat.

If there were Yankee boats on the Mississippi, guarding the mouth of the Red, they might have to sneak across somehow. Might have to go down the Atchafalaya a ways to find a place to wiggle through the bayous, cross the Mississippi, and then work their way back up. How long would that take, and would the food hold out?

It seemed hours before the boat came up, though he knew it was only minutes. He felt the way he did before a battle, wondering if he would be alive in another hour. He sat silent, straining to hear every sound from above. At last he heard a hail, followed by the slowing of the *Ellie Mae*'s engine.

The voices were muddled at first, then all too clear. "Heave to and prepare to be boarded," a sharp voice demanded.

On instinct, Jamie took off his hat with the Texas star pin, shrugged out of his coat and removed his gun belt, tucking them behind Hawkland's coffin. A risk; if he were taken prisoner out of uniform it could go badly for him, but shedding the marks of a soldier might be his only chance of escaping capture. He felt the boat move with the new weight of the boarder, listened tensely as Cooper identified himself and explained that he was taking Mrs. Hawkland home.

"Sorry to disturb you, ma'am," the stranger outside said. "Is your husband aboard?"

"Yes—that is, he is below—"

Jamie propelled himself onto the deck before Mrs. Hawkland could say any more. She looked startled, but at his warning glance she fell silent. He stepped toward the stranger—a Yankee officer, younger than himself by the looks of him—and put out his hand.

"How can I help you?" Jamie said.

The young man's eyes narrowed. He did not shake Jamie's hand. "What have you got down in there?"

Jamie glanced toward the hold, where the hatch gaped open from his pushing it aside as he came out. He could just see a corner of the coffin. "Just an old man dead of scarlet fever. Taking him home to be buried."

"Scarlet fever?" The look of dread on the Yankee's face was gratifying. Jamie held back the smile he felt, and instead nodded gravely.

"Have a look if you like."

The man's eyes flicked toward the hold and widened slightly, then shifted to Cooper. "Is that right? Just that coffin, nothing more?"

Cooper gave a lazy nod. "Not even no fish. Like the man says you can see for yourself."

"No. That will not be necessary." The Yankee strode back toward his own boat, a sleek steam-powered launch, smaller than the *Ellie Mae*, with a bronze howitzer sitting in its bow. He stopped and turned, his glance sweeping among them all as if he were reluctant to let them go. "I have orders to burn every boat on this river."

"Oh, no," Mrs. Hawkland said in a faint voice. "Please, this man would not have brought his boat down here if we had not hired him to take us to Rosehall."

The Yankee turned to Cooper. "It is your boat?" Cooper nodded, and the man asked, "Have you ever carried goods for the Rebels?"

"No, sir. Nor I wouldn't, neither. Seen a lot of Rebels on the river, though."

The man's eyes grew intense. "You have? Where?"

"Up at Alexandria, two day ago. They all headin' north."

Jamie watched him in silence, annoyed, but he doubted the information was news to the Yankees. When the officer turned to him for confirmation, he gave a shrug and a nod.

"Where did you say you were going?" the Yankee demanded.

"Rosehall," Jamie told him. "Belle View Plantation. Just across the Mississippi."

"Colonel Ellet was there some weeks ago," Mrs. Hawkland said. "We sold him cotton to protect his boat."

"Colonel Ellet?" The man's brows rose, then drew together. "Which Colonel Ellet?"

"Which?" Mrs. Hawkland frowned slightly. She looked faint, and Jamie stepped toward her, concerned that she might fall. He could feel his heart pounding as he helped her sit down on the baggage.

"Rivers?" she said, looking up at the Yankee. "Charles Rivers Ellet? I believe that was the name."

The young man's expression softened a little. He glanced at Jamie, who thought, *Go away. We are not enough to interest you.* He hoped the Yankee wouldn't notice the disparity between his clothing and Mrs. Hawkland's. He felt his every hair standing on end.

"All right," the man said at last. "I will escort you to the mouth of the river."

Jamie made himself smile and nod. "That is very kind of you. Thank you."

The Yankee returned to his own boat, and looked relieved to be there. "You move on ahead. I will follow."

While the negro started the boat downstream again, Jamie walked aft to the box that held the provisions and opened it, deliberately holding the lid so that the Yankee could see its contents. He took out a cracker and bit it in half, the crumbs sticking in his dry mouth. Closing the box, he stood up and tried to look casual as he picked up his valise and returned to Mrs. Hawkland's makeshift couch. When he got there his knees threatened to give and he had to sit down. He put the half-eaten cracker aside and managed to swallow what was in his mouth.

Mrs. Hawkland turned to him, eyes wide. "What would they have done . . . ?" she whispered.

Jamie shrugged and ran a hand through his hair. He kept his voice low. "Taken me prisoner. Maybe shot me for a spy. It could still happen."

She looked horrified. "There were no boats here when we left. I had not thought you would be coming into such danger! I would never have asked it of you."

Her voice was so chagrined Jamie had to laugh. "It was a chance. I knew that."

"What will you do? How will you get past them going back?"

"I will figure that out when I get there. I am more concerned about there being more Yankee boats on the Mississippi, whatever boat this fellow came from, for one. They might not be as accommodating as he."

Jamie glanced aft at the launch, and saw that the Yankee officer was watching them, holding a spyglass in his hand. With a shiver, he wondered if that glass had been trained on the *Ellie Mae* earlier, before he had taken off his coat. He turned to Mrs. Hawkland and took her hands in his. Small, pretty hands. They were trembling.

"Thank you for what you said about Colonel Ellet," he said softly. "I think that tipped the balance in our favor."

She looked up at him unhappily. He smiled at her.

"Don't look so worried. He's watching. That's better, you're prettiest when you smile. Will you do something for me?" She nodded. "Two things, actually. Give me your purse again, so I can pay Cooper when we get to Rosehall. No, not now. I'll come back in a minute. First I want you to call your girl over and brush out your hair."

"My hair? Why?" She frowned at the improper suggestion.

"Just do it." Jamie realized he had spoken to her as he would to a subordinate. He moderated his tone, and added, "Please. I need to put my coat in my bag, and I want that Yankee to be watching you, not me."

"Oh. Of course." She smiled up at him bravely, and he felt it like a stab in his heart.

"Thank you. Wait till I've been with Cooper a while."

"All right."

He kissed both her hands for the Yankee's benefit. She squeezed his fingers before he let go. He stood up, legs a bit shaky but they supported him, and went forward to speak to Cooper, taking the valise with him. The negro looked up as he approached. Jamie sat beside him and spoke quietly.

"Thanks for the warning."

Cooper nodded toward the maid seated by the funnel. "You can thank Miss Sarah there. She the one told me you been good to her mistress. Yanks can have you for all I care."

Jamie swallowed, but took this calmly. He turned to the girl and gave her a nod. "Thank you, Sarah."

She smiled shyly, then glanced away as if unsure whether she should be looking at him. He noticed Cooper was watching her with a fond expression on his face. At first he had thought Cooper's interest in the girl was the usual animal kind, but the look on his face just now was more fatherly.

Cooper looked up at him and his smile faded some. "She reminds me of my Ellie Mae, back when Ellie were younger."

Jamie nodded. He was willing to listen, but Cooper seemed to have no more to say. Whether Ellie Mae was a sweetheart or daughter, alive or dead, Cooper kept it to himself.

"Sarah?" Mrs. Hawkland called. "Come here please."

The girl got up and went to her. Jamie stared straight ahead, watching the river. There was more water here, wider and deeper. Cottonwoods hung gnarled branches out over the banks. He remembered going through here before—the Old River, just above the Mississippi. One way or another, it would end soon.

He glanced back and saw Mrs. Hawkland taking down her hair. Beautiful hair—long, rich chestnut-colored hair—the Yankee officer and his men would enjoy watching her brush it, he hoped. A memory flicked through his mind of how her hair felt, how it smelled. Turning away, he stood up slowly and carried his valise down into the hold.

Out of sight of the hatch, he scrambled to grab his things from behind the coffin and cram them into the bag, mashing his hat all out of shape on top of the coat and gun belt. He closed the bag, took a deep breath, and casually carried it up again. As he emerged he saw Mrs. Hawkland holding up a hand mirror, her other hand pulling her loose hair away from her long, white throat. Despite everything, he felt himself responding to that sight, and he hoped all the Yankees did, too.

He walked toward her and set the valise down with the other baggage. She was pinning her hair up, now, with the maid's help. Jamie stood watching, and when she was finished he sat down beside her again. She reached out a hand and he took it, felt the hard coins pressing into his palm through the purse. He held onto her hand.

"I will get it back to you on the shore."

"Keep it," she said. Her lips smiled, but her eyes were troubled.

"I do not want your money."

"You may need it."

Jamie swallowed, unwilling to argue, unable to face his snarled feelings about her on top of his present danger. It was too much.

"Now it is you who look worried," she said quietly.

His head came up, and he managed to smile. She smiled back and squeezed his hand, then slipped hers away, leaving the purse behind.

"You will have to come up to the house, you know," she said. "You have made them think you are my husband."

"I-I am sorry—"

"No, it was a wise thing to do, but you must carry it through now. I will find a way to get you back across the river."

Jamie glanced at Cooper. He had planned to return to Alexandria with the man, but Mrs. Hawkland was right, it would look peculiar. Besides, he could not be sure that Cooper wouldn't just hand him over to the Yankees.

He turned back to Mrs. Hawkland. "Thank you."

She smiled, and this time her eyes were soft. "We will get through this."

"Yes."

He gazed at her, admiring her courage. She must know that if he was discovered she would be blamed for aiding him. She seemed not to fear the Yankees—well, of course she did not. She had been smuggling cotton under their noses for months. She and her husband.

He glanced toward the hold at the reminder, and noticed they were coming to the Mississippi. Ahead he could see the wide water, and in it a big sidewheeler, its lower deck enclosed, guns protruding from ports on the upper deck. Beyond, on the far shore, Mrs. Hawkland's house gleamed white on the hilltop through the hazy heat, paradise just out of reach.

The Yankee launch drew abreast of the *Ellie Mae,* and the officer shouted through a trumpet, "Follow me."

Jamie sat silent as the negro guided his boat into the Mississipi after the launch and followed it to the side of the big steamer. The Yankee officer climbed out onto the deck of the boat, where an older officer met him. This man was tall with a long, dark beard, and wore the uniform of a lieutenant-colonel in the Yankee army. The two men conversed briefly, then walked toward the *Ellie Mae.* Jamie felt his shoulders tightening, tried to counter it and look relaxed.

"You, there," the senior Yankee said, pointing straight at him.

Jamie stood and came toward him. He felt Mrs. Hawkland's hand brush his as he stepped away.

"You have scarlet fever aboard?"

Relieved at the question, Jamie tilted his head toward the hold. "A man dead of scarlet fever."

"And where are you going?"

"That house right there," Jamie told him, gesturing toward Rosehall.

The army officer looked at the house, then back at Jamie. "What were you doing away from home?"

Jamie's heart rose into his throat. He cast frantic thoughts back to the awkward dinner party aboard the packet, and said, "Mrs. Hawkland wished to visit her aunt in Shreveport."

A hand slid around his elbow. He glanced down to see Mrs. Hawkland smiling sadly up at him. His other hand came up to cover hers as she looked at the Yankees.

"The fever broke out on our boat after we left Alexandria," she said. "Poor old Mr. Hawkland died." She gave Jamie a pitying glance, laced with a glint of warning, then looked at the officer again. Jamie stared at his boots, trying to appear brokenhearted.

"We wanted to bring him home to rest right away," Mrs. Hawkland continued, "and of course, we did not wish to risk introducing fever into my aunt's home. This was the only boat we could get to bring us down. Please do not destroy it—Mr. Cooper is an honest man."

"I am not concerned with his honesty, but with the use to which the Rebels may put his boat."

"I'll die 'fore I let the Rebs have it," Cooper put in fiercely.

Mrs. Hawkland tilted her head a little as she regarded the officer. "Are you by chance a relation of Colonel Ellet, sir? You remind me of him somewhat."

Jamie saw the man's brows twitch in surprise, but he made no reply, instead walking the *Ellie Mae*'s length on the deck of his own vessel. Jamie waited in silence. Mrs. Hawkland squeezed his arm and he looked at her. In that moment he loved her, for her courage, her strength, her cleverness. She gazed tenderly up at him, heavy with his child, and he felt as if he were drowning. He could not afford this; not when they both stood on the brink of disaster.

"Very well, you may go," the Yankee said.

Jamie felt a wave of relief so strong it almost made him dizzy. He looked at the officer, who had already shifted his attention to Cooper.

"You there—I expect to see you go back up the Red as soon as you have set them ashore."

"That just exactly what you gonna see," Cooper answered.

"If I find you anywhere below Alexandria again I will burn your boat. Understand?"

"Yessir."

The officer returned his attention to Jamie, staring narrowly at him, frowning a little. "Carry on," he said at last, and turned away.

Jamie stood still, afraid to move, afraid the Yankee would change his mind. The sailors in the launch climbed out of it and brought their boat aboard the steamer. Cooper started the *Ellie Mae* across the Mississippi.

"May we sit down?" Mrs. Hawkland asked in a weary voice.

Jamie helped her to her couch and sat with her, feeling Yankee eyes on his back. He resisted the temptation to glance back at the gunboat, instead watching the eastern bank slowly loom closer. Late afternoon light set the white drive aglow and lit up the columns of the house. With each passing minute he breathed a little easier.

A crowd of negro children gathered at the landing to greet them, waving and shouting in high, excited voices. Cooper cut his engine and brought the boat drifting to the shore, then dropped his anchor overboard. Jamie helped Mrs. Hawkland to her feet, helped her ashore, and stood on the landing dazed with relief.

The children crowded around them. Mrs. Hawkland spoke to one of the taller ones. "Seth, run up to the house and tell Damien to send the carriage down. Tell him to send two men to move the baggage. And the wagon," she added as the boy darted off up the drive.

"Madame?"

Jamie turned to see the maid standing at the edge of the boat, holding Mrs. Hawkland's open parasol. He moved to help her ashore.

"Sarah, you gonna come away?" Cooper said sharply.

The girl hesitated. Jamie stopped, watching the boatman come up to her. Was this what they had spent all those hours talking about? Was he offering to help her run?

"Sarah!" Mrs. Hawkland sounded shocked and angry.

The maid stood still in the parasol's shade, frowning in thought. She looked at Cooper, at her mistress, and finally at Jamie. He glanced at the Yankee gunboat, wondering how many glasses were trained on them. They could not afford an altercation under that scrutiny, and Cooper knew it.

"Now's your chance, child," the fisherman said softly. "You come with me you be free for sure. Wait for some boy to rescue you, might be waiting a long while."

The slave gave him a long, silent look, then turned to Jamie and reached out her hand. He helped her out of the boat and watched her go to her mistress, holding out the parasol. Mrs. Hawkland accepted it, still surprised, no longer angry. The maid stepped behind her and stared at the ground. Jamie glanced at Cooper, who met his gaze with hard eyes.

"You owe me thirty-five dollars," the man said coldly.

Jamie took out Mrs. Hawkland's purse and counted out the coins. "Here's ten more, for your help."

"Keep it. I didn't do it for you."

Jamie looked up at him sharply. Cooper's expression was downright hostile.

"I done it 'cause I give Miss Sarah my word I won't betray you. She asked me not to tell them Yankees and I won't, not today. I ever see you again, though, better watch out."

"Fair enough," Jamie said. He put the coins in Cooper's hand.

The negro gazed at Sarah for a moment, then turned away. He did not look at them again, the whole time Mrs. Hawkland's servants were unloading the baggage. Jamie supervised this, taking his own valise and checking to be certain nothing was left behind. When he stepped ashore for the last time, Cooper hauled up his anchor and started back across the river.

The sun was beginning to set by now, and the baggage was all strapped atop the carriage. Mrs. Hawkland and Sarah were already inside. All that remained on the landing was Hawkland's coffin. Even as he looked at it, Jamie heard the sound of another vehicle coming down the drive. He looked up to see a wagon arrive, driven by a tall negro who despite his wiriness looked as if he could break a man's arm with his bare hands. The driver stared at Jamie, then looked to the carriage as Mrs. Hawkland spoke.

"Thank you, Damien. Please bring the coffin up to the house."

The negro nodded and got down from the box, looking at Jamie. "Whose coffin is this?" His voice was deep.

Jamie swallowed. "Colonel Hawkland's."

The dark eyes sharpened briefly, then the man turned away to direct the loading of the coffin into the wagon. Jamie climbed into the waiting carriage.

No one spoke on the way up the drive. Mrs. Hawkland looked exhausted, the maid lost in her own thoughts. Jamie watched out the window as the sun sank behind the gunboat that once again stood between him and where he wanted to be.

18

I would not die in Spring time
When all is bright around.
And fair young flowers are peeping
From out the silent ground
   —"I Would Not Die in Spring Time," Stephen Collins Foster

The carriage stopped, and Marie opened her eyes. Mr. Russell got out and offered her his hands. With his help she got down, then stood looking at the house. It had never loomed so large before. She gazed up at its white pillars gilded by the setting sun, its tall windows, its broad steps. She must enter it without Theodore. Live in it without Theodore.

"Madame?"

Lucinde was beside her, dark eyes questioning. Marie found she could not speak, nor could she stop the flow of tears she had held back for so long.

"Madame, where is Monsieur?"

"Colonel Hawkland is dead," said Mr. Russell's voice behind her. The words were like a blow, though the voice was quiet. Marie took a step forward and nearly lost her balance; Lucinde caught her around the waist and helped her up the steps and into the house.

She waited in the parlor, aware of the movements and voices of servants, unaware of what they meant. When she saw the coffin being carried into the house she stood up.

"Bring it in here, please." Her voice was unsteady but she tried to give it authority.

Lucinde came toward her, concern on her face. "Madame—"

"We will wake him in here."

Marie turned and picked up an ornament from the sofa table—a little dog statue Theodore had been fond of. Lucinde hurried to clear the rest of the things off the table while Marie sank into a chair by the door, holding the dog in one hand. She watched Damien and Victor move the furniture back, making room for the coffin. Lucinde returned and cast a black cloth over the mantel clock before allowing two of the garden boys to carry in the coffin and set it on the table.

"Candles," Marie said to Lucinde. "Bring in candles, please. And send Zeb to town to fetch Father Clément." St. Francisville was twenty miles away, and the chapel of St. Francis was beyond it, across the river. The priest would not arrive until tomorrow, or perhaps the day after.

"Oui, Madame. Will you come up now and change your dress?"

"No. Leave me, please." She was too tired to move, too hurt to do anything but stare, dry-eyed now, at the black box with Theodore inside. When she thought back over the last few days she was amazed at all that she had been able to do with this great wound in her soul.

She was aware that time was passing. She heard the clock strike—muffled beneath its covering—saw the light fade from the tiny gap in the drapes that Lucinde had pulled across the windows. Servants came offering food and drink; she refused all. Finally a different step approached from the hall, went silent on the carpet. Marie looked up to see Mr. Russell standing before her, holding a tray.

"I am an ambassador," he said, in a voice that implied he did not relish his mission.

Marie closed her eyes. "Go away."

"I will, as soon as you have eaten something."

She felt anger at his intrusion, and sat rigid while he put the tray on the little table someone had moved next to her chair. He squatted beside it and lifted the cover from a plate of food, which he picked up and held out to her. She looked at it, then flung it away from her, knocking the plate out of his hands and across the room where it shattered against the leg of a chair. Marie gasped, then sobbed, blinded by new tears. She felt his hands pressing a handkerchief into hers and clung to them, unable to stop the racking sobs. His shoulder was near, and without thought she reached for it, hung on it, wept into it. She felt his arms go around her, felt their comforting warmth and strength, and yielded. It was wrong; it was unwise, but she could not let go. She could no longer do anything but grieve.

Jamie waited for the storm to subside, aware of the servants watching from the hall. He did not speak, only held her and thought of his own sorrows, of Martin and Daniel and Colonel Reily. After a while her sobs grew quieter, then ended. At the first suggestion she might pull away he let her go, sitting back on his heels.

"I broke the dish," she said in a quavering voice.

Jamie nodded. "Never mind."

She looked at him, then at her husband's coffin. He had never seen her look so broken, even that awful morning on the riverboat.

"You should try and get some sleep," he told her gently. She shook her head, so he tried again. "Lie on the sofa, then. Rest a little."

After a moment she nodded, and held out a trembling hand. Jamie got up and helped her out of the chair, guided her to the velvet covered sofa where she lay on her side, staring at the coffin. Candles on the mantel behind her head cast a soft glow through the room, glinting on gilt furniture. Above the candles, a life-sized portrait of Mrs. Hawkland looked out at him with a smile he remembered all too well, though he had not seen it lately. He swallowed and looked down at her lying on the sofa in the rumpled dress she had worn for four days now, one hand draped over her swollen belly. How could he have guessed that his indiscretion would bring him here? He shook his head to clear it of useless questions, stepped back, and quietly went out.

A footman carried a dustpan into the room as Jamie left it, going to clean up the broken plate. Three other servants waited in the hall with anxious faces: the butler, the tall woman, and the wiry negro they called Damien who had driven the wagon.

Jamie looked at the woman and gave an apologetic shrug. "Bring her some milk."

She nodded and hurried away. The butler's face underwent a transformation; deep concern vanished, replaced by a stiff formality.

"Your supper is ready, sah. Will you take it in the dining room?"

Jamie hesitated a second, but was overruled by his empty stomach. "Yes. Thank you."

He followed the butler across the hall to a large room at the back of the house that was almost completely filled by a long, polished table of dark wood. Like the rest of the house, it intimidated him. A lonely branch of candles sat at one end of the table where a single place setting was laid. A black cloth had been draped over a huge mirror on one wall. Jamie sat down, glancing up at a large, ornately carved wooden paddle above the table that moved slowly back and forth, causing the candles to flicker. He followed the rope that moved it down to the hands of a young slave boy who stood against the wall.

His hunger had first awakened at the smell of the food they had asked him to take to Mrs. Hawkland. Now he appeased it on sliced sausage, cold potato soup, a rabbit haunch and greens, trout with almonds, and cheese, all of which he consumed with a gusto more appropriate to a soldier's fare of bacon and beans. The dishes came and went; he was given white wine, then red, then brandy which the butler poured for him just as the footman took away a dainty plate from which Jamie had cleaned every crumb of a strawberry tart.

"Coffee, sah?"

"No, thank you."

The butler set the decanter at Jamie's elbow and retired. Jamie sipped the brandy—smooth fire on the tongue—and looked at the slave boy who still stood pulling his rope, gazing at nothing. Boy and paddle moved in absolute silence, making a breeze for Jamie's sole benefit. He wondered if the boy's arms ached.

What day was it? He had to concentrate to remember. Natchitoches had been Sunday, so this must be Tuesday. John would be in Shreveport by now, might even have gone on to Marshall. Jamie hoped his friend had remembered to send word to General Green for him, otherwise he would catch hell when he got back to the battery. If he got back.

He finished his brandy, thought about pouring more and decided he didn't need it. This was confirmed when he stood up and found his head swimming. He steadied himself, then walked slowly from the room.

Candlelight spilled from the parlor's open door. Jamie crossed the length of the huge hall and stood in the doorway looking in. Mrs. Hawkland lay where he had left her, but her eyes were now closed. He backed away. There was nothing more he could do for her.

Nothing much he could do for himself, either, with the Yankee gunboat out in the river. He stepped to a window by the front doors and moved the lace curtain aside. There it was—dark shape against the darker trees behind. He let the curtain fall.

Weariness overtook him. He blinked hard to keep himself awake long enough to get upstairs. An oil lamp burned low beside the gigantic bed in his gigantic room. Never had he enjoyed such luxury, even as his Aunt May's guest. Someone had unpacked his bag and hung his jacket, his spare shirt, and his two extra pairs of threadbare drawers in a wardrobe that seemed big enough to hold all the clothing his family owned. The mirrors on its doors had been covered with black cloth, carefully pinned to allow them to close properly. It must be some local custom of mourning, to cover all the mirrors. The hall clock downstairs had been draped as well; he had noticed it as he came up.

He found his gun, socks, and other things in a drawer in the wardrobe, and on a shelf above the clothes lay his hat. Unseen hands had tried to put it back into shape, and even brushed it. He reached up to touch the star pin, feeling a rush of homesickness. His eyes threatened to close, so he pulled off his boots and his clothing, left them lying in a heap on the floor, and crawled naked into the feather bed, instantly falling asleep.

Cairo was hot, muggy, and looked to be muddy as ever, despite the fact that the river had fallen somewhat during Nat's leave. He did not bother to climb the sodden levee upon disembarking from the transport, but proceeded, portmanteau in hand, directly to the wharfboat that housed the Mississippi Squadron's offices. This, like the rest of the navy's facilities, lay on the eastern side of the point of land where the Ohio river met the Mississippi. There were always a number of boats present. The *Eastport* and the *Chillicothe* were where he had seen them on his way home—still on the ways, undergoing repairs—and the receiving ship *Clara Dolsen* lay at her permanent station. Nearby, next to the store ship *Abraham,* another boat was moored—a river monitor, brand new by the looks of her. She lay low in the muddy water, almost flat, with a round gun-turret near her bow, smokestack amidships, and pilot house perched precariously on a pair of braces that jutted forward from a peculiar, flat-topped, armored pyramid at the stern. It took Nat a moment to realize that this was a wheelhouse; the boat was a sternwheel monitor, something he had not previously heard of. Not a soul was to be seen aboard her. She looked forlorn, almost forbidding, with her sloping, inhospitable deck.

Fleet Headquarters was as busy as it had been on his previous visit, but this time the clerk who acknowledged him requested that he wait, and after a few minutes ushered him into the commandant's office. He set his bag down by the door and stood, a bit nervous, waiting while the commandant finished writing a letter.

Nat had not previously met Captain Pennock, though he had heard a great deal about the man who directed the fleet's business from this place. Whatever the navy's river forces needed—be it boats, supplies, or men—passed through Pennock's control. He was a powerful man, connected by marriage to Admiral Farragut, and looked to be a man one should not cross. Nat observed him and his office as he waited, listening to the scratch of his pen on the paper.

The room was furnished without embellishment: a desk, a few chairs, shelves of books and files, and a clock mounted upon the wall. The desk was laden with paperwork, but all of it was orderly. Captain Pennock's person was neat, his countenance firm though it seemed to be permanently etched into a frown of concentration. He was perhaps fifty, Nat thought, from the silver at his temples and amidst his side whiskers.

The pen's scratching ceased, the pen itself was returned to the inkwell, and Captain Pennock looked up, regarding Nat with an expectant expression. "Yes?"

"My name is Wheat, sir. I was carpenter aboard the *Queen of the West,* and am here to be reassigned."

"Pity about the *Queen,*" Pennock said, picking up a sheaf of papers and flipping through them.

Nat swallowed. "Yes, sir, but perhaps she will be recaptured."

Pennock paused and looked up at Nat with one eyebrow quirked. "Where have you been, young man? The *Queen* was destroyed two weeks ago."

Nat felt a rush of dismay, but tried not to let it show in his face. "I— have been home on leave."

"Ah." Pennock returned his attention to the papers. "She encountered some of our boats on Grand Lake. They tried to capture her but an unlucky shell cut a steam pipe and set her cotton afire, and there was nothing to be done. She burned two hours, then her magazine exploded. A great pity, for we could have used her, but one cannot conduct a war without some loss. Ah, here it is." He extracted a sheet from the papers, setting the rest aside and taking up his pen. "I am getting up a crew for the *Neosho,* which you may have seen at the wharf here."

"The monitor?"

"Yes. She won't be ready for another week or so, but there is much you could do on board."

"With respect, sir, I . . ."

The fleet captain's expectant gaze stopped Nat's words in his throat. He did not quite have the nerve to reject outright an assignment offered by this man. He coughed.

"I was wondering if I might possibly train as a junior pilot."

Pennock frowned. "A pilot? Have you any experience?"

"Some, yes. Nothing formal. My uncle was a pilot, and taught me the Ohio, and the Mississippi down to Natchez. It was some years ago—"

"Do you think you could handle the Mississippi today?" Pennock's voice had acquired an edge, and his eyes a sharp glint.

Nat drew a deep breath. "With some practice, I believe I could."

Pennock let the page fall to his desk and returned his pen to the inkwell, then leaned back in his chair and laced his fingers across his flat stomach. "Please sit down, Mr. . . . ?"

"Wheat," Nat said, drawing a chair forward.

The commandant's frown deepened a little. "Wheat? Nathaniel Wheat's boy?"

"Yes, sir." Nat felt his jaw tightening, and made an effort to relax it.

"I'm surprised he hasn't kept you in Cincinnati, building tin-clads."

"So is he, sir."

Pennock's gaze held his for a moment, one eyebrow slowly rising, then a smile broke across his face and all signs of care and authority vanished as he laughed aloud. Nat laughed, too, mostly out of surprise, and some nervousness.

"I have met your father, Mr. Wheat," said Captain Pennock. "He is—a determined man. If you have succeeded in defying him, you have my respect."

"Success might not be the best name for it," Nat said, half to himself.

Pennock's smile softened and his eyes narrowed a bit. "Well, the navy is a good home for orphans of every description. You will find your place. Do you really think it is in the pilot house? Or is it just that you do not care for a monitor?"

Nat glanced up sharply. "I am afraid I do not care for them," he admitted.

"Nor do I. Beastly things. Have you ever been in one? Like a floating coffin. Someone must sail them, however." Pennock retrieved his paper, scanned it, then dropped it again and leaned forward, resting his elbows upon the desk. "Are you serious about piloting?"

"I am interested, sir, though I have no certification whatever—" Nat paused as Pennock laughed again.

"My dear fellow, we have been using flatboat men. We cannot get any better; the navy will not match river rates of pay. Do you think you could outpilot a raftsman?"

"Possibly," Nat said, feeling a grin creeping onto his face.

"And you do not mind the danger? Even the most heavily armored pilot house will not stop every shell."

Nat hesitated, thinking of Renata. This, though, was the reason he had not actually proposed to her. If something should happen to him, she would be free.

"How much did you say the pay was?"

Pennock's eyes crinkled with laughter. "I see you are your father's son after all. Well, it is nowhere near what a first-class river pilot gets, but I think you will find it an agreeable increase over a carpenter's pay. What do you say to a hundred a month?"

Nat's heart gave a decided jump. His present pay was only eight hundred dollars a year, after a reduction he had been forced to accept when he transferred from the army's service to the navy. A hundred a month was indeed an agreeable increase.

"When do I begin?" he said quietly.

"As soon as I can get you a berth. Of course, I should consider assigning you to the *Neosho* . . ."

Nat held back a grimace. "I would be much more confident in a familiar class of vessel, sir. A tinclad, or even a tug. I have never handled such a craft as a sternwheel monitor."

"No one has ever handled such a craft. She and her sister *Osage* are the first of their kind. She only draws four feet, laden," Pennock added in a tone of amusement.

"But she is bottom-heavy," Nat said. "I fear I might do her a harm, as inexperienced as I am. That would not look well for either of us, with a brand new vessel."

Pennock chuckled. "Yes, very like your father." His glance went to the clock, and Nat followed it, surprised to see that it was nearly six. "Well, come around in the morning and you shall take the *Abraham* for a short tour. If you manage not to ground her, I will see what I can do for you."

Pennock stood up, and Nat quickly followed suit. "Thank you, sir!"

"Seven o'clock sharp," Pennock said. The gaze he fixed on Nat was piercing, but the hand he extended was friendly. Nat shook it, liking the firm, warm grip.

"Seven sharp," he said. "Yes, sir."

Pennock dismissed him with a nod and sat down again, returning to his paperwork. Nat retrieved his portmanteau and quietly left, his spirits much higher than they had been when he came in. He would see if his usual boardinghouse could accommodate him tonight, but first he would take a good look at the *Abraham*.

19

Jadyè, jadyè chèr frèr,
No senyèr m'a dit Il ora pitchye de noun.
(Good-bye, good-bye dear Brother,
Our Lord told me He will have pity on us.)
——Creole Wake Song

Someone was singing. Marie opened her eyes, saw the black wall of
the coffin before her, and closed them again. She was stiff from lying
on the sofa, which was too narrow for comfort. She lay listening—it
was Lucinde's voice, and the song an old wake song—until she felt
able to open her eyes again and slowly sit up.

Lucinde stopped singing and rose from the chair by the door, coming to Marie's side with long, silent strides. "Madame?"

Marie looked toward the mantel clock, but it was draped. She had
forgotten that custom, a superstition, really. All clocks and mirrors in
the house draped during the wake, so that the coffin would not be
reflected and spread death further through the household. She
remembered when her father had died, it had seemed the whole
house dripped with black crape. Her mother had gone into permanent mourning, scarcely speaking, never again setting foot outside the
house. That, too, was a common custom among her people, but not
one Marie intended to keep. She could not afford to keep it, even had
she desired to.

She opened her mouth to ask what time it was, then changed her
mind. It did not matter. She did not want to know.

"Come upstairs, Madame," Lucinde said. "You will sleep better in
your own bed."

A part of her wanted to stay and watch over Theodore through the
night. She knew she had not the strength, though. She needed to rest.

"Come up, cher," Lucinde said, her voice a low croon. "Come up

229

and let Lucinde make you comfortable. You do not want to look like this when the priest comes."

Marie glanced up at that, but saw only concern in Lucinde's dark eyes. She held out her hands to be helped up and went upstairs with her servant, slowly, for her feet were unsteady. Her chamber glowed with soft lamplight and she felt a flood of relief upon entering it; felt safe, though she knew that was illusion. Damien had brought up the copper bathtub, which sat waiting with pitchers and a steaming kettle nearby. Marie allowed Lucinde to undress her and help her into the tub, already partly filled with warm water. A shiver went through her as she relaxed into the bath. Lucinde added more water from the pitchers and the kettle, handed Marie soap and a sponge, then began to take down her hair, humming softly as she smoothed out the tangles while Marie washed herself. Her scalp ached, and she sighed with pleasure as Lucinde poured warm water over it and rubbed in a shampoo of lavender and rosemary. She had forgotten how good it felt to be clean; forgotten to pay attention to her body, being so absorbed in her pain. The body felt no pain, though. The body continued in health, though her inability to eat had weakened it. The child stirred within her and her hand went to soothe it. She would have to eat soon, for the child, but first she would rest.

Lucinde dried her with soft towels, dressed her in a nightgown and wrapper, and made her lie on the chaise while she brushed her hair dry. Marie gazed sleepily at the empty fireplace.

"Madame, who is that man who came with you?"

Marie froze, then drew a careful breath. "An acquaintance. A soldier. He is a friend of Mr. Lawford's. He offered to escort me, made all the arrangements." She was saying too much. A simple question did not require so many answers. "I needed help," she added, excusing herself more to herself than to her servant, feeling tightness rise in her throat. She should not have brought him here, but she had been too shocked to manage things for herself. She would have to get rid of him soon, for she had foolishly told him the truth about her child, and that gave him power over her should he choose to wield it. Also, she acknowledged only in the silence of her heart, she feared he might gain power over her in other ways. He was young and strong, with eyes that haunted her. She flinched from the feelings that stirred. The body reacted without regard to her sensibilities, but the body did not rule her. She would not yield. She had a husband, a precious beloved husband, who was not yet under ground. The Texan had no place in her life.

Perhaps he would demand one, she thought, and swallowed. She would face that when she came to it. Not now.

She felt Lucinde begin to braid her hair, and closed her eyes. She had done wrong, and God had punished her. A most cruel punishment, but she was beginning to understand it, though she could not yet accept it. She would make the best of what she had left. It was all she could do.

"Bed, now, Madame," Lucinde said softly, and Marie complied. From the depths of her feather bed she watched the woman pick up the dress she had been wearing.

"Dye that black," she said. It was a good dress, but she would never be able to wear it again without thinking of Theodore.

"Oui, Madame. Good night."

It seemed only a moment later that she awoke. The room was dark, but sunlight slipping in around the edges of the drapes told her it was morning. She closed her eyes but sleep evaded her, weary though she still was. Too many questions and problems chased through her mind. She was hot, and threw aside her sheet.

"Good morning, Madame," said a voice nearby, startling her.

Marie turned her head to see Sarah sitting beside her bed. "Where is Lucinde?"

"Talking to Cook. I ask for the honor to dress you today."

Marie gazed at the girl. She had spoken deferentially, but that she would put herself forward at all was unusual. Marie remembered Sarah's hesitation at the river landing, her own astonishment that the girl would even consider running before her very eyes. A month ago—even a week ago—she could not have imagined such a thing.

"Is it because you have something to say to me?"

The girl met her gaze and nodded once, slowly. Marie could still see the shadow of a bruise about one eye.

"Madame, I ask a favor from you. Lucinde ask for me before, but now I ask for myself. I ask let me be your dresser still, and let me sleep in the house."

"None of the servants sleep in the house." At once Marie regretted the sharpness with which she had spoken. She knew perfectly well the girl's reason.

Sarah's gaze dropped to the floor. "Soon the bébé will come. You will need someone to watch over him. I could do that." When Marie did not answer, Sarah looked up at her. "Please, Madame. I help when

Monsieur was sick, no? I stay because I believe you are kind, you are generous—"

"You stayed because you expect Adams to purchase your freedom. Is that not so?" Marie spoke quietly, but still an edge of fear came into the girl's eyes. "What if he never returns?"

"Madame is kind," the girl said in a hollow voice. "Madame will not let me be hurt again. Lucinde says so, and I believe."

Marie stifled a sigh. She did not need this annoyance on top of all the rest. She got out of the bed, and Sarah hastened around it, snatching up Marie's wrapper.

"No, I will dress at once," Marie said.

Sarah laid the wrapper on the foot of the bed and went to the wardrobe. When Marie was dressed to her petticoats, Sarah hunted through the wardrobe and produced a black dinner dress from its recesses. Marie nodded; she had no black day dress, and while this was of taffeta rather than a plain fabric, it would do for today. She must choose some more dresses to dye, she thought as she held up her arms while Sarah slipped the gown over her head. The girl made a sound of dismay when she discovered it would not close over Marie's stomach.

"Never mind," Marie said. "Fetch me that black mantelet."

The loose overgarment concealed the deficiency of the dress, and was of a duller fabric. Marie turned toward the wardrobe before remembering that the mirrors had been covered. No matter; she scarcely cared how she looked. She sat on the chaise longue while the maid did her hair. She was already warm in the black dress and mantelet, but it did not matter. She did not expect to be comfortable in any way today.

When her hair was coiffed she arose and stepped into the black slippers Sarah brought out for her. The girl had gone silent, and despite her own troubles Marie could not help but pity her.

"I will do what I can to see that you are not hurt again," she said quietly. It was a qualified promise, and she saw understanding of that in the girl's face after her first hopeful glance.

"Thank you, Madame," Sarah whispered, head bowed.

Marie left the room and went downstairs, leaning heavily on the bannister, feeling dissatisfied. She now had an unpleasant interview with Mr. Shelton to look forward to. At the foot of the stairs she stopped, unsure where to go—not to the parlor where Theodore lay, not yet—nor to the library with bills and ledgers for her to try to comprehend. She looked toward the dining room, wondering if Mr. Russell was there. She did not yet wish to face him either.

"Good morning, Madame." Lucinde came toward her from the butler's pantry. "Would you like a little coffee, or some tea? You could sit in the music room. No one will bother you there."

Marie smiled with relief. "Yes, thank you. Tea."

She followed Lucinde to the music room across the hall from the parlor. She glanced that way before going in, saw the candles still burning. She would have to send word to the neighbors that she was holding a veillée, though perhaps there would be no need. She had summoned the priest; that might be enough to spread the news. There would be visitors soon, one way or another.

The music room's drapes were partially open, just enough to allow daylight to filter through the lace curtains beneath. The piano and harp had been covered before her departure last week and in consequence the room felt somewhat lonely, but Marie sat with her back to them on a sofa facing the window and was able to relax a little. Lucinde brought tea and a small bowl of gruel, at which Marie gave a rueful smile.

"Brave Lucinde. Do you not fear I might throw it at you?"

Lucinde shrugged, her face impassive. "If throwing it will make Madame feel better, eh bien. But perhaps Madame would consider eating it instead."

Marie laughed softly. "Madame would. Thank you."

She managed to eat half the gruel before her shrunken stomach rebelled. Setting it aside, she took up her teacup and leaned back against the cushioned sofa. She saw an empty stretch of years before her and it frightened her; she turned her mind away from it, taking refuge in smaller, more immediate problems. She must send for Mr. Shelton. She must prepare to receive visitors for the wake—Lucinde had perhaps already set the cook to making food. She must welcome Father Clément, and she must find some way to send Mr. Russell back across the river.

Grief overwhelmed her, as sudden as a summer squall. She put the teacup down with a clatter and searched her pockets and sleeves in vain for a handkerchief. Sarah had forgotten to give her one. She caught up the napkin from the tea tray and held it to her mouth, angry at her loss of self-control even as she wept.

Nat stood at the *Abraham*'s wheel, constantly examining the water's surface as he guided the sidewheeler up the Mississippi. His eye caught on a ripple that could be a reef building, but after watching it briefly he decided it was only the breeze. Though he was out of practice, he found he had not lost the ability to read the water that Uncle Charlie had drummed into him. Nor had he lost the habit of noting the river's perpetual changes; now that he was concentrating on the banks he realized he was more familiar with their present state than he had expected. He had spent as much time as he could on deck, both during his time on the *Queen* and on his return here after her loss, and must have been marking the river without realizing it.

A memory came to him of Uncle Charlie in the pilot house of the *Columbine,* quizzing him and Quincy on their marks on a warm summer day. The sun's heat, the buzz of cicadas, Charlie's fragrant pipe tobacco all returned to him easily—too easily, for he did not want their distraction, pleasant as they were. He brought his attention to the present and began to turn the wheel as the *Abraham* approached Cairo from below.

"Do not return to the depot yet," said the boat's captain, Acting Ensign Wagner. "Continue up the river a while."

Nat corrected the wheel and glanced at Wagner, a volunteer officer a bit younger than himself, inclining toward stoutness, who looked more like a clerk than a commander. He had stood beside Nat all the morning, observing his progress impassively and occasionally directing him to change course. The river was still fairly high, and Nat had encountered no difficulties in piloting the steamer down to Bayou du Chien, turning her, and coming back up. This instruction to continue up past Cairo he could only presume was a test of his nerve, as he had informed both Wagner and Captain Pennock that he had not been above Cairo in the past year and more. He was sorry Pennock had not come along, for he would have enjoyed his company more than that of the *Abraham*'s rather stoic commander, but Pennock had of course many more important things to do than cruise about the river.

Nat watched both the eastern bank and the water ahead closely, looking for signs of hidden shoals or obstructions. The river narrowed as it curved around the point on which Cairo was built. Soon a long towhead came in sight up ahead—almost an island, though at this stage of the river the feet of the trees growing on it were still underwater—and Nat guessed that this was Wagner's objective. A short while later, when he had the *Abraham* in the gentle water between the towhead and the bank, his suspicion was proved right.

Wagner drew his watch from his pocket and consulted it. "Well, I think that will do. Bring her about and return to Cairo, please, Mr. Wheat."

Nat acknowledged the order with a single nod. He was being given the opportunity to demonstrate both his piloting skill and his courage. There was a good deal of water inside the towhead, but the *Abraham* was a sizeable boat, and to turn her here where he did not know the river was to risk grounding or even snagging her, though he doubted there were many snags in this part of the river, as Cairo was a busy port and inconvenient obstructions in the vicinity would have been dealt with. Uncle Charlie would not have hesitated to turn her, but Charlie would have known the river; Nat did not. Conscious of Wagner's scrutiny, Nat held his course for a few minutes until the *Abraham*'s bow was just abreast of the towhead's top end. He glanced downriver to assure himself no other boats were nearby, then signaled to the engineer to slow the port wheel and began his turn. The water showed no sign of any debris snagged up against the towhead, so Nat trimmed it pretty closely, enough to make Wagner step forward to peer out of the window at the young trees sliding past, though he said nothing. That was risk enough for Nat, and once past the towhead he brought the boat out into the current, letting it carry her swiftly back down toward Cairo. He drew out of the fast water just above the bar, rounded the point neatly and turned up into the Ohio where he brought the steamer back to the wharf. He took his time landing her, as this was an operation he had not practiced much in his youth. Still, he was pleased at the speed with which he had accomplished the return. Turning the boat inside the towhead would have taken longer; he had chosen correctly, at least in his own judgment.

Wagner nodded, checking his watch once again. "Very good. I will inform Captain Pennock of your satisfactory performance."

"Thank you, sir."

Wagner smiled, an expression that did not appear at home on his face. "Good luck to you. We need every good pilot we can get."

Nat thanked him again and took his leave. On the wharf, he paused to look back at the *Abraham*. She was a little larger than the *Columbine* had been, and nowhere near as pretty.

Turning away from that sadness, Nat fixed his gaze on the muddy levee. It was too early to seek his dinner, and though he had an appointment with the fleet captain later in the afternoon, he knew better than to annoy him before Captain Wagner had made his report.

He had a few hours on his hands, and could think of nothing he preferred to do with them than to write to Renata and tell her of his start at piloting. Nat smiled as he thought of her. Brave, loyal, and true. His patriotic girl. Looking forward to composing a good, long letter, he began the muddy climb up the levee and back into town.

Jamie picked up the coffeepot, only to find it was empty. Offered the choice of having breakfast in the dining room or on a tray in his bedroom he had requested the latter, fully aware it was craven of him. He didn't want to face another meal in that great, gloomy room, alone or in company with his hostess.

He put the empty pot down again and got up, going over to the window. Drawing the curtain aside just enough to look out, he saw to his surprise that the steamer was gone. In its place two masted ships rode at anchor, the larger flying a blue flag along with the Yankee colors. Oceangoing ships looked out of place on the Mississippi; they reminded him of Galveston, the last place he had seen such vessels. He frowned, remembering the bombardment of Galveston, the navy's guns wreaking havoc, the streets littered with bricks and splintered wood.

As long as the Yankees were blockading the Red, he could not get across here. It was not wise to stay, either; Mrs. Hawkland had mentioned a Yankee officer's previous visit, and if the commanders of those ships decided to call on her now he could be discovered and she punished for harboring him. The sooner he left, the better.

He went to the wardrobe and began packing his things into his valise, not knowing where he would go but feeling better at being prepared. He packed his coat, knowing it would be a liability if he ran into any Federals. His vest was sufficient for decency's sake. When the footman came in to take away his tray, Jamie asked him where the nearest town was.

"About twenty miles to the south, sir. St. Francisville, and Bayou Sara also, at the riverside."

"Thank you."

Bayou Sara he had heard of; it was a cotton port. Maybe he could get across there. He finished packing, picked up his hat, and carried his bag downstairs. As he neared the ground floor he heard Mrs. Hawkland speaking nearby and a man answering. He set his bag by the foot of the stairs and stepped toward the voices.

"Ah, now ma'am, it was just a bit of fun—"

"Fun for you, perhaps, but it has caused considerable inconvenience in my household. I wish it to cease."

Jamie found himself looking through the open doorway of a room furnished up as an office and sitting room. With a start he remembered it was the room where he had encountered Mrs. Hawkland when he first came to this house, weeks ago. She stood near the desk, her face a bit pale above her black dress, addressing a tall man Jamie had not seen before. The stranger was attired in the sort of clothes Jamie would have worn for ranch work. He held a slouch hat, and he wore a mustache and shaggy goatee. His eyes were narrowed and he was smiling in a way Jamie disliked.

"Ma'am, I don't think you realize what is necessary to make these niggers respect authority," the man said.

"Do not patronize me, Mr. Shelton," she said in a severe tone. "It is not a question of authority. Over my household servants you have none."

Jamie had been about to withdraw, but something in Mrs. Hawkland's posture prompted him instead to knock on the open door. "Excuse me—Mrs. Hawkland?"

She glanced his way, and he thought he glimpsed relief in her eyes. "Come in, Mr. Russell," she said, then returned her attention to the stranger. "As you see, Mr. Shelton, I have a great deal to attend to. I believe I have made myself clear on this subject, so there is no more for us to discuss. I will not tolerate interference with the house servants, and I will not warn you again. Good morning."

Shelton's smile faded and he chewed absently at his mustache, then gave a small nod that could have been meant as an excuse for a bow. He turned toward the door, shooting a dark glance at Jamie as he passed. Jamie looked after him, listening to his footsteps recede toward the back of the house. When they were gone he turned to Mrs. Hawkland, who was now leaning against the desk.

"Pardon the interruption."

She looked up with a small smile. "It was welcome. As you may guess, my overseer is not much inclined to take me seriously."

"Maybe you should consider hiring a new one."

"I wish it were possible. So many men have gone into the army . . ." She shook her head slightly, and drew herself up. "You wished to speak to me?"

"Yes," he said, but found himself reluctant to do so. He turned his own hat in his hands, one point of the star pin grazing a fingertip. Some of the things he wanted to tell her were best left unsaid, and some of his feelings defied being put into words at all. Here in her home, surrounded by her wealth and the marks of her bereavement, she seemed farther than ever beyond his touch. He gave it up, and went straight to the point.

"I was hoping you might lend me a horse to get to Bayou Sara. Figure I have a better chance at getting across the river there."

"Oh. Certainly. Or I can have Damien drive you."

"A horse or a mule would be faster, if you don't mind. Is there someone in town I could leave it with?"

She nodded, then glanced in the direction of the river. "There may be Yankee boats at Bayou Sara, too."

Jamie shrugged. "Chance I will have to take. At least I will not be putting you in danger any longer."

Something in her face softened, and she looked away, then moved to pull a bell rope by the fireplace. Jamie felt an urge to comfort her as he had the night before, and silently cussed himself for a fool. He had every reason to be angry with her still. He was angry, wasn't he?

"I wanted to thank you for protecting me yesterday," he said somewhat stiffly. "You took a risk, and I'm grateful."

Her hand flicked in a small gesture of dismissal. "I am grateful to you as well, for everything you have done."

The butler came in answer to the bell. Jamie stood silent while Mrs. Hawkland gave the elderly negro instructions for providing him with a mount. When the servant had gone away, she met his gaze and they stood regarding each other.

"Will you be all right?" Jamie asked quietly.

Her hand moved to her belly. "Yes."

He glanced toward the back of the house. "That overseer—he will give you trouble."

"I can handle him."

"I just wish I could be of more help."

"That will not be necessary."

Her tone was unmistakably cold; her gaze had become wary. Jamie felt offended. Yes, he decided, he was still angry. How could she assume he would simply forget about this child?

"I will come back when this is all over," he said in a careful voice. "There are things we should discuss—"

"No." She turned to face him squarely, and raised her chin as he had seen her do when addressing the overseer. "We have nothing to discuss. You are not responsible."

He stepped closer to her and dropped his voice. "That is not how I see it."

"No? But that is how it is." The edge in her voice was matched by a hard glint in her eye. "I know what you are thinking," she said, her whisper almost a hiss. "You are thinking maybe you would like to marry me, and be master of five plantations, no?"

Jamie shook his head. "That is not what I meant—"

"Of course it is." Her lips smiled, but her eyes were like two bits of flint. "It would make you the richest man in Louisiana!"

Stung, he replied without thinking. "Or the most expensive whore!"

The shock on her face matched his own. Before he could speak again her hand flew out and slapped him. Chagrined, his cheek stinging, he stared at her, struggling to master his anger. A moment was long enough for him to realize there was nothing he could say. More words would only make it worse. He took a step backward, then turned and went out of the room, retrieving his bag from the stairwell and striding toward the back door, where he hoped to hell his horse was waiting.

20

How sweet the hours I passed away,
With the girl I left behind me.
        —"The Girl I Left Behind Me," Traditional

Marie hastened to the hall, the taffeta of her skirts whispering against the doorway as she stepped through it. She was about to call after Mr. Russell when she saw him pause at the back doors, which were open to the breeze. She waited, watching him, wanting to apologize, wanting him to turn and do the same. Instead he reached into his pocket, tossed something from it onto the table by the butler's pantry where it landed with a thud that made her wince, then strode out.

Slowly she went to the table and picked up the stocking purse that he had thrown there. The coins slid beneath the crochet, glinting through the threads, hard against her fingers. She had known all along he did not desire her money; she had used the accusation to push him away. His reaction, the hateful words he had flung at her, his last furious glance, returned to make her face burn. She drew a shaky breath.

So. He is gone. That is what I wanted, no? That is what is best.

She closed her eyes, trying to shut out the tumult of her feelings. Too much had happened too quickly—she could not comprehend it all—she felt dizzy, almost sick. She turned and made her way with unsteady steps to the parlor, where she would be free to weep.

It took Jamie three hours to reach Bayou Sara, by which time he had cooled down some. The woods that surrounded the grounds of Rosehall gave way to a field of cotton being worked by gangs of slaves. A few white men watched over them, but he did not see Mrs. Hawkland's overseer among them. He passed field after field of cotton, then cane. He did not know whether he was still on her land. He did not care, either.

The horse sensed his anger and surged ahead; Jamie had held it to a trot, but now that he was out of sight of the Yankee ships he let it stretch its legs. It was a fine animal, a high-spirited bay gelding that must have been one of Colonel Hawkland's own mounts, for it was surely not a work horse. He let it have a long gallop, noting that the levee had given way to bluffs that gradually rose to a height of forty or fifty feet above the river.

He saw a vehicle approaching and reined in. The small open carriage was driven by a negro and occupied by a grim-faced priest who shot a suspicious glance at Jamie as they passed. Jamie gave a nod, though he doubted the priest had seen it.

After a time the road curved away from the river and dropped abruptly down the chalky side of the bluffs to gently rolling woodlands that were still well above the river, though not quite so high. The road turned farther inland, running southward through a dense forest broken by occasional fields and houses. The horse was now content with a slower pace, and Jamie walked and trotted it through woodlands filled with countless birds singing and flitting through the branches. He crossed a railroad track, of all things, just before he reached the village of St. Francisville.

Most of the town was clustered along its main street. Jamie encountered a church, a schoolhouse, an open market, and several shops, one of which—the blacksmith's—was where he'd been told to leave the horse. The smith confirmed that the main street continued on to Bayou Sara, and Jamie headed off westward, valise in hand, pausing only to buy a boudin sausage from a vendor at the market. He ate this as he walked, the spices combining with the afternoon's heat to make him sweat. He was grateful when he left the town for the shade of the woods, even though the air was stifling beneath the trees.

After a short distance the road dropped steeply down off the bluff, and Jamie found himself in a village that ran alongside a wide bayou. A short way to the south this emptied into the Mississippi. He peered out through the trees at the big river, seeing no sign of any gunboats. Northward, where the bayou was still and broad, he could see where the railroad ended. The warehouses clustered around the terminus and the houses and businesses of the village all showed evidence of recent flood waters. He saw no boats of any kind. The place seemed largely deserted. Two boys—one about his brother Gabe's age, the other a couple of years older—sat on a rock with fishing lines cast into the green water.

Bayou Sara was indeed a port town, and looked the part. No churches here; this village was less civilized than its straitlaced sister up the hill. Jamie peered at the buildings, looking for a saloon. The sausage had made him thirsty, and he was tired and out of ideas. He had hoped there would be a boat here that he could hire to take him across the river, but there was not so much as a raft. He most earnestly hoped he would not have go back to Rosehall and ask Mrs. Hawkland for help.

He walked up to an unimposing wooden building with a faded signboard that read O'MALLEY'S. The doors stood open, and Jamie could hear a murmur of voices from inside. He went in and stood a minute while his eyes adjusted to the dimness. The conversation stopped, then gradually resumed. Once he could see to confirm the place was a saloon, Jamie went up to the bar where a man with a lean face and thin brown hair that was already gone from the top of his head was cleaning glasses.

"Beer, please."

The man gave him a long look, then silently filled a glass. Jamie took a moment to quench his thirst, conscious of the gaze of the other patrons. When he judged their conversations had returned to normal he spoke quietly to the barkeeper.

"Do you know of anyone who might take me across the river?"

"No one gets across the river," the man said gruffly, wiping out a glass with a rag. "Yankees burned all the boats."

Jamie felt a sharp pang of dismay, which he hoped didn't show in his face. "Every boat from here to New Orleans?"

The barkeeper shrugged. "Might be some boats at Port Hudson, but you couldn't get across there either. Yankees are mounting a siege."

Jamie ran a hand through his hair. "Are you sure there is no way of getting across here? I do not have a lot of money, but I could take an oar."

Instead of answering, the man gave him another long look. Jamie got the feeling he was being weighed.

"Whereabouts are you from?" the barkeeper said at last.

"Texas." That was obvious, more or less, from his clothes and his speech, but Jamie decided to risk admitting more. "I am trying to get back to my unit."

"Soldier, are you? How did you get separated from the army, then?"

"That is a long and tedious story." Jamie took a pull of his beer. This conversation was not getting him anywhere, and it was straying too near subjects he didn't want to think about, much less talk about.

The sound in the room dropped again and Jamie glanced over his shoulder to see who had come in. Instead he saw everyone in the place staring out the door toward the river, where a ship was gliding by downstream. Jamie recognized it.

"I saw that ship this morning," he said.

"Where?" the barkeeper demanded. Surprised by the sharpness in his voice, Jamie turned to him.

"Up at—up at the Red River. That's where I came across. There were two Yankee ships there, that one and a larger one."

"No others?"

"I saw a gunboat there yesterday, but it was gone this morning."

Jamie realized no one else was talking. He glanced around, and saw every soul in the place watching him.

"Ben," said the barkeeper, with a jerk of his head.

A man at one of the tables got up with a dull scrape of his chair along the mud-caked floorboards. Jamie turned to watch him go out, and noticed that the daylight was slanting in the door now. The afternoon was getting on. Everyone in the saloon was still, as if they were all holding their breath. When a sharp whistle sounded from outside the room suddenly emptied, men jumping from their chairs and scrambling to get outside.

Jamie dug a hand in his pocket. "How much for the beer?" he said, turning back to the barkeeper, whom he found pointing a pistol at him.

"On the house," the man said, "because either you just gave us the all clear to get a shipment over, or you're a Yankee spy and that's the last beer you'll enjoy."

Jamie slowly placed his hands on the bar. "I'm no spy. What do you mean I gave you the all clear?"

The barkeeper gestured toward the door with the pistol as he came around the bar. "That was the *Albatross* just went down," he said. "Ben's whistle means she's out of sight, likely on her way down to Port Hudson. If there is only one boat left at the Red it is probably the *Hartford,* the admiral's boat."

"It had a blue flag," Jamie said.

The man nodded. "That's her. She'll stay on blockade at the Red until the *Albatross* comes back or another boat joins her. We have tonight to get a shipment over, and the next hour is our best shot. Still want that ride?"

"Yes," Jamie said at once. It might be his only chance.

"Fine, then. Come along. If you are wrong and we get attacked you're going over the side with a bullet in your head."

Jamie felt his pulse quicken at the threat. "Another Yankee boat could come down from up the river," he said.

"That would be your tough luck, wouldn't it?"

The barkeeper gestured toward the door, and Jamie preceded him outside. The sleepy bayou town had become a storm of activity. The two boys Jamie had seen fishing were gone, their lines abandoned. Far up the bayou he saw them running along the bank, and beyond them a man on horseback was riding up the opposite bank between the bayou and the river. Closer at hand the men who had been in the bar were making their way toward the railroad track. The barkeeper motioned to Jamie to follow them. Some sort of signal must have been made along the rail, because before they reached the depot a train came in, laden with cotton and hogsheads that Jamie guessed probably contained molasses. He wondered briefly if the cotton was Mrs. Hawkland's, then decided not to think about it.

A few minutes later he saw two long flatboats coming down the bayou with the fishing boys riding on the front of the first. They tied up at a landing where the tracks ended, and men instantly began moving cargo from the train to the boat. Jamie watched, thinking he would have stowed things a little differently, but it was none of his business and the men seemed to have done this before.

"I could pitch in," he said to the barkeeper, who had holstered his pistol, which Jamie was glad to see.

The man shook his head. "Ben's got a good crew together. They'll have it done soon enough."

Jamie nodded, watching how smoothly the loading proceeded. In under half an hour the first boat was laden and had moved down the bayou to make room for the second. The barkeeper and Jamie went aboard. A half dozen men poled the boat down the bayou to the village, where they stopped. The crew all looked up the Mississippi, and Jamie, doing likewise, had to squint against the setting sun. After a few minutes had passed, a light appeared on the near shore at a point where the river turned northward—Jamie assumed it was the rider, signaling that the river above the point was clear—and the polemen moved the boat out into the Mississippi. Poles were drawn up, and long-bladed oars brought out to help guide the boat across the river.

Jamie could not help looking northward, though Rosehall was far out of sight. He was beginning to regret his hasty departure. He still felt angry with Mrs. Hawkland, hurt that she would think he coveted her money though it was a natural enough suspicion. More, though, he wondered about the child, whether he would ever see it, whether he could bear not to.

This part of the river flowed west, and consequently the sun was almost straight ahead, sinking into the river itself in a blaze of reddish gold that spread itself over the yellow water. Jamie felt an odd sense of calm as the boat glided across the current. He could see the landing they would make for now, a little way down the shore. He had a long way to go to get back to the battery, but at least he was on his way.

Nat whistled as he strode into fleet headquarters, and flashed a smile at the clerk. "Captain Pennock sent for me."

The clerk nodded and waved him toward Pennock's office, so Nat tucked the newspaper he had brought along under his arm. One good thing about being in Cairo was the access to current news, which was half bad, half hopeful. Chancellorsville had been a disaster, but it had resulted in the recent demise of Stonewall Jackson, a blow to the Rebels. A few days since, General Grant had taken Jackson, Mississippi, and just this morning word had come in that he had laid siege to Vicksburg.

Nat had become quite at home here in the past few weeks, in between trips down the river and back aboard dispatch boats, supply boats, couriers—any boat that would soon be returning to Cairo. These journeys he had spent in the pilot houses of the various vessels, acquainting himself more particularly with the current state of the river. The pilots—all unlicensed men, as Pennock had said— regarded him with suspicion at first, but once they learned he was no threat to them they were willing enough to share what they knew. He had twice been down as far as Vicksburg, and felt much more comfortable with his understanding of the intervening portion of the river, enough to mind the wheel now and then for a pilot who needed a moment's respite.

At Vicksburg the tension had been thick; the fleet lying above the bend out of range of the Rebel batteries was restive and wanted nothing more than the signal to come down and shell the city in cooperation with a general assault. Vicksburg was the single greatest hindrance to the navy's operations along the Mississippi, followed by Port Hudson, then a handful of minor shore batteries that in themselves were not much of a threat. With Grant closing in on Vicksburg, it was possible that by summer's end the river would be entirely in the navy's control.

Pennock was alone in his office, and glanced up from his usual daunting stack of correspondence. "Ah, Wheat. Sit down, I will be with you in a moment."

Nat helped himself to a chair, wondering what sort of boat the commandant would send him to this time. He rather hoped it would be the *Forest Rose,* for he'd enjoyed his one jaunt in her; her captain was a gentleman, her pilot a good fellow with whom he had spent a few jolly days on a trip to the Yazoo and back.

Pennock signed a paper with a flourish and placed his pen in the stand. "Here you are," he said, offering the page to Nat, who took it, somewhat surprised as previously he had only been given verbal assignments. Looking at it he saw it bore formal orders for him to report for duty aboard the U.S.S. *Cricket.*

"She is a tinclad, not terribly speedy, but I expect you will like her. Been in for repairs to her boilers. They were finished this morning. You are to report aboard at once, they are waiting for you. Please give my respects to Lieutenant Langthorne, and good luck to you."

Nat glanced up from the orders, his heart jittering a little. Pennock was smiling, offering a hand. Nat shook it.

"Thank you, sir."

"Stop in and say hello, when you are next in Cairo."

"I will, sir. Thank you. Thank you for everything."

Pennock gave him a friendly nod and turned to the next document awaiting his attention. Nat withdrew, feeling slightly stunned, and stood in the outer office staring at the paper in his hand.

I am really going to do this. I am really a pilot.

A weight of responsibility descended on him. These last weeks he had treated as something of a holiday, though that mood had vanished the moment he had realized what Pennock was handing him. He knew that he could pilot better than half of the fellows whom he had lately accompanied down the river and back. Now he had the means to prove it.

He thought of Uncle Charlie and of his father. He would have to let his parents know that he actually had a berth. He would write to his mother, and hope that his father let her read his letter before destroying it.

He strode out of the office and up the sodden levee, making for his boardinghouse. His few possessions were quickly packed into his portmanteau, and after settling his bill he returned to the wharf and sought out the *Cricket.*

She was smaller than the *Forest Rose,* and not as tidy. The iron case-mates surrounding her lower deck were put together with less preci-sion than Wheat, Sr. would have demanded, and her open forward doors looked like nothing so much as the entrance to a storm cellar. She was about a hundred and fifty feet long and perhaps thirty abeam, and her draft was light even with six guns aboard. Her pilot house was square and unlovely, with high narrow windows and walls that looked too thin to Nat, though they did appear to be armored. Copper, probably, he thought with a grimace.

She had not been a luxury steamer; the railings on her boiler deck were plain rather than ornate, without gingerbread. Her single ornament was a five-pointed star hanging between her smokestacks.

A bright star.

Nat stood gazing at it, a smile creeping onto his face even as his throat tightened. Drawing a deep breath, he squared his shoulders and went aboard.

21

The Mosquito Fleet, termed so by the members of the "forlorn hope," or those who were engaged in the storming of Brashear City . . . consisted of 53 skiffs, dugouts, bateaux, flats, etc., collected along the banks of the different bayous.
—Randolph Howell, Private, Company C, 5th Texas Cavalry

Jamie guided his section into position on the edge of Berwick Bay in the half-dark before dawn, serenaded by a deafening barrage of frog-song from a nearby stand of rushes. It was good to be back with the battery, though he thought it ironic that after he had worked his way across half of Louisiana to rejoin them, and after all the heartbreak and struggle of the retreat from Bayou Teche three months since, here they were back again, barely ten miles from Camp Bisland where they had started. This time, though, they were on the offensive.

General Banks was off besieging Port Hudson with most of his forces, and General Taylor had conceived the notion of visiting New Orleans while the Federal commander was away. He had not stated this objective in his orders, but the whole army knew he wished to go there; he had proposed it earlier in the spring to General Smith, who had instead sent Taylor on a wild goose chase up to Vicksburg. Smith, Taylor's superior officer, had his own ideas of how to use the forces in the department, which seemed to diverge from Taylor's more often than not. Ellsberry Lane had happened to be present at Taylor's headquarters when the general received notice that Smith would not permit him to use Waller's division in southern Louisiana, and had described to Jamie in reverent terms Taylor's ability to swear in multiple languages.

Taylor had a plantation near New Orleans, and everyone knew he still hoped to reclaim it. There wasn't a man in the army who was against it. Like most of the Texans under Taylor's command, Jamie had never been to the Crescent City. It made no difference; Louisianans and Texans alike savored the idea of marching into New Orleans.

First, though, they must take Brashear City, which lay across Berwick Bay from where they now stood. A railroad into New Orleans terminated there, and the Yankees had established a depot stuffed with supplies and provisions, much of it looted from plantations along the Teche. The quartermaster in Jamie looked forward to its capture with both pleasure and trepidation: on the one hand, rations had become mighty lean; on the other, the men were likely to go a bit wild. That was not his problem, however, save in respect to his own section, and if they got into the town at all they would not be in the van.

He had left Cocoa back in camp; all the Valverde Battery's officers were on foot, as they wanted to avoid giving their presence away to the Yankees across the bay and on the gunboat anchored nearby. The frogs were a boon in that respect. As long as they kept up their racket, the creak of carriage wheels and the stray grunts of the men as they ran up the guns by hand would be masked. He squinted through the mist rising off the south end of the bay, trying to make out his target, the Federal earthworks. The Yanks had heavier guns than the Valverde's, but that didn't matter much. Only a fool would fail to realize that in firing at them across the bay the battery had no intention of trying to capture the works.

That task would fall to Major Sherod Hunter's "Mosquito Fleet," mostly Texas cavalry with a handful of Louisianans, who had silently gone down the bay a couple of hours before in a motley collection of boats, rafts, canoes, even sugar coolers—anything that would float. When the guns began to fire Hunter would attack, and with any luck take the Federals by surprise. Their garrison was small and half made up of convalescents, if rumor told true.

The daylight was coming up now, and the frogs were settling down. The sound of hoofbeats muffled by the damp made Jamie turn his head to look back toward Lieutenant Nettles, who stood just behind the battery in a stand of cypress trees. Nettles greeted the rider—Lane, probably, from the look of his horse—with a nod and a word that was drowned by the racket of the frogs. Nettles had command of the battery in the absence of Captain Sayers, whose shattered ankle would take time to mend and who was back home in Texas, recuperating. Jamie wondered if John Reily had found time to visit him; the late colonel's son was still on leave, comforting his grieving mother.

The image carried him back to Rosehall and Mrs. Hawkland, who still haunted his thoughts despite his best efforts to put her out of mind. Was she a mother by now? Possibly. It was late in June, almost two months since he had escorted her home.

Wrenching his thoughts back to the present, he watched the dismounted rider leave Nettles and move toward his section while Nettles strode over to speak to Lieutenant Hume. As he had thought, it was Lane. Jamie smiled and raised a hand in welcome.

"You'll fire at five," Lane said, joining him.

Jamie looked at his watch. "I have a quarter to."

"Twelve to," Lane corrected, consulting his own timepiece. Jamie adjusted his watch and returned it to his pocket.

"Meet for dinner in town?" Lane said, grinning.

Jamie laughed. "If Hunter's boys leave anything for us."

"Don't you worry. All Green's Brigade couldn't gobble up everything in that depot." He looked toward Brashear with an acquisitive gleam in his eye, and Jamie had to smile. He waved a lazy farewell as Lane returned to his horse to ride back to Green's headquarters. When his friend's form was lost in the dim light under the trees, Jamie started forward to pass the orders to his gun captains.

Green's Brigade. It still sounded strange to him, though the change was a welcome one. By the time he'd rejoined them, the brigade had been calling themselves that for some time. Poor old Sibley was all but forgotten, and good riddance to him was the view of your average Texan. Give them Tom Green any day—*he* had never fallen ill just as the brigade was going into a fight. He was much more likely to be in the thick of it, bellowing like a bear.

Jamie told his sergeants of the imminent order to fire and had them load their guns to the ready, then took his place between them. Nettles gave the order to fire on the dot of five o'clock, and Jamie had barely passed it on when the guns roared and his heart leapt with excitement. In the dim morning light the muzzle-flashes were brilliant, smokey red-orange lashing out from the guns—his own and the rest of the battery's—six guns shattering the morning and driving the frogs into submission. A gust of breeze sent acrid smoke past him; Jamie inhaled its familiar powder smell with a sense of homecoming. The battery's orders were to fire at will once the bombardment began, so he had nothing to do but watch where the shots fell and decide if they were doing any harm at all to the earthworks or the men inside them. Not that it mattered; his purpose this morning was merely to hold their attention until Hunter's little armada could get behind them.

He glanced at Hume's section to his left and Nettles's to his right. It felt right to be here—he knew the men he was fighting beside and he knew what to expect. He drew a deep breath of powder smoke and sighed with satisfaction. He was beginning to actually enjoy this, he realized, and the thought bothered him a bit. He could be killing men by the dozen for all he knew.

The Yankees in the fort began firing back, shells passing with their peculiar banshee shriek or smacking into treetops and raining down a wreckage of twigs, leaves, and moss. One burst near enough to Jamie's section to shake the ground underfoot and make him flinch from the threat of shrapnel. He felt the blast against his face. None of his men were hurt by it; they kept right on loading and firing. He watched on, checking the time now and then. The Yankees scurried around in the earthworks. O'Niell's crew ran their limber back for a fresh chest of ammunition. Jamie wondered if Hunter had run into trouble—surely they should have reached the earthworks by now. His watch told him it was nearly seven, though he found it hard to believe he had been firing for almost two hours. Taylor's main force would be advancing on Brashear soon. He thought the Yankees might be slackening their fire. Looking toward Nettles, he saw a staff officer gallop up to him.

Nettles looked up and signaled to cease firing, and Jamie hastened to convey the order to his crews. One by one the battery's guns fell silent. Jamie strained to hear across the water, finding a sound but not quite able to tell whether it was the echoes of the cannonade still in his ears or something else. He trained his field glasses on the works, now clearly visible in the growing daylight. The Yankee guns were silent, and the works looked abandoned. He lowered the glasses and smiled as he recognized the sound at last. It was Green's Brigade, cheering.

Marie sat in the library, trying to concentrate on the ledger books which recorded the workings of her plantations. The heat of the day oppressed her spirits more than it did her body; she had been constantly uncomfortable for over a month now, and was resigned to it. The child was packed so tightly within her that she could scarcely eat, and false pains had troubled her for days. She had not slept well, and had to force herself to get out of bed each morning. The distraction of plantation business gave her a welcome reason to overcome the tendency to lethargy.

Not wishing to increase the heat in the room by lighting a lamp, she worked by the muted daylight that filtered down through the trees and into the library windows. One of these was open to the breezes, such as they were.

A glass of lemonade sat at her elbow and she sipped at it now and then, though sparingly, for her stomach was unsettled this morning and inclined to cramp.

The books were not entirely strange to her; she had helped Theodore with the records since shortly after their marriage, but had not previously needed to grasp all their detail and import. She was discovering how much she did not know about the workings of the plantations. The one occasion on which she had summoned Mr. Shelton to confer with her about such issues had left her with more questions unanswered than answered, and she had not bothered to speak to him again. She mistrusted him, and found his attitude toward her infuriating. Had she not been with child Mr. Shelton would perhaps have been surprised at how quickly she took matters into her own hands. She had even contemplated driving out in her carriage to observe the condition of her holdings, but instinct had warned her that to do so would have no good effect upon the field hands and their overseers.

She paused, a finger tapping the shaft of her pen. Once this child was born, Shelton would learn that she was no passive owner. Theodore had not been, and neither would she be.

She looked toward the fireplace, above which hung a painting of Theodore, serenely confident, dressed in his favorite linen suit and holding a Panama hat and malacca cane. How she missed him. She felt a sudden intense desire to be held; she had not been held since—she had wanted to think since Theo had died, but that was not quite true. Mr. Russell had held her once since then. The memory made her arms tingle and made her want to cry. She shook it off, gazing up at Theodore instead. It was him she really wanted, and all she had left was his picture. Beyond the wall on which it hung, beyond the rest of the house, out in the river the Yankee gunboats were now a constant presence. She had baled cotton and hogsheads of sugar sitting useless while the next crops ripened under the hot July sun.

Tomorrow was Independence Day. When the war had begun, she and Theodore had discussed whether the holiday would become a national celebration of the Confederacy (they had agreed that it would), and speculated upon how long it would take for their new country to gain its own independence. This was the third July since that time, and there was still no conclusion in sight.

A gentle knock fell on the open door and she looked up to find Damien there. She nodded for him to come in and carefully recorded the sum she had been making, then put up her pen.

"Did you get the wagon repaired?" she asked, looking up at the slave standing before her.

"Yes, Madame," Damien said in his deep, quiet voice. "I drove it back out to Panola fields like you wish."

"And what is the condition of the fields?"

"Cotton coming along, Madame."

"What about the indigo?"

He shook his head. "Not so good. Weeds coming in on it. Field hands work slow from the heat. One fell down while I was there."

"What happened?" Marie watched his face, knowing that as little as a flicker of an eyelid could mean a great deal. Damien was reticent; like Lucinde, he rarely voiced a complaint and never did so on his own account. She knew, though, that he saw much more than he told her. For now he was her best informant about the present state of her holdings; she continually found tasks for him that took him to the different plantations, and questioned him upon his return. By his tacit, unsurprised manner during these interviews he showed that he understood her purpose, and though she knew it set him behind in his regular work as the household's handyman, he never expressed surprise or concern.

"Madame, I think he had not had enough water to drink. He could not be roused. They put him in the wagon and then I left."

"Was Mr. Shelton present?"

"No, Madame."

"Was the field hand abused?"

To this Damien returned no answer, but looked at the floor. Marie pressed her lips together as a painful cramp seized her. When it had passed, she drew a breath, as deep as her crowded lungs could manage.

"Was he kicked?"

"No, Madame."

"Beaten?"

Damien's eyes flicked to hers, then away. "Mr. Monroe slap him some to wake him up. But he did not wake up."

"I see." Marie asked him a few more questions, then dismissed him, thanking him. She found it frustrating that she could not investigate such problems herself, and must rely on a slave's assistance. Soon, though, she would be able to take these matters in hand. She reached for the pen, then realized Damien had not left.

"What is it?" She raised an eyebrow, but kept her temper in check. Damien certainly did not deserve that she should take out her ill humor on him.

"Pardon, Madame. We wished to give you a small thing. May I bring it in here?"

Resisting the urge to snap out a refusal, she folded her hands. "Very well."

Damien nodded and left the room. Marie sipped her lemonade, then put it down with a grimace. It was too sour; her stomach protested. She was perspiring and her back ached. This day was becoming more miserable than usual. Perhaps she would take a nap and finish her accounts in the evening, when the air might be a little cooler.

Damien returned with Victor, helping him carry what she at first thought was a large bench into the study. Marie stood, about to protest, when she realized it was not a bench but a cradle. The two slaves set it down gently on the carpet before the fireplace. Marie stepped toward it, astonished.

It was made of yellow pine, polished smooth and glowing softly in the dappled daylight from the window, smelling faintly of linseed oil. Damien's handiwork, she knew. Inside were a small quilt and mattress, the former made of scraps she recognized from cast-offs she had given to Lucinde. Marie looked up and saw her in the doorway, along with Sarah and Alphonse.

"We know you want to have nice things for the bébé, Madame," Damien said softly. "We know you have no time since Mars Theo died. These are not as nice as you could make or buy in New Orleans, but maybe they help some."

Marie ran a hand along the back of the cradle. The wood was satiny smooth to the touch. "I certainly could not make something like this. I do not know when you found time to work on it."

"Little here, little there. Victor help some. Alphonse give some fabric for the quilt Lucinde make. Cook save all the feathers from the kitchen and Sarah she make the mattress."

Marie looked up, meeting each anxious face in turn. She knew an absurd impulse to cry, but mastered it and cleared her throat. "Thank you, all of you. It is a lovely gift."

Lucinde's face relaxed; Sarah's flickered a smile. Victor gave a little bow and Damien nodded in his serious way. She knew them all so well—better than any others, now that Theodore was gone. They were more than mere property. In a sense they were a second family. She was touched by this mark of their affection for her, and felt a warmth toward them in response.

"It is beautiful," she whispered, and leaned down to reach for the quilt.

A strong cramp clutched at her and she gasped, doubled over, unable to rise. She grabbed at the cradle but it moved—she was falling—then Damien's strong hands gripped her shoulders and guided her to the sofa where she sat, eyes clenched shut, until the pain ebbed. When she opened her eyes she saw Lucinde kneeling before her, watching her. She blinked stupidly at the woman, who gave a little smile.

"Better now, Madame?"

Marie took a short breath, let it out, and nodded. The pain had frightened her, but now that it was gone she felt foolish. She looked up and found that Sarah, Victor, and Alphonse had gone. Damien stood nearby, silently watching.

"Thank you, Damien," she said, a little unsteadily, and moved to get up.

"Perhaps you should rest a while, Madame," Lucinde said.

"I have too much to do." She reached a hand out for support, but instead Lucinde took it between both of hers.

"I think maybe you should not work any more today, Madame."

Marie looked up at her. "Oh."

Everything was ready. Lucinde had been midwife in the slaves' quarters for many years; Marie trusted her to help her. There was a white midwife in St. Francisville, a white doctor also. She did not want them. She would rather have Lucinde by her than a stranger.

A shiver went through her, ending in a pain in her lower back which grew and swelled to envelop her whole abdomen. She squeezed her eyes shut and tried to breathe, but could only get short gulps of air. She tried to pray, though it was hard to think of words, even prayers she knew by heart. She wound up thinking only, *Theo, Theo,* over and over as she clung to Lucinde's hand, waiting for the spasm to pass.

At last it faded and she felt a cool cloth touch her face. Opening her eyes, she saw that Sarah had returned with a basin and a handful of handkerchiefs. Lucinde dabbed the cool water—a fleeting scent of roses—to Marie's forehead and cheeks. Marie sighed gratefully.

"Would you like to go to your chamber, Madame?" Lucinde asked.

Marie nodded. "Yes."

Lucinde helped her to her feet and kept an arm around her waist. Marie stood still for a moment, feeling slightly dizzy, then slowly walked out to the hall. Halfway up the first flight of stairs another pain struck her, so swiftly she cried out in surprise. The next moment Damien caught her, this time lifting her in his strong arms, and carried her up to her room.

22

Sleep my child and peace attend thee,
All through the night
> — "All Through the Night," Traditional

Marie remembered how, after her father's death, her mother's life had seemed to fold in upon itself. Maman had confined herself to her home and family, seeing fewer and fewer visitors, until in her final days her entire world comprised a single bedchamber and the niece who waited upon her there. Something similar was happening to Marie now, not from grief over Theodore's death, but from the impending birth of her child. She no longer knew what was passing in the greater world—could not spare a moment's concern for Shelton or the other problems of managing her own estates—her attention was focused on the upheaval gripping her body. All her world was reduced to her bedchamber, its white draperies and linens, the thick carpet she paced between spasms of pain, the fine wood of the furniture she leaned on in her restlessness. She had asked Lucinde to draw the curtains, not wanting to see the Yankees hovering in the river, thus depriving herself of even the view of her gardens. Night was falling now; Sarah brought in a candle and lit the lamps, her manner hushed and awed. Lucinde sent her away again and turned down the wicks, making the light gentler.

Patient Lucinde—she sang from time to time, seemed to know what Marie wanted before she could ask for it, and ignored her fits of temper. Marie had already said several spiteful things she did not mean; she was not in control of what was happening to her, a circumstance she detested even more than the physical suffering. Lucinde ignored her moods and for the most part stayed out of her way, but was instantly beside her when pain and helplessness overwhelmed her.

At last even a sense of time was lost to her; she gave up on walking and lay on the bed, drifting between spasms, half-dreaming in her exhaustion, thinking of Theodore. She could imagine him watching her ordeal from heaven, whispering praises, rallying her with his bright smile. Tears came and went. She could afford tears in this private place and indulged in them silently, finding some relief though nothing could redress Theo's physical absence. Yet she felt he was with her, even now. More, probably, than he would have been had he lived, she thought with a wry, weary smile. She hoped he had forgiven her for the way she had gotten this child; surely from heaven he could see all the circumstances and perhaps could even hear her secret thoughts.

The soft, golden glow in her chamber seemed peopled with angels. She could hear them singing and wondered idly if she were going mad—or if perhaps she would die and go to join Theodore, forsaking all the trivial cares of this world—then the pain struck again and her thoughts collapsed once more to *Theo, Theo, Theo.*

Dimly Marie became aware of Lucinde's voice speaking to her, of a change in the way that she hurt and of the need to push the child out of her. Other voices chattered excitedly; Lucinde hushed them. Marie wished they would leave her in peace. She was so tired, but still the pains came, wave after wave, until she felt a sudden movement.

"One more, Madame." Lucinde's voice was like cool water on her frayed sensibilities. "Just one more."

The pain came on again, she yielded to it, forcing her aching body to push, and the child slid free. Marie struggled up, frantic to see it. Blood was everywhere, all over the bed and the tiny squirming body in Lucinde's hands.

"Is it a boy?"

"Oui, Madame. A beautiful boy."

A thin wail of complaint rose into the night. Lucinde caught up a cloth and wiped the blood from the child, then laid it on Marie's bosom. It was tiny, the fragile body topped by a red, blotched and wrinkled apple of a face, frowning crossly. Marie gazed in weary surprise at the strange little creature while Lucinde raised her up and heaped pillows behind her back. The infant coughed and whimpered.

"What will you name him, Madame?" Lucinde asked.

The question nearly overwhelmed her, for it made her think of all the arrangements that must be made. The priest must be summoned to baptize the child; should it be done here, or in town? Yankee boats had made it impossible to cross the river to the Chapel of St. Francis, and there was no Catholic church on this side—

The infant wriggled within the blanket, reminding Marie so strongly of how it had once moved inside her that all other thoughts were swept away. This is my child, she realized all at once. This is my son. He let out a small, unhappy sound and she shushed him, holding him a little closer, touching his face with a fingertip, marveling at the perfection of his tiny features. What would she name him? There was no question.

"Théo," she said. "Théodore."

Jamie sat at the table in the battery officers' mess tent, drinking coffee and watching Foster read his three letters from home. Jamie had received no letters in the recent mail, and had been inspired by Foster's good fortune to try to improve his future chances, but he had gotten no farther than "Dear Emma" on the page of lined notepaper in front of him.

Outside he could hear the sounds of the camp settling down for the night. The wild celebration that had followed the capture of Brashear City and its two million dollars worth of supplies—including enough whiskey to light up Green's Brigade for a couple of days before the quartermasters had wrested the source away from them— had largely subsided. Green had moved on, pushing the fleeing Yankees ahead of him and leaving the Valverde Battery with the main column, though the word was they might be brought up to the Mississippi to fire on the Yankee ships and try to prevent them from supplying their forces at Port Hudson.

Taylor's army was better fed and better clothed than it had been for some time and had continued to move toward New Orleans, but the prevailing mood tonight was gloomy. Rumors, which at all times were worth less than the breath expended in their promulgation, had for some days predicted the fall of Vicksburg, and even the staunchest patriots were beginning to believe it.

Jamie took another sip of coffee and tried to think of something to write. Nothing came to mind that was not pathetically trite. The things he felt most deeply were hard to put into words, and platitudes made for poor correspondence.

He got up to refill his coffee and offered to do the same for Foster, who shook his head. As he was returning to his seat he heard footsteps outside, and looked up to see Captain Cornay enter the tent.

"Cornay! Come in—would you care for some coffee?"

Cornay smiled. "Thank you, yes. I was hoping I would find you."

Jamie scrounged another cup and filled it. "This is Lieutenant Foster. John, this is Captain Cornay—St. Mary's Cannoneers—I told you about him."

Foster nodded. "I remember. How do you do, Captain?"

"How do you do?" Cornay shook Foster's hand, then sat down and took a sip of the coffee Jamie handed him. "I am sorry not to find all of your battery's officers together—I wished to thank you all."

Jamie raised an eyebrow. "What for?"

"For your work at Berwick. One of the pieces you captured was the 12-pounder siege gun I had to leave on the field at Bisland. My men are most happy to have it returned to them."

"Well, you are welcome, though it is Green and Major Hunter you should be thanking," Jamie said. "We just provided the distraction."

"I have already thanked General Green. He is taking the gun with him to the river, though it may not make a difference now."

Jamie paused in the act of lifting his cup. "You have heard some news?"

Cornay nodded. "It is confirmed. Vicksburg has surrendered."

Jamie put the cup down. So much for New Orleans. So much for cutting off the Yankees at Port Hudson—with Vicksburg gone, they could now supply their forces there from above. Port Hudson would not be able to stand against both Banks and Grant, which meant the entire Mississippi was lost. For the first time Jamie wondered how long the Confederate Army would last, though he kept the thought to himself.

"Thank you for telling us," he said.

Cornay nodded. "I am only sorry it is not better news."

Foster stood up, tucking his letters into his coat. "Think I'll turn in. Pleasure meeting you, Captain."

Jamie watched him go, then took a swig of coffee. "How are your family?"

"They are safe," Cornay told him. "Thank you for asking."

"Have you seen them?"

"Briefly."

Jamie heard an edge of bitterness in Cornay's voice, and wondered if his home had been ravaged by Banks's army. He could not ask such a question, so instead he said, "How many children do you have?"

Cornay's face softened in a smile. "Three. A girl and two boys. And you?"

Jamie looked down into his coffee. "I am not married." He took another swallow and coughed.

"Ah. I recommend it, mon ami. They—my family—are what make it worthwhile to be in service to the country."

Jamie looked up at him, surprised by a pang of envy. Cornay gave a small shrug.

"I do not mean to say I do not care about our country. I would serve in any case, but it is for mes petites that I fight." He shook his head. "Bah, I am not making sense."

"Yes, you are."

Cornay looked up at Jamie. "You have a sweetheart at home, maybe?"

"Uh—not really."

"But you would like to, eh? When you return a hero, you may find she likes you better than you thought."

Jamie shook his head, smiling. Impossible to explain his situation. There were no sweethearts at home, only a firebrand up at Belle View who was far beyond his reach. He missed her, he realized, and the thought froze his heart.

Cornay was watching him. Jamie tried to shape his face into a smile as he glanced up at the Louisianan. The captain's pale eyes were half lidded. He spoke softly.

"I would not presume to advise you, Lieutenant Russell—"

"Call me Jamie."

"Jamie?" Cornay's accent made it sound odd.

"Well, James."

"Ah, Jacques." Cornay smiled and leaned toward him across the table. "Well, mon cher Jacques, if you will bear my interference, I would say to you, finish that letter to your sweetheart—"

"This is to my sister," Jamie put in.

"Tear it up, then, and write to your sweetheart. Tell her it is the thought of her shining eyes that carries you through every battle. Tell her you kiss her a thousand times, and when you see her again she will already be yours."

Jamie laughed, shaking his head. "I—well, thank you for your advice."

"Ah, what you want to say is go to the devil, Cornay. Bien, I will go, but not au diable." He drained his cup and stood up. "Thank you for the coffee."

Jamie rose and walked with him to the door. "Thank you for visiting. Please come again."

"I would like to. Give my compliments and my thanks to your comrades, please. I will hope to meet them another time. Au revoir."

They shook hands, and Jamie watched Cornay walk away into the night. Returning to the table, he picked up his pencil and smiled. Beneath "Dear Emma" he wrote, "I have just had a visit from an amusing friend, who recommends that I acquire a sweetheart. Perhaps you could look about you for someone suitable."

Nat stood beside the pilot house on the *Cricket*'s hurricane deck, watching the infantry she had been carrying set fire to a pile of pontoon boats. He had taken to leaving the pilot house whenever the boat was at rest, it being cooler out on deck than inside that small, close box. Its exterior had recently been painted with a large numeral "6" in accordance with Admiral Porter's orders, which added nothing to its aesthetic appeal.

The *Cricket*'s venture today up the Little Red River, a tiny tributary to the White River, had been a success; she had captured two steamers, *Tom Sugg* and *Kaskaskia,* which the Rebels had been using as troop transports. It had been slow going coming up—Nat did not know this stream at all and no local pilot could be found, so he had kept the boats out sounding the narrow channel the whole way—but so far they had not been troubled by the Confederates known to be in the area. A number of the Arkansas farmers along the shore had displayed U.S. flags and made other demonstrations of loyalty. Nat suspected some of them did so more out of fear for their property and the hope of being spared than from actual patriotic sentiment.

He yawned and rubbed at his eyes. He was tired, having been at his station since four in the morning. None of the fleet's gunboats had more than one pilot; consequently, Nat stood long hours of duty when the *Cricket* was moving. He did not mind, as this was much better than the tedium of cruising back and forth at their station on the Mississippi near the mouth of the White.

Lieutenant Langthorne walked up to him just as he was stifling a second yawn. "I am surprised you did not retire for an hour," he said.

Nat shrugged. "I don't sleep well in the daytime. Besides, I have been enjoying the show."

Langthorne looked over his shoulder at the burning pontoons, and his mouth twisted wryly. "Let us hope no ill comes of it. Marmaduke will not like having his forces divided."

The pontoons had been in use as a bridge by Rebels crossing the river; they had abandoned it in haste at the *Cricket*'s approach, and some of them remained trapped on the east side. They would have a jolly time getting across now, with both their transports and their bridge lost to them.

Nat checked his watch, which told him it was half past two. "Will we be here much longer? Perhaps I will go below for a while."

"Half an hour at most," Langthorne told him. "I want to get our prizes back to the White as soon as possible."

Nat nodded, feeling inclined to agree. The gunboats *Lexington* and *Marmora* were waiting in the White, their drafts being too great for the Little Red. Best to rejoin them before sunset and get back to the Mississippi, away from these close shores where snipers would be emboldened by darkness.

Half an hour being too little time to nap, Nat remained on deck and amused himself between watching the pontoons burn and gazing at the carte-de-visite Renata had sent him in her last letter. In it she wore a rather dreamy expression, very pretty though unlike her personality which was usually lively. It made him homesick and a little sad to look at it, but this self-inflicted torment was voluntary and he had no regrets. He was glad to be in service, thought his contribution worthwhile, and would have been sorry to be obliged to leave the *Cricket* just now. Apart from her being fired into by a handful of guerrillas late in June, this expedition was the most interesting event in her tour since Nat had come aboard.

He gave a sigh which turned into another yawn. The August heat added to his languor. Down in the bowels of the boat some hammering was going on; the carpenter's gang fighting the leaks that had plagued the *Cricket* in recent weeks. Nat smiled to himself, glad to have escaped that task.

By three o'clock the *Cricket* was gliding down the river with *Tom Sugg* and *Kaskaskia* close behind under command of officers and troops Langthorne had sent aboard. They had gone some ten miles when Nat was startled by the crack of a rifle, causing him to glance away from his course.

As he looked at the puff of smoke drifting up above the east bank a rattling volley shivered the drooping leaves of the trees—dozens, maybe hundreds of rifles—a hailstorm of musket balls flew at the *Cricket,* thudding into her sides, some punching through the copper armor of the pilot house or flying in through the window slots. Nat gasped and tore his gaze away, staring forward at the river channel, hands suddenly slick with sweat on the wheel. He heard cries of dismay, shouting, someone screaming. The rifle fire continued, not in volleys but as a constant peppering as the hidden Rebels loaded and fired as fast as they were able. Answering musketry came from the infantry aboard the *Cricket* and the other boats, a small comfort. Every time he heard the whine of a bullet Nat flinched, but he kept his eyes on the river. If he thought about his situation—trapped in the inviting target of the pilot house—his heart hammered too painfully so he tried to think of other things, tried to focus on the channel and remember the marks he had taken that morning on the way up. He wondered if he dared ask the engineer for more speed. He decided against it; if they grounded within range of the rifles the crew would be sitting ducks, and in all probability the *Cricket* would be captured. Nat clenched his jaw. That would not happen, not if he could help it.

The port-side howitzers began to fire, making the deck shake beneath his feet with each round. Nat was never more glad of anything in his life. The Rebels on the shore kept up their fire; they must be running along the bank through the cover of the woods, following the boats downstream. A ball knocked off Nat's cap; he left it lie as he negotiated a bend in the river. Beyond was a straight stretch, and he set the wheel and risked a look back at the two prizes. He could not help uttering a cry of dismay as he watched the *Kaskaskia* swing around, out of control, headed for the shoal water near the bank. Shouts of alarm from out on deck echoed his feelings. Either the *Kaskaskia*'s rudder had somehow been disabled, or her pilot was hit.

The enemy's fire began to slacken. The howitzers continued to fling canister at the shore, each round shredding foliage as it passed into the woods where the Rebels were hiding. At last there were no more rifle shots, and Nat heard the order to cease firing.

Acting Master Jenner, the *Cricket*'s XO, entered the pilot house out of breath. "Captain's compliments, and we're to take the *Kaskaskia* in tow, if she don't ground first. You are not hurt, are you?"

Nat picked up his cap and dusted it off. There was a ragged hole in it. "No."

"Very good." Jenner hurried away, leaving Nat to communicate with the engineer and bring the *Cricket* to a stop. When that was done he looked at his watch. It was just past four-thirty. The fight couldn't have lasted more than half an hour. It had seemed an eternity.

He took inventory of the damage to the pilot house, counting seven places where musket balls had punched through and finding two of the balls rattling on the floor. These he pocketed. He then went outside and walked around the pilot house, finding another fifty-eight hits where the balls had penetrated the copper armor but not the wood behind it. Thinking of the number of rifles that had been trained on him made him feel a bit ill. He took out Renata's picture and gazed at it a long while.

Thank God I survived to write you another letter, he thought. He would tell her about the two balls that came into the pilot house, but perhaps not the seven that pierced the walls, and certainly not the other fifty-eight. He was almost inclined not to mention the fight at all, not wishing to distress her, but if he did not she might hear of it from other sources. Better that he tell her himself.

He glanced up at the wooded bank, silent and peaceful now. He must tell Mother as well, and she would inform his father. Wheat, Sr. had not reacted well to the news of Nat's assignment to the *Cricket,* but her last letter had hinted that he no longer forbade her to speak of her eldest son at all. She considered this an encouraging sign. That was her way; never to confront, but slowly to persuade, with tiny advances, until the change she desired was made almost without Father's awareness. Nat hoped the news of this fight would not cause her too much setback.

Lieutenant Langthorne was approaching. Nat put Renata's picture back in his pocket and acknowledged the captain.

"We are taking *Kaskaskia* in tow," Langthorne said. "Can you handle it?"

"I believe so." Nat glanced up at the captured steamer, whose crew had prevented her from grounding once the Rebels had been chased off. She was coming slowly down toward the *Cricket.* "What happened?"

Langthorne glazed at him briefly, as if weighing his response. "Her pilot was wounded in the head and arm. The surgeon expects him to recover."

Nat nodded, swallowing. "Thank you."

"All right yourself? Jenner told me you were not hurt."

"Just shaken up a bit."

Langthorne gave him a wry, understanding smile, and gripped his shoulder briefly before moving on. Nat returned to the pilot house, and in a few minutes the *Kaskaskia* was secured in tow and the order came to proceed.

Nat had not previously piloted a towing vessel, so he went forward cautiously, especially when negotiating the Little Red's sinuous twists. The water was deepening a bit, which told him they were nearing the lower portion of the stream, a hopeful sign. The sooner they were back in the White, the better he would be pleased.

He found his gaze straying to the bank, caught himself imagining flickers of movement beyond the trees. His heart would lurch with each such distraction, until he became annoyed with himself and set his attention on the course ahead, forbidding himself to look at the bank. Some ten miles downstream he saw another boat coming up. It proved to be the *Lexington*, Lieutenant Bache's boat. He was in command of the expedition. She rounded to and led them downstream toward the White.

The sun was beginning to drop in the west. A cabin boy brought Nat some cold beef and bread, which he ate while at the wheel. The boats had progressed some five miles downriver and the sun had just set when muskets again fired on them from the east bank.

Nat jumped and could not help uttering a sound of dismay which he was glad no one could hear. All the terror he had felt during the first attack returned in full force, though he could tell just from the sound that this volley was smaller. The howitzers began firing almost at once, and the *Lexington* joined in with her big eight-inch guns. The Rebels withdrew immediately; the fight was over almost before it had begun. Nat breathed a shuddering sigh.

He stayed at the wheel, keeping his eyes on the river and trying not to think at all. Lieutenant Langthorne came to see that he was all right. Someone brought him coffee. The day's light slowly faded as they neared the White, where Langthorne had told him they would anchor for the night. Everything was strangely normal, strangely quiet, except for the pounding of the carpenter's gang far below. They were plugging new leaks, new holes made by the musket fire, Nat was sure. He remembered his earlier smug thoughts with a grim smile, and concluded he had been in error. While he still preferred it to carpentry, piloting most definitely had its disadvantages.

23

It's a long time coming
But I know, yes I know
If you keep on living, change will come
　　　　— "A Change Is Gonna Come," Negro Spiritual

Marie stood on the gallery at Rosehall with Théo asleep in her arms, gazing at rosebushes once more ablaze with blossoms that scented the cooler, autumn air. In three quick months Théo had grown from a pudding-faced newborn into a robust, energetic infant. Plantation business, her ledgers and accounts, and her correspondence had largely gone unattended, and what surprised Marie most about this was how little she cared. She had no time to worry about the Federal boats on the river; they remained a constant presence, but she ignored them. Théo was the center of her life, the sun around whom she and all her servants revolved. She was often tired and sometimes dispirited, but these small woes were eclipsed by the joy she felt whenever she looked into his eyes, and saw the light of his soul shining back.

Today would be somewhat different, she thought, and instinctively hugged him closer. In the morning she had worked in the library with her son's cradle beside her—she had asked Damien and Zeb to build a second one, for she spent so much time in the library that it was necessary—and while Théo slept she had gone through enough of her neglected correspondence to know that it was imperative for her to sell some cotton, and soon. Bills that had remained unpaid through the summer weighed on her conscience. Now it was October, and she felt keenly uncomfortable with the state into which her affairs had fallen.

The sugar harvest had begun, and though she had Damien's reports to tell her how it was going, her conscience whispered that she ought to supervise the sugaring in person. Theodore had always done so, but in past years Marie had usually come to the sugarhouse only for the festival day after the work was finished. That must change; she had made up her mind to pay a visit to Angola to observe how the sugaring progressed, and would take advantage of the occasion to try to further the sale of some cotton.

It was not only good business, but a matter of honor and personal pride that she clear her debts. If she did not, there would soon be whisperings that she was incompetent to run her plantations, and however capable she knew herself to be, it would not do for her employees and slaves—and perhaps even her neighbors—to believe otherwise. At first she had considered swallowing her pride and her patriotism and contacting the captain of the boat that prowled the river opposite Belle View, but remembering how Colonel Ellet had paid for his cotton with empty promises she felt reluctant to trade with the Federals. A search through all her unopened letters had yielded not a single message from Mr. Lawford; the last word that had arrived from him had been in April, just before she and Theodore had departed on their evil-fated journey up the Red River. Nevertheless, she was determined to continue with the most recent transaction Lawford had initiated, another trade of cotton to Europe in exchange for arms and gold. The prospect of arms would persuade the Confederate Army to assist her in procuring transportation and to protect her shipment in transit, or so she hoped.

She had therefore, after feeding Théo, spent the remainder of the morning composing a letter which now resided in the pocket of her riding habit, and which she must seek to have carried across the river to its addressee, General Richard Taylor, the Confederate commander of forces in western Louisiana. She remembered Mr. Russell speaking well of him, affirming that he was a gentleman and a valiant commander. Had Mr. Russell been at hand she might have applied to him for assistance in contacting the general; the thought brought heat into her cheeks, and she hastily dismissed it. As it was, she knew of only one person on her estates who could help her achieve this, and naturally he was the individual she least desired to seek out: Mr. Shelton.

Théo wriggled and fussed a little, and Marie hastened to soothe him, not wanting him to wake. It was hard to contemplate leaving him even for a short time. Except for walks in the immediate grounds—around the garden, the home farm, and the orchards, or visiting Theodore's grave in the little fenced enclosure beneath an old, spreading oak—she had not left Rosehall since the birth. Today, though, she would go out, and only her trust in Lucinde enabled her to leave Théo behind.

Lucinde waited nearby, silent and patient, ready to take charge of the bébé. Marie knew it was time and beyond that she should choose a slave for the child, to be his nursemaid now and his servant later in life, as Lucinde had done for her. Sarah was the obvious choice, being an experienced house servant. Marie had hesitated, though, and knew it was because of Sarah's hopes for freedom. However futile they might be, however piteously Sarah begged to be Théo's nursemaid, and however much Lucinde hoped she would choose the girl, Marie could not rid herself of the feeling that Sarah's ambition would interfere with her devotion to Théo. It was to Lucinde, therefore, and not to Sarah that she turned today.

Théo was quiet again. Marie kissed him and with a small pang gave him into Lucinde's embrace. "Take care of him."

"I will, Madame. Hurry back."

Marie merely nodded. She turned away—an act which required some strength of will—and walked down the steps to where Theodore's bay gelding waited beside the mounting block. In the past she had always disdained the use of this article, preferring the assistance of a leg up from her groom or from Theodore. Just now, though, she wanted the additional security of the block. Her health was nearly recovered since the birth, or she would not have been able to ride out today, but she still felt a little unsteady and wished to take no chances.

I suppose I am getting old, she thought. Annoyed with herself, she drew aside the skirt of her riding habit and set her foot in the stirrup.

The bay sidled a little as she mounted, perhaps out of unfamiliarity with the sidesaddle. She had horses of her own—a sweet old mare and a couple of feisty hunters—but she wanted to ride a mount that the workers, and Mr. Shelton in particular, would recognize as Theodore's. It was a symbolic gesture, and one that she knew would have effect. She indulged in a small, wry smile as she gathered the reins. She knew her people; no one could say that she did not. She knew how they would respond.

Once she was in the saddle Damien mounted the mule she had reserved for his use, and sat waiting to follow her. Marie dared a glance toward the house, saw Lucinde slowly swaying back and forth, singing to Théo in a voice too low to carry out to her. She swallowed and looked ahead, touching the bay's flank with her whip to start him down the drive with Damien following a short way behind. Passing between the rosebushes she recalled when they were first planted, when everything at Rosehall was new, including her marriage. Love for Theodore ached within her, though time had softened it a little. It had already been five months and more since his death. She could scarcely believe it.

The drive joined the road that ran along the levee. Marie threw a frowning glance toward the Yankee gunboat hovering by the mouth of the Red, then turned the bay southward. She let the horse stretch its legs, speeding past fields of dark brown cotton plants, bare after the harvest, with only scraps of white clinging here and there to the branches. The air was delicious, with just a nip of coolness that foretold frost before many more weeks passed. The cane growing on Angola plantation must all be got in before then and rendered in the big sugarhouse. Marie hoped she would be able to evaluate the state of the sugaring on the basis of what little she knew. Her own family had grown mostly cotton, but her uncle had planted cane. She remembered getting underfoot during the sugaring at Lindens Plantation when she was a child, but such recollections yielded little practical understanding. She would have to look back through Theodore's notes from last year's harvest. Then there were the yams to be dealt with, though that was a smaller crop, mostly grown to feed the slaves. She must also think about the indigo and decide whether to try it again next year.

Recognizing the familiar numbness of being overwhelmed beginning to creep over her, Marie shook her head and looked about her. Damien was there a few paces back, a comforting presence. They had passed from Belle View Plantation onto Angola, the Hawklands' largest holding, which made up all the south side of their property and most of the west. Marie gazed eastward a bit longingly, thinking of Killarney Plantation and the Creole-style cottage Theodore had built for her beside the lake, with its cheerful yellow paint, green shutters, and white trim. Sometimes she thought of withdrawing there and hiding from all the world, but she could not do so, not now. She had too much to do. Perhaps after the harvests were in and the sugaring done she would take Théo there for a month, if she could get her affairs into good enough order. In the past she and Theodore had wintered in New Orleans, but she did not wish to go there now. Even had she not been in mourning, with the Yankees in control there was no gaiety there anymore, no laughter, and the house would seem so empty without Theodore.

The cotton fields gave way abruptly to cane, and Marie began to look out for the road that led away from the river to the sugarhouse. She almost rode past it—it was becoming so choked with weeds as to be hard to spot from the river road. She would have to speak to Mr. Shelton about that. Reining in the bay, she turned down the track with Damien close behind.

Tall cane grew jungle-thick on both sides of the narrow road, rising almost to her shoulder. It would have been above her head were she not mounted. She knew it was customary to leave the crop in the field until the last possible moment, so that it would be as sweet as possible when finally cut.

Harvesting and sugaring were always a race against frost, at least this far north where frost was a danger. The sugarhouse, which Theodore had built at enormous expense before their marriage, was steam-powered and could run all day and night, and did so every year during the sugaring. Ordinarily Damien stayed at the sugarhouse at harvest time, overseeing the carpenters who worked to keep machinery, vats, and barrels in repair. This week he had ridden out each morning and come back to Belle View late at night in order to keep Marie apprised of the harvest's progress. When she knew she would visit Angola she had sent for him to accompany her, so this was his second ride out today.

Suddenly the cane to her right disappeared. A line of wagons stood waiting along the road a short way ahead, and across the open field of stubble she saw slaves working, some windrowing cane, some topping and trimming, others carrying stalks to the wagons to be driven to the sugarhouse. Marie was surprised at how few seemed to be working this field; she knew she had many more slaves than were present. Sugar required tending year-round; there were some three hundred slaves who lived on Angola and did nothing else, while others were moved from one plantation to another as necessity demanded. At sugar harvest, every hand that could be spared should be at labor here until the cane was in, yet she judged there were fewer than two hundred at work.

Three men on horseback sat watching the harvest. When Marie reined in the bay and set it walking toward them across the stubble, one of the riders started forward to meet her. She recognized him as Mr. Shelton well before they met.

"Good afternoon," she said to him, smiling.

Shelton nodded his head. "Surprised to see you out here, ma'am."

"Are you? I thought I should know how the sugaring is progressing. Is this the first field to be cut?"

The overseer glanced back toward the slaves. "Yes."

Marie made some quick mental calculations. In a week's time perhaps fifty acres had been harvested, out of some two thousand in sugar. At that rate it would take months to bring in the cane.

"We shall have to step up the pace," she said pleasantly. "Where are the rest of the slaves working?"

Shelton's eyes narrowed. "At Killarney, bringing in the last of the cotton."

The cotton should all have come in by now; that harvest had begun in August. Marie bit back a sharp question and took a moment to phrase a gentler command.

"I see. Well, it is getting late, so we had better bring them all here until the sugaring is done."

"The cotton will lose quality if it sits in the field, ma'am."

Marie ignored the note of condescension in his voice. "Yes, it is a great pity, but if we must lose quality somewhere it should be in cotton. We still have cotton from last year in the sheds. The sugar is more imperative, and will bring a greater profit. You may bring all the slaves over from Killarney tomorrow, along with any others that are available. I believe there are some two hundred at the Panola farms, are there not? I am sure at least half of them could come down while the rest tend the food crops."

Shelton stared at the slaves, a muscle in his jaw tightening. Marie thought his eyes showed anger, but when he turned back to her they were hooded, and the shade cast by his hat brim made it hard to see his expression.

"If that's how you want it, ma'am."

"It is indeed. Thank you," Marie said crisply. "Now, I have another matter to discuss with you. Will you ride with me to the sugarhouse?"

They returned to the road together, and Damien, who had waited there, fell in behind them. Marie was glad of his presence. She disliked Mr. Shelton, and was beginning to wonder about his competence as well. He was not a stupid man—Theodore would not have tolerated incompetence in his overseer—yet he had badly mismanaged the cotton harvest, if what he had told her was true. She would have to pay closer attention, that was clear.

"I need to get a letter across the river," she said in the same pleasant tone she had used earlier. "Is your friend in Bayou Sara still able to cross?"

"On occasion."

"Excellent. The letter is to go to General Taylor. I will pay one dollar each for you and your friend, and another dollar when I receive a reply from the general."

Shelton made no reply. Marie knew a moment's fear that she had offered too much—that she had betrayed how very important this letter was to her—but she resolutely dismissed it. Express letters cost more under normal circumstances, and these were hardly normal. In any case, she could not unsay it, so she preserved a serene expression and hoped Mr. Shelton's curiosity had not been aroused.

They arrived at the sugarhouse, a massive brick structure with chimney stacks emitting a trickle of smoke. Marie and Shelton dismounted and went in, and Damien accompanied them, moving to talk with the skilled slaves who were operating the steam engine that powered the mill. Marie withdrew her letter from her pocket and gave it to Mr. Shelton, along with two gold dollars. He glanced up at her sharply; he must have expected Confederate money, but Theodore had preferred to trade in specie, and Marie had followed his custom.

"If there is any difficulty, please apprise me at once," she told him.

"Yes, ma'am."

She began to stroll the length of the sugarhouse, casting an eye over the machinery. "I presume the cotton yield from Angola and Loch Lomond was satisfactory?"

"Yes. Some rot on the plants nearest the river." Mr. Shelton's voice sounded slightly more respectful.

"What do you make of the indigo failure? Should we attempt it again next year?"

"Cotton is easier."

"I have enough acres in cotton for now. I might consider more yams. What went wrong with the indigo, do you know?" She had let an edge of challenge creep into her voice, and from the way his head snapped up it was not lost on Shelton. He met her gaze with narrowed eyes.

"Weeds choked it out," he said shortly.

"Ah. Yes, the weeding has fallen off a bit. I noticed it on the road in. When the sugaring is finished, you may set a gang or two to clear all the farm roads, then have them attend to the indigo fields. We may as well try another year."

She continued a pace or two, then turned when she realized Shelton had not kept up with her. He was standing, glaring at her; he had not acknowledged her last instruction. No overseer liked to be told his business, but she had not insulted him. She had spoken to him just as she had heard Theodore do on countless occasions, with pleasant formality and respect. She raised a questioning eyebrow. After a moment he looked away.

Marie's attention shifted to the cane carrier, a moving belt that brought the cane to the rollers that would crush it to squeeze out the juice. A solitary slave boy—a lad of ten or twelve—was unloading cane from a wagon onto the carrier, scattering the stalks sparsely across the wide belt.

"We must make better use of the carrier," she said, half to herself. "It should be kept filled."

Shelton crossed the distance to the carrier in a few quick strides and before she could protest smacked the boy's face with the back of his hand, hard. "Get a move on, fool!" he shouted. "Can't you see your mistress is watching? Fill that carrier, you lazy little bastard!"

The boy, tears glistening on his dark cheeks, cast a terrified glance at Marie and began throwing cane onto the carrier as fast as he could grab it from the wagon. Stalks rolled off the belt and slid to the floor. Marie clenched her teeth.

"Mr. Shelton!" she said when she could command a steady voice. She summoned him with a gesture and stepped a few paces away, out of the boy's hearing. Shelton followed, looking smug.

"That was unnecessary," she said in a low voice. "I meant that we should have more slaves at work. That boy cannot fill the carrier by himself."

"It's good to remind them who is boss," Shelton answered.

"Do not make me remind you who is boss, Mr. Shelton." She was angry and held his gaze, saw the depths of uncaring in his cold, dead eyes. A tingle of fear ran along her forearms, but the thought of her pistol, which rested in her pocket, chased that weakness away. She almost wished he would give her a reason to use it, but he backed down, looking sidelong at the carrier.

"My apologies, ma'am. I misunderstood your instructions." His voice was tinged with insolence.

"I will try to make them plainer, then. Take that boy off the carrier and give him an hour's rest. Have two field hands take his place for now; by tomorrow you will need half a dozen to keep up with the harvest. Is that clear enough?"

"Yes," Shelton said through clenched teeth. Marie raised an eyebrow again, fixing him with her haughtiest gaze. "Yes, ma'am," he amended at last.

"Good." Marie put on her gloves and turned to depart. "I will speak to you again soon," she added over her shoulder. That was to ensure that he would indeed bring the sugar harvest up to full speed by tomorrow. She had not planned to ride out again this week, but perhaps she had better; Shelton needed watching.

Damien followed her outside and, there being no mounting block here, carefully helped her into her saddle. Shelton did not join them, and Marie was just as glad not to be obliged to endure his company any longer. She waited until they had passed the harvesters and reached the river again, then gestured for Damien to move up beside her as they turned north.

"When were you last at Killarney?" she asked.

"Ten days ago."

"What was the state of the cotton harvest then?"

"Cotton was all in the week before, Madame."

Marie looked at him, astonished, then looked out at the river. Afternoon light glinted on the water, just beginning to become tinged with gold.

So Shelton had lied to her. Where were the slaves he had said were at Killarney? A cold heaviness settled in her heart, and she wished she had not given him the letter to General Taylor, but it was too late now. She could not get it back.

"Damien, I have instructed Mr. Shelton to bring all available slaves to Angola tomorrow to harvest the sugar. After they have arrived, I want you to talk to the drivers and find out where they have been. Do not let Mr. Shelton overhear you."

"Oui, Madame."

She looked at him, steady and solid as he rode, showing no surprise, showing no thoughts at all as he gazed at a spot between his mule's ears. The very picture of a stupid servitor, though Marie knew he was no such thing. She wished she could make Damien her overseer; she trusted him more than than Shelton.

Well, why not? He could lead; all the slaves at Belle View looked up to him, though perhaps his stature at Rosehall might make the field hands less likely to trust him. He would need influence enough to win him the respect of hundreds if he were overseer of five plantations.

If she were to pursue that course other adjustments would be necessary; she doubted the white overseers at each of the plantations would accept a negro over them, slave or free. She could not think of three slaves, or even two, who would be able to take their places.

Marie frowned, weary with thinking and with the unaccustomed activity of the day. Her breasts ached and she wanted only to be home again, holding Théo while he fed, comfortable and safe. How she wished she did not have so many decisions to make. How terribly she missed her husband. Swallowing the sudden tightness in her throat, she lifted her chin and spurred the bay toward home, proud and erect, as befitting a woman of her station.

Nat was running through the gunboat, climbing companionways, dashing from stateroom to stateroom through adjoining doors, desperate to escape the rushing steam that pursued him, but no matter how many doors he wrenched open or how many steps he climbed, he could not find a way out. The screams of scalded men hung in his ears, his skin was slick and his clothing drenched with sweat and steam both, and ever the roar and the heat increased behind him like the breath of some monstrous dragon.

He awoke sweating. He was pretty sure he had yelled himself awake, and he propped himself up listening for a moment, sucking deep breaths of cool air and wondering if anyone would come to check on him. After a couple of minutes he knew they would not, and lay back with a groan.

The nightmares had begun right after the *Cricket* was attacked and had continued to trouble him since, though it was close on two months ago now. They varied; sometimes the boilers exploded, sometimes the ship was riddled by rifle fire and he crawled around its decks bleeding from a hundred bullet wounds. Occasionally Charlie was with him and he woke when he failed to drag his uncle clear of the murderous steam. Once it had been Quincy and the bullets. The effect was the same in any case: he was robbed of sleep for hours, sometimes for the rest of the night. He had tried drinking himself into a state of unconsciousness, but that rendered him unfit for duty the next day. Instead he had taken to rising after a nightmare and walking the deck, or writing the letters he had no time for during the day.

He sat up, rubbing his neck, and reached for his clothes. The river damp made the nights chilly; he would have to get a heavy overcoat for winter when they got back to Cairo. The *Cricket* was there, still undergoing repairs of the leaks and the damage from the fight. She had been on the ways for over a month now, and while she was out of service Nat was piloting the *New National,* a sidewheeler captured from the Rebels a year or so before, currently hauling stores to the boats on blockade. Her crew had learned to ignore Nat's nightmares; when he stepped out on deck not a soul was stirring save the guard, who merely glanced his way and then went back to watching the shore.

Nat paced the small deck slowly, taking in the night sounds of water lapping and a few crickets feebly protesting the cold. They were off Helena, anchored beside the gunboat *Tyler* for the night. In the morning they would start back to Cairo.

He turned up the collar of his coat and leaned against a smokestack, hoping for a little warmth from it, though the fires were banked. For perhaps the hundredth time he wondered why the nightmares haunted him so—was it guilt over running counter to his father's wishes, or renewed grief over Charlie's terrible death? Or had being so helpless during the attack on the *Cricket* made a coward of him for good and all?

He thought it wasn't the latter, despite vivid memories of the fight and the shakes he had experienced for days afterward. Charlie was so often in his thoughts these days that he suspected the dreams had something to do with his uncle. He remembered how shattered the whole family had been when they received the news of the *Columbine*'s disaster. It was the only time he had ever seen his father weep.

Charlie, laughing Charlie whom everyone loved and dismissed as a ne'er-do-well, had been piloting the *Columbine* when her boilers exploded, sending steam throughout the boat and straight up into the pilot house. He got out quickly, his face scalded pink but seeming all right, and helped carry out some of the less fortunate crew and passengers from the lower decks, setting them outside in the cool air. When the boat was towed into port at Louisville, despite a persistent cough, Charlie again helped to take the victims—those who had lived—ashore. A day or two later he developed a fever. Father had been sent for and had left at once, though he would not permit Nat or Quincy to accompany him. He had arrived at the cheap boardinghouse where Charlie lay in time to watch his brother die. Nat remembered his silence on returning home, and his answer when Nat had finally dared to question him.

He breathed steam when the boiler blew. He thought he had gotten out in time, but it burned his lungs enough to kill him. Pneumonia, the doctor said.

Nat frowned to himself. Wheat, Sr. was not the easiest man to deal with, and God knew Nat had reason upon reason to be angry with him, but of late he had begun to remember just how much Charlie's death had to do with their enmity. Before that time Nat had often pushed the limits of parental authority, and as often been punished, but without rancor on either part. After the *Columbine* exploded there had been more tears in the Wheat home, more arguments, a new bitterness that hung in the air the way the smell of smoke clung to a forest that had burned even as new green growth concealed the scars. He had been sixteen.

He closed his eyes and sighed. In becoming a pilot, he had defied his father out of sheer cussedness as much as the desire to serve his country. Now he was tired and feeling somewhat less fired with patriotism, though still determined to see it through. He was proud of being a pilot, proud of the use he had made of Charlie's gift of knowledge. Standing in the pilot house was at times like standing a vigil—his own private tribute to his uncle and the boyhood hopes that had died with him. Realizing this, and remembering his father's grief over the death of the brother who had so exasperated him, Nat felt some of the anger that had dwelt inside him for so long drain away.

If only there were some way to communicate these feelings to his father, it might bring them closer to an understanding. Nat had not the first notion how to do it, though. Not in a letter—the thought of trying to commit such sentiments to paper made him shudder. It was sure to sound melodramatic, or maudlin, or both. He could not write such stuff, not even to his mother or Renata.

He looked up at the stars, misty through a light, cold haze. Heaven held no answers for him—no immediate ones, at any rate—but he found comfort in the eternal and uncaring existence of something far beyond the reach of the petty wars of men, be the contenders armies and navies or father and son. Perhaps he would someday find his way back to an open and unreserved affection for his father. He hoped so, though he could not see it now. He thought of Charlie dwelling up among the stars, and could not help thinking that if he were truly there, looking down on Nat and his family and their squabbles, he would be laughing. Smiling at the thought, Nat went below again to try for another hour or so of sleep.

A knock fell on the door of the library, where Marie sat with Théo on the sofa before the fire. It was late, almost midnight. She had been poring over Theodore's records of the previous year's sugar harvest, but had paused in this effort when Théo had awakened and informed her in no uncertain terms that he was hungry.

"One moment," she called, then gently coaxed Théo, who was half asleep again, into giving up her breast. She fastened the front of her dress, wrapped her shawl around her shoulders, and settled Théo beside her on the sofa, then said, "Come in."

Damien entered quietly, appearing to have just gotten off his mule. The firelight flickered on his dark skin and on the heavy wool coat she had given him to wear when riding at night.

"You look as if you haven't eaten," she told him. "Is Lucinde getting you something?"

A small smile flicked across his face. "Oui, Madame. I thought you would want to hear right away what I learned from the drivers."

"Yes. I take it the slaves are all at Angola?"

"All but a few, Madame. Harvest going on well now."

"How many are there, would you say?" Marie asked, following a whim to test the extent of Damien's knowledge.

Damien gave her a measured look before answering. "All the Angola slaves are there again, Madame. Killarney, too, Loch Lomond, too, and the cotton pickers from Belle View. About a hundred from Panola, also. Six, close to seven hundred, all."

Marie nodded; this sounded right. "Thank you. What did you learn?"

"All the others been where they should be, Madame, except Angola field hands. They all been down to Newton's place for two weeks, the drivers say."

"Newton's? What were they doing there?" Marie frowned in surprise. Mr. Newton was a neighbor to the south, who had a plantation of about a thousand acres.

"Harvesting sugar, they say, Madame."

"Indeed?" Marie stared at the fire, feeling a rising wrath. Théo fussed and she rubbed his belly to quieten him. "Did you learn anything more?"

"No, Madame, except Mr. Shelton been having dinner with Mr. Newton most every day."

Marie nodded. So, Shelton had decided to conduct a little business on his own, at her expense. She wondered how much Newton had paid him for the use of Angola's slaves.

"Sit down, Damien. I want to talk to you." She gestured to a chair that stood against the wall by the door.

He looked surprised for a moment, then brought the chair forward and sat in it, facing her. Marie regarded him, debating with herself. Damien looked away from her gaze after a few seconds. Ever discreet, ever deferential.

"I believe I have had enough of Mr. Shelton," she said, more to herself than to Damien, but he looked up nonetheless. "I think you might do a better job running the plantations. Do you think you could manage it?"

Damien's eyes widened and he swallowed, still not meeting her gaze except in a brief flicker. "Not over Mr. Weeks, and Mr. Petrie, and—"

Marie waved a hand in dismissal. "Oh, they will go as well. They are all thick with Mr. Shelton, and would be of no use. I thought Big George might make a good junior overseer—he manages the groundsmen at Belle View well enough. You are familiar with the skilled men in the sugarhouse. Is there one who would be able to oversee all of Angola?"

Damien blinked at her, seeming in his astonishment to have forgotten his submissive habit. "Joe Daly, yes. He could do it."

Marie nodded. "With those two, would you be able to at least make a start?"

"Madame, you want to fire all your white men and put slaves in charge?"

Marie smiled. "Yes, I believe I do. Except for the senior overseer. He must not be a slave."

Damien's face fell. Marie tried to suppress a smile, but failed. "I am asking a great deal of you, my old friend," she said softly. "If you can do it, if you keep my plantations running through this harvest and next year's, I will set you free." She swallowed, her heart fluttering a little at what she'd just said. "Do you agree?"

Myriad emotions crossed Damien's face, too swift for her to recognize, then his usual cautious expression returned. "Don't mean much to me to be free if Lucinde is a slave," he said.

Marie nodded. He was no fool, and she was glad of that, for she needed a man of wit to take on this task. "Lucinde will be free as well, come the end of next year's sugaring. You have my word on it." She extended a hand toward him.

Damien stared at her hand a long time, then slowly took it in his, barely clasping it, shaking once and letting go. Then he smiled. "Where do I begin?"

24

Where are you goin' my sisters? / Where are you goin' now?
Oh well we're goin' on down to the river Jordan
Gonna wash our sins away
     — "March Down to Jordan," Negro Spiritual

Marie rode toward Angola again, this time with a small cavalcade at her back. A brisk breeze blew from the southwest, warning of change in the weather. It ruffled her cravat and caught at her hair through the snood she wore beneath her hat.

She and Damien had needed a full day to make all the preparations she thought prudent, which included handpicking an escort of a dozen slaves from Belle View and arming them with shotguns and hunting rifles from Theodore's collection. Big George, a slave of imposing size and lamblike disposition who was head groundskeeper at Belle View, had at first been astonished with the news that he was now to oversee Belle View Plantation in addition to the home farm, and Panola Plantation as well. The idea had taken time for him to comprehend, but Marie's promise of a small salary (a third of what she currently paid to Mr. Monroe) had gone far to inspire him with enthusiasm for this new role. It was another risk; by paying him, she was in essence inviting him to save up the price of his freedom. Mamere would simply have ordered him to do the work—but Mamere would never have placed a slave in charge of an entire plantation. Marie could see no other choice, though, and felt that for a task attended by so much responsibility she would get better service by offering some reward.

When they reached the Angola road Marie paused to look back at her escort. Some of the slaves looked nervous, others—like Zeb, who assisted Damien about the house and grounds and knew of Mr. Shelton's abuse of Sarah—grimly determined. Damien was as placid as ever, save for a sharper glint in his eye. Marie turned to him and Big George, who were riding just behind her.

"You remember what to do, George?"

The big negro nodded. "When you send Mr. Shelton away I go talk to the drivers, keep the work going."

"That's right. Damien, the others all know their tasks?"

He nodded. "They know."

Marie drew a breath and squared her shoulders. "Very well. Let us proceed."

There was a certain exhilaration to taking great risks, a feeling she had often enjoyed. Today she was taking as great a risk as she ever had—perhaps the greatest of her life. She hoped she was doing right.

They reached the harvesting sooner than she had expected, coming suddenly on a field of cut cane lying in long windrows. The stubble fields now extended far down to the southern edge of Angola. Hundreds of slaves were at work, more than Marie had ever seen together in one place, and for a moment the sight startled her. She felt a stab of dismay at the knowledge that these hundreds belonged to her, that she controlled their very lives; for an instant she wished she did not, but reason swiftly reasserted itself. These slaves represented a large part of her assets—over a million dollars of value—money she could not part with lightly. Without them her plantations could not be harvested, and all the promise of cotton and sugar would rot and go to waste.

Mr. Shelton had seen her. She rode toward him with Damien and the others at her back. Mr. Weeks, a weedy, wiry individual who had spent a number of years running auctions in New Orleans before Theodore had hired him, and Mr. Monroe who was somewhat younger and tended toward a constant frown, came forward with Shelton. She did not see Mr. Petrie; perhaps he was at Killarney. She would have to find him, but first she must deal with the others.

She stopped, making Shelton come to her, listening to the rustle of cane leaves beneath his horse's hooves. The other two hung back slightly, but within hearing. She debated whether to speak with them separately, then decided to push forward. If Shelton resisted then the others would witness the result and perhaps benefit by it. Damien knew exactly what she expected, though she hoped to avoid the use of force. She lifted her chin and gazed at the head overseer, waiting.

Shelton at first stared back, then fidgeted a little. "Good morning, ma'am," he said at last. "All the hands we could bring are at work here." He gestured toward the field.

"So I see," Marie said. "I would like to know when you intended to inform me that they had been leased to Mr. Newton."

Shelton's face showed surprise for only a second, then became a mask, with eyes narrowed. "I don't understand, ma'am."

"Nor do I. I thought at first it might have been an arrangement about which you and my husband had an understanding, but I have checked his records for the last five years and found no mention of an agreement with Mr. Newton, nor any payment for the use of my slaves. Nor do I think it wise to have leased slaves to Mr. Newton before bringing in our own sugar. Have you an explanation?"

His eyes spat bitter hatred. Marie was glad to see it, for it meant he had no sly plan to evade her accusation.

"I don't expect a lady like yourself to understand—"

"No, it is quite evident that you do not. Mr. Newton has not yet told me what he has paid you, but as it cannot be less than your annual salary I will presume it to have covered your pay for the year. Any additional amount you may consider your severance." Marie raised her hand, and Damien moved forward with Zeb and two others. "These men will escort you to the overseer's house and assist you in packing your belongings. You may use one of the sugar wagons, but it must be returned by tomorrow."

"You can't do this!" Shelton said.

Marie raised an eyebrow. "What makes you think I cannot? I promise you, if I take you to court over the misappropriation of my slaves you will fare much worse."

She saw him swallow and permitted herself a small, wry smile. "You will, of course, refrain from setting foot on any of my properties henceforth. My new overseers have been instructed to deal harshly with trespassers." She watched him closely, saw his gaze flick from her to the armed slaves behind her, and slid her hand into her pocket to grasp her pistol.

He reached for the gun at his own belt. Before he could bring it up a half-dozen hammers cocked. Shelton froze, staring at the small pistol in Marie's hand. She knew that Damien and the others she had brought with her were ready to shoot.

"I would reconsider, if I were you, Mr. Shelton."

He glared at her, eyes burning with fury, but appeared to decide it was not worth the risk to attack. He slowly moved his hands out to his sides.

"Very wise. Damien, please see him to the overseer's house and help him pack up."

She watched the small party away. Shelton—stiff in every muscle by the looks of his back—tamely followed Damien and the other three to the road. When they were out of sight she moved toward the two junior overseers.

"Mr. Monroe, Mr. Weeks. I believe Mr. Shelton must have had your cooperation in his little venture, otherwise you would surely have brought it to my attention. You will therefore depart under the same terms as he. You may apply to him for any compensation you feel is due to you. These men will assist you in moving out of your quarters."

She gestured to her escort and six of them moved forward, their guns in their hands. The two white men exchanged a glance. Monroe looked alarmed, Weeks surly, but neither of them offered any protest. Marie watched them depart, and when they and their wagons were gone, drew a deep breath of relief. She would not be entirely easy until Damien and the others reported back to her, but she thought she had made sure they would have the advantage.

She turned toward the field, a breeze brushing her face and sighing through the cane. A few of the field hands were working but most were standing, staring, or whispering among themselves. Sensing trouble, Marie glanced toward Big George, who had dismounted and stood talking with some of the drivers. She nudged the bay to a walk and started toward them, feeling a tightness in her belly. The hands must be made to work—they must obey Big George or all would fall to disorder.

As she approached, the drivers, whose job it was to keep the other slaves working, dispersed to the fields. Marie heard them shouting to the field hands, saw the hands slowly returning to their tasks. Her gaze fell on a female slave, belly swollen in pregnancy, eyes dull in a face shining with sweat as she bent to cut cane. Marie wondered whether Shelton or one of his cronies had got her with child. A foolish thought—the child could as easily have been fathered by another slave—but she could not help feeling a pang of sympathy for the woman's misery. All at once she was angry, and regretful that she had not rid herself of Shelton sooner, that she had been content with banishing him from Belle View and had not thought of what suffering he might have caused elsewhere. She knew the slaves led hard lives, despite her father's and later Theodore's best efforts to shield her from unpleasant knowledge. She had never previously felt the weight of responsibility, though.

She swallowed. It was weariness, and the tension of confronting

Mr. Shelton, that had made her weak and confused. She would overcome it. She must.

The pregnant woman paused as her neighbor whispered to her. She looked up toward the road where Shelton and the others had gone, then at Marie. The eyes that had been so flat and dull a moment earlier now sparked with emotion that Marie could not read. The slave's face took on a strange, fierce half-smile and she spoke to the next hand in line, then bent to her task with what seemed to Marie to be greater energy. The man she had spoken to let out a wild yip.

Marie became aware of a restless motion among the field hands, a disruption in the rhythm of their work, like a breeze rippling through the cane. Word was spreading through the fields. It occurred to Marie that she was in the presence of hundreds of negroes wielding sharp knives, but she banished the thought. To show fear would be fatal.

Another field hand gave a wordless, elated yelp, then another, then all the slaves began to shout. All work ceased as hundreds of voices rose in a chaos of noise. The bay tossed his head at the racket and Marie shortened her reins, ready to bolt if need be, but the slaves did not seem to be angry. Some of them began waving their arms in the air, and as she watched one or two started jumping in a crazy dance.

Big George came riding up to her, grinning broadly. "They cheering for you, Madame. They cheering because Shelton is gone."

Relief flooded through Marie. Feeling a little breathless, she rode a bit closer to the nearest slaves; there was no way she could make all of them hear her, but those who did would repeat what she said to the others. She raised a hand and the shouting fell away into silence.

"Thank you all," she called out to them, looking across the dozens of dark faces turned toward her. "I trust your new overseers will do a better job than the old." She paused to let a spate of shouting die down. "If you will all work hard to bring in the sugar, you will have a day's rest for the festival. If we lose no sugar to frost, you will have two days' rest."

An unequivocal cheer answered her. She felt strange addressing the field hands; she had never done so before, except for the few sick she visited in the hospital at Panola. Theodore had always dealt with the workers in the fields, and while she had helped with the accounts and made appearances at festivals and holidays, she saw now that she was just beginning to learn what it really meant to own plantations.

She raised her voice to address Big George over the cheering. "Thank you, George. Keep them working."

He nodded, still grinning. With a wave of her hand Marie turned away and rode back to the road. Three mounted and armed slaves remained to escort her; they would be sufficient to accompany her to Mr. Newton's plantation, after which she would seek Mr. Petrie. Relegating the dozens more tasks that crowded her thoughts to the future, she set the bay to a brisk canter and started back toward the river road.

Nat's arms tingled with suppressed excitement as he landed the *Cricket* at Vicksburg. Her new captain, Acting Master Gorringe, had granted him permission to stop here for an hour on the way down to their new station at Red River. Though Nat was impatient to get ashore he took care in landing the gunboat; only when he had her gently snuggled against the battered dock and the crew had secured her there did he go out on deck and look to Gorringe, who nodded. Nat smiled back his thanks and strode to the companionway, dashing down the steps as fast as he dared.

As he climbed to the city, white scars on the chalk cliffs presented ample evidence of the destruction wrought by months of cannon fire. When he reached the top he saw that the buildings were equally battered. Piles of splintered wood and rubble remained though it had been six months since the city's surrender, and the hillsides were pocked with dugouts where the citizens had sought shelter from the barrage. Vicksburg was in a dreary condition, and the impression was strengthened by a chill December wind that made Nat pull his new coat closer to himself. The sky was overcast with heavy gray cloud, and dampness in the air threatened rain. Few people were about.

Nat asked directions of a soldier standing guard at the courthouse, who pointed out the way to a boardinghouse that was serving as a hospital for officers. Nat paused in the vestibule, grateful to be out of the wind, and looked about for someone connected with the place. A narrow hall divided the house, with narrow stairs running up to the second floor. To his right was a small dining room, to the left a parlor inhabited by a jaundiced-looking army major sleeping in a chair by the fireplace, a rug pulled up to his chest to supplement the feeble embers of the dying fire. Nat was about to start down the hall when he heard a step above. Looking up, he saw a thin young man with curling brown hair coming down the stairs, leaning against the railing. Had it not been for the navy coat he wore and the brightness of his eyes, Nat might never have recognized his brother.

"There you are!" He hurried forward, wincing at how frail Quincy looked. They met and embraced at the foot of the stairs.

"I saw you from the window," Quincy said, his smile folding lines into his face that Nat did not remember seeing there before.

"Lord, haven't they been feeding you? You are as thin as a rail!"

Quincy grinned. "I have put on weight since I arrived here. You should have seen me a month ago." He looked into the parlor, decided against disturbing the major, and beckoned Nat into the dining room. "I would take you up to my room, but I share it with another fellow and he's sleeping. Lost an arm, poor devil—he sleeps most of the time."

Nat, who had been watching with dismay while his brother limped ahead of him, merely nodded. He knew Quincy had been shot in the thigh at Galveston, but that was nearly a year ago; a year Quincy had passed mostly in a Texas prison camp. It was only a few days ago, when the *Cricket* had come in to Cairo, that Nat had learned his brother had at last been released on parole of honor and was in Vicksburg.

They pulled two chairs over to the front window which looked out at the dismal street. "Still healing up?" Nat asked as Quincy carefully lowered himself into a chair.

"Mostly healed. It took a while, and I'll always have a bit of a limp. The muscle was damaged, and—well, we did not have the best of medical attention, shall we say?" His smile took on a wry twist, but his voice remained cheerful. "I intend to try if a course of dancing will improve it. Must do something with myself while I am waiting to be exchanged."

Nat smiled back as best he could. "Trying to make me jealous?"

"Naturally."

Nat glanced out of the window. A woman was walking slowly down the street, huddled in a shawl, her bonnet pulled forward to conceal her face. Nat watched her out of sight, trying to think of how best to tell Quincy about himself and Renata. It was awkward; Quincy and Renata had flirted in school and corresponded after Quincy went to the Naval Academy. Nat looked at his brother, wondering whether he was about to hurt him.

Quincy smiled at him. "You are lucky to have found me here," he said. "Next week I leave for home."

Nat knew a pang of jealousy; Quincy would be home for Christmas. He gave an apologetic shrug. "I only just got your letter. They had it at Fleet Headquarters, since it was addressed to the *Queen of the West*."

"You changed boats?"

Nat laughed. "You have been out of touch!" He explained about the *Queen*'s capture and eventual destruction, then told of his visit home, passing over certain points for the moment, though he did describe his father's anger at his decision to return to the navy instead of accepting a partnership.

"Glad I was not there," Quincy said, grimacing.

"You will probably get the same offer. Or command, rather."

"And Father will get the same answer."

Nat raised an eyebrow. "He'll be overjoyed. You still want a naval career, then?" Even after what happened, he thought, but did not say it aloud.

A determined glint came into Quincy's eye. "I have a chance at a lieutenancy, if I can get back into a ship. The problem is getting exchanged."

"Well, don't let it worry you. Go home, rest, and fatten up. You deserve a holiday."

Quincy's quicksilver grin lit up his face. "Oh, yes. I intend to enthrall all the young ladies. By the time you get home Renata won't even remember you." He laughed, but when Nat glanced down instead of joining him, a shade of concern crept into his face. "She is well, isn't she? You must have seen her during your leave."

Nat shifted in his chair. "Oh, yes. She is well. Very well indeed." He felt his color rising. He decided to meet the issue square on, and looked Quincy in the eyes. "We spent a great deal of time together, in fact. Nothing is official yet, but after the war we intend to be married."

For an instant Quincy looked dismayed, then he gave an awkward laugh. "Is that a fact? Well, congratulations, then."

Nat held up a hand as if to forbid Quincy from expressing happiness when what he felt was disappointment. "Nothing is certain," he said, though already he felt jealous of the time his brother would spend at home, the time he would no doubt spend with Renata, even if only in friendship. "I have not told you everything. When I went back to Cairo for a new assignment I asked about piloting, and as the navy is short of experienced men I was received with open arms."

"You mean to give up carpentry?"

"Have given it up. I have been piloting since May."

Quincy's eyes widened. "What did Father say?" he asked in an awed voice.

"I have not communicated with him since, though I gather he has said a great deal to Mother on the subject. None of it pleasant, I expect."

Quincy shook his head slowly. "You are braver than I."

"Or stupider."

Their gaze held for a moment, then they both laughed. Nat gave a rueful grin. "Don't despise me, will you?"

Quincy's smile was genuine this time. "Of course not. I am all admiration. And I'm glad for you and Renata, truly. She is not the only girl I have been thinking of." He glanced toward the window, an odd smile lingering on his thin lips. "In fact I was—rather distracted, for a time."

Nat waited, curious but aware that Quincy might shy away from saying more if he was pressed. He had always been mercurial of temperament, and his confiding mood could swiftly change to cold reserve. He gazed out of the window a while, seeing something far away, Nat thought. At last he drew a deep breath.

"You remember I wrote to you about Mrs. Hawkland? The cotton planter's wife? I described her portrait in my letter."

Nat nodded, suddenly feeling unsettled. "I was at Belle View last spring."

"Were you?" Quincy looked surprised.

"Yes, and I met Mrs. Hawkland briefly. I have been wondering how it could be that she thought my name familiar."

Quincy looked down at his hands, his face flushing. "I chanced to meet her in New Orleans."

"Oh. You never mentioned it."

"No, well . . ."

Nat was surprised to see Quincy, who was a pretty accomplished flirt, so embarrassed. A flicker of concern woke in him.

"She is even more striking in person than in her portrait, wouldn't you say?" Quincy said softly.

"I did not happen to see the portrait."

"No? Well, you may take my word for it. I saw her on the wharf at New Orleans, recognized her from the portrait, and introduced myself. How do you like that for brass?"

"Outrageous," Nat said, trying for a lightness he did not feel.

Quincy laughed. "I half expected her to think so. She didn't, though—she invited me to visit her at home there, and the next time we were in port, I did."

"Was her husband in town?"

"No."

Nat's concern grew. To call alone on a married lady at home without her husband present was not quite the thing. Even an innocent visit could lead to malicious talk, and Nat suspected Quincy's visit had not been entirely innocent.

The color in Quincy's cheeks rose higher. "To be honest, I think she was only interested in getting me to write a letter recommending she be given a permit to sell cotton."

"And did you?"

"I did. I would have jumped over the moon if she had asked me, or tried to."

"What else happened?" Nat gazed unblinking at his brother, and was relieved when Quincy gave a soft laugh.

"Nothing. I went back to the *Lane*. If we had come to port there again . . . but we never did."

"That is fortunate."

"I know. I made rather a fool of myself, I'm afraid, but Commander Lea said no harm would come of it."

Nat watched him for a moment. "I didn't think her that lovely."

Quincy gave a soft laugh. "No? I found her quite bewitching."

Nat frowned. Quincy had fallen in and out of love countless times during boyhood, but had always found a new flirt or some fascinating project to distract him from heartache. Nat had never known him to be this hard hit. He began to conceive anger toward Mrs. Hawkland.

As if shaking himself out of reverie, Quincy grinned. "And there was another young lady I admired, a Rebel spitfire, in Galveston. So you see, I have not suffered any boredom."

Nat smiled, unconvinced. All these interactions had occurred before his imprisonment last January; the present year must have been tedious and uncomfortable for Quincy, but he seemed not to want to discuss that.

The hall clock struck and Nat looked at his watch. Two o'clock already—where had the hour gone?

"I must get back. I have already overstayed my leave."

Disappointment flicked across Quincy's face, quickly banished by a smile. "Well, thank you for visiting. You must be high in your captain's esteem, if you stopped just for this."

Nat stood up and put his watch back into his pocket. "Not I; that's your distinction. He knows all about the *Harriet Lane*'s capture. No escaping it, old man—you are a hero."

Quincy laughed, shaking his head, and got up to see Nat to the door. "Where should I write to you?"

"U.S.S. *Cricket*," Nat told him. "We are going down to the mouth of the Red—that is our new station."

Quincy's brows rose. "Well, if you see Mrs. Hawkland—don't let her coax you into anything."

Nat smiled. "Never fear. My heart belongs to another."

He stood gazing at his brother, reluctant to leave, knowing he would miss him now more sharply than he had before. Quincy put out a hand; Nat shook it, then caught him in a tight hug. "I will see you in Cincinnati," he said, stepping back.

"For your wedding, if not before."

Nat nodded, not trusting his voice. The army major in the parlor stirred and muttered in his sleep. Quincy glanced at him, then leaned forward to whisper to Nat.

"Do you ever think of Charlie?"

Nat's shoulders tightened. "Only every time I step into the pilot house," he answered softly.

A shadow of sadness crept into Quincy's eyes. "Take care of yourself," he said.

Nat was suddenly glad he had not told Quincy about being fired upon, or about the dreams that still troubled him. "You do the same. Give my love to Mother and—and tell Father hello."

Quincy smiled. "I will."

Nat opened the door and winced at the blast of damp, chilly wind that struck him in the face. He hurried down the steps to the street. Glancing back, he saw Quincy standing on the top step and waved to him to go inside, but Quincy shook his head and raised a hand in farewell. Nat strode down the street quickly, the faster to get his brother back in out of the cold. At the corner he looked back and saw Quincy still standing there, watching him away. With a final wave, Nat turned the corner out of sight and let go a sigh as he hastened back toward the river.

On Christmas day Green's Brigade began to arrive in Houston, having been ordered there by General Kirby Smith, the department commander, at the request of General Magruder, who commanded defenses in Texas. The weather was bitter—unusually so, for Texas— and the men were exhausted after a forced march for which Jamie could see no good reason. There was no immediate threat to Houston, despite the rumor that General Banks was planning to launch an attack against the Texas coast. The thought of defending Galveston all over again made Jamie weary.

He told himself he should be happy to be closer to home, happy to be back in Texas. Louisiana would have to look after itself, he supposed, though he had been sorry to leave General Taylor's command and to have to say farewell to Captain Cornay. Two and a half years of soldiering had taught him the unwisdom of forming close friendships outside his own unit—you never knew when you would be uprooted and sent marching hundreds of miles, and there were more permanent ways to lose friends as well—but the knowledge had not kept him from liking the Louisianan.

He did acknowledge a degree of relief at being well away from Rosehall, though a part of him hoped to return there. That was an uncomfortable thought, and he put it aside, happy to have the distraction of getting the battery into camp. It was well after dark by the time they were settled and Jamie sought out the battery commander's tent. He found Captain Nettles hunting through his camp desk. Nettles had been made captain and given permanent command of the Valverde Battery when Sayers, now recovered from his wound, was promoted to major and joined Green's staff.

"Sir, would it be all right if I went into town for an hour or so?"

Nettles glanced up, his frown changing to a swift grin. "Tired of Baker's cooking?"

Jamie shrugged. "I'd like to have a meal indoors."

"Go ahead. Have the best Christmas dinner you can buy."

Jamie watched Nettles scoop up a handful of papers and stuff them into a cubbyhole. "You are welcome to join me if you like," he added.

"I would love to, but Green has called a staff meeting."

"Tonight?"

Nettles nodded and grimaced. "Have a whiskey and think of me shivering in the staff tent."

"I could bring something back for you. . . ."

"I accept." Nettles dug in his pocket and produced two crumpled Confederate bills. "Have a drink on me, and get what you can with the rest. Thanks."

Jamie smiled and pocketed the money. "Merry Christmas," he said over his shoulder as he left. Nettles's reply was a grunt.

In the officers' mess tent Jamie found Foster huddled in a blanket by the stove, dipping a hard cracker into his coffee while he watched Baker, the cook, making supper. The bacon smelled good even though Jamie was heartily sick of bacon, but he shook his head when Baker looked up at him. "Don't make any for me. I'm going into Houston."

Foster looked up at him. "Visiting friends?"

"Just visiting. Care to come along?"

Foster opened his blanket, revealing his sash which he had slung over his shoulder, indicating he was serving as officer of the day. "Can't. I'm on duty till morning."

"Oh, sorry. Is Hume in camp?"

"He turned in. Worn out from the march."

Jamie nodded, resigning himself to dinner alone. "Good night, then. See you in the morning."

"Mm. Merry Christmas."

Jamie walked to the picket line where Cocoa was tied. She tossed her head when she recognized his step.

"Hey, girl," he said, acknowledging her greeting. "Care to spend an hour in a nice, warm stable? I know you're tired, but it won't take long to get into town."

Cocoa made no objection beyond a heavy sigh when he began to saddle her, and before long they were headed toward Houston on the muddy road through the brigade's camp. Jamie glimpsed fires here and there among the lines of tents, with weary soldiers clustered close around them. He thought about looking for Ellsberry Lane, with whom he had celebrated the past two Christmases in camp, but as Lane was adjutant of the 4th he would probably be at Green's staff meeting.

Houston seemed to be huddled against the cold, though lights gleamed from enough windows to cast a measure of cheer into the wintry street. The main avenues were paved with shell that crunched wetly beneath Cocoa's hooves and hissed under the wheels of a passing carraige, reminding Jamie of when he had come here with Emma to meet their Aunt May. She had been staying at the Capitol Hotel preparatory to moving to Galveston, and they had been her guests there, enjoying the most luxurious accommodations. The hotel was just down the street ahead of him; Jamie rode up to it and reined in, wishing he could afford to buy his dinner there. His gaze traveled to the corner suite on the top floor and he swallowed, remembering another occasion on which he had spent the night in that hotel.

The window facing the street was that of the parlor; the bedroom was behind. The curtains—heavy red velvet, he remembered—were drawn, though he could see a gleam of light at the window's edge. He wondered if Mrs. Hawkland's invitation to share her dinner in that parlor had been as innocent as it had seemed. He thought it must have been, but some time during the evening she had changed her mind. Jamie closed his eyes, remembering champagne and oysters and how he had forgotten his honor, forgotten everything but pure, ecstatic physical pleasure. He had not left the hotel that night. He had tried to slip away the next morning, when reason had returned and he began to regret what he'd done, but she had heard him and come out to say good-bye. She had thanked him, he remembered, and said that she had never done this before.

Jamie opened his eyes, looking up at the window again. He had forgotten that—had not understood at the time what she had meant— had thought it unimportant, just as he'd thought he could forget that night's indiscretion and put it behind him. He gave a soft, bitter laugh. He would never forget it; he knew that now. Far away in Louisiana there was now a child with his blood in its veins, and he could never forget that. A terrible loneliness descended on him, worse than any he could remember. He was lonely for a love that, as far as he knew, did not exist, at least not for him.

Cocoa sidled; it was cold standing still, and she could often sense his moods, so he was probably upsetting her. He no longer felt hungry but he knew he needed to eat so he nudged her into a walk, seeking a hostelry more in keeping with his financial condition, and less likely to evoke painful memories than the Capitol Hotel.

25

On the 7th of March I had assembled at the mouth of the Red River a large fleet of ironclads...
        —David D. Porter, Rear-Admiral, U.S. Navy

Marie stood at her bedchamber window looking out at the Yankee boats in the river. Her robe was not quite sufficient to ward off the chill of an early March morning, but the boats were an equal cause for the shiver that ran through her. There were more now—many more than there had been yesterday, when she had first noticed them gathering. Usually there were at most three boats present at any time, and often only one. She now counted a dozen at least, despite the shrouding rain. Something was happening, or about to happen, and she could not imagine that it would be anything but bad for her interests.

The boats varied somewhat in size and shape, but they were almost all gunboats. Some were the big, heavy ironclads, riding low in the water like turtles, or monitors with round turrets that could rotate to aim their guns at any threat. There were also a few of the converted river steamers—she had heard that the Yankees called them tinclads—with armored plating over their lower decks and portholes through which the barrels of cannon glowered. A couple of coal barges lay along the far bank just below the mouth of the Red River.

Marie turned at the sound of the door opening. Lucinde came in carrying a tray with Marie's morning cocoa, and raised her brows in surprise to see her out of bed. "Are you not cold, Madame?"

"Yes. Has Damien left for Killarney yet?"

"Not yet, but soon."

"Please ask him to wait. I want to speak to him." Marie hurried back to the bed and climbed in, shoving her chilled feet under the blankets and accepting the tray from Lucinde. She picked up the cup, then paused before drinking. "Don't worry about the fire yet. Hurry and catch Damien before he leaves."

Lucinde, who had started toward the fireplace, gave Marie a brief, measured look and went to the door. "Oui, Madame."

Marie sipped her cocoa. Its warmth spread through her chest and she relaxed a little, but she suspected the day ahead would be difficult. She had planned for Damien to begin loading cotton on wagons to be taken down to Mobile. From there, if all went as planned, the cotton would go to sea on a blockade runner that Mr. Lawford assured her was fast enough to evade any Federal vessel on the water.

Marie sighed. Why she should dislike this method, when it was little different than shipping the cotton up the Red River and through Texas to Mexico, she was not certain. Perhaps the added risk, or perhaps the more palpable underhandedness of it. She had little choice, however; she must sell cotton or face financial ruin. A year or two ago she would have felt it was all a grand adventure, but Theodore had been alive then, and had any difficulty arisen he would have handled it. Managing such transactions on her own was much less appealing, though Mr. Lawford's reappearance in Louisiana had been a blessing.

She had not seen him in person, but he had written several times from New Orleans. Of the cotton he had taken to Brownsville on her and Theodore's behalf the previous spring, something less than half had gone to France; the rest had been confiscated when Federal ships had invaded the port. He had forwarded to her the money he had received, but as half the payment had been in weapons that Theodore had promised to the Confederacy, the remaining sum had been only enough to cover her most pressing obligations. She needed more money, therefore she must sell more cotton.

A soft knock fell on the door. "Come in," Marie called, and set the tray aside.

Sarah entered, shyly smiling as she brought Théo to the bed. Marie took him into her arms and kissed his rosy cheeks.

Sarah hastened to the windows and closed the drapes again. "So cold! Lucinde did not make the fire?"

"I sent her on an errand. Would you mind?"

Sarah smiled and shook her head as she moved to the fireplace. Marie settled Théo to nurse, then watched the girl build up a fresh fire with practiced ease—one of the few tasks she had learned as a parlor maid that had remained useful once she became Théo's nursemaid.

Marie had finally yielded, not to the combined persuasions of Sarah and Lucinde, but to Alphonse's earnest request that someone be assigned to keep watch over the child while Madame was busy with plantation management duties. Since he had begun to crawl, Théo had terrorized the house servants with getting into every place he should not be. Marie had meant to keep closer watch over him, but she had thrice become absorbed in her accounts after placing him on a blanket on the floor with a toy or two when he had expressed discontent with being confined in his cradle. On two occasions he had narrowly escaped injuring himself, or some priceless ornament, or both. The third time he was not so lucky, and Alphonse had come to her nearly in tears over the shattered fragments of a Delft candy dish. It was the realization that her son's misadventures had seriously disturbed her butler's normally serene state of mind that had at last convinced Marie to make Sarah Théo's personal servant. The girl was pathetically grateful, despite the fact that Shelton had long since ceased to be a threat to her. Marie could only assume she yearned for the higher status that belonging to the hope of the house would bring.

Lucinde returned and crossed the room to the wardrobe. "Damien is waiting in the library, Madame."

"Thank you. Théo is almost finished, non, petit?" Marie tickled his nose, causing him to frown and grab more greedily at her breast. She resigned herself to a few more minutes, and watched Lucinde lay out the clothes she would wear that day. The merino morning dress was becoming a little worn, but it was the warmest of the gowns she had dyed for mourning, and the day was likely to remain chilly and wet. Its wide, bell-like sleeves were two years out of fashion, though that was a matter of depressing unimportance as it would be seen only by her own servants. Perhaps she would go to New Orleans later in the spring, after the cotton sale went through, and visit her favorite dressmaker to order some new clothes.

As soon as the thought occurred she realized she could do no such thing. She could not afford it, nor did she care to go to New Orleans just now; indeed, she could not be absent from the plantations at this time. It was March, and the cotton planting would soon begin.

With a small shock she realized the anniversary of Theodore's death was less than two months away. She would soon be out of deep mourning. Strangely, that frightened her. She cuddled Théo closer.

Half an hour later she entered the library where Damien, dressed for riding, was patiently waiting. He had hung his heavy coat over the back of his chair and moved it close to the fire. He stood up when she came in.

"Thank you for waiting," she said, gesturing to him to resume his seat as she sat on the sofa. "I think perhaps we had better not move the cotton today. There are too many gunboats in the river. I do not like the look of them."

Damien nodded agreement, watching her sidelong as he often did. "I will go tell Mr. Petrie."

Marie nodded. Mr. Petrie had protested so vehemently against being classed with Mr. Shelton that she had decided to risk retaining him as overseer of Killarney Plantation. He had not disappointed her, even adjusting to Damien's supervision with surprising grace.

"Take care not to catch cold in this rain," she said. "Have you a warm scarf?"

A small smile came to Damien's lips. "Madame is kind to be concerned."

"Madame cannot afford to lose her overseer, even for a week, merci beaucoup. If you haven't got a scarf I will give you one of Theodore's."

Damien's smile widened as he stood up. "Mars Theo gave me a scarf Christmas a year ago."

Marie felt a sharp pang of loneliness, but stood up to shake it off, and managed to smile. "Well, I am not surprised. He was well aware of your worth. Keep warm and hurry back."

"Oui, Madame."

She watched him go, tempted to follow him into the hall to look out at the boats again. Looking at them would gain her nothing but more worry, however, so instead she went to her desk to begin the day's work.

Jamie sat with his back against the sandy earthwork of Fort Scurry on Galveston Island, trying to stay out of the wind as he read a letter from his sister. The weather had remained cold, and while the breeze off the gulf was gentle it was chilly enough to make him want to shelter in the lee of the work. His cannoneers were huddling as well, except for the man on lookout who had the joy of standing and shivering as he looked over the barbette, watching the gulf for any sign of a ship. Jamie's section had left their own guns in town and were manning the heavy guns in the fort—two 8-inch Columbiads and two 9-inch Dahlgrens—which meant using the drivers as cannoneers, as his two platoons ordinarily handled one gun apiece. It was good for them to be doing something a little different, though. Boredom was one of the soldier's worst enemies.

Jamie brushed a strand of hair out of his eyes and sighed. Emma's letter was troubling. Momma and Daisy were not getting along well. Daisy had been Aunt May's dresser, but Momma was not as fashionable as May had been and didn't need a body servant. Since Daisy could not cook she had been given housework and scullery duties, which didn't suit her notion of her own importance. Emma described her performance as lackluster. She didn't say so in her letter but Jamie could tell that the friction Daisy was creating was making her life unpleasant, and he suspected that she would have gotten rid of Daisy if not for Aunt May's wish that the slaves not be sold.

Rupert, on the other hand, was shaping up into a fine ranch hand. Jamie was glad to know it, and got the impression that Emma was spending as much time in the saddle as she could. Poppa had been unwell, she said, and had handed more of his responsibilities over to her and Gabe. To her, is what she meant. Gabe was just fifteen this month. Jamie would have to write to him tonight and wish him a happy birthday.

Fifteen. Gabe had been twelve when Jamie first joined the army. Was it naive of him not to have known how much of his life he would be spending in service to his country, how much he would miss of his family's life? He had not really thought about it at the time. He had been caught up in the excitement of making a new army and launching it on a campaign, flags flying and trumpets blaring, off to find glory and riches, or so they had all thought.

The sound of hoofbeats in the sand outside the work made him glance up. The lookout turned toward town, then called to Jamie, "Courier coming, sir."

Jamie stood up, tucked the letter into his coat pocket and brushed the sand from his trousers, then walked out to meet the rider. It was one of the orderlies from headquarters in town—Jamie recognized him but didn't know his name. He watched the man dismount and hurry toward him, returned his hasty salute.

"Captain Nettles's compliments, sir, and you are to bring your section into town at once."

"Are we changing posts?" Jamie asked, wondering if they would be rotating to another of the network of earthwork forts that defended the island, but the courier shook his head.

"I don't think so, sir. All the Valverde Battery has been called in. Captain Nettles received a dispatch from General Magruder, but I do not know what it said."

"I see. Thank you, we will start immediately."

Jamie returned to the fort to give his sergeants the necessary instructions, then retrieved Cocoa from where she was picketed grazing on sparse clumps of sand grass, and rode into town. He could still see the marks of Yankee shells on some of the buildings near the bay, though the worst of the damage had been repaired. For a moment his gut tightened with the memory of the fight on New Year's Eve in 'sixty-two: shells screaming from the guns of the Yankee ships in the bay, rubble falling from the buildings as they were struck, bodies floating in the water beneath the docks from the failed attempt at storming the Yankees on Kuhn's Wharf. He squeezed his eyes shut and shook his head to banish the images, then drew a deep breath and rode on.

The house the army was using as its headquarters was buzzing with activity. He met Foster coming out of Nettles's office, looking annoyed.

"What's the matter, John?"

Foster grimaced. "We might as well never have come back. I would have had two weeks leave come Monday." He brushed past before Jamie could ask him more questions, so Jamie went in to report to Nettles, who was scrawling a letter and looking slightly harassed.

"My section is on its way in," Jamie said.

"Good. Have them pack up at once, then move your guns to the depot and put them onto the train that is waiting there. We are to get to Houston as fast as possible."

Jamie was startled—he would have to get to his quarters and pack up his own things, if they were leaving the island that soon. "What's the hurry?"

Nettles glanced up at him. "We're going back to Louisiana. Taylor wants the whole brigade as quickly as possible. General Banks is moving on the Red River."

Nat sat huddled in his overcoat in the stern of the *Cricket*'s second yawl, rain dripping off the bill of his cap as he watched the *Benton* loom closer. Acting Master Gorringe had taken the first yawl out to Admiral Porter's flagship, the *Black Hawk,* for a meeting of commanders, but before he left Nat had secured his permission to visit the *Benton,* on which Adams was still serving as far as he knew. Nat had heard nothing of his former mate since they had lost the *Queen* just over a year ago, and wanted to know how he was faring.

For himself, 1864 had passed fairly quietly so far, apart from chasing the occasional Rebel boat that ventured out of the Red River, and a couple of excursions in search of cotton to confiscate or information about enemy movements. He freely admitted, if only to himself, that he would be content to spend the rest of his tour cruising their station off the mouth of the Red without further excitement. It was as comfortable a station as one could find on the Mississippi short of being in a port, having woodyards close by and a fair prospect. Rosehall inexorably drew the eye; Nat had spent hours gazing at it, chatting with Gorringe about its reported beauties, including its mistress.

He liked Gorringe, who was a few years younger than himself and seemed inexhaustible. The *Cricket*'s commander had been born to English parents in Barbados, had been a merchant marine, and had joined the navy as common sailor shortly after Nat had signed on as the *Queen*'s carpenter. Experience and his unflagging energy had propelled Gorringe to his present rank and command, which Nat envied but could not begrudge him.

Gorringe had pressed him for details about the ravishing Mrs. Hawkland, but Nat was reluctant to talk about her. Besides the awkwardness of his own encounter with her, he could not forget Quincy's melancholy over her. Since being stationed near her home he had found her intruding more and more upon his thoughts. That she owned slaves would not have bothered him much two years ago, but she owned Adams's sweetheart, and that was somehow a different matter.

The yawl reached the *Benton,* and Nat went aboard and identified himself to the pinch-faced midshipman who was officer of the watch. "Is George Adams still serving aboard?"

The midshipman frowned. "Adams?"

"A carpenter's mate. A negro," Nat added a bit impatiently.

The youth's brow cleared. "Oh, Adams. Yes, he is aboard. He'll be below, they are all patching leaks today. Should I fetch him up?"

"If you would, please. I will not keep him long."

"Step into the gun deck if you like, and get out of the rain. I'll send him to you there."

Nat thanked him and went inside. The *Benton* was a former snag boat that had been converted to an ironclad by her builder, James Eads. She rode low in the water, with only a peaked metal shade, through which the funnels poked, roofing her upper deck. Nat was deeply envious of her heavily armored pilot house, but of course the whole boat was covered in thick plates of iron, much heavier than a tinclad's. He noticed the closeness this caused immediately upon stepping inside the gun deck. The guns, of which there were sixteen, varied from Parrotts to IX-inch rifles and were all in excellent trim.

"Mr. Wheat?"

Nat turned and saw Adams approaching, a shadow of strain in his face. He wondered how Adams felt about being back at Belle View, but that was too intimate a question. Nat hesitated, then offered a hand. Adams shook it.

"How do you like serving on the *Benton*?" Nat asked. "I have been admiring her guns."

"She is all right, though she will spring a leak if you stare at her too hard."

"Design problem?"

Adams shook his head. "Seams keep opening up. She needs to go on the ways. Commander Greer is aware but so far we stay on duty."

"Maybe after this expedition you will get the chance."

"What boat are you on?" Adams asked. "Did you come looking for a mate?"

"No, I'm piloting now, on the *Cricket*. I think our carpenter has all the men he needs, but I could ask—"

"Mr. Wheat?" called a voice from the forward part of the deck. Nat looked up to see a tall man in a commander's insignia coming toward him, with the midshipman on watch tagging behind.

Beside him Adams stiffened to attention. "Commander Greer," he said in an undervoice.

Nat straightened. "Yes, sir, I'm Wheat."

"Admiral Porter wishes to speak to you. My gig will take you to the *Black Hawk*."

"Me?" Nat was astonished; he had not thought the admiral even knew of his existence.

Greer nodded. "He has some questions to ask you about Belle View Plantation. Gorringe said you had been there."

"Yes." Nat glanced at Adams. "Yes, I have been there once, but if the admiral has questions he would profit more by asking them of Adams, here. He lived on the plantation."

Greer's brows rose. He looked at Adams, briefly considering the suggestion. "Very well, go along with him," he said to Adams. "The boat is waiting."

The midshipman escorted them to the forward deck, where they entered the captain's gig, a fine, long boat with a crew of ten on the oars. The rain had lightened somewhat. The gig moved away from the *Benton* and threaded its way among the other vessels toward the flagship, an enormous tinclad with two gun decks. Nat looked at Adams, hoping he had not done him a disservice by causing him to be sent along.

"Have you been back to Belle View before this?" he asked quietly.

Adams shook his head. "I was going to come when I had enough money. I have been saving the prize money." His slight frown grew more pronounced.

Nat wished he could comfort him. He would gladly have loaned Adams some of his own prize money toward Sarah's purchase, and wondered if he could convince any others to do the same. Technically Adams had no need to purchase her, but President Lincoln's emancipation of the slaves was in this part of the country still more a theory than a reality, although Nat had noticed more and more of his acquaintances in the navy had come to view slavery as an evil that should be actively corrected.

The gig reached the *Black Hawk,* an enormous vessel, over four times the *Cricket*'s weight. The *Black Hawk* had begun life as a civilian steamboat, and was grand in every sense of the word, worthy of the fleet commander's dignity. Her pilot house sat atop an elegant Texas deck, a feature absent from the lowly *Cricket*. Only boats of this scale even had Texas decks, where the exclusive and luxurious quarters of their captains were located. Nat and Adams debarked and were escorted up a series of companionways to the admiral's quarters also on the Texas deck.

Admiral Porter's sitting room was large and somewhat cluttered, a number of empty chairs testifying to the recent meeting of captains. A midshipman was in the act of moving the chairs against the wall when Nat and Adams were ushered in. He immediately retired to wait beside the door.

Nat had expected the admiral to be even more imposing than his flagship, but in fact he was a slight man whose coat was comfortably loose rather than tailored, and who was presently slumped in a chair behind a desk loaded with correspondence. His hair and long beard were dark, and the frown he wore seemed habitual, though Nat guessed it was the result not of ill-nature but of the admiral's constantly having to give his attention to numerous matters concerning the management of his river fleet. The eyes that glanced up at Nat were piercing, but the slight, questioning smile in them took away any sense of intimidation.

"Nathaniel Wheat, sir, pilot of the *Cricket*. You sent for me."

"Yes." Porter glanced at Adams.

"This is George Adams, carpenter's mate on the *Benton,* sir. He has lived at Belle View, and came along on the understanding that you have questions about the plantation."

Adams made a stiff bow toward the admiral, who sat blinking at him for a moment. Porter picked up a letter from the scatter of papers before him, glanced through it, then put it down.

"Questions about its owner, actually. Do you know Mrs. Hawkland?"

"Not really," Adams said. "I saw her a few times. The colonel talked to me sometimes, but not Madame."

"Yes, well, I am informed that Colonel Hawkland is dead, so it is— Madame—about whom I wish to know. Would you say that she is loyal to the Union?"

Adams looked confounded. Porter turned his gaze to Nat, who coughed. "I only met her very briefly, sir. My brother knew her a little—"

"Is your brother here?"

"No, he is in Cincinnati, waiting to be exchanged. He served aboard the *Harriet Lane.*"

"Ah." Porter's nod and smile were kindly. He picked up the letter again. "I have information from a man claiming to have been Mrs. Hawkland's overseer, one Peter Shelton."

Adams stiffened, and Nat glanced his way, seeing his jaw tighten. Apparently the admiral saw it as well.

"You know Mr. Shelton?" When Adams nodded, Porter asked, "Would you say that he is trustworthy?"

Adams did not answer immediately. He seemed to be struggling to control his emotions. He was breathing rather quickly, and when he spoke his voice was rough. "I am not the one to ask."

Porter gazed at him thoughtfully. "Were you a slave at Belle View?"

"Yes, until my father bought my freedom."

"Ah. I see." Porter's voice was quiet, though not weak. "How would you describe this Mr. Shelton?"

Adams frowned, blinking. "Cruel," he said, finally.

A flash of memory returned to Nat, of the thin-faced man who had punched Adams in the kitchen out behind Rosehall. Had that been Shelton? He glanced toward Adams, but his friend was still watching Admiral Porter.

"Cruel." Porter looked at the letter in his hand, tapping it with one finger. "So he would not be above slandering his former employer."

Adams gave the ghost of a smile. "He would not be above that, no."

"Hm." Porter's frown deepened, and he pressed his lips together. Nat received the impression that he was disappointed. Porter dropped the letter to the desk and leaned back in his chair, lacing his fingers over his stomach. "Mrs. Hawkland is in possession of a vast quantity of cotton. If she were found to be disloyal, as this Shelton claims, it would be subject to confiscation. You would like a share in that prize, would you not?" Porter looked from Adams to Nat.

"Yes," Nat said, then honesty made him add, "if it could be proved that she is disloyal."

"Have either of you any reason to believe that she is?"

Adams said nothing; his gaze was fixed on the floor. Nat answered slowly, trying to balance the facts he knew against the distrust he felt in his heart.

"No . . . in fact, I have reason to believe the opposite. She asked my brother for help in obtaining permission to sell cotton to Federal interests in New Orleans."

"And did he assist her?"

"He wrote a letter recommending she be given permission."

Porter's gaze remained on Nat's face, as if he was trying to read him. "Did your brother have anything more to say of her?"

Nat hesitated an instant. "Only that she was extraordinarily lovely. Bewitching, he said." He hoped the admiral would not ask for further elaboration.

Porter's brows rose. "My curiosity to meet her increases." His eyes narrowed as if in calculation, and after a moment he sat up and said, "Yes, I wish to meet her, and judge for myself whether she is loyal. You shall accompany me, Mr. Wheat. I would like to see her reaction to meeting the brother of the man who aided her."

"Yes, sir." Nat swallowed, wanting nothing less than to visit Mrs. Hawkland, but unable to think of a way out of it. He sensed Adams stiffening with tension beside him. "May Adams accompany us, sir? He has family at the plantation."

Adams shot him an intense, grateful glance, which was not lost on Porter. The admiral's face took on a wry smile. "Why not? Billings, have my gig readied, and fetch me my overcoat." He stood up as the midshipman by the door sprang to activity. Porter came out from behind the desk, looking well pleased. "We are going to pay a call of courtesy at Belle View."

26

I received communications from General Banks informing
me that he would be in Alexandria on the 17th March, and I
made my dispositions to meet him there.
—David D. Porter, Rear-Admiral, U.S. Navy

Marie's eyes widened as she looked out the front window toward the
river, not because there were even more gunboats there now, but
because a smaller boat was crossing the river toward Belle View landing. Ever since the Yankee boats had started haunting the river she
had dreaded receiving a visit from some bluecoat captain. So far she
had been relieved to have been spared. Now and then lesser officers
came ashore to buy vegetables from the slaves—Damien had spoken
with them a few times—but they had not intruded upon her privacy.
Now it appeared her good fortune was about to change.

The boat was a handsome craft, with a large crew and a mast from
which floated a Yankee flag and a solid blue pennant. Marie frowned
and turned to Alphonse, who had alerted her to its approach.

"I think you had better order coffee, Alphonse."

"Oui, Madame. I will tell Cook, and have Victor make a fire in the
parlor."

Marie went into the parlor to await her uninvited guests, and paced
between the window and the empty fireplace, too agitated to sit down.
She had spent little time in this room during the past year, a change
from her previous habit. It had once been her favorite room in the
house, for she loved to entertain and had always made a point to maintain social contact with her neighbors—not an easy thing in plantation
country, where many miles could separate families. Since Theodore's
death, though, she no longer had time or inclination for such pursuits.

The footman came in. Marie moved out of his way and stood by the
window, silently watching the boat make its way toward the landing.

One would think Yankees would know better than to come calling in a rainstorm. Luckily for them Rosehall's drive was paved with shell, or their clothes would have become steeped in mud by the time they reached the house. Should she send the carriage for them, perhaps? It would be a nice attention, but she was not obliged to call out her carriage for persons who came to her home unbidden. She wondered what they wanted of her. Perhaps cotton—she might sell it to them, if she could get any cash at all. She swallowed, nervous and unhappy, and suddenly realized how vulnerable she was. Suppose those dozen men at the oars all came up to the house and forced their way in. Suppose they offered her violence. Alphonse and Victor could not withstand a dozen strong men. She thought wildly of fetching her pistol, but that was folly. The only effective use she could make of it in such a situation would be against herself.

"Pardon, Madame?"

Marie turned at Lucinde's voice and saw her standing nearby, holding the widow's cap she had made for Marie to wear at Théo's christening. "Oh! Yes, thank you."

Lucinde placed the cap over the black snood Marie had taken to wearing most days—it was less formal than a cap, but kept her hair tidy and out of reach of Théo's eager hands—and arranged the long black streamers down her back. Marie wondered if she should have changed her dress for a better one, but it was too late now. The Yankees would not know the difference.

She smiled at Lucinde, grateful for her calming presence, her gentle touch. How foolish she had been to panic so a moment ago. She would get through this; she had faced worse than a visit from Yankee sailors.

Victor stood up from the hearth, where the fire he had made was already sending warmth into the room. Marie thanked him and he went out.

"Is there anything else you need, Madame?" Lucinde asked.

"No, thank you Lucinde."

Lucinde smiled as if to reassure her, then followed Victor out. Marie went to the window again. The boat had landed, and three men had got out and started up the drive, one of them carrying an umbrella. The oarsmen remained behind. Marie relaxed a little.

She moved away from the window and took out her rosary, a pretty thing that Theodore had given her, each bead a perfect rose blossom. She smiled at the memory, and began a silent prayer.

Nat trudged between the admiral and Adams up the long, wide driveway, thinking it strange that the only time he ever came here was when the famous roses were not in bloom. The bushes on either side of the drive were leafing out—he could see the dark, reddish leaves where buds would develop—but it would be some time before there were blossoms. He was reminded of his mother, who was very fond of flowers, an inclination she had passed on to Quincy.

Feeling homesick, he looked at Rosehall to distract himself. It was larger than he remembered. The drive was a good quarter of a mile long, and by the time they reached the top of it his legs had begun to protest the unaccustomed exertion. Must get ashore more often and take some exercise, he thought as they mounted the steps and passed between round, white columns. He remembered the back of the house, shadowed in night. It had seemed different then—less gracious, more forbidding.

The porch was deep, the front of the house adorned with tall windows flanking double doors of oak. These were opened by a gray-haired negro butler whose manner was so stiff-rumped Nat had to hide a smile.

"May I help you, gentlemen?"

The admiral, who had been occupied in closing his umbrella, looked up. "Yes, I am Admiral Porter; this is Mr. Wheat and Mr. Adams. We have come to pay a call upon your mistress, if she is at home."

The butler's eyes flickered as he glanced at Adams. He made a stately bow to the admiral. "Please come in, sah."

The hall was enormous, with painted pastoral scenes on all the walls, chandeliers depending from the ceiling, and an elaborate parquetry medallion in the center of the floor. Nat yielded his wet coat and hat to a footman whose clothes looked more costly than any of his own.

The room to which the butler showed them, immediately to the right of the front doors, was furnished with breathtaking opulence which formed a striking contrast to the sober gown of the woman who stepped forward to greet them.

Nat recognized her at once, and wondered nervously if she would remember him. She was certainly lovely enough to justify Quincy's raptures, though she seemed rather pale. Perhaps that was the effect of a black dress unrelieved by any ornament. Nat felt a tug of sympathy for no other reason than that she was attractive and in mourning.

The butler announced their names in the order in which Porter had given them. She looked sharply at Nat, then from him to Adams with an expression of dawning understanding as the butler said Adams's name, his tone dropping with disapproval. For a second her eyes flashed with indignation, then she looked down, concealing it with graciousness. Nat felt guilty for having asked to bring Adams along—he had not thought about how awkward it would be. Adams's rank was higher than that of a common sailor, but not much higher, and it would have been a bit odd for the admiral to include such an individual in his party even if he were white. Add to that Adams's race, and the fact he had once been a slave of Mrs. Hawkland's, and Nat found reason to admire the composure with which she met her unexpected visitors.

She turned to the admiral and smiled. "How do you do, Admiral Porter? I am honored by your visit."

"The honor is mine, ma'am." Porter bowed with casual grace over the hand she extended.

Mrs. Hawkland turned to Nat. "I remember you."

Nat bowed. She gazed at him a long while, then looked at Adams, who stood silently beside him. After a moment she inclined her head slightly, then returned her attention to the admiral.

"May I offer you some coffee?"

"That would be most welcome," Porter said.

Mrs. Hawkland glanced at her butler, who bowed and withdrew. "Please be seated," she said, moving to a chair near the fire.

Nat followed Porter to a gilt sofa upholstered in cobalt velvet, which he hoped would not suffer from the dampness of his clothes. Adams perched on the edge of a matching chair.

"You have a beautiful home, Mrs. Hawkland," Porter said.

"Thank you. My late husband designed it."

"Please accept my condolences on his passing, ma'am. I never met him, but have heard others speak highly of him."

"Thank you." Mrs. Hawkland's gaze dropped and Nat thought her face looked a bit strained, but after a moment she straightened in her chair and turned to him with a small smile. "I met a young man named Wheat in New Orleans. Could he be a relative of yours?"

"My brother, ma'am."

"Ah."

Admiral Porter leaned back on the sofa. "Are you well acquainted with Acting Master Wheat, ma'am?"

"No, not at all. We met only twice, but he did me a service for which I am most grateful."

"What service was that?" Porter's voice and face showed only innocent curiosity; Nat admired his subtlety.

"He helped me acquire a permit to sell cotton." Mrs. Hawkland's eyes took on a slight brightness as she gazed at the admiral. "Is that what you are here about? Cotton?"

Porter hesitated an instant, then replied, "I am here to pay a call of courtesy, ma'am, having brought my fleet to this place. Also to permit Mr. Wheat to further his family's acquaintance with yours, and to enable Mr. Adams to visit his own family who are here."

She stiffened slightly, though her smile remained gracious. "I believe you have been misinformed. Mr. Adams's family were all bought free some years ago."

Nat saw the admiral's eyebrow twitch and hastened to speak. "He wishes to visit his fiancée, ma'am."

Mrs. Hawkland glanced at him, then at Adams, who returned her gaze at first, then looked away. Her lids dropped slightly, veiling her eyes with long lashes as she watched his discomfort. After a moment she looked at the admiral, then reached for a long-handled silver bell on the table beside her. "Very well."

She rang the bell and a moment later the footman appeared in the doorway. "Victor, ask Sarah to bring Théo down, please." Nat thought he detected an edge in her voice.

"Oui, Madame."

The footman departed and the room fell silent. Nat looked around at the fine furnishings, heavy blue drapes pulled back from tall windows and gauze curtains that softened the daylight to a cool glow. A gilt clock on the mantel chimed the quarter-hour, a pretty tone that hung in the air briefly before fading.

"Yes, a call of courtesy," Porter said, as if there had been no interruption. "I thought you might wonder, perhaps, at seeing so many vessels in the river."

Mrs. Hawkland smiled. "I have become accustomed to seeing boats here, but I confess it is surprising to see so many at once."

Porter nodded, smiling. "Just so. I am about to lead an expedition up the Red River."

Her delicate brows rose a little. "Do you not fear opposition? There is an army west of this river."

"There is an army on its way up from New Orleans as well, even as we speak. General Banks is leading it. My fleet will cooperate with him in opening the Red River to Shreveport."

Her mouth formed a silent "O" of surprise, then returned to a smile. "Then you have nothing to fear from General Taylor."

"Do you know the general, ma'am?"

"No, though I have met Mrs. Taylor." She glanced down, a sudden sadness coming into her eyes. Nat felt a sympathetic tug at his heart, and began to understand Quincy's infatuation. She could not be unconscious of the effect of her charms, but she made no obvious use of them, as many a younger coquette would have done.

The butler returned with a large silver tray which he set on the table before his mistress. She whispered some instruction to him to which he nodded before going out. She then smiled at her guests and proceeded to pour the coffee. Nat savored its scent even before receiving his cup. No shipboard sludge or chicory-cut brew this; it was fine coffee, probably straight from Brazil. He drank it slowly, thinking of home.

Admiral Porter sipped, then set his cup down on the table. "You mentioned cotton, ma'am. I have heard that you might be selling it."

Mrs. Hawkland nodded. "Do you need some to protect your boats? We have sold to the navy before—"

"Which navy?" Porter asked, his eye a little sharper, his manner a trifle less affable than a moment ago. Nat looked to Mrs. Hawkland, who seemed surprised.

"I have never sold cotton to the Confederate navy."

"I have heard you might be selling to the Rebel army," Porter said in a quiet voice.

Mrs. Hawkland put down her cup and folded her hands in her lap, her face very solemn. "I have not done so. Who accuses me?"

Porter did not answer; it was Adams who said, "Shelton."

A flash of anger came into the lady's eyes as she glanced at Adams. She addressed Admiral Porter crisply. "Mr. Shelton is no doubt vexed with me for having dismissed him. I fear he is not a man to be taken at his word."

"Why did you dismiss him, ma'am, if I may ask?" Porter's voice was gentle, almost sympathetic.

Her eyes narrowed. Nat felt a small thrill at the passion she displayed, even though she kept it tightly reined.

"For leasing my slaves to another planter without my knowledge or permission, and in the midst of my own harvest."

"Are not overseers expected to make independent decisions regarding plantation management?" Porter asked.

"Yes, but not to keep the profits for themselves," she returned. "And even if it were innocent, which it was not, it would have been a bad decision. Had I not discovered what he had done and retrieved my slaves, I would have lost most of my cane harvest to frost. Nor was this Mr. Shelton's only transgression." She glanced toward Adams, who nodded, his own eyes suddenly hot with anger.

"I do not know how my husband contrived to control him," Mrs. Hawkland continued. "I have not been able to, and found it necessary to dismiss him. I must beg you to be cautious of accepting his word."

Porter, watching her narrowly, gave a small nod. "Thank you, ma'am. I will take it into consideration."

A negro woman came into the room, carrying a baby who was fussing sleepily. She hesitated when her gaze fell on Adams, and Nat realized with a small shock that it was Sarah. He had not recognized her; she looked happy and well, and he had last seen her miserable with fright.

"Bring him in, Sarah," Mrs. Hawkland said. The girl carried the baby to her chair and gave him into her arms. "My son, Théodore," Mrs. Hawkland said to the admiral, then smiled down at the child and murmured to him in French. "Sarah, you have a visitor," she added without looking up. "You may speak with him in the pantry."

Adams stood up at once, and Nat watched him follow Sarah out of the room and into the vast hall, where they disappeared from view. Admiral Porter leaned toward his hostess, elbows on his knees and his fingers knit between them, smiling as he watched her gently rock her child.

"A fine little fellow. How old is he?"

"Just over eight months. He was born on Independence Day." She smiled as she said it, but there was a hint of something else in her voice. Nat wondered if Quincy could have interpreted it; he could not.

"Ah yes, independence," the admiral said. "As you know ma'am, our president has declared the slaves in this state to be free. Your girl Sarah there could come away with her man today if she chose to."

Mrs. Hawkland looked up, and Nat sensed tension between them. The admiral's voice was deceptively soft; the lady gazed at him, her bosom moving with her breath but her face betraying only watchfulness, until at last it relaxed into a small smile.

"I believe Mr. Adams considers it a point of honor to purchase her freedom," she said quietly. "His own father freed his family, and the accomplishment was much admired."

"Slavery will end, ma'am. You must know that."

"I do," she said slowly, a shadow coming into her face. "I would have ended it here myself, could I have done so without facing ruin."

"Ruin may yet come. You had best be prepared."

She made no answer, only gazed at Porter for a moment, then looked down at her sleeping son. Nat felt a strong desire to comfort her, which was madness, of course. She was rich beyond his wildest imaginings; she needed no sympathy from him. He realized he was holding his empty cup and saucer on his knees, and leaned forward to place them on the table. The movement drew her attention and she looked up with a quick smile.

"May I fill your cup, Mr. Wheat?"

Nat glanced at Porter, who had leaned back again and was watching their hostess through hooded eyes. He seemed in no hurry to depart.

"Thank you, but will you not let me help myself? Your hands are full."

She nodded assent, and Nat poured more coffee for himself and the admiral. Mrs. Hawkland remarked on the rain, expressing the hope that the crews of the boats were not suffering, and for the remainder of the visit she and the admiral conversed on such innocuous subjects. Nat put in a word now and then, but between feeling cowed at being in company with his fleet commander and the confused emotions inspired by Mrs. Hawkland, he found himself with little to say. He only hoped neither of them concluded he was stupid because of it.

The baby woke and began to fuss. A couple of minutes later Adams and Sarah returned, both silent and unsmiling. The maid at once went to her mistress and took away the whimpering child, exchanging a glance with Adams as she left the room. Adams watched after her hungrily, then returned to his chair and lowered himself onto it, looking unhappy.

"May I freshen your coffee, Mr. Adams?"

Nat glanced sharply at Mrs. Hawkland, watchful for any sign of irony, but saw none in her face. In fact, as near as he could tell she pitied Adams. The former slave looked up at his former mistress and the tension in his face changed to sadness. He shook his head. "No thank you, Madame."

Porter, who had watched all this in silence, now sat up. "I fear we must be getting back. There are matters I must attend to—none of them as interesting as yourself, Mrs. Hawkland, but alas, they are inescapable." He rose, and the others followed suit. "Thank you for the coffee, and for taking the time to entertain us."

"It was my pleasure. I hope you will visit again."

He looked at her, eyelids lazy and a smile spreading his beard. "I hope I may."

Porter bowed again over her hand. When she offered it to Nat he followed suit, glancing up at her in time to see a glint of amusement in her eyes. It lit up her face and made him catch his breath. He felt himself blushing as he released her hand, and could well understand Quincy's succumbing to her.

She at once turned and offered her hand to Adams, saying, "I am glad to know you are doing well in the navy, Mr. Adams."

Adams hesitated, then gingerly shook her hand and immediately let go of it, stepping back. Nat looked at Mrs. Hawkland, liking her more for this small act of kindness than for anything he had yet seen or heard of her.

The butler and footman arrived with their coats and hats. Mrs. Hawkland bid them farewell and remained standing in her parlor while the three navy men went into the hall to don their outer clothing. Bracing himself for another drenching, Nat was surprised when the butler, retaining the admiral's umbrella, led them out onto the porch and escorted them to a closed carriage waiting at the foot of the steps. When Porter had entered the vehicle the butler stepped back to allow Nat and Adams to follow, and to close the umbrella which he then handed in to its owner.

"Thank you, my man," said the admiral as the butler closed the door. He tapped the carriage wall twice with the umbrella handle to signal the driver, and the vehicle smoothly started forward and down the drive.

"Well, that was most interesting," Porter said. "What is your opinion of the lady, Wheat?"

Nat hesitated. "I cannot say whether she is loyal," he said slowly, "but I-I do believe that she is good." He frowned, not quite sure how he had reached this opinion.

The admiral's eyes narrowed. "Hm. Have you anything to add to that, Mr. Adams?"

Adams, gazing at the floor, shook his head. Nat watched him, concerned. It seemed his private visit had not gone well.

"Shall we go back and fetch your fiancée away?" Porter asked him. Adams swallowed. "I cannot keep her on the *Benton*."

"Well, that is true enough. Perhaps when we return from this expedition. I think I shall have to defer my decision regarding Mrs. Hawkland's cotton, and hope the Rebels don't burn it in the meantime."

The carriage slowed to a stop at the landing, and the three men got out and returned to the admiral's gig. They crossed the river back to the *Black Hawk* in silence, then Nat and Adams parted from the admiral to return to the *Benton*.

Nat watched his friend, sorry to see his sadness. "Sarah looked well," he said gently.

Adams looked up at him and smiled a little. "Yes. She is happy—says Madame is very kind to her." The smile faded. "I told her I will come for her as soon as I have enough money. She asked where I would take her. I have no house for her to live in, and I cannot bring her with me in the Navy. She said she does not want to be alone in a city full of Yankees."

Nat bit his lip, unable to think of any consoling advice. "She still loves you, doesn't she?"

"Yes. She says so."

"You will think of something."

Not a very helpful statement, but Adams nodded agreement and put on a brave smile. Nat bid him farewell at the *Benton* and returned to the *Cricket,* chilled once more from boating about the river in the rain. The other yawl was back; he should report to Gorringe, who doubtless would want to hear all about his visit to Rosehall. Pausing on the main deck to look back at the mansion, he almost felt as if it had been a dream. Had he really been sitting on a velvet couch sipping coffee from fine china just an hour ago?

He shivered, realizing with a start just how cold he was. The rain seemed to be increasing again, and the gray sky was heavier. He hastened into the *Cricket*'s main deck, where a visit to the engine room would chase the chill from his bones.

"Do you wish me to close the drapes, Madame?"

Marie, feeding Théo in the rocking chair by the fire in her bedchamber, glanced up at Sarah. "No, I wish to see the river. You may bring me my shawl instead."

The girl seemed nervous since the Yankees had left. Marie watched her fetch the shawl, wondering if she had misinterpreted the silent exchange between her and Little George—Mr. Adams, which sounded so strange—after they had returned to the parlor. He must have urged Sarah to come away with him, even as Admiral Porter had suggested. Marie had thought from Sarah's manner that she had refused, but now she was not so certain. Perhaps she was planning to slip away at night. Perhaps Marie would not bother to constrain her; if the girl was that discontented, she would not be a good servant to Théo.

She closed her eyes. Eight hundred, nine hundred dollars the girl was worth. Was she really willing to let that walk away? She could not, according to the relentless account books downstairs, but the difference between the numbers in those books and the actual lives of her slaves was becoming more and more apparent to her.

She had not the heart to treat them cruelly—had never wanted to treat anyone cruelly—yet the nature of slavery called for it at times, and she could see the effect of it on Damien, Big George, and the others who were her agents in the governance of her plantations. The field hands mistrusted them, men of their own race, because they were trusted by Marie. She wanted problems brought to her attention and resolved, but sometimes she did not know about them until they became so bad that punishment was necessary. She had made small changes. Pregnant women were no longer beaten; she had been appalled when she learned that under Mr. Shelton's administration transgressors who were with child were routinely made to lie with their bellies in holes dug for the purpose, so that the valuable unborn would not be harmed by the whipping. Now they were punished by confinement away from their families instead. She could imagine that in time this would result in more of the female slaves bearing children, hoping to avoid beatings by getting themselves with child. That would mean more profits, assuming plantation business continued as it was. Marie was not confident that it would.

Had Theodore known about such practices? He must have. How could he have lived with the knowledge, she wondered. She feared she was not a very good planter.

No; that was untrue. She was a fine planter. If she lacked anything it was the hard-heartedness required of a slaver, but she sensed change coming in that respect.

Admiral Porter's warning had frightened her; she was not certain that it had not been a threat. What had Shelton told him, she wondered? At first she had feared that he still possessed her letter to General Taylor, but if that were so it would have damned her completely in Admiral Porter's eyes, and he would not have bothered to visit her but would have seized her cotton outright. She was disturbed by his visit nonetheless, for he seemed to be probing her. She had told no untruths; indeed, she had not sold cotton to the Confederate armed forces, only to foreign nations for their benefit. If Admiral Porter had questioned her more closely she might have been forced to deceive him, a detestable thought, even though he was an enemy.

Shelton had read her letter to Taylor—that much was clear. That he had contacted the Yankee commander surprised her. Apparently his hatred of her was so complete that he would use any means at all to strike at her, even accusations for which he had no proof.

Théo hiccupped and let out a little mewling cry. She sat him up on her knee, bouncing him gently. She had begun to see familiar things in his face, most notably his eyes, which were a clear, glowing hazel, very like the ones that haunted her still. She wondered where Mr. Russell was—with Taylor's forces somewhere, she presumed—and whether he knew of the coming threat. She felt an urge to send a warning across the river, but dismissed it. Admiral Porter had been careful to tell her nothing that could not easily have been deduced. There were plenty of watchers west of the river; she would only compromise herself by attempting to communicate with Taylor's army. Mr. Russell would have to fend for himself.

She wondered if she would ever see him again. She had done her best to ensure that she would not, but more and more she had grown to regret that act. She liked him, after all. Who would not? He was a pleasant young man with a kind heart. Looking at the echoes of his face in her son's, she realized how foolish she had been to think she could forget him. She would be reminded of him every day.

Such thoughts were dangerous; she pulled her shawl closer about her and carried Théo to the window. Another boat had just arrived—one of the heavily armed ironclads. There were now boats all over the river as far as she could see. Admiral Porter's fleet was assuming formidable proportions. Soon they would start up the Red River, and God help those in their path. Marie thought of her aunt in Shreveport and breathed a silent prayer for her safety. She added a hope for the safety and success of Taylor's army, and thought heaven could not blame her if she prayed for one soldier in particular.

Jamie slumped in the saddle, weary and sore from the long march. Pine woods flanked the road on either side and the air was thick with dust kicked up by Bagby's regiment—once the 7th Texas Mounted Volunteers, now the 7th Texas Cavalry—who rode ahead of Jamie's section. The 5th and part of Bush's newly recruited regiment were behind him—some seven hundred cavalry in all in the little column, the regiments being severely under strength. The rest of the Valverde Battery was with Taylor at Pleasant Hill.

Green's Brigade had arrived in Louisiana after eighteen days of not quite forced marching, which had been miserable enough. From Houston to where they had crossed the Sabine River was nearly two hundred miles, and they had come another fifty miles into Louisiana. Some of the cavalry were as yet unarmed. Magruder, possibly jealous of having to give up his troops to Taylor, had issued a ludicrous order for a number of the wagons to remain on the Texas side of the Sabine, an order Jamie would have been sorely tempted to disregard had he been in charge.

Earlier in the day Colonel Bagby had come back and ridden with him a while, which was kind of him. Bagby had been with the brigade from the start, serving as a major with the 7th in New Mexico, moving up to lieutenant-colonel and then taking command of the regiment when Colonel Steel resigned. He was about thirty, slim with clear eyes set deep in his face. His manner was cordial though a little distant, which Jamie attributed to his having been a West-Pointer.

The column had marched early that morning, and had already made at least ten miles in Jamie's judgment. He felt every one of them in his bones, and knew Cocoa was weary as well. Her head was low as they trudged up the Natchitoches road toward Spanish Lake, where they were to hold a bridge against the enemy's advance. Jamie wondered when Bagby would call a halt. There was enough dust in the air that he could not see the colonel riding at the head of the column. He looked at his watch, saw that it was only two, and sighed, resigned to a few more hours in the saddle. Maybe he would get down and walk for a while—except that his legs were so sore he was not sure he would be able to keep up. His men, afoot except for the noncoms and the drivers, were grimly silent as they marched.

A rumbling up ahead startled him; he heard a wild shout, then a bullet sang past his head. Instantly his heart was pounding, terror pumping through him as pistol fire, then musket fire thickened to a constant crackle and whine of projectiles. The thundering of charging horses dissolved into a chaotic clash of cavalry in the road ahead.

A horseman came charging back along the edge of the road, pulling up so hard when he spotted Jamie that his mount squealed in protest. "Colonel says deploy here in the road," he gasped, waiting only for Jamie's nod before riding on toward the rear of the column.

Jamie ordered his sergeants to unlimber the guns, his throat tight with fear. Who were they fighting, and how many were there, he wondered? They were not supposed to have met the enemy this side of Spanish Lake. A whiff of powder smoke came to him. The fighting was close.

The drivers and cannoneers moved swiftly, all weariness banished by the urgency of acting under fire. The men unlimbered the two guns and the drivers took the limbers down the road. It was narrow; it would be difficult to turn. Jamie hoped he wouldn't have to, at least not under fire. He could hear Bagby's cavalry behind him moving away into the woods. No infantry support to protect his guns. He felt horribly exposed here, but there was no help for it.

A riderless horse galloped past, heading back toward Pleasant Hill. Jamie swallowed, wondering what unfortunate trooper had lost it. When his guns were in battery he took his place behind them and took out his field glasses knowing it would be futile but trying anyway to see what was happening ahead. He could do nothing while Bagby's men were in front of him.

Bagby himself rode up a few minutes later, thick red dust coating his clothing and beard. "The cavalry are moving into line on either side of the road," he told Jamie. "They should be out of your way now. The enemy have horse and foot. Fire as soon as you have a target."

"Yes, sir!"

Bagby was gone even as Jamie replied. He peered through the glasses again, trying to make sense of the swirling dust ahead. He could still hear the sound of the skirmishing, though it was muffled now that the cavalry were off the road and into the woods. The musketry continued, though it seemed random. He could fire a round at the road ahead and see what resulted, but it would give his position away. Better to know his first rounds would have an effect.

He summoned his sergeants, who reported their platoons ready. "Load with canister," he told O'Niell. "Schroeder, load one round of shell and fire on my order. Be ready to switch to canister if they show close in our front."

"Yes, sir," Schroeder said. He and O'Niell returned to their stations.

Jamie wiped dust from his eyes and squinted once more through the glasses. He saw something moving—couldn't tell what. He squeezed his eyes shut and opened them again, trying to see better. Dust was puffing up again, obscuring his view. Dust puffing up . . .

"Number one!" he screamed to Schroeder, raising his hand in the air as he looked at the 6-pounder's chief of piece. Schroeder's face turned toward him, pale in the dust. "Fire!" Jamie shouted, swinging his arm down at the same time. Schroeder relayed the order and the gun roared. Cocoa reacted but stood firm. Jamie could not see the flame as he was staring through the glasses at the spinning dust again, dust kicked up by legs in blue. A moment later the shell burst, the legs moved in startled confusion, and the dust billowed forward.

Jamie looked up at O'Niell who was ready and watching, and signaled him to fire the howitzer. He didn't bother to raise his glasses for he knew he would not be able to see, but he could hear a distant scream through the ringing of the cannon fire in his ears and imagined the blue legs being riddled with musket balls. He swallowed bile, aware that he would never like this and equally aware that he dared not hesitate to send more death out from his guns. He rode to Schroeder and shouted to him to switch to canister and to fire at will, then went to O'Niell and told him to keep firing canister.

Jamie could no longer hear the cavalry, could see next to nothing but trusted that he was making way against the enemy. Until he received further orders from Bagby or found his section in imminent danger of being captured, he must continue as he was doing. He wished he could see—thought about sending a man up a tree—decided against it.

A stray ball whizzed past him, making him realize the musketry had dwindled to almost nothing. Either he had successfully routed the Yankee infantry, or—

A heavy boom and a hail of balls reached the section almost together. Jamie flinched, fully expecting to feel the sudden pain of a wound. The number two man on the howitzer went down, shrieking, and was dragged aside by the number seven, who grabbed his implement and took his place. Jamie recovered his wits enough to think wryly that Bagby had been wrong. The enemy had not only horse and foot, but artillery as well.

27

... *Colonel Bagby, commanding his own, McNeill's, and some*
companies of Bush's newly raised regiment, with a section of
the Valverde Battery, was attacked on the Natchitoches road
by cavalry, infantry, and artillery.
— Richard Taylor, Major-General C.S. Army

Sun was slanting over Jamie's shoulders from behind, stabbing in between the treetops. He could hear the skirmish getting louder, which meant the cavalry were falling back again, which meant in a minute he would be limbering up. He sent a runner back to warn the drivers, who had taken to lying down with the reins in their hands on account of the shells the Yankee artillery were firing. Another of these howled in and burst just a dozen yards short of the guns, sending deadly bits of metal hurtling in all directions. Jamie had stopped flinching a long time ago, for there was not a thing he could do to evade the effects of a shell. He kept watching his guns, kept in touch with his sergeants, kept an eye on the limbers and caissons behind him. He would continue until he was hit or it ended.

His eyes stung with the smoke and dust of the fight, and he coughed now and then, taking sparing sips from his canteen only when he needed to speak. He had lost count of the wounded cavalrymen he had seen limping back to the rear where Bagby's surgeon was looking after them as best he could, or slung over their saddles on mounts led by comrades, their blood dripping onto the road. More than a dozen, he was certain. He had sent two of his own men back to the surgeon as well.

He heard a commotion in the underbrush to his right and turned, a hand to his pistol, then relaxed when he saw Colonel Bagby riding out of the woods toward him. The colonel's coat was was torn, a long gash near the elbow. "How much ammunition do you have left?" he called as he joined Jamie.

"I am on my last chests," Jamie told him. "Forty rounds each gun, no more."

Bagby squinted back up the road toward Pleasant Hill. "General Taylor has sent supports forward to us. We should meet them any time now. Fall back another hundred yards, and conserve ammunition."

"Yes, sir."

Bagby crossed the road and disappeared into the opposite woods. Jamie rode to his sergeants and ordered them to limber up, then turned Cocoa toward the rear to select a new position.

A shell burst nearby and a piercing, loud shriek knocked his hat off; it tumbled into his lap and he caught it against his chest with one hand to keep from losing it, aware of the sudden pounding of his heart. Cocoa had jumped and he reached forward to stroke her neck, then looked over his shoulder at the guns. Two men had been hit—their comrades were already attending to them—and he could see bits of the fragmented shell lying in the road. The teams had not yet come up, thank goodness. Screaming, plunging horses in harness were a nightmare to manage. He sighed and brushed the sweat out of his eyes before putting on his hat, then realized he hadn't been sweating.

He stared at the dark smear on his glove, then pulled it off and touched his forehead with his fingertips. They came away wet with blood. Breathing hard, he felt up into his scalp until his fingers found the cut and made it sting with the salt from his skin. He hissed, but forced himself to explore the wound. It was a couple of inches long and not too deep. He hoped there was nothing inside it—he was bleeding enough that there shouldn't be. Wiping his hand on his coat, he looked up to see the limbers coming toward him. He moved out of the way, noticing the shocked expression of one of the drivers as they passed.

"It looks worse than it is," he called after the man, who probably didn't hear him.

He took out his handkerchief and held it to the cut, wincing at the pain. He meant to wipe his face as well but the kerchief came away pretty well soaked, and he tossed it aside into the woods. Momma would be angry at his so casually discarding her handiwork, but he sure didn't want to put it back in his pocket. He jammed his hat on over the wound, noticing a new hole made by the shell fragment that had hit him, hoping the hat wouldn't be ruined completely by the blood. At least it would keep the mess out of his eyes. He glanced back to make sure his sergeants had everything in hand, then nudged Cocoa forward.

She grunted and tossed her head; she could smell the blood. He spoke to her, murmuring soothing nothings as they trotted away from the fighting. The cavalry's wagons had already pulled back out of his way. He chose the top of a slight rise for his new position; behind it the road curved gently northward. He saw no sign of the promised supports, only the column's wagons well to the rear. Having selected his position, he started toward the section again, only to meet Sergeant Schroeder riding back to him, frowning with concern.

"Biggs said you were wounded!"

"It's just a scratch," Jamie told him. "We will place the guns there, on that rise."

"Shall I take charge while you go to the surgeon?"

"No, I'm all right. Go start the guns back, I will stay here."

In fact, he was feeling a little light-headed. He walked Cocoa back to the rise and took two deep swallows from his canteen, then sat breathing, listening. The sound of the fight was muted. Some small animal scurried through the woods nearby, running from the chaos. Jamie resisted the temptation to take his hat off again—he could do nothing more for himself, and the wound would be better left alone until he could get it cleaned up. His scalp was throbbing now, and his head ached generally. Blood had trickled down alongside his nose and reached his lip; he licked at it, tasting the sulphur tang of gunpowder on his skin along with the copper-salt.

Long pine shadows lay across the road ahead. The sun would set soon and the air was getting damp—probably it would rain. Jamie shivered in anticipation, considered getting out his greatcoat, decided to wait until he really needed it. Cocoa sidled restlessly; he leaned forward to pat her neck. When he straightened up again his head swam. He closed his eyes and took a deep breath, trying to regain his balance.

Rumbling. He looked up and saw his guns coming. He waited where he was, marking the spot where he wanted them until he had to move out of the way of the limbers and was joined by his sergeants at the side of the road.

"I must look like hell," he said, grinning at O'Niell, who was staring at him aghast.

"You sure do!"

"How many rounds do you have left?"

They reported the numbers. The howitzer was down to shell except for two rounds of canister which would be reserved for a final stand. The 6-pounder had shot, shell, and a few rounds of case. Jamie discussed strategy with the sergeants, told them to be conservative with their remaining rounds, then left the decisions to them. They all knew what sort of troops they were fighting by now. The solid shot and the shell, if well aimed, could disrupt the enemy's artillery, who like themselves had remained in the road. The other rounds could be fired into the woods where they would be effective against the cavalry and infantry, taking care of course not to fire when their own cavalry were present. If Bagby had any clear idea of the numbers that opposed them he had not shared it with Jamie, but as they had been falling back steadily for hours it seemed pretty obvious they were outnumbered.

The guns were in battery; the sergeants dismounted and sent their horses back with the drivers, and Jamie walked Cocoa back onto the road to take up his position. It would be quiet for a little while, until the cavalry fell back closer to them. Jamie felt tired and a bit stupid—he had felt that way even before getting hit. He would sure sleep well tonight, he thought, smiling a little to himself.

He could hear musketry now. The cavalry were retiring, and in another minute Bagby came loping back to Jamie's position. The colonel reined in and opened his mouth to speak, frowned, then said, "Report to the surgeon."

"I—"

"That's an order, Lieutenant. Sergeant?" Bagby turned toward the 6-pounder.

"Schroeder," Jamie called, and waved the man over. Schroeder jogged up to them and looked at Jamie, who told him, "You're in command of the section."

Schroeder's eyes widened a bit but he nodded and turned to Bagby for orders. Jamie saw O'Niell watching from his post and shot him a sheepish grin, then started toward the rear. His head was aching pretty badly now and he would be glad to get cleaned up. Didn't want to keep frightening the men, he thought, and laughed a little, which hurt.

He heard the moaning of the wounded long before he reached them. Bagby's surgeon had the worst cases—about eight fellows—in a wagon that was still half filled with crates, and most of the groans were coming from there. More than a dozen others were sitting on the ground with their backs against pine trees or lying down, some looking like they were sleeping. A handful of horses grazed on the grass at the side of the road.

The surgeon, hands bloodied halfway to the elbows, was sewing shut a long cut on a cavalryman's thigh. He looked up as Jamie dismounted and leaned against Cocoa to get his breath. The surgeon started to rise, but Jamie waved him back.

"Go ahead, I can wait."

He led Cocoa over to the grass, thought about hobbling her but decided he had better not. Might want to leave in a hurry. He scratched her neck and praised her for a brave girl. Feeling tired, he sat under a tree and took another swallow of water, then leaned back gingerly and closed his eyes.

"Show me where you are wounded."

Jamie looked up to see the surgeon bending over him. Hadn't heard him come up. He sucked in a breath and took off his hat, or tried to. It was stuck to his hair, matted with blood. He pulled it free and winced at the pain in his scalp.

A hand shoved a canteen in front of his face. "Drink."

Jamie could smell the whiskey. Normally he didn't care for the stuff, but just now he was willing to oblige. He took a swallow, then a bigger one, and felt stupidity washing through his mind even as the liquor burned down his chest. The canteen was heavy so he lowered it to rest on the ground, holding it upright. He thought he should cork it, and searched with clumsy fingers for the chain.

Pain seared through his scalp and he gasped, muscles tightening in his chest. "Sorry," the surgeon muttered, but he kept fumbling at Jamie's head, sending lances of pain through him, white-hot behind his eyes. Jamie thought he would vomit, but before that could happen another flash sank him into darkness.

"The channel through the falls lies here," said Mr. Withenbury, laying a finger to his map.

Nat crowded close to the *Cricket*'s wardroom table with a dozen other pilots, peering at the chart Withenbury had brought. Admiral Porter was in the room as well; it was he who had engaged the services of the Red River pilot to guide the fleet through the rapids above Alexandria. He had been lucky to find Withenbury. A pilot with knowledge of the region was absolutely necessary to the expedition's success; some of the boats had already grounded below the city on their way up from Fort De Russy, which was supposed to have been their first fight. Instead the fort had fallen to Banks's army even as the fleet was arriving, leaving the navy little to do but scour the adjacent countryside for cotton.

On this side of the Mississippi there was no consideration of loyalties; cotton was confiscated wherever it was found, regardless of the owner's reputed patriotism or lack thereof. The reasoning was that if it were left alone the Rebel army would burn it to keep it out of Union hands. Nat knew that greed played at least an equal part in the scramble. A number of speculators had accompanied the navy, some apparently friends of the admiral's. Nat thought them despicable. Bales of questionable ownership were stenciled with "CSA," then claimed by the navy as contraband of war and labeled "USN" as well. Since the *Cricket*'s arrival at Alexandria in mid-March Nat had twice spent the evening ashore, and both times had heard the joke that the initials stood for "Cotton Stealing Association of the United States Navy." Though he stood to gain financially by the practice, it left a bad taste in his mouth. He wondered if Mrs. Hawkland realized how fortunate she was that Admiral Porter had refrained from molesting her cotton.

Porter had transferred his flag to the *Cricket* for the coming expedition, as the *Black Hawk* was by far too heavy to go over the falls. Nat was a little nervous at the thought of piloting the flagship, but comforted himself with the knowledge that, excepting Withenbury, none of the pilots present knew a lick more than he about the upper Red.

Withenbury, a local, spoke slowly in a quiet, slightly drawling voice. He seemed the sort of fellow who was never in a hurry. He described the falls in detail, pointing out hazards on the chart and answering anxious questions from the assembled pilots. Nat listened in silence, wishing the wardroom were not so stuffy; it still smelled vaguely of last night's supper.

"When will the water rise?" someone asked.

Withenbury looked up, cocking an eyebrow. "Usually the rise begins in January or February. This year it started late, and has been slow."

"It *will* rise, will it not?"

"It has risen every year since 'fifty-five."

Nat frowned, thinking that a noncommittal answer, but he would hardly have wanted to promise a rise in the river had he been in Withenbury's place. The success of the entire campaign could be at stake. Nat happened to know that Admiral Porter did not wish to take his fleet up the river, but General Banks had insisted, and Porter was gallant enough—or clever enough—to want no responsibility for any disaster that might befall the army if it were deprived of the fleet's protection. Capturing Shreveport would require gunboats, or at least would be much easier with their help. Porter, who had often been heard to say he could take his river fleet wherever the sand was damp, had agreed to go up.

He had chosen a dozen gunboats to go, which would be accompanied by a number of transports carrying troops borrowed from General Sherman's army for the expedition. These were rough fellows who had celebrated the capture of DeRussy by looting a nearby plantation while their commander, A. J. Smith, looked on with amusement. It had set the tone for the army's behavior whenever they went ashore.

Also present were the Mississippi Marine Brigade, now under Alfred Ellet's command. Nat had been saddened to hear that his former commander aboard the *Queen,* Charles Rivers Ellet, had died at his aunt's home in Illinois the previous October, where he had gone to recuperate from typhoid fever. He had been only twenty.

Withenbury fell silent, having finished his discourse and answered everyone's questions. Porter, who had remained in the background, now came to the table, rubbing his hands together briskly.

"Very good. If there are no more questions, we may as well get underway. The *Eastport* shall go first up the rapids."

Withenbury smoothed his mustache, letting thumb and forefinger rest on his chin a moment. "Beg pardon, Admiral, but if you ask for my judgment, I would say it is bad policy to put the largest boat into the chute first. She might get aground, and if she did it would hinder the passage of the other vessels."

Porter fixed narrowed eyes on the pilot. "I want you to go on board and take her over the falls."

The air prickled with silent tension. Nat knew he would not have had the courage to defy the admiral, and neither did Withenbury, it seemed. The Louisiana pilot raised his shoulders slightly, and said, "If that is your decision."

Porter gave a curt nod. "It is. Gentlemen." He swept the room with a glance, then went out, taking the tension with him.

The pilots began to disperse, thanking Withenbury for his advice. Nat walked with him to the main deck and saw him onto his boat.

"Maybe the river will come up another inch or two."

Withenbury glanced upstream, then looked back at Nat with a wry smile. "We shall have to hope for that."

"If anyone can get the *Eastport* up it is you."

Withenbury didn't answer, only raised a hand in farewell as the boat's crew pushed off from the *Cricket.* Nat watched him away, then went up to the upper deck and stood outside the pilot house looking over the fleet. He could not see how the heavier vessels were to get up the river. The falls looked impassable, rusty water churning white in a dozen places. He looked for the channel Withenbury had shown them on the chart, a narrow band of faster moving water, smoother than the rest. It looked too narrow to Nat.

Porter and Gorringe came up onto the deck, the admiral moving forward to the bow. Gorringe joined Nat and flashed him a grin. "So, here we go, eh?"

Nat turned a grimace into a smile and nodded, looking out at the *Eastport* which had started forward, slowly beginning to thread her way through the rapids. She was a big ironclad ram, nearly twice the length of the *Cricket,* with eight heavy guns. Her draft was all of six feet if it was an inch, Nat judged. He would not have been willing to swear that there were six feet of water in the chute.

"It will be good to get out of Alexandria," Gorringe remarked. "We have been idle too long."

Nat involuntarily glanced toward the left bank, where pines crowded together above a dense undergrowth. Somewhere beyond those woods Banks's army was preparing to march toward Shreveport, and somewhere beyond that were the Rebels. He kept to himself the hope that Banks would remain between Taylor's army and the river.

A loud grinding made him look up. *Eastport* was in trouble; her wheels churned up water as she labored to get over a rocky place, then she stopped with a jolt that must have knocked a few sailors off balance. Gorringe muttered a curse under his breath and strode forward to join Porter, who was already looking at the gunboat through his glass. Nat crossed his arms and leaned against the pilot house, watching in silence. *Eastport* reversed her wheels, chuffing smoke as she tried to back off the rocks. It was no good; after a few minutes her engines slackened, and she hoisted a signal indicating that she had grounded.

Withenbury had been right. Now the river was effectively blocked; there was not enough water for any of the other boats to pass the *Eastport.* Nat frowned, remembering Garvey, the pilot who had run the *Queen of the West* onto shoals right under Fort De Russy's guns. Garvey had been a traitor—that had become clear. Nat was certain he had grounded the *Queen* deliberately. Had Withenbury just done the same with the *Eastport?* If so, he was clever enough to have warned Porter in advance, in front of a roomful of witnesses.

Gorringe came back, looking disgusted. "It will take hours to bring her off."

Nat nodded agreement. "We'll be lucky to do it today. Can't get another steamer in to tow her."

"Maybe the tugboats can do it."

Nat sighed, unwilling to state aloud his thought that it was more likely her crew would have to bring her off by their own sweat. She would have to be lightened, all of her cargo removed and carried above the falls by wagon, along with her guns. It was an inauspicious beginning to the expedition.

Gorringe shook his head. "Well, I had better tell the engineer to bank his fires. Join me for coffee?"

Nat gave a reluctant smile. "Red River coffee?"

Gorringe assumed an affronted expression. "I know you have been spoiled by your visit to paradise, but I maintain that the Red tastes better than the Mississippi. The silt has a fineness, a piquancy—"

"Yes, yes. It is everything you say." Nat laughed, and followed his captain below.

Jamie woke to a rumbling that made his heart quicken until he realized it was thunder. He had been dreaming of battle, a confused dream, for even as the guns were firing he heard the grave diggers at work. The sound—chop of shovels into wet earth—continued although he was now wide awake, and it wasn't until he heard rain against canvas that he realized it must be men trenching around his tent. He opened his eyes and saw that he was right, he was in a tent, except it wasn't his; the roof was too high.

"Bonjour, Jacques! Not quite dead yet, eh?"

Jamie turned his head, wincing as he did, and saw Captain Cornay sitting beside him on the ground, gently smiling. Beyond him were other wounded men laid out on blankets—Jamie could see one of his own cannoneers.

"The head hurts, no? Try some of this." Cornay held out a flask.

"No—no whiskey, thanks." Jamie's voice came out in a croak and he cleared his throat.

Cornay grinned, blue eyes glinting. "Whiskey? Bah. You are in sugar country, mon ami. This is Louisiana rum."

Amused, Jamie carefully hauled himself up on one elbow and accepted the flask, curious to try a liquor he hadn't tasted. It was smooth on his tongue, had little aroma and an unfamiliar aftertaste, and sent fumes rising straight into his head. He handed it back, coughing a little and smiling his thanks.

"Where are we?"

"North of Mansfield. There will be a battle in a day or so."

Memories of the skirmish rushed in on Jamie; he tried to sit up too fast and was stopped by a throbbing in his head. He sank down again, hoping it would quit. "My section—"

"They are fine. The Yankees desisted just after you were wounded. Your little mare is safe also, I saw her this morning."

Relieved, Jamie gave a wry smile. "My hat?"

Cornay reached past Jamie's head and retrieved a battered and blood-encrusted mess, which he dropped onto Jamie's chest. Jamie frowned at it.

"It's the pin I want." He turned the hat until he found the little star pin that Emma had given to Martin, whose hat it had been before he was killed. She had given Jamie one, too, but it had been on his own hat that he had lost at Valverde. He unpinned the little silver star and tried to rub off some of the tarnish with the cuff of his shirtsleeve.

Cornay picked up the hat and examined it. "You could brush off the blood. A hat is better than no hat, eh? Here—it has two holes in it." He poked his fingers up through them and looked at Jamie with a raised eyebrow. "One from yesterday, the other . . . ?"

"Galveston." Jamie breathed on the star pin and polished it some more.

"Is that pin from your sweetheart?"

Jamie looked at Cornay, whose mouth was curving up into a smile on one side. He felt an answering smile threatening and frowned to subdue it. "From my sister."

"I think I do not believe in this sister."

"She would be quite annoyed to hear that." Jamie held the pin at arm's length and looked at it critically. It was better, the best he could do without any sort of real polish. He fastened it to his shirt, then grinned up at Cornay. "Come to San Antonio some time and I will introduce you to her."

"I will. And . . ." Cornay's smile faded and he looked away briefly. "I was going to ask you to my home in return, but I think it will not be fit for visitors for a while."

Jamie felt his heart constrict with sympathy. "Are your family all right?"

Cornay nodded. "They are out of the way. I went down to see them at Christmas. My father is not taking it well. His house was burned—everything lost."

A woman wearing an apron over a brown dress came toward them, carrying a bowl of something steaming. She made Jamie think of Momma, though she didn't really look anything like her. She smiled. "Can you sit up and eat a little?"

"Yes, ma'am."

With Cornay's help, Jamie carefully got himself upright, letting the blanket that had been covering him fall to his lap. His head felt a little soggy but didn't throb too much. The woman handed him the bowl, which contained a thin stew and a spoon. He thanked her and started in on the stew, grateful for its warmth.

"What were you saying about a battle?" he said around a bite of beef.

Cornay drew his knees up and wrapped his arms around them. "Everyone says this is where we will whip the Yankees. I hope it is so, for we have given up too much ground already, waiting for you Texans to arrive. No," he added holding up a hand as Jamie was about to protest, "I mean no offense to you. Do not let us argue about things we cannot control. General Taylor has to fight not only the Yankees but his superior officers. He has been begging for months for enough troops to face Banks. He knew last year that the Yankees would come up the Red River in the spring. I am frustrated, me. The whole army feels so. We are ready to fight."

Jamie nodded. He would go back into the field as well, as soon as the surgeon allowed it, and fight beside his friends. This stand could have as easily been made in Texas as in Louisiana. Indeed, if they failed here they might well be pushed back into Texas. Shreveport was not so very far from Marshall. Marshall was but three hundred miles from Austin, the capital, and San Antonio was less than a hundred miles beyond that.

Jamie looked down at the bowl, which had a couple of bites of stew left in it. He wasn't hungry anymore but he gulped it down anyway, then set the bowl aside. His gaze met Cornay's and held, sharing silent understanding.

"We'll whip them," Jamie said, his voice rough.

Cornay's smile flashed. "Your General Green is already biting at their heels."

"That's Green. Point him at an enemy and he'll attack." Jamie picked up his battered hat. He'd kept it in memory of Martin who had fallen at Valverde, charging the guns that later became the Valverde Battery. That had been Jamie's first fight, and it was Green who had led that charge.

Cornay sighed. "I had better get back to my camp."

"Thank you for coming to see me."

"But of course. We are brothers, no?" Cornay offered a hand, and Jamie shook it, smiling.

"Yes."

28

Action, prompt, vigorous action is required. While we are deliberating the enemy is marching. King James lost three kingdoms for a mass. We may lose three states without a battle.
—Richard Taylor, Major-General, C.S. Army

Jamie leaned on the rail fence in front of his section, weary of waiting for the battle to begin. Nearby Cocoa grazed on the wet grass. Beneath the trees the brush still glistened with moisture from rain that had fallen all the previous day and night. The roads and the field in front of him, which had been muddy early in the day, were beginning to dry.

General Taylor had drawn up his forces that morning on the ground he had chosen, a large open field straddling the stage road from Shreveport to Natchitoches, three miles southeast of Mansfield. Many roads crossed at Mansfield, and Taylor had no wish to yield such access to Banks's army. Just now the Federals were strung out for miles on a single road through the dense pine woods, and the Confederate commander liked it that way.

The field was farmland, cut out of the woods in a lopsided right angle with the stage road bisecting it roughly on the diagonal. At its widest east-west it was about a mile; most places it was closer to half a mile across. Rail fences ran all along its edges and on either side of the stage road, and also divided the field in several places. Taylor had placed his forces along the north and west edges where the woods met the field. The Yankee line was on the south and east within the woods, on a hilltop behind the fence.

Earlier in the day Jamie had stood out in the sun for a while, but now the shade of the woods was welcome. The smell of damp grass was strong, partly from the trampling of skirmishers who had been active more or less all afternoon.

He glanced to his right, down the ranks of Mouton's division of infantry. Cornay's and another Louisiana battery were nearby, just forward of Polignac's and Gray's brigades. He could see Captain Cornay standing beside his black horse, patiently waiting. Beyond Mouton, Walker's Division of Texas infantry and dismounted cavalry were spread around the angle at the back of the field and down its west side. The stage road ran to the northwest toward Mansfield, dividing Walker's troops. Two batteries flanked the road and a third faced east between Waul's and Scurry's brigades—Jamie looked for General Scurry but could not spot him—with the far right held by two regiments of cavalry under Terrel and the redoubtable old Prussian, Buchel.

The Confederate left was held by Green's cavalry division, including Bagby's brigade, formerly Green's brigade, formerly Sibley's. Even with the addition of an extra battalion the entire brigade numbered just over a thousand, the size of Green's original 5th regiment. That was a sad thought, but Jamie didn't linger on it. The whole war was a sad business; however, they could not quit now.

Indeed, gazing at Taylor's army of almost nine thousand, Jamie had no wish to quit. An old feeling stirred in him, a ghost of the thrill it had been early on with Sibley's brigade, when all the flags were new and the troops untried with no notion of what was before them. He would never be so callow again, but he could admire the spectacle of thousands of men and horses and guns poised for combat. Today, on this field, the biggest battle Jamie had yet seen would unfold.

He hoped it would be today, anyway. The battle lines had been drawn since midmorning; it was now four in the afternoon and still nothing had happened. There were only a few hours of daylight left. Jamie's scalp itched where the wound was healing. He resisted the urge to remove his hat, which he had cleaned as well as he could though it was so battered now that there wasn't much shape to it.

A familiar figure on horseback drew Jamie's gaze to his right. General Taylor, in his black greatcoat, was riding down the line of Gray's brigade of Louisiana infantry, talking to them. Jamie strolled that way, curious to hear what the general was telling his countrymen.

He heard Taylor say, "As you are fighting in defense of your own soil I wish the Louisiana troops to draw the first blood." A roaring cheer greeted the general's words. At almost the same moment a knot of Yankee cavalry skirmishers made a rush against the line right before the Louisianans. Minié balls whined and Jamie instinctively sprinted toward his guns, but Gray's men responded before he could get more than a few steps away. A concentrated volley of musketry filled the air beneath the trees with smoke and sent the Yankee horsemen reeling back with heavy losses. One poor bastard went down just beyond the fence, himself and his horse both riddled, both screaming.

Jamie noticed Bagby's brigade moving on his left. They had been in the open a hundred yards or so forward of the line at a place where the edge of the field jogged, and were now retiring to the woods on their left. He approved of the change, as it got them out of the Valverde Battery's way and opened more of the Yankee line to his field of fire. A few minutes later he thought he detected activity in the enemy line opposite, and peered through his field glasses trying to see what they were up to. Possibly concentrating forces on their right; it was hard to tell with the woods screening them.

Taylor responded by shifting more cavalry and infantry to the left of his line. Debray's regiment, which had been in reserve, came forward to replace a brigade that moved from the center to the left. Jamie could see Colonel Debray, his former mathematics instructor, standing beneath his colors as his regiment came up on both sides of the road. Debray had visited Jamie at the field hospital a couple of days earlier, and told him that his men had been skirmishing with the enemy at the same time Jamie and Bagby's brigade were doing so, and only a few miles away. It had been their first taste of combat.

So many friends on this field, old and new. Jamie had spent nearly three years in the army now; it had become his normal way of life. He glanced over at Captain Nettles and Lieutenants Hume and Foster, sitting under the trees rolling dice. They, along with the sergeants and men of his section, were his day-to-day family. How many of them would be alive at the end of this day's work? It was taboo to speak of that but every man on the field must wonder silently in his heart.

Something was happening; Jamie saw Mouton and his commanders mounting their horses. A minute later Mouton's division advanced into the field, knocking down the rail fence in their front and stepping over the rails out into the sun. It was beginning.

A little tingle of anticipation ran down Jamie's arms. He felt relief and disappointment both; with the infantry moving in their front, the artillery would not be firing immediately. Mouton had been given the privilege of opening the ball, but as he liked and admired the general, Jamie could not wish it otherwise. Gray's brigade began to run across the field, anxious to close with the enemy at last. Mouton and Gray had to spur their horses to catch up.

The men of the Valverde Battery, who had been resting beneath the trees, began to gather at the fence to watch the advance. The first of Gray's regiments rushed down a slope toward a shallow ravine that ran through the middle of the field. Before they reached it they came under fierce fire from the Yankees which slowed them, even pushing them back in one place. Jamie heard a deep report and saw canister rip through one company, winced at the sudden loss of twenty men or more. The Yankees had guns in the woods, then. He raised his glasses to try to locate them, wondering if it would be feasible to fire shell over the heads of Mouton's men. There was too much smoke for him to see clearly; he would have a better chance of spotting a muzzle flash without the glasses, so he lowered them.

The color bearer of the lead regiment fell. An officer picked up the flag; in a moment he was hit as well. Jamie watched as man after man picked up the colors, only to be shot down. The Louisianans struggled up the hill toward the Yankee line, paying a bitter price in the fallen they left behind.

A cheer made Jamie look up to see Mouton leap his horse over a rail fence and dash up the slope. His men and officers rallied and followed, charging toward the wooded hill and disappearing into the smoke that clung about the trees. Jamie's heart rose with exhilaration mixed with fear—they had closed with the Yankees at last. The chaos of sound that reached him was muted by distance, but he had no trouble imagining what it must be like. He had been in a similar place a few days ago.

Now there was movement on the Confederate right. Jamie watched Waul's and Scurry's brigades start across the field toward the Federal left. Terrel's and Buchel's cavalry went with them, advancing in unison with their flags bright in the clear air, a fine sight. They must be making for the Federal left, trying to flank them. Soon they were hidden from Jamie's view by the woods at the angle of the field.

Walker's infantry broke into a run. Jamie caught a glimpse of Scurry out in front of the line on horseback with his hat in his hand, urging his men on and screaming—obscenities, no doubt. Jamie grinned. The infantry charged up into the woods as Mouton's men had done.

The Yankee guns had not fired in some time; Jamie wondered if they had been withdrawn. A heavy report dispelled that notion, but its sound was different. Maybe the guns had been captured, and were now being fired on their former owners by Scurry and his men, just as they had done in New Mexico. Jamie felt a flash of sick memory of the carnage at Valverde together with a thrill of excitement at the hope of such a fine prize. He glanced toward the center of the field and saw General Taylor and his staff advancing. The artillery on the right were limbering up, and Jamie's pulse quickened.

Green's cavalry had gone into the woods on the left. Except for the batteries, which could not maneuver well in the heavy brush under the trees, and Debray's regiment in reserve, who were also advancing, all of Taylor's army had gone into the woods. Only the crackle of musketry, the occasional boom of the heavy guns, and puffs of smoke rising above the pines attested to the continuing fight.

Jamie found Nettles and stood beside him to wait for the orders that would come soon. They could hear the wounded now, calling for help, calling for water. Jamie's heart ached for them, but it was not his duty to help them; helping them would in fact interfere with his duty. There were others ready to do that, and they were not far away. At night, though—after the battle was over—men from the ranks would go out to search for their friends among the fallen.

"Here he comes."

Nettles's voice jarred him; Jamie looked up to see a staff officer galloping along the fence toward their position. Beyond him Cornay's battery was moving. Jamie didn't wait for the actual order but started back to his section at once. There was only one place they could be going—back to the road and down it to join the fight. He found his sergeants and told them to limber up, then went to Cocoa who had strayed a little way along the fence. He scratched her neck, taking comfort in the warmth of her hide, the smell of grass on her breath. He gave her a quick hug for luck and got up in the saddle.

The battery fell in at the rear of the artillery column. Walking wounded passed them at the sides of the road, some openly weeping with pain, most silent and grim. As they neared the woods a straggling column of wounded Louisianans emerged from it, their faces masks of anguish and grief. Many of them wept, and some called out angry words to the sky. Maybe they were just emotional, being Frenchmen, but Jamie thought it strange.

"What is it?" he called down to a dark-haired rifleman who was cradling his wounded arm against his chest, a dark bloodstain spreading on his gray coat. The man looked up at him, eyes flashing anger.

"They have killed Mouton."

Jamie sucked in a breath, and could only nod his thanks to the soldier as he passed. His throat tightened; now he understood their grief. General Mouton was a gallant commander who would be greatly missed. Jamie remembered a year ago down along the Teche, when they had almost been caught by the Yankees, and Mouton had waited until every man was across the burning bridge before crossing it himself.

The column slowed ahead of him, then halted. Jamie rode forward to Nettles to find out what was happening.

"The road is blocked," the captain told him. "Yanks abandoned their train."

Jamie's eyes widened. "How many wagons?" he demanded, quartermaster instinct taking over.

"No idea, but it isn't just wagons. The wagons blocked the road, so they had to abandon their guns. No way to get them through the woods."

Jamie grinned, and Nettles grinned back. It was a victory, then.

With the road blocked there was no way the batteries would fight today. Orders came to retire, and all the artillery returned to the battleground and bivouacked there. The sun was setting by the time the captured guns began to come down the road. Jamie watched them roll past one by one, his delight growing as each new team appeared. He counted twenty guns, all with their limbers and caissons. That nearly doubled the army's artillery. Maybe he could retire his little mountain howitzer now, and replace it with another 6-pounder.

Word came that the batteries would advance as soon as the road was clear, but after the guns came wagons loaded with arms, ammunition, supplies. After an hour of watching them lumber out of the woods, Nettles told Jamie and the other officers to let the men build fires and cook whatever they had left of their rations. The smell of bacon and corn cakes rose in the camp, blocking out less appealing battlefield smells. The latter would eventually overwhelm, but for now the camp was almost pleasant, if you could forget about the casualties lying beyond the firelight.

It took half the night before the wagons were all out of the woods. Jamie was certain the captured train was bigger than the train Sibley's brigade had taken to New Mexico. He was not able to sleep much with the rumbling of wagons in his ears, and had given up by the time orders came for the battery to march. It was still dark when the column formed in the road once more and started forward to join the rest of the army.

News filtered back in scraps. Mouton had been shot from his horse by a Yankee infantryman in a company whose surrender he was trying to accept; the Louisianans had instantly turned their rifles on the Yankees, and their officers had had to restrain them from slaughtering every last prisoner. The whole 13th Corps of Banks's army—the men who had been on the wooded hill—had crumbled and run before Taylor's advance. A second corps of Yankee cavalry had fallen back, but a third had been strong enough to halt Green, and there had been an hour or two of sharp fighting before the Yankees finally yielded control of the only stream for twenty miles. Jamie nodded when he heard that; it was the sort of thing Taylor would do. The general knew the country and would make sure to secure any advantage to his own army. The Yankees would not be enjoying their dry camp tonight.

The artillery column halted briefly near the captured stream while the battery in the van fired a few rounds into the Yankees' camping place. Apparently they had gone looking for water because there was no response. The column moved forward again, filling canteens as they crossed the precious stream. A small sliver of a moon came out, casting just enough light to set the pale petals of peach and plum trees aglow. It would have been lovely but for the dark shapes lying on the orchard grounds.

After a time the sky began to lighten generally, and now the chaos of the Federal rout became apparent. Knapsacks, blankets, and weapons littered the forest floor. The woods were filled with the smell of the smoldering wagons the column occasionally passed. Shortly before noon they reached another open field with some summer homes scattered along a gentle ridge called Pleasant Hill. Jamie had been through here before, and the Valverde Battery had camped here with Green for a couple of nights while he was in the hospital at Mansfield. The road intersected in the midst of the houses with another road coming down from Sabine. A little to the south a third road branched off westward.

The column halted and after conferring with General Taylor the chief of artillery began positioning the batteries. The Valverde and two others, Moseley's and West's, were stationed just within the woods to the right of the Mansfield road. From there Jamie could see most of the enemy's batteries on the ridge west of the junction. One stood much closer, posted under a handful of pines on a hill just the other side of the road, well in front of the houses. A large quantity of infantry supported this battery, some behind it, some in line to its left. This field was smaller than the last, with patches of pines scattered through it. Colonel Major's cavalry held the left, Debray's and Buchel's cavalry under General Bee stood on the Mansfield road with Mouton's hard-used infantry division—now commanded by Polignac—in reserve. On the right were Walker's division, and two fresh divisions of Arkansans and Missourians come down from Shreveport too late for the previous day's battle, along with some cavalry.

The Yankee line extended into the woods on either side of the structures. Jamie wondered where the owners of the houses were— far away if they had a particle of sense. The buildings could be used for cover by sharpshooters; they were probably stuffed full of Yanks already. He peered at them, gauging the distance and thinking about the timing of the fuses he would use if he had a chance to fire on them.

Skirmishers flirted back and forth while the armies formed their lines. Jamie had begun to wonder again if anything would happen before sundown when he saw Green riding along the edge of the woods. The general dismounted to speak to his artillery chief, Major Semmes, and the batteries' officers gathered around him. Jamie hastened to join them. Green glanced up as he arrived, looking tired but by no means ready to quit. He gave Jamie a nod.

"Howdy, Russell. How's the head?"

"Better, sir, thanks."

Green grinned, then turned to Major Semmes. "Which battery is that on your left, against the road?"

"The Valverde, sir."

"They get the honor of opening the ball. Move all three of these batteries out to face those Yankee guns on the hill there." Green turned to Captain Nettles. "Tim, open up as soon as you are in position and fire on them with all you've got. When the rest of you boys get in place you join in. Lots of noise, gentlemen. We want all the Yanks looking your way."

Jamie gave a nod, feeling the muscles of his back start to tighten. They were to distract the enemy to cover some other movement, no doubt. It would make them a target, but that was part of the job, and after standing idle the previous day while the infantry and cavalry took hell from the Yankees, it was only right that the batteries should do their part. It would be good to get in a few licks of their own.

Green gave a few more instructions to Semmes, then mounted up and rode off toward the woods. Jamie returned to the battery with Nettles, Hume, and Foster, then summoned his sergeants and gave them their orders. In a few minutes they were moving onto the road. Jamie sat erect in the saddle as the battery formed in column and started forward, passing between Buchel's and Debray's regiments, who moved out of the road to let them by. He caught Debray's eye as they passed and they exchanged a nod.

The battery advanced at a brisk pace, and when they were past the cavalry Major Semmes directed them to turn off to the right of the road. Jamie was conscious of thousands of eyes watching their deployment. There were even more men on the field than there had been yesterday—more Yankees, certainly. The very air seemed charged with electricity; he saw everything with crystal clarity, from the pale edges of drying clay along the red mud gashes made by his carriage wheels in the grass to the gleam of distant muskets carried by the Yankee infantry. His gaze fell on Sergeant O'Niell, on Private Biggs, on other men of his command, and to each he thought silently, *Don't die.*

He glanced up at the Yankee battery and thought he saw movement there; they might already be preparing to fire. He adjusted the howitzer's position slightly, then ordered his sergeants to load to the ready. Watching his men move smoothly through their routine, he felt a swell of pride. They were ready; he turned to Nettles, who sat his mount behind his old section, which he still commanded. Nettles was watching Hume, whose guns were just getting into battery, having been in the rear. Beside Hume Moseley's battery was moving into position. Nettles glanced at Jamie, then gave the signal to fire.

The first volley was almost in unison. Jamie had his glasses trained on the enemy battery and saw the shells burst, one high, two others short; the rest were out of his sight.

In seconds the Yankee infantry opened fire. Most of the bullets passed overhead, but a few found their marks and Jamie swallowed at the sudden cries of the wounded. The Yankee battery fired and their first volley got close enough to make him flinch. He glanced to his left, hoping the other batteries would open soon. The butcher's bill would be steep for this fight.

Smoke heavy with the smell of powder drifted around him and faded. His cannoneers were loading the next round. Their orders were to fire at will, so the howitzer barked again before the 6-pounder or the other sections were ready, the shell bursting close enough to the enemy battery to cause a bit of stir among the Yankee cannoneers. Jamie gave a grim little smile. He liked that gun. If he could replace it, he'd arrange to send it back to San Antonio, at his own expense if need be. It shouldn't be given away or melted down, not with the names of the honored dead, Martin's included, engraved on its barrel. It was a monument to their sacrifice.

The barrage intensified, minié balls whining, shells roaring overhead or thudding deep into the soft ground to burst in showers of mud. Jamie saw one of his gunners go down and winced; Sergeant Schroeder stepped into his place, took the hausse from the fallen man's hand and calmly sighted the piece. After the round was fired the sergeant moved another man into the gunner's position, and the dance continued.

A round of case shot burst overhead and spat musket balls in all directions, thudding into the ground like a sudden squall of hail. Cocoa flinched and squealed; Jamie needed a quick hand to keep her from bolting. She let out a loud, frightened neigh. He cast a glance over her and found what he feared—a long, ugly gash on her left hindquarter. He reached forward to pat her neck, feeling her trembling beneath his hand. "Don't die," he murmured, though she wouldn't hear him over the din.

Moseley's battery opened and the pressure eased a bit as some of the Yankee infantry shifted their attention away from the Valverde guns. When West's battery opened as well, the Yankee battery panicked and fled, leaving two of their guns on the hilltop. Jamie whooped and shouted the news to his men, who raised a loud cheer.

"Direct your fire on that infantry battalion," Jamie told his sergeants, and watched them comply, wondering if there was any chance of capturing the abandoned guns. To do so they would have to convince the Yankee infantry to retire, which was a hard proposition. General Green seemed to have the same idea in mind, though; within a few minutes he sent orders for all three batteries to advance. Jamie passed the word to cease firing and limber up, then took a swallow of water to moisten his throat.

Minié balls hummed all around and Jamie kept expecting to halt, but it wasn't until they were within two hundred yards of the hilltop that Major Semmes ordered them into battery. By that time the noise of the rifle balls was constant. Jamie expected to be hit any minute, being mounted. He remembered Mouton and his staff getting on their horses the previous day, the better to lead their charge. Every one of them had been struck.

Such thoughts did him no good. With an effort he put them aside and concentrated his attention on his section. On Nettles's order he opened fire on the infantry supports directly behind where the Yankee battery had been, his object to keep them from withdrawing the abandoned guns. He wondered if the action the artillery movement was masking had begun. If it had not, it must soon, before the batterymen were used up.

As if in answer to his thoughts he heard a rumble of hoofbeats from behind, and glanced back to see General Bee leading Debray's and Buchel's cavalry up the road. His heart leapt, but at once he thought they were too few. He looked toward the left to see if more cavalry would join the charge, but saw none there—they had moved elsewhere—Debray and Buchel were alone. Heart thundering, Jamie urged Cocoa to Schroeder, then to O'Niell, ordering them both to lay covering fire for the charge. There was no more he could do but watch as the two small brigades dashed forward. He expected to see them form and hurl themselves against the Yankee line and be broken like a wave on rocks, but they did not make it that far. A regiment of Yankee infantry rose up from concealment behind a fence that paralleled the road, and fired into the cavalry column, bringing the charge to a halt. Wounded horses reared and screamed, their riders tumbling to the ground. Those who had not been hit moved into the sparse shelter of a few pines east of the road. Buchel, who had been in the rear and not taken the full force of the volley, pulled his cavalry back. Jamie saw General Bee's horse shot under him. Bee caught another whose rider had fallen and mounted it, only to have it killed as well. Debray's horse went down with him; neither got up. Jamie's throat began to ache and he realized his face had formed a frowning mask. The remnants of cavalry were between him and the Yankees who had caused such havoc; his guns could not help them. He glanced at his section, still firing at the main Yankee line, then looked back in time to see Debray alive, on foot, leaning on his sword as he limped to the rear. He gave a gasp of relief.

Buchel had dismounted his troopers. Leaving his horses behind, the Prussian commander led his men on foot to attack the Yankee ambuscade. Jamie felt a thrill when, a few minutes later, the attack succeeded and the Yankees were driven back to their line. Bee withdrew the remaining cavalry and Buchel's dismounted men in fairly good order, but Jamie watched in growing dismay as he realized Colonel Buchel had not returned with his men.

What had gone wrong? Something must have—Taylor could not have planned to send only Bee's cavalry against the whole Yankee line. A minié ball's hornet whine reminded Jamie he had no leisure to think about it; with Bee's retreat, the Yankees returned their full attention to the artillery. A shell from the more distant batteries ploughed the ground, passing within six feet of one of his caissons before bursting. He caught his breath and glanced toward Nettles. All the batteries were taking casualties; they were too close to the Yankee line. Jamie let go of the last shred of hope that they could capture two more Yankee guns. He would settle for getting out of this alive.

Nat eased the *Cricket* around a bend in the river, moving slowly not only because of the unfamiliar channel but with the memory of the *Queen*'s misadventure at DeRussy in mind. They were high in the Red, having spent several days navigating its tortuous course to bring supplies and additional troops to a planned juncture with General Banks at Loggy Bayou. The expedition, which included twenty-six army transports escorted by six of the lightest-draft gunboats, had reached the appointed place after numerous groundings and delays early in the afternoon on April 10th. They had found no waiting envoy from Banks, but surprised a Confederate scout and nearly captured them as a landing party from the *Cricket* rushed ashore. While the Rebels ran, the sailors collected their abandoned property including some letters from General Taylor which seemed to amuse Admiral Porter. The Admiral had set the transports to unloading their cargo, then decided to reconnoiter upstream in the *Cricket*.

As a new length of the river came in view Nat's heart tried to leap out of his chest. He grabbed at the bell-cord and signaled all stop. Immediately she slowed, and Nat stood gripping the wheel, staring at the alarming sight of an enormous steamer crossways in the river, completely blocking the channel.

He heard excited voices and hurried footsteps. Having seen the *Cricket* safely to a stop, he came out of the pilot house to get a better look at the obstruction. Gorringe and Admiral Porter joined him at the fore of the hurricane deck.

It was the steamboat *New Falls City*, as proclaimed in grand letters on her wheelhouse. She was not only sideways, but so large that her bow and stern rested on either shore, and she had been broken in the middle to further ensure she would block the river. A banner made from what looked like several bedsheets adorned her upper deck, and on it was painted in large letters a cordial invitation to attend a ball in Shreveport.

Admiral Porter let out a crack of laughter. "That is the smartest thing I have ever known the Rebels to do."

"Can we remove her?" Gorringe asked.

Porter fingered his beard, frowning slightly. "We have the means. It will take days, though, and we may have to dredge the channel. I'll give you odds there's a sand bar making below her there."

As they discussed the removal of the wreck Nat cast an uneasy glance toward the shore, wondering how General Banks would react to this development. Doubtless he would be displeased to learn that his naval support would be delayed by a week or more in arriving at Shreveport.

"Wheat, take us back to the landing," Porter told him, then turned back to Gorringe. "We will send up the tugboats and have their crews start work at once."

Nat returned to the pilot house. The river was too low for the *Cricket* to turn; he would have to back her downstream. Tedious work, as the pilot house was farther from the stern than the bow and he had also to account for the paddle wheel, which was out of his view. He signaled reverse slow to the engine room, and stood beside the wheel facing astern. The pilot house was small enough that this was an awkward position, and by the time the *Cricket* had crept back down to the landing his shoulder was becoming stiff.

The transports had already disgorged a large quantity of cargo, mostly crates of rations, onto the shore. Nat took the *Cricket* below, out of the way of the tugboats that would soon be sent up to the wreck. Once he had landed her he went down to the wardroom and asked the steward for coffee. A couple of the gunboat's officers were at the table chatting about the *New Falls City*. Nat joined them, sipping his coffee and debating whether to retire to his cabin in the hope of catching an hour or so of sleep, or stay up on the probability that Porter would want to accompany the tugs back to the wreck. Before he could make up his mind, Gorringe appeared and cast a glance around the wardroom. "Wheat, come with me," he said a bit sharply.

Nat left his coffee on the wardroom table and followed Gorringe out. "Banks's messenger arrived," the captain told him. "He has just been with the admiral."

Gorringe gave him no time to ask questions, but took him straight to the admiral's quarters. The army captain had delivered his message and gone, it seemed, for Admiral Porter sat at his desk, frowning over a letter. He put this down when Nat and Gorringe came in.

"Mr. Wheat, in your opinion may the boats safely be turned at this point?"

Nat considered briefly, then shook his head. "Some of the smaller vessels could use the mouth of the bayou to turn, but there is not enough water for the gunboats."

Porter gave a nod, as if this were the answer he expected. "We shall have to back them down to Coushatta, then. As soon as the transports are loaded we will depart." He glanced up and must have seen Nat's confusion, for he added, "Banks was whipped, and is falling back on Grand Ecore."

Nat's heart sank. It no longer mattered that the expedition could not proceed to Shreveport; the difficulty would be in getting them back down the river to safety. Without the army's protection they were vulnerable to attacks from the shore. Nat swallowed, remembering a half dozen places they had passed on the way up where the riverbanks were higher than the *Cricket*'s pilot house. In a place like that the Rebels could pour hell down on them, and the gunboats would not be able to elevate their guns enough to reply.

"By the way," Porter said, sifting through the papers on his desk, "that scout we nearly bagged left behind a letter you might find interesting. One of Taylor's staff was a member of the party, and he abandoned his correspondence along with his supper." He found a single page, oft folded and with battered edges, which he proffered to Nat.

The outside of the page was addressed to General Richard Taylor, and endorsed with a note from Taylor instructing his staff officer to respond. Nat unfolded it and read a request that he imagined Taylor must have received scores of times from frightened and desperate planters, a request for assistance in shipping cotton to Mexico to be sold to the French. It was not until he read the signature that Nat understood why Porter had given it to him. He swallowed and looked up at the admiral, who was watching him with a wry expression.

"That's right. It is from our kind and pleasant hostess at Belle View. Curious that she didn't mention it to us, wouldn't you say? Her old overseer was telling the truth after all."

Nat handed the letter back. "What will you do?"

Porter gave a short, sharp laugh. "Ask me again when we have extricated ourselves from this thrice-cursed river."

29

I do not see why a fleet should not have the protection of an army as well as an army have the protection of a fleet.
—David D. Porter, Rear-Admiral, U.S. Navy

Jamie urged his men forward through the woods with as much speed as they could muster though he was dog-tired himself. General Green wanted his guns at the river right away, and Jamie could hear cannon fire already. He had just this hour got his section across a deep bayou, there being only one flatboat ferry with which to cross the two batteries and several regiments of infantry Green had brought with him from Pleasant Hill. They had left that place of misery at six the previous night and marched through the dark hours, then snatched what sleep they could while waiting to cross the bayou.

Green's impatience was clear; he had sent word to Jamie not to wait for the rest of the battery to cross but to bring his section up to the river at once, as the Yankee gunboats were already arrived near Blair's Landing. Jamie was beginning to get an inkling of what life must be like for Green's cavalrymen, and was privately glad he was not one of them.

He had not slept well the night after the battle. Shortly after Bee's disastrous charge at Pleasant Hill the Valverde battery and its neighbors had been pulled back from their advanced position, and thereafter took part in the fight only at a distance. They had suffered heavy casualties during their time of exposure; Jamie's section alone had lost two men killed and five wounded. He now had no extra men left. They were all in the gun crews, which were still short. He had also lost one horse killed and two so badly hurt that they had to be put down. He was grateful not to have lost Cocoa; her wound had not damaged bone, and though she was favoring her left hind she seemed to be healing all right.

The fight at Pleasant Hill had not gone well for General Taylor. Bee's charge had been meant to occur after the Confederate right had attacked and demoralized the Federal left flank, and Green had indeed ordered it forward at the sound of fighting from that direction, but the flank attack had gone wrong and the division making it had ended up in between two lines of Yankees, and suffered accordingly. The whole battle had been plagued with mistakes and misunderstandings. Taylor had finally called it off at dusk, after two of his divisions fired on each other in the twilight. Both armies spent the night on the field, shivering in the dark and listening to the anguish of the wounded. The following day Taylor sent his cavalry back to Mansfield to find fodder for their starving horses, and Banks began to withdraw. The Yankees left their wounded and dead on the field, but Taylor declined to take prisoner the Yankee surgeons who had remained behind, and instead supplied their wants and left them to their work.

With Banks in retreat the Yankee fleet had started back down the Red, according to the staff officer Taylor had set to watch them. Taylor wanted them stopped. Green had taken up the march on the road that led from Pleasant Hill to Blair's Landing. He had two infantry brigades—one of raw recruits fresh from Texas who had arrived too late for the battles—and Cornay's and Nettles's batteries with which to oppose the gunboats, but it looked as if they would not all get across the bayou in time.

The sound of cannon fire intensified as Jamie's section drew near to the river. He could already smell the water's-edge odor of rotting wood. He drew a deep breath, feeling less than prepared for another fight. Part of him was so weary he just wanted to quit—turn around and ride back home to Texas—but he could not do that. Those were Cornay's guns firing; he could not abandon his friend, much less go home carrying the shame of having failed General Green.

He reached the shore and found Green's infantry in line along the riverbank beneath sheltering cottonwoods, while Cornay was exchanging brisk compliments with the guns on a handful of Yankee boats. Two of these—a low floating contraption armored over in steel plates, and a steamer heavily laden with cavalry horses—were apparently stuck on sandbars in the middle of the stream; other steamers lay nearby trying to help float the distressed vessels. Most of them, except for the armored gunboat, were unprotected but for makeshift barricades of cotton bales, sacks of grain, and bundled hay, which provided cover to sharpshooters. Each steamer had a field piece mounted on its uppermost deck, and these and the gunboats were harassing Cornay. Jamie saw that the Louisiana captain was on foot and his guns were being moved by their cannoneers; Cornay's horses must have been killed by the Yankees. He decided to waste no time getting his section into battery. Green could move him if he didn't like his position. He chose a spot that afforded a good sweep of the river, and placed his guns beneath the cottonwoods and the caissons back in the woods, hoping that a little distance would offer some protection for the teams.

Even before he opened fire his section drew the attention of the gunners on the boats. Jamie kept moving, having no wish to make a perfect target of himself for some sharpshooter. He was already tempting, being possibly the only mounted figure in sight. He thought of sending Cocoa back to the caissons, but she would only be marginally safer there, and he needed her. She was nervous at being under fire again, but steady enough.

"Fire on the gun ports," Jamie told his sergeants, hoping to ease the pressure on Cornay.

The gunboats flung canister and grapeshot at the shore; Jamie replied with shell, knowing that each round he got into the interior of a boat would cause havoc when it exploded. The fight stormed on for an hour and more. Jamie moved his section several times, whenever the Yankee guns found his range too accurately. Once he rode to Cornay and offered a horse, but the Louisianan shook his head, grinning, eyes alight with battle-fire.

"I will stay on foot, me. My men cannot move fast enough to escape me!"

Jamie laughed, wished him well, and rode back into the woods to look for a new position for his own guns. The armored gunboat managed to get itself free and float down the river, sweeping the shore with canister from its heavy guns. Jamie saw Green striding along the infantry line, shouting encouragement to the recruits, who were cowering behind the trees trying to evade the gunboat's fire. He remembered cowering in just such a way himself, in his first fight, then finding the courage to follow Colonel Green into the fray at Valverde.

Green got hold of a horse and mounted it, yelling, "I'll show you how to fight!" With a bloodcurdling yell he rode along the riverbank in front of the recruits. Some of them took heart and came forward to fire at the boats, which responded with more rounds of canister and case. One of these, aimed at a company of infantry, exploded just as Green was riding in front of them and took off top of his head.

Green's horse panicked and spun round in a circle, the force of its motion strong enough that the general's body remained upright for a few seconds, flinging blood in all directions. Jamie gasped, then choked at the horrible sight. At last the body collapsed, sliding to the ground where the horse, calm now though its flanks dripped with blood, stood quietly over its fallen master.

Jamie stared in shock at General Green's corpse, finding it hard to breathe. The batterymen stood at their posts in stunned silence. The infantry had already vanished into the woods, which would have been a disaster except that the Yankees had also ceased firing. No one was much inclined to fight anymore today, it seemed. The battle faded to nothing as the sun began to set, sending tree shadows across the glimmering river. A surgeon came forward to confirm what everyone knew; Tom Green, hero of San Jacinto and Valverde, was dead.

Biting his lip to keep his jaw from shaking, Jamie rode to his sergeants and ordered them to withdraw the guns into the woods. He should go to Green's next in command for orders. He could not remember who that was.

One by one the boats glided away, except for the cavalry transport, still stuck on the bar. Jamie accompanied his guns back from the shore and encountered Cornay in the woods, the laughter gone from his face.

"I am sorry, mon ami."

Jamie felt the tears finally coming forward. "Mouton, now Green," he said in a strangled voice.

"Yes."

And Reily, and dozens of others. Daniel, too. They were all blending into one deep pain that it seemed would never go away.

Silently Cornay offered Jamie his flask. Silently Jamie took it, raised it to Green and drank enough to make his eyes sting. They remained together, not talking, not needing words. It was dusk before they received orders to limber up and move down the river road. They would march through the night again to get ahead of the Yankee fleet, which tended to prefer navigating in daylight. Tomorrow they would try again to destroy the fleet that had killed General Green.

Marie rubbed her eyes, weary of struggling to find hopeful news in her accounts. The numbers had begun to blur together in the ledgers. She considered lighting an additional lamp, but her supply of oil was low. She had sent Zeb, who had assumed many of Damien's handyman duties, to St. Francisville for this and other supplies that morning, though she suspected there was no lamp oil to be had. He had not yet returned, which was one reason she had gone back to work after supper, so as to be available when he arrived. If he arrived. Perhaps it was weariness, but she had begun to wonder whether Zeb had taken advantage of the opportunity to run. About a dozen of the field hands had done so this spring, after a rumor that Yankees would lift them up into a place of plenty had spread through the quarters. About half the truants had wandered back, having discovered no benevolent Yankees waiting to welcome them within twenty miles.

A soft knock at the library door made her look up. "Come in."

Alphonse entered. "Madame, Mr. Petrie is here."

"Mr. Petrie? At this hour?"

Alphonse's expression was normally unreadable, but she saw a grim glint in his eyes. "He has brought Zeb. He found him on the Angola road. He had been robbed and beaten."

Marie rose from her chair in sudden alarm, then clasped her hands together, seeking self-command. "Is Zeb alive?"

Alphonse nodded. "Damien and Lucinde are caring for him."

"Ask Mr. Petrie to come in."

She walked to the fireplace, where a small blaze was burning to keep back the evening chill, and rested her hands upon the mantel, looking up at Theodore's portrait. A moment later she turned to face the door as Alphonse showed Mr. Petrie into the room.

He was only a year or so older than she, a very serious young man with straight dark hair and whiskers, all of which he kept trimmed short. She knew that he was reading law in the hope of applying for the bar. He stayed near the door, perhaps conscious of his rough outdoor clothing.

"Please sit down, Mr. Petrie." Marie took a chair by the fire, and watched him sit somewhat hesitantly on the sofa.

"I apologize for intruding upon you at this hour—"

"Do not consider it. I understand I have to thank you for rescuing my servant."

The overseer nodded. "Yes, ma'am. I was just coming in from Angola—I had gone to consult with Daly about the cotton planting—and I found your boy in the ditch beside the road. He had been trying to walk to the sugarhouse, but collapsed before he could reach it."

Marie swallowed. "Did he tell you what happened?"

"Yes, ma'am. Apparently he encountered Mr. Shelton in the village, and was forced to listen to his nonsense for a time. Your boy went about his business, but when he left for home Shelton followed him, took his horse, and beat him near senseless."

Marie closed her eyes briefly, then opened them and frowned into the fire. She should have known that Shelton would continue to annoy her.

"How badly was Zeb hurt?"

"I think he will recover, though I am fairly certain one or two ribs were broken. He is greatly concerned about the loss of the horse."

Marie smiled, shaking her head. "I will speak to him."

"Ma'am?"

She looked up at Mr. Petrie, whose face showed deep concern. He leaned forward a little and cleared his throat.

"Your boy said that Shelton made threats. I do not know if they were idle or not. He said—well, a number of things, but the main idea seems to have been that he means to come up here and take your cotton, and sell it to the Yankees."

Marie felt anger stiffening her shoulders. She threw them back, and with effort relaxed her hands, which had clenched the arms of her chair. "I have no doubt that he would like to do so. Idle or not, I will take his threat seriously. Mr. Petrie, what would you do in case of an attempt to take cotton from Killarney Plantation?"

"I have a pistol and a shotgun in my possession. Other than that, I have no defenses."

"Would you trust any of your drivers to be armed, or would providing them with weapons only encourage them to start an uprising in the slave quarters?"

He looked at her in growing surprise, then considered the question. "There are three or four I would trust with firearms, and we have a number of machetes, if it came to that. An uprising is not likely, I think. Particularly if the threat came from Shelton." He smiled slightly. "You are pretty highly regarded in the quarters, ma'am."

Marie was surprised at how much this pleased her, but let it pass for the moment. She had larger matters to think of, such as how best to protect her resources, which were scattered over five plantations.

"I have two dozen shotguns, with about five hundred rounds of ammunition. I have also my husband's sporting rifles, and his pistols."

She rose and went to the cabinet where Theodore's guns were kept, beckoning to Mr. Petrie to follow her. Withdrawing her keys from her pocket, she found the one that unlocked the cabinet and threw open its door, then turned to Mr. Petrie, whose face had gone grave.

"You may choose one for yourself. How many shotguns do you think you may need?"

"Six?"

She nodded. "I will have them brought to you, with ammunition. Please keep me advised of any unusual activity near Killarney. You might consider setting a watch at night."

"I will."

Marie looked at him expectantly. He hesitated, then selected a rifle. She gave him a box of cartridges from the shelf above the guns and locked the cabinet once more. She asked him a few more questions about the state of Killarney, then saw him out, thanking him again for bringing Zeb home as she walked with him to the back door.

"Mr. Petrie," she said as he reached for the handle, "when you have occasion to go into the village, may I suggest that you carry your pistol? Mr. Shelton may be emboldened by his success against an unarmed servant."

His eyes flashed with an emotion she could not quite read. Indignation, perhaps. "Yes, ma'am. You are right, of course. I will be cautious."

"Good night, Mr. Petrie."

"Good night, Mrs. Hawkland."

She watched him carry the rifle down the steps to where his horse was tied. A quarter moon was rising, casting just enough light to enable her to see Mr. Petrie pause to load the rifle and lash it to his saddle in such a way that he could quickly free it, before riding away.

Across the yard she saw a light burning in the upper storey of the household slaves' quarters—Zeb's room. She must visit him, find out from him what Shelton had said that Mr. Petrie had been too gentlemanly to tell her—personal threats against herself, she suspected—and allay his concerns about the horse. She sighed, turning back to the library to fetch her shawl. This night was far from over.

Nat stood on deck with a cup of coffee in hand, watching the preparations being made for the destruction of the *Eastport*. It was midmorning, and the flagship, along with the gunboats *Fort Hindman* and *Juliet*, and transports *Champion No. 5* and *Champion No. 3,* had spent five weary days accompanying the ironclad as she limped downstream toward Alexandria, now only sixty miles away. Admiral Porter was unwilling to give up on her, but today he had finally admitted defeat.

Ten days since she had been hulled by a torpedo the Rebels had placed in the river, and sunk up to her gun deck. Pumps had been taken aboard her and the *Champion No. 5* had taken her in tow. Enormous effort had been expended to get her afloat and drag her down the river over rocks, bars, and a multitude of logs. She had grounded badly no less than eight times. The ninth, and final, time she stuck fast right across the channel and Admiral Porter had at last been forced to conclude she could not be saved. A thousand pounds of powder were now being distributed about her, enough to render her useless to the Rebels, though with time and effort they might be able to salvage her iron plates. Porter had even entertained hopes of bringing these away, but Nat's experience at the shipyard had enabled him to provide the admiral with an accurate estimate of the time and labor that would be required for such an undertaking. Porter had abandoned the idea.

Nat sighed, glancing toward the river's right bank, to which the *Cricket* had made fast. A slight movement there caught his attention and he paused, peering at the trees. Rebel guerrillas had plagued the fleet throughout their descent of the river over the last two weeks; they made especial targets of the unarmored transports, but the gunboats were not immune to their attentions. Nat set his cup on the deck and took out his glass, peering at the shore. What he saw made him leap to the deck bell and ring it sharply to get the attention of all hands, then dash into the pilot house and signal the engine room to bring up full steam.

Gorringe called up the ladder well from the wardroom below. "What is it?"

"Guerrillas," Nat shouted back. "Better cast off!"

Even as he said it, the first crackle of rifle fire began from on shore. The Rebels had abandoned their cover in the trees and were making a rush to board the *Cricket*. Nat felt a moment's panic, then a broadside of canister and shrapnel from the *Cricket*'s guns greeted the Rebels, checking their charge. The deck hands that had gone out to cast off from the shore scurried inside through the forward doors, which closed after them with a heavy clang. Immediately Nat signaled ahead half, and drew away from the bank as quickly as he dared, his heart thundering. The Rebels continued to fire and the *Cricket*'s guns answered, joined by those of the *Juliet* and *Fort Hindman,* sweeping the woods. Gorringe came into the pilot house, eyes alight with excitement.

"Did you see them fall back? They are no match for our guns!"

Nat raised an eyebrow. "Lucky they had no artillery. Some of the Rebel bands have."

"Field pieces. They cannot compete with our heavy guns."

Nat declined to take up the argument. After another half hour, Gorringe at last convinced himself that the Rebels had gone, and reluctantly called off the bombardment of the shore. The *Cricket* returned to the bank and a watch was posted. The activity on the *Eastport* resumed.

Nat went out on the hurricane deck again, and soon Gorringe joined him, saying, "I am surprised Admiral Porter didn't destroy her sooner. He was on the verge of ordering it two days ago, did you know?"

Nat shook his head. "We should never have brought her above the rapids. We keep hearing the river will rise, but instead it continues to fall."

Gorringe's face grew serious. "The admiral has received some intelligence with regard to that. The Rebels have been diverting the water into the lakes up near Shreveport."

Appalled, Nat looked at the shore. Lines of white sediment striped the rocks and the bare roots of cottonwood trees that had once stood in water. The river was not just low, it was being killed.

"We'll never get the ironclads over the falls."

Most of the fleet was above the Alexandria rapids. The *Cricket* had been all the way down to the city before returning to assist the *Eastport,* but she had scraped bottom coming back up, and she drew only four feet. Nat's stomach sank as he realized they might lose more than just the *Eastport.*

In silence he and Gorringe watched the final preparations for the ironclad's destruction. By midafternoon all was ready. The small boats drew back, and all prepared for the shock of the blast. After twenty minutes, nothing had happened. Watching through their glasses, Nat and Gorringe saw Commander Phelps, the *Eastport*'s captain, return to the gunboat.

"That electrical gadget must have failed," Gorringe said. "Phelps will have to light the fuse by hand."

Nat nodded. "I hope he gets clear in time."

Porter's launch drew near to the *Eastport* as well, and the admiral appeared to exchange words with Phelps. The commander disappeared into *Eastport*'s main deck, then returned almost at once and leaped into his boat. The oarsmen had not pulled more than twice when an explosion ripped through the gunboat's guts, flinging splinters in all directions, all over both the small boats. Nat winced for their occupants, but if anyone was hurt it seemed not to be serious. The boats quickly pulled away from the *Eastport* as a second explosion, then a third, followed. More blasts went off as the various caches of powder detonated, then flames engulfed what remained of the upper decks. Despite all the frustration she had caused, Nat was saddened by the sight. It was sad to see any vessel perish, and grim to think that this scene might be played again many times over before long.

Admiral Porter returned to the *Cricket,* looking weary and dispirited. Dinner was piped. Nat swallowed a hasty meal for which he had little appetite, then returned to the pilot house. After filling her hold with fence rails for fuel—the fleet having long since run out of coal—the *Cricket* cast off and slowly moved downstream with the other boats, abandoning the wreckage that was all that remained of the *Eastport.*

Jamie lowered his field glasses and turned Cocoa southward, clicking to her for a trot. The road ran along a bluff at this part of the river, and he had volunteered to stand watch at a bend upstream of where his section and the St. Mary's Cannoneers stood, just above the mouth of the Cane River. Cornay's battery was still without horses. A detachment of two hundred Louisiana infantrymen had been posted with them, the Texas recruits who had witnessed Green's death being utterly demoralized and useless. They had gone back to the army, which was pursuing Banks's retreat toward Alexandria.

"Whoa," Jamie called softly as they reached the battery, and Cocoa dropped to a walk, then halted and blew a sigh. Jamie dismounted and went to where Cornay was standing with Lieutenant-Colonel Caudle, a Texan, in command of the detachment.

"They are coming," Jamie told them. "Five boats at least."

Caudle gave a nod. "Good. Get your men to their posts. We'll see if we can relieve them of a boat or two." He strode off toward his riflemen.

Jamie turned to Cornay. In the past two weeks, as they had dogged the boats down the river, he had taken to treating the captain as his commander, though his section had not formally been assigned to Cornay's battery. It made sense to function as a six-gun battery, and Jamie had found himself usually in accord with the Louisianan, who was both shrewd and daring. He had even taught Jamie a few words of French—commands, mostly.

Cornay smiled, blue eyes glinting. "Bon chance, Jacques."

"And good luck to you."

"You will get a boat today, I think."

"If you don't get 'em first with those 12-pounders. I'll be lucky if I get to mop up after you."

Cornay laughed. "C'est la guerre."

"What does that mean?"

"It means, 'That is war.'"

Cornay offered a hand, and Jamie shook it, smiling. They parted, Cornay striding off calling for his own lieutenants, and Jamie going to where his men sat resting beneath the trees. He called his section to attention and had them load to the ready, then mounted Cocoa and watched through his glasses for the first sign of a boat rounding the bend. Evening was coming on but there would still be another hour or so of light, enough to get in a few licks on the Yankee boats.

Within minutes he could see a thin trail of smoke, and soon afterward the bow of a boat came around the bend. It was one of the lightly armored tinclads, and was flying a blue flag. Jamie recalled someone telling him that meant it was an admiral's boat. He held his fire, waiting for the boat to come closer, but she must have seen the battery for she opened fire with two bow guns. Cornay's four guns replied at once, and Jamie signaled his sergeants to fire.

The gunboat came on slowly, giving the battery ample time to fire at her. Jamie had Schroeder aim at a small gun on her uppermost deck, quickly dispersing its crew. The guns on the lowest deck were protected by the armor, but it was not very thick and though it repelled the infantry's bullets the shells had little trouble getting through it.

The boat's fire slackened even as she drew closer to the battery. Jamie saw a shell from one of Cornay's guns go right through a gun port and explode within the boat in a flash of fire and smoke. He glanced over at Cornay, grinning. The Louisianan grinned back, then shouted to his men, urging them on in words Jamie couldn't hear. Probably French. He was turning back to his own guns when the sound of a shell bursting made him look back.

Cornay was gone. The men he had been standing near had been knocked to the ground, leaving their gun unattended.

"No!" Jamie screamed, a futile sound at once swallowed up by the roar of the guns.

Nat clung to the wheel, sweating with fear as the *Cricket* drifted slowly past the battery on the shore. The engine room was not responding to his signals, and Gorringe and Porter had both disappeared below when the *Cricket*'s guns had stopped firing. A minié ball whined through the air in front of his face, so close he could feel the draft. He glanced back at the transport behind him; it was unarmored and crowded with negro refugees. With the *Cricket* in their way they would be sitting ducks for the Rebel artillery. Nat turned forward again, keeping his eyes on the river, not daring to look at the shore. He rang the bell again, hoping for some response. All he could do was keep the boat in the channel and pray that her engine would come up.

Another explosion ripped into the lower decks; Nat felt it through his feet. Bullets pelted the pilot house constantly. One came in and ricocheted around before rattling to a stop on the floor. It was worse than in the Little Red; it was the worst fire he had ever been under, and he felt his mind becoming numb with fear.

"Renata," he said, over and over. Her name was a talisman he clung to, a window to a world that was not madness and hellfire. He didn't dare take out her picture for fear of losing it, but he knew every detail from the many hours he had spent staring at it, so he held it in his mind while his hands tended the wheel.

A horrendous crash struck the pilot house above and behind him. Nat felt a blow in his right side, followed an instant later by searing pain. He reached for the wound and the pain flashed brighter, making him cry out as his hand brushed against something rough. He could feel blood slipping down inside his coat. Swallowing, he gripped the wheel tightly, made sure the boat was still on course, then made himself look beneath his right arm. A jagged, inch-thick splinter of wood protruded about three inches from the wound at an upward angle. He could feel the rest of it inside him with every movement. He looked forward again, then rang another urgent peal on the bell.

His breath came in sharp gasps, each sending a wave of pain through him. The bullets kept coming, and he almost wished one would strike his head and end it all, but it would seem that was not his fate. He clung to the wheel.

One of the *Cricket*'s guns began firing again, somewhat erratically. Nat heard a noise from below; someone was coming up the ladder. He felt faint with relief. Glancing down, he saw that it was Admiral Porter. He tried to collect his wits.

"She's not making way, sir," he shouted above the noise of the bullets.

"Yes, I know," Porter told him, joining him at the wheel. The admiral's face was fierce with concentration. "The chief engineer was killed and his hand was on the valve when he fell," he told Nat. "I have put one of the firemen to bringing up steam. You should have way again in a moment. What is this? Are you wounded?"

"I fear so, sir."

"Give me the wheel."

Nat complied, stumbling backward. He felt the bench against the back of his legs and sank onto it, gingerly leaning back so as not to disturb the splinter, grateful to be relieved of responsibility for the boat, hoping he would not bleed to death before the day was out.

Jamie glanced at his section, saw both guns still firing away, and turned Cocoa so sharply toward where Cornay had stood that she was startled into running the few strides it took to cover the distance. He reined her to a halt, far more roughly than she deserved, and sat staring at the mangled flesh that a moment before had been his friend.

Cornay's body had been pierced by dozens of musket balls. Case shot, Jamie thought numbly. His face was unrecognizable, all one side a bleeding pulp. He must have died instantly.

Jamie became aware of the surviving cannoneers standing, staring. He looked up at them. "Did he tell you to stop? No, so get back to your posts!" His gaze swept their stunned faces, looking for the chief of the piece. He spotted a sergeant.

"You there—get this gun back into action! Kill those bastards, God damn it!"

That meant something to the cannoneers. Determination replaced the shock in their faces. They turned to work, the sergeant detailing two men to carry Cornay to the rear. One of Cornay's lieutenants dashed up as they were lifting the captain's remains onto a blanket. He stared, then turned a stricken face to Jamie. Gordy, Jamie remembered. That was his name.

"You're in command," Jamie told him.

Gordy stood a moment longer, then woke up and began to shout orders in French. Jamie turned back to his guns.

He had no leisure to think about what had happened, and no wish to. He rode between Schroeder and O'Niell, constantly moving, pointing out the gunboat's most vulnerable spots. She had started moving a bit faster, and more boats were coming down, presenting better targets, but Jamie fired on the first boat until it was impractical to continue. He pushed his crews to their limits, wanting to hurt the Yankees as much as possible. O'Niell and Schroeder sensed his rage, for they obeyed silently and without question.

The lead gunboat was nearing a bend and would soon be out of sight. Jamie turned his attention to the next boat, an unarmored steamer. Her decks were crowded with negroes—refugees, from what he could tell through his glasses. He had little interest in them, and after throwing a few shots at the wheelhouses, he turned his attention to the next boats, a steamer and a tinclad lashed together. He wanted the gunboat disabled. He wanted every gunner aboard her dead. He pressed his sergeants to fire at her lower deck, aiming at the gun ports.

A tremendous explosion drew his gaze to the first steamer, the one carrying the negroes. She was instantly enveloped in steam, huge clouds of boiling air billowing out of her lowest deck, bodies jumping or falling from all her decks into the river. Cornay's men cheered at first, then stopped when they realized the horrible fate of those trapped on board.

Jamie returned his attention to the two boats lashed together and fired on the tinclad. He struck her wheelhouse and she seemed to lose control; he kept firing. Soon he was rewarded with a hit that shrouded her with steam, though not so violently as the exploding boiler had done on the transport. Sergeant Schroeder turned an inquiring look his way. Jamie signaled to keep firing. He didn't care if a round or a dozen were wasted; he wanted to do as much damage as possible. Cornay's mangled face flashed in his mind and he clenched his teeth.

A third gunboat sent a shell into the woods just yards from Jamie's guns. He ordered his sergeants to turn their fire on that vessel. The sunset interfered with his vision; he stared through his glasses and realized the two other boats were retreating upstream, the steamer towing the tinclad. The other gunboat kept firing on the battery as it too retreated, covering its two companions. Jamie and the St. Mary's Cannoneers returned shot for shot and then some until the boats passed above the bend. Even then Jamie would not give up; he ordered Schroeder to elevate his 6-pounder to fire over the point.

"Cease firing," a voice said nearby. Jamie looked up to see Lieutenant-Colonel Caudle beside him, mounted on a bay horse.

"They are gone, son," the colonel said gently.

Jamie swallowed. He felt numb, aggrieved, dissatisfied. He looked toward the river, where the St. Mary's Cannoneers were at work hauling victims of the boiler explosion out of the water.

"We will get another crack at them tomorrow," Caudle said. "Pull your guns back thirty yards and bivouac."

Jamie nodded, not trusting his voice. He passed on the order, rode Cocoa back to where the guns would spend the night, and dismounted. He watered her from the Cane River—he did not want her drinking from the Red—and found a grassy spot where she could graze. He untacked her and started to rub her down. The ordinary activity was in such contrast to the fight that it suddenly took his breath away and he stood for a moment with his hands on the mare's back, his mind filled with blood and horror.

Footsteps crunched softly on the forest floor; someone was coming. Jamie drew a shattered breath and squeezed his eyes shut for a second, then turned.

It was Gordy, Cornay's lieutenant, carrying a lantern. Jamie hadn't realized it was that dark. The yellow light dug sharp shadows across the Louisianan's face. He stood looking at Jamie for a moment, then quietly spoke.

"We would like you to come to the wake."

Jamie's gut, which had been clenched in a hard knot, let go a little. He nodded, and slowly followed Gordy back toward the camp.

30

One of my officers has already been asked if "we would not burn our gunboats as soon as the army left," speaking as if a gunboat was a very ordinary affair and could be burned with indifference.

—David D. Porter, Rear-Admiral, U.S. Navy

Steam reached out toward Nat, a living monster that howled with a thousand voices of the scalded dead. He could not run, could not move—he was pinned to the wall by jagged spikes of wood, watching helplessly as his doom approached to claim him. He screamed a wordless protest, his cry rising to blend with the roaring steam as it billowed up to swallow him.

Nat woke with a boat's whistle still echoing in his ears. Sunlight poured across his face from skylights in the cabin of a riverboat. He gasped a few times, catching his breath, and tried to reach up to cover his eyes but a jab of pain in his right side stopped him.

"You all right, sir? Thought I heard you call."

Nat shaded his eyes with his left hand and saw a sandy-haired young man in army uniform standing over him. He had a vague impression of having seen him before.

"Yes."

"Would you like me to bring you anything? Some milk?"

"No. Yes—yes, some milk, thank you."

The fellow gave him a brisk smile and went away. Nat slowly sat up, his side twinging with pain at any sharp movement. He remembered now—he was on a hospital boat at Alexandria. Porter had arranged for him to be carried there along with the rest of the wounded from the *Cricket*. A few wounded from the transport that had exploded were there as well—or had been. Looking around, he saw that most of the beds were now empty.

Nat closed his eyes, remembering the horror of the transport's explosion. He had watched helplessly as the *Cricket,* powerless to help them, had gone on down the river. He had wept for the poor, tormented souls on board and in the water, some who did not know that they were already killed. Like Charlie, they had tried to help the other victims. A few had been fished out of the river by the *Cricket,* but most had been left behind.

His throat tightened. He had been sick, but vague memories of the suffering victims remained with him, some whose scalded skin sloughed off leaving them raw and tormented, some who looked normal but had breathed in steam and died slowly from the damage to their lungs.

Like Charlie. His father had watched his own brother die that way. Nat felt tears returning; he could understand, now, why Father had forbidden him and Quincy to pursue a career that would place them at risk of such a death every day of their lives.

Footsteps sounded on the staircase nearby. Nat wiped at his face with his shirtsleeve, and looked up as Gorringe arrived.

"Good morning! Up and about today, eh? How's the rib?"

Nat swallowed. "Hurts."

Gorringe fixed him with a critical eye. "I came to see if you are fit for an excursion. Looks like perhaps not just yet."

"What sort of excursion?"

"Up to look at the dam. It is set to be finished today."

Nat blinked. "Dam?"

"The army's dam. I told you about it—though you were a bit drifty at the time."

Nat sighed, then winced. "Sorry, I don't remember."

"It is the brainchild of Banks's chief engineer—one Colonel Bailey. They have been working on it nearly two weeks, and it has raised five feet of water above the falls. It is supposed to be the fleet's salvation, though we shall see."

The army orderly returned with a glass of milk. Nat drank it greedily, then gingerly leaned forward to set the empty glass on the deck. When he straightened, wincing at a ripple of pain, he saw Gorringe watching him and managed a smile.

"Are you going up in the *Cricket?*"

"Yes, the admiral wants to inspect the work. I should get back, in fact. Sorry you are not quite up to it."

"I am up to it. I would like to go."

Gorringe looked skeptical. Nat stood up and walked over to fetch his coat, which was hanging on a peg above his bed. He was able to take it down with his left hand, but putting it on defeated him. A surgeon hurried over and took the coat away, shooting an accusing glance toward Gorringe.

"My captain is here to take me for a little exercise," Nat explained.

Gorringe crossed his arms. "I am not here to help you throw yourself back into a fever."

Nat glanced at the surgeon, who said, "You were in a fever for several days. The splinter that struck you cracked a rib, and it was lucky you had a rib just there. It left some wood behind, which we didn't know for a few days. Not to worry, it is all out now and you are mending again."

"Some air will do me good, then, won't it? I will just sit on the deck."

The surgeon gazed at him for a moment, then turned to Gorringe. "You will bring him back by this evening?"

Gorringe sighed. "I cannot promise that, but I will bring him as soon as we return."

The surgeon helped Nat into his coat and handed him his cap. "I hope you will not be sorry presently."

"I won't. Thank you."

Nat started down the stairs with Gorringe, finding it necessary to go down sideways one step at a time, like an old man. Gorringe started to run lightly down the steps, then paused halfway down to turn and wait for him.

"Are you sure about this?"

"Yes, yes. Tell me about this dam. What is it made of?"

Gorringe laughed. "Name it. Rocks, rubble, trees, a sugarhouse that was handy. At least a dozen buildings have been pulled down. Four empty coal barges loaded with boulders. And cotton—that made the speculators happy, as you may imagine."

Nat chuckled, wincing a little. They reached the bottom of the stairs and crossed the stage to the dock. Gorringe let Nat set the pace as they walked along the landing toward the *Cricket*.

The admiral's flag was still on her, hanging limp from the jackstaff. Nat marveled at the damage; she truly had been shot to hell. It was a wonder she had made it past that battery at all.

"She is pretty cut up," he remarked to Gorringe.

"Yes, we took thirty-eight rounds of shot and shell in that fight, and lost half our crew. Her bottom is badly scraped as well. I am only glad she still floats. Lord knows when we may be able to take her up to Cairo for repairs."

They boarded and went up the companionway. By the time they reached the hurricane deck Nat's breath was coming in short chops and he was starting to feel dizzy. Gorringe procured a chair for him and scrounged up a rug to lay over his knees, though the day was getting warm. Nat sank into the chair, deeply grateful to stop moving.

"Thank you. Don't let me be a nuisance."

"You are not. I must go, however; we will cast off soon. Oh—I nearly forgot."

Gorringe reached into his breast pocket and produced three letters, which he handed to Nat. Nat glanced up at him, flushed with sudden pleasure.

"Thank you!"

Gorringe smiled back and cocked an eyebrow. "Enjoy them. We will not be getting any more for a while—the Rebels have blockaded the river below us."

He went away, leaving Nat with a sense of dismay, but this could not last when he had letters from home in his hands. One was from Quincy and two from Renata. He devoured them eagerly. They were all dated in March, around the time the fleet had started up the Red. Renata's were cheerful and loving, filled with Cincinnati gossip, silly stories that made him smile with fond memories and homesickness. Quincy had stuck a damned crocus into his. Nat laughed as it fell out, then tucked the withered bloom behind his ear as he read Quincy's news, which consisted largely of his hopes to return to service soon. Arrangements for his exchange were in train, and he was already in communication with the navy about getting a berth. With any luck he would get a promotion as well. Father was predictably displeased.

The deck bell rang loudly behind him, and Nat carefully turned his head to look back at the pilot house. He did not recognize the man at the wheel. Now that he thought of it, a number of the men he had seen aboard the boat were unfamiliar to him. Perhaps some of the *Eastport*'s crew had transferred to the *Cricket* to make up for her losses.

The trip to the falls was accomplished in under half an hour. The *Cricket* tied up to the right bank, opposite a rocky patch below the dam. The shore was crowded with spectators, military and civilian both.

Nat was amazed at the change that had been wrought. The dam, reaching out from either bank, had created a wide pool at the foot of the lower rapids. On the west it was built of cribbed stone and brick; an endless stream of wagons brought these materials to the shore, where flatboats loaded them and took them out into the river. Hundreds of men from the engineer corps—mostly negro troops—stood shoulder-deep in the water as they added more material to the structure.

On the left bank there were no buildings to be demolished, so the dam on that side was made of trees stacked lengthwise with the current, their boles elevated by intervening crosswise logs that raised the foot end of the dam. The four barges lay side by side in between these two structures, and the only water coming down now was that pouring through the narrow gaps between the barges, which the engineers were working to fill.

Admiral Porter came up onto the hurricane deck accompanied by two aides and stepped to the bow, glancing at Nat as he took out his glass. "Good to see you, Wheat! How are you feeling?"

"Much better, sir. Thank you."

"Come to see what Banks's fellows are up to, eh? Quite a show. Of course, if damming would get the fleet off, we would have been afloat long before this."

Porter's aides laughed. Nat merely smiled, as laughing was painful to him just now. Despite his skepticism, the admiral peered through his glass with an intensity that indicated his interest in the proceedings.

Remembering his own glass, Nat reached into his coat pocket and with only a few twinges was able to get it out and examine the activity on the dam. Gorringe came up on the deck along with his executive officer and a few others. There was much speculation as to whether the dam would work or was a stupendous waste of effort and resources, but as the afternoon wore on it became evident that the water in the pool was rapidly rising.

Porter sent one of his aides off with a message. More of the crew gathered on the decks—Nat could hear voices from the boiler deck below. Their excitement echoed his own; if the dam worked the ironclads would be saved, and the navy and Banks's army would have the might to force their way through any Confederate blockade and get back to the Mississippi.

In the middle of the afternoon three of the gunboats—the *Osage*, *Neosho*, and *Fort Hindman*—were able to pass the upper falls and enter the pool above the dam. The event sparked even greater interest, and attracted more spectators to line the shore. Nothing further occurred, however. Porter's aide returned with the news that another foot of water was needed before the boats could safely pass the falls. Porter went below, and the officers who had gathered on the deck gradually dispersed as the crew returned to their routines.

The dinner pipe sounded, making Nat realize that he was hungry. He got up, somewhat stiff from sitting all afternoon, and put his chair out of the way, then went down to the wardroom where he was made welcome by the *Cricket*'s officers, some of whom were new to him. He learned that the gunboat had received a number of transfers from the crew of the tinclad *Covington,* which had been destroyed three days since by Rebels—cavalry and a four-gun battery—thirty miles below Alexandria. They shared an animated conversation over dinner, discussing how long it would take for the dam to build up another foot of water and whether it would withstand the pressure.

After the meal the officers went about their duties, and Nat, having nothing else to do, repaired to his quarters. He discovered he was sharing them, he presumed with the new pilot. As his things had not been disturbed further than was necessary to add a second cot to the narrow stateroom, he did not mind. He took down Renata's picture—the Patriotic Girl—and gazed at it, smiling softly, feeling a little more hopeful of getting home again before very long.

A knock on the door was followed by Gorringe poking his head in. "There you are. Sorry, old man, but it looks as though we will be here through the night. Do you need anything? Want the surgeon to have a look at you?"

"No, I am all right, thanks. Think I'll rest a bit."

Gorringe nodded. "Tired eh? See you in the morning then."

Nat was indeed tired, and his wound had begun to ache, probably from moving around so much. With some effort he was able to get out of his coat. He hung it on its usual peg, then got into bed with a weary sigh.

Running footsteps woke him to the dim light of early morning and a strange roaring sound. Looking around, he saw that the other cot was empty; it appeared that its occupant had left in a hurry. Nat eased himself up, draped his coat around his shoulders, and went out onto the boiler deck. Many others were there, watching water rush through a large gap in the dam.

Nat stepped to the railing. Someone jostled him, causing him to hiss with sudden pain.

"Sorry."

Nat shook his head in dismissal, unable to move his gaze from the sight of the caged river roaring to freedom. Two of the barges had broken loose and swung down to rest against the rocks below the tree dam on the east side, leaving a wide gap in the center. Nat's hopes seemed to be pouring away with the water.

The crowd stood on the deck, mostly silent. The sun rose, glinting from the spilling water and revealing a large crowd gathered on the bank, growing by the minute.

"Look!" someone said.

Nat glanced up and saw a boat moving near the upper falls. He took out his glass and peered through it.

"It's the *Lexington*!"

Dozens of faces were turned toward the vessel. No one spoke. The *Lexington* scraped her way over the upper falls, evaded a rapid near the middle of the stream, and headed past the three ironclads in the pool, straight toward the gap left by the barges the river had pushed aside. Nat held his breath as she approached the dam under full steam. If she went down wrong, or had not enough water, she could stave in her bows. She pitched forward over the cascade and slid down it, rolled queasily from side to side, hung on the rocks for a moment and then swept through into deep water.

Everyone on the *Cricket* cheered, echoing a roar from the crowds on the bank. Nat joined in with as loud a shout as he could manage, ignoring the twinge it cost him. He watched the *Lexington* glide to the bank, and laughed with relief.

The three boats in the pool quickly moved to follow. *Neosho,* the river monitor on which Nat had declined to serve, took the gap too slowly and submerged, evoking a groan from the watchers. A moment later she rose to the surface again, and was greeted with cheering. The *Osage* and *Fort Hindman* followed without incident, and a general celebration commenced.

The man next to Nat grabbed his hand and shook it, grinning. It hurt him but Nat didn't care. Although the dam had broken, it had proved that the ironclads could come down. There was hope for the fleet after all.

Marie paced the gallery with Théo squalling in her arms. It had rained in the morning, then the day had turned sultry, and Théo could not be made comfortable. She and Sarah had tried singing to him, bathing him, feeding him, distracting him with toys. He cried harder with each new attempt, and at last Marie had given up on anything but walking back and forth, hoping he would exhaust himself. So far he had not.

For days she had tried to think of a plan to protect her cotton. She had sent a message to Mr. Lawford, but feared it would not even reach him before Shelton made some attempt against her. She knew he had friends in Bayou Sara, and that one of them had a flatboat. She was almost ready to let him have as many bales as the boat would carry, except that she knew he would only come back for more. She feared very much that she was about to be forced into a war, and was at a loss to know how she could conduct it with two dozen shotguns and a handful of rifles.

Théo howled into her ear; she shifted him to her other hip, bouncing him a little, kissing his brow, murmuring to him. Nothing helped. She looked out at her rosebushes, now blooming, and longed to run down the drive between them. Yes, she decided.

"Sarah!"

Marie turned and strode toward the front doors, where the girl was sitting on the steps stitching a jacket for Théo. She looked up as her mistress approached.

"Take him. I am going for a ride."

"Now? But it is so warm—"

"I need the exercise, and I need to think. I will not be out long."

She gave Théo into his maid's arms and went into the house, passing through the hall and out the back doors. She looked about the yard intending to summon the handyman, but saw only the cook, plucking a chicken. Returning to the house she called to her footman. He came out of the butler's pantry, looking startled.

"Victor, run to the stables and tell them to saddle my mare. Where is Zeb?"

His face went blank, reminding her strongly of Alphonse. "I do not know, Madame."

"Never mind. Is Lucinde downstairs? Ask her to come up to my chamber."

"Oui, Madame."

Marie ran up the stairs. In her bedchamber she began to undress, and had already pulled her habit and riding breeches out of the wardrobe by the time Lucinde arrived.

"Ah, bien. Fetch my riding boots, please."

"Madame, I think it is too warm for you to ride."

"Nonsense. I ride in warmer weather than this. My mare has not been out all week, and neither have I." Marie stepped out of her skirt, letting it collapse onto the floor as she picked up her breeches and put them on.

"But, Madame . . ."

Marie looked up at her servant, who seemed upset. It was unlike Lucinde to fret. Marie gazed at her a moment, then spoke more gently. "Do not be a mother hen, cher. I will not stay out long. I just need to shake out the fidgets."

"Oui, Madame."

Lucinde bent to collect the abandoned skirt, then silently helped her into her habit. Marie watched her, wondering if something was wrong—some trouble in the quarters, perhaps. Usually Lucinde came to her if there was something very wrong.

Lucinde brought out a beaver hat, set it on Marie's head and pinned it to her coiffure, then arranged the veil over her shoulder where she could reach it. Not once did she meet Marie's gaze. When all was done, she stepped back out of the way.

Marie stood watching her for a moment. "Are you all right, Lucinde?"

At that Lucinde looked up in surprise. "Oui, Madame." She conjured a smile. "I hope you enjoy your ride."

"Merci."

Marie went out into the upper hall. She saw Sarah standing in the door of the nursery, holding Théo who had finally stopped crying, though he still fussed. Marie stepped toward him and laid a hand to his cheek, then went down the stairs, pulling on her gloves.

A groom had her horse waiting at the front of the house. The mare tossed her head when she saw her mistress, obviously anxious for a run. As Marie approached, the groom made a step for her with his hands. She allowed him to throw her into the saddle, accepted her whip from him, and with a twitch of the reins started down the drive at a trot, then a canter. She reveled in the breeze made by the mare's pace, smiling as she caught a whiff of rose scent. At the foot of the drive she glanced up at the boats—two today, one the very large gunboat that had lately made itself at home at the mouth of the Red River—and turned south.

Summer was fast approaching. The springtime flowers at the roadside were already fading, and new crops were well underway in the fields. If she could only sell cotton and sugar, everything would be all right. The thought brought her back to her troubles, and she reined the mare in to a trot, thinking.

"Bonjour, Madame!"

Looking up, Marie saw Big George riding across a cotton field to join her, wearing a wide straw hat and mounted on the large mule she had given him. She smiled and halted the mare.

"Bonjour. How is everything at Panola?"

George smiled, showing large white teeth with a gap in the middle. "Going well, Madame. Indigo all in. Do you like to ride over and see?"

"Not today. I do not have time. I just want to ride along the river, let Giselle stretch her legs."

"May I ride with you, Madame?"

Marie turned a quizzical look at him. The big overseer made haste to explain.

"You should not go unescorted, Madame. There are bad people about."

"I doubt I am in danger on my own property."

"But on the road, Madame—we do not know who may come riding. There were Yankees over from one of those boats the other day."

"Yankees? Doing what?"

"Buying carrots and onions from the slave farms, Madame."

"Oh." She sighed. "Very well, you may ride along."

She set the mare in motion again, and Big George's mule easily kept pace. She supposed she should have brought a groom to accompany her, though she hated the idea that her plantations were unsafe for her to travel. Sometimes it seemed that civilization was crumbling around her, that she was living in a ruined world despite the richness of her lands.

After giving her mare a good gallop, Marie reined in to a walk and gazed out at the river below the bluffs. The afternoon sun was becoming quite warm. She came to the road that led to the Angola sugarhouse and Killarney Plantation beyond. It had been cleared of all weeds and newly ditched during the winter. Big George reined in, half-turning his mule down the road.

"Madame, I remember Mr. Petrie wants to speak with you. Will you come?"

Marie circled the mare. "Not today, George. I do not have time."

"It is time for you to turn back, maybe?"

Marie halted the mare and frowned. She looked down the river road, which she had ridden many times. It proceeded along rising bluffs, curved around the lower fields of Angola Plantation, then dropped down the bluff into the woods and ran on to St. Francisville. She looked at George.

"Why do you wish me not to ride on this road?"

George gave a nervous laugh. "I did not say that, Madame."

"Is something wrong at Angola?"

He swallowed, opened his mouth, and closed it without answering. Marie felt a sudden dread.

"What is happening?" she demanded.

Big George looked down at his hands. "You do not want to go there, Madame."

In response she turned and sent the mare galloping down the road. She heard the mule's hoofbeats behind her, but knew George would not dare to lay a hand on her or her mare. She was angry, frightened. Could Shelton have already come to Angola? The cotton sheds were all toward the north side of the plantation, nearer to the river landing, for the bales could not be carried down the bluff. What, then, could be happening in the south fields? She put a hand to her hip, reassuring herself that her pistol still rested in her pocket.

A mile down the road a big live oak was visible off in the field, a landmark between the two lowest fields of Angola. Marie glanced that way and saw movement, so she reined in and started the mare across the field, letting her pick her way through the sharp clumps of new-planted sugar.

"Madame, please—"

She turned to look at George. "Will you tell me what is happening?"

"I . . ."

Marie turned her attention back to the field. What had at first glance appeared to be a work gang now seemed too large for it— more like three or four gangs, and what were they all doing in a field that was already planted? She urged the mare forward, heading toward a man on horseback beneath the tree. She thought it was Damien, but before she could be certain a rumble of hoofbeats drew her gaze farther south. Five men on horseback were galloping across the field—her own slaves, she thought—in fact, one of them looked like Zeb. They were leading a sixth horse with its rider lying across its saddle. The slaves near the oak saw them coming, and a roar rose from them that frightened Marie into reining in.

George halted beside her, breathless now. "Come away, Madame."

"Tell me what is happening!"

He met her gaze this time, eyes narrowing. "No."

Marie was shocked. George had never defied her, not in the smallest thing. Something was terribly wrong.

She started forward again, determined to find out for herself what George would not tell her. The horsemen reached the tree, and the slaves pulled the limp body down from the saddle. Marie urged the mare to a trot. The figure was tied up, she thought as she came closer. It was a white man. It was Shelton; she saw his face, eyes alive with terror, before it was swallowed by the mass of black bodies.

Damien glanced up and rode toward her, blocking her way. "Go back, Madame," he said in a voice she did not recognize.

"What are you doing?" she demanded, aware that she sounded panicked. She took a deep breath and tried for a calmer tone. "Damien, what is the meaning of this?"

"Unfinished business. It need not concern you."

"It does concern me! This is my land, those are my slaves, and that man was once in my employ! I will be held responsible for anything—"

"No one will know."

His tone chilled her. She stared at him, realizing this man, whom she thought she had known, was a stranger.

Damien's eyes were hard and flint-sharp. "He followed Zeb from town again, but he got lost this time. Poor man. He fell into the river, we think, but no one saw. No one saw anything."

"Damien, no—"

"Go back, Madame. Go home to Belle View. You did not come to Angola today."

A shout from hundreds of voices drew their attention to the oak. Someone had thrown a rope over one of its branches, and Marie gasped as a dozen hands hauled on it, pulling Shelton by the neck high above the field where he kicked at the air. The slaves cheered and danced. The men on the rope began lowering Shelton and for a moment Marie thought she might yet have a chance to save him, but they were only bringing him within reach of those on the ground, who crowded toward him swinging clubs, tree branches, axe handles—anything they could use to hit back at the man who had tormented them. Marie put a hand to her mouth. She felt sick, but could not look away from the horror. The mare, aware something was wrong, let out a nervous neigh.

In a few minutes Shelton stopped thrashing, but the slaves continued to beat at him. Marie sat stunned in the saddle, staring at the mangled body, now swinging back and forth as the slaves hit it with their clubs, making a game of it. Finally the neck gave way and the head and body fell separately to the ground. A moment later the head appeared impaled on the end of a stick, bobbing above the crowd of cheering, dancing slaves.

Marie looked at Damien, finding her voice. "This was wrong."

He turned stony eyes toward her. "Do not tell me you wish he was still alive."

She shook her head. "I loathed him, but this was wrong. Evil will come of this."

"Pardon, Madame, but you know nothing of evil."

Damien held her gaze a moment, then slowly rode away. Marie watched him go to the five riders who had brought Shelton to his doom. She looked at the seething, dancing crowd of slaves, parading their grisly trophy about the fields, and wondered with a shiver of fear if she would be next. She glanced toward Big George, who sat silently watching her.

"Ready to go home, now, Madame?"

Marie swallowed. The sun beat down hot on her back, on the gleaming black bodies dancing in the field, and on the young sugar plants below. She hated this, she realized. This was wrong. She could not blame her slaves for their wrath. Had she been one of them, she would have done the same. It must cease, this wicked practice. It must end.

Shelton was gone, but that was not enough. This field had drunk blood before, probably more than she had ever imagined. One white man's blood would not begin to make up for it.

She closed her eyes briefly, then nodded. She would go home and pray for forgiveness, for all the wrongs she had done and for those that had been done in her name. Despite the sun's heat, she shivered as she turned the mare back toward the river.

Jamie stood with Sergeant O'Niell in the woods near the riverbank, frowning at the splintered wreck that had been the howitzer's gun carriage. Today's exchange with the gunboats had been brief, but a lucky shell from a Yankee gun had dismounted the howitzer and shattered the axle and one wheel of its carriage. The tube was all right, but there was no way to get it back into service.

"We could lash it onto the limber," O'Niell suggested.

Jamie shot him a doubtful look, imagining dragging a useless tube around for weeks and months. As far as he knew this was the only mountain howitzer remaining in all of Taylor's artillery. There were no replacement carriages to be had, and not likely to be any. With more captured Yankee guns available than men to fire them, it would be foolish to keep the howitzer merely for sentimental reasons. His horses would be better employed in hauling a serviceable gun.

Jamie stepped toward the howitzer, which was leaning crazily on the ruined wheel, and ran a hand along the tube. It was still a bit warm from the last time it had been fired. Beneath his fingers the names of Valverde's honored dead were engraved in the bronze. His hand went to Martin's, as it always did.

Footsteps approaching made him look up. Major Semmes came toward them and Jamie straightened and saluted.

Semmes looked at the gun. "Done for, eh? Well, you will have to leave it. We are moving tonight. The Yankees have camped about five miles up the river road. The general wants to make a stand near DeRussy tomorrow."

Jamie nodded, disliking the orders, but there was not much to like about the way this campaign was ending. The Yankees outnumbered Taylor's army four to one—too many to attempt to defeat them in a general engagement. While Taylor had succeeded in stopping their advance on Shreveport and had chased them back out of the Red, he could not destroy them. All the army could do was see them to the door and wish them good riddance.

It made Jamie angry. He had lost too much—Louisiana had lost too much—to be content with letting the Yankees go. They had burned Alexandria as they left it, an entire city razed for no reason except spitefulness, its residents cowering on the levee with their few remaining possessions in piles at their feet as they watched their homes eaten up by the flames. The Yankees had pillaged and burned their way all down the river, leaving not even the lowliest slave cabin untouched, and Taylor's army did not have the strength to do more than snap at their heels.

Semmes left, and Jamie looked out at the river where an hour before he had fired on the passing gunboats. Their dams up at Alexandria had worked and all of the Yankee boats had escaped, another source of dissatisfaction. If more troops had been given to Taylor, he might have had the strength to capture the Yankee boats. With a few of those gunboats, the Mississippi might have been freed from the Yankee stranglehold.

If wishes were horses. Jamie grimaced, then stepped toward the riverbank, looking down at the water. Here in the lower Red it was deep, filled with backflooding from the Mississippi which dimmed its brilliant rusty color a little. The bank he stood on was only about four feet above the water.

"O'Niell, hitch your team to the limber, then have your men assemble here."

"Yes, sir."

O'Niell went away, and Jamie got up on Cocoa and rode to Schroeder to order him to limber up the 6-pounder. When that was done he summoned all the men of his section to the riverbank. He looked them over as they gathered there: tired, dusty, somewhat dispirited but not yet ready to quit. Of the forty men he had first brought from Texas more than a year ago, twenty-three were left. Many of them had been with the army in New Mexico where the guns were captured and the Valverde Battery first formed. Those who had joined the battery since were yet fully aware of the blood that had been shed for its guns.

It was Sunday, Jamie realized with mild surprise. It had been so long since there was time for religious observances that Sunday had become like any other day. He did not consider himself a fit person to lead any such, but it felt right to be doing this on a Sunday. Not being much of one for speeches, he planned to keep his short. When all the men were assembled he stood beside the howitzer to address them.

"You all know the history of this gun. We can no longer take it with us, and I don't want the Yankees to lay their hands on it." He paused for the rumble of agreement to subside. "So we'll spike it and throw it in the river. If we get an opportunity to come back for it, we will. Anybody wants to take a last look at the names, now's your chance."

He stood aside and watched as the men filed forward to touch the gun, some squatting down and running fingers along the tube to find a favorite name. O'Niell came to stand beside him.

"Sorry, Evan," Jamie said.

O'Niell nodded understanding. "Has to be done. I'm glad you are not leaving it to the Yanks." He took out his pocket diary and made a note of their position. "Just in case we get back," he said with a rueful grin.

The sun was starting to set as O'Niell stepped to the gun and called its crew forward. With ceremony the number three man dropped a spike into the vent, the number two struck it with the handspike, and the number one drove his rammer down the barrel, bending the spike inside. Four cannoneers came forward and lashed ropes around the tube. It weighed only a couple hundred pounds, so it was easy enough for them to lift by the ropes and carry to the river-bank. At O'Niell's direction they swung it back and forth, building up momentum until with a shout they let it fly out over the water, trailing the ropes like fluttering pennants. The tube gleamed gold as the setting sun hit it, then struck the water a dozen yards out from the shore and sank without a trace.

Jamie and his men stood silent, gazing at the river where the gun had disappeared. Not until the sun had set and the light began to fade did they turn to their one remaining gun and start for the next place from which they would harass the Yankees.

31

I enclose two notes I received from Generals Banks and Stone. There is a faint attempt to make a victory out of this, but two or three such victories would cost us our existence.
—David D. Porter, Rear-Admiral, U.S. Navy

The *Cricket* slipped out of the Red and into the Mississippi just before midnight on May the 15th. Nat eased her up to the side of the *Black Hawk* and signaled all stop to the engine room as the deck crew made her fast to the larger vessel. His duty done, he could not help looking toward the east bank and Rosehall. A waxing moon hung above it, setting the white columns aglow, though no lights were showing across the vast water of the Mississippi.

Such a wealth of water was almost overpowering after weeks spent scraping around in the upper Red. The gunboats and transports all had plenty of room now, though in order to get over the falls the ironclads had been forced to remove their armor and leave it behind. It had given the crews something to do while they waited for the dam to be rebuilt and additional dams to be thrown out higher up in the falls to raise the water in the channel. Ultimately they had all escaped, and that was enough of a victory.

The *Benton* was present among the vessels at anchor in the river. Nat had expected this, and had already obtained Gorringe's permission to visit her. He had reached a decision about how to assist Adams.

Now, though, he went below, hoping to see Admiral Porter and wish him farewell before he transferred his flag to the *Black Hawk*. Though Porter certainly had his faults Nat had found him inspiring as a commander, and liked his brusque humor. He was sorry to see him leave the *Cricket*.

He arrived at the door to Porter's stateroom simultaneously with a tall, dark-haired, and clean shaven gentleman in the uniform of an army major-general. Nat hastened to step back with a deferential nod. The general smiled and quietly thanked him, then knocked on the stateroom door. It was opened by an aide.

"Yes, sir?"

"I am General Canby. I came to pay my respects to the admiral."

"Yes, sir! Of course, please come in."

Resigned, Nat started to turn away but was stopped by Porter's voice from within the room. "You there! Wheat! Come in here a moment."

Nat glanced at the aide, who swung open the door. Stepping in Nat saw Porter, who had lately been ill, packing up his correspondence. Nat thought he looked extremely tired.

Abandoning a heap of papers on his desk, the admiral came forward to greet his ranking guest, shaking his hand. "How do you do, General? I cannot tell you how pleased I am to welcome you. This district desperately wants a competent commander."

"Thank you, Admiral. Allow me to congratulate you on extricating your fleet from a difficult position."

"Thank you, yes—though the credit goes to Colonel Bailey. We will talk more of that anon. Let me introduce you to the young fellow who piloted this vessel past a Rebel battery with a seven-inch splinter in his side. Mr. Wheat, this is Major-General Canby. He is to replace General Banks."

"That is not quite the case," the general temporized. "General Banks's district and some others are being consolidated. He will continue to serve under me. How do you do, Mr. Wheat?"

Nat shook Canby's hand, finding his grip firm and friendly. "I am honored to meet you, General." He turned to Porter. "I do not wish to take up your valuable time, sir—I only wanted to wish you well, and to say that I hope you are feeling better."

"Kind of you. I have told Gorringe to send you home while the *Cricket* is on the ways at Cairo. No sense in having you sit about eating your head off at the navy's expense."

Nat laughed. "Thank you, sir."

"What more may I do for you?"

Seizing the chance he had hoped for, Nat smiled. "Nothing, sir, unless you would care to put in a kind word for my brother with Admiral Farragut."

"That's the brother who served on the *Harriet Lane*? The one who helped our friend Mrs. Hawkland sell her cotton?"

Nat felt his cheeks flush. "Yes, sir."

Porter laughed. "I'll mention him, and never mind the cotton. We have more important business."

Nat looked up at him, curious. "Does that mean you will not be visiting Belle View again?"

The admiral's eyes narrowed. "Quite right. I have had enough of Belle View for the present, though who knows. Perhaps we will return. In the meantime we will give Madame something to remember us by, and content ourselves with that. Good luck to you, Wheat."

Porter offered a hand, and Nat shook it. "Thank you, sir. It has been an honor to serve with you."

The admiral smiled and turned his attention to General Canby. Thus dismissed, Nat retreated, wondering exactly what Porter had meant by "something to remember us by."

He left the *Cricket* and ordered the yawl's crew to make for the *Benton*. A few words with her XO got him permission to borrow Adams, though he received a curious look as well. He did not bother with explanations. The *Benton*'s officers had no need to know his plans; they affected the *Cricket* only, and he had already made arrangements with her captain for what he intended to do.

Adams appeared on deck, frowning as he blinked away sleep. Nat directed him to enter the yawl.

"We have an errand ashore."

Adams glanced toward Belle View, and Nat nodded. "That's right. Come along, we have no time to waste."

Adams climbed into the boat and sat in the stern, where Nat joined him. Leaning forward, Nat spoke quietly into his ear.

"How much money have you got?"

Adams gave him a sharp look, then whispered back. "Here? Twenty-seven dollar."

"Give me eighteen, that will even the figure." Nat took a rather heavy cloth purse from his pocket and quietly showed it to Adams. "I have borrowed from the paymaster against my prize money, and collected a few donations. I will give you a list of the men you should thank and may wish to repay."

"You borrowed eight—"

"No," Nat whispered back, glancing at the oarsmen. "Not nearly. But I think it will be enough. We will make sure that it is."

Adams stared at Nat, his look of painful hope so intense that Nat had to smile. A moment later the negro dug in his own pockets and squinted at a small handful of coins in the light of a setting quarter-moon, picking out several to give to Nat, who put them in the purse and restored it to his vest pocket.

"But what will I do—"

"I have everything arranged," Nat said quietly. "The *Cricket's* ward-room needs a laundress. She will not object to that for a short while, will she? Just until we reach Cairo."

"Can't keep her in Cairo."

"I know. I will take her on to Cincinnati and find her a place there until your enlistment is up. When is that?"

"Two months."

"Good. When you are free come to Cincinnati and apply for a job at Wheat's Shipyard. I believe you will get it, with your experience. I will do what I can to help."

Adams swallowed. "Why? Why you doing this?"

Nat hesitated, wondering which of several reasons had tipped the balance. A wish to make up for past prejudice, perhaps, or to be free of indebtedness for Adams's saving him from the steam aboard the *Queen*. He suspected, though, that it was the way Mrs. Hawkland had used his brother—hurt him, really—that he most wanted to address. As a gentleman he would not actually harm her—to do so would rob the act of any satisfaction—but he would gladly inconvenience her, and shame her if he could.

To Adams he said merely, "You did me a service. Now I am able to return the favor."

Marie started awake at the sound of heavy pounding on the front door. Hurried footsteps belowstairs were followed by voices, some loud and insistent. Getting up, she pulled on her dressing gown and over it a heavy robe. Lucinde appeared in her night wrap as Marie was stepping into her slippers.

"Who is it?"

Lucinde caught up a lace cap from the dressing table. "Yankee sailors, Madame—one I think was here before, and Little George is with him."

Pausing, Marie let Lucinde place the cap on her head while she thought through the possibilities of what might happen next. She heard Alphonse's strident tones rising up from below, vibrating with indignation. It brought from her a grim little smile, though there was little to be amused at. She retrieved her pistol from the drawer of her bedside table, checked it, and slipped it into the pocket of her robe.

Leaving her bedchamber she looked into the nursery next door where Sarah was sitting up, rocking the cradle with her foot to soothe Théo, who had been wakened by the noise. The girl cast a frightened glance toward Marie.

Stepping to the stairwell, Marie stood listening. In a moment she heard someone coming up the stairs. At the landing a dark figure appeared—Victor, carrying a candle. He glanced up at her and hesitated. Marie beckoned him to come up. He did so, looking nervous but managing a bow, and addressed her quietly.

"Madame, a Mr. Wheat desires to speak with you at once. He says he is from the U.S.S. *Cricket,* and he has brought some men with him . . ." A fleeting look of anger crossed the footman's face. "Alphonse is staying in the hall, Madame, and Zeb has gone to fetch Damien."

"Very good. Thank you, Victor. You may tell Alphonse that I will be down presently."

She watched him return downstairs at a slow pace, nearly as stately as Alphonse would have done. When the light from his candle faded away from the stairwell she waited still, counting slowly to one hundred. Lucinde had kindled her own candle and brought it out to her. She accepted it, and slowly descended.

Light glowed from a branch of candles on a table near the front doors. Victor stood there, and the sound of voices and shifting feet on the gallery outside told her why. Just inside the hall Alphonse had placed himself like a bristling terrier before the Yankee sailor and Little George, blocking them from intruding farther into the house. Marie crossed the darkened hall toward them. She addressed Mr. Wheat.

"I trust you have some explanation for awakening my household at this hour."

"My apologies, ma'am, but my boat will leave before dawn and our business with you is urgent."

She stared at him, aware that she was frowning, wondering how he planned to induce her to yield Sarah up to him. The back doors opened and with a glance she saw Damien and Zeb come in, Damien with his shotgun. Grateful for their presence, she turned.

"Come into the parlor, then. It is drafty here."

The butler lifted the candelabrum and carried it into the parlor. Marie followed him, leaving Victor and the others in darkness. She set her candle on a side table, then walked to the fireplace and turned to stand before it. She did not invite Mr. Wheat or Little George to sit, but waited while Alphonse carefully lit candles on the mantel, the tables, the sconces, until the room blazed with light. When he finally walked out to take up a position in the hall, Marie spoke.

"What is your urgent business, sir?"

Mr. Wheat, whose jaw had begun to tick with impatience, looked at her with narrowed eyes. "We are here to purchase the freedom of your serving-girl, Sarah."

"And if she is not for sale?" Marie said softly.

"I think you will sell her." The Yankee sailor reached into his coat. Marie's heart stirred with fright and she put her hand into her pocket to grasp her pistol, but released it when she saw the Yankee withdraw a bulging purse from his coat. He dropped it into his other hand with a chink of metal. Coin, not paper. Not promises.

"I am offering four hundred dollars."

Marie swallowed, looking from the purse to Wheat's face. "She is worth twice that."

A mirthless smile curved his lips. "Maybe, but I'll wager you have not seen four hundred in specie for many a day." He walked to the sofa and spilled the purse's contents onto it, gold and silver glinting in the light of many candles.

Marie paced slowly from the cold hearth to the curtained window and back, resisting the impulse to stare at the money. A glance had told her that the amount was what Mr. Wheat had claimed, or near enough. The uses to which she could put that money silently assailed her, tormenting her as the sight of a feast would rack a starving man.

The sailors watched her in silence. Mr. Wheat was quite correct in his presumption that her financial straits would make his offer attractive. She suspected he was also capable of coercion; there was a suggestion of ruthlessness about him. Doubtless that was why he had brought with him the men who stood outside. She wished she knew their number, and whether they were armed. She had but four manservants, with one shotgun and her pistol ready. The only other within call of the house was Cook. Marie smiled inwardly at the thought of the old woman brandishing her kitchen knives, but realized at the same moment that Cook would not necessarily fight to retain Sarah. Perhaps none of them would, or at best would only make a show of it. Swallowing this uncomfortable thought, she looked past her uninvited visitors toward the hall.

"Victor, come here."

The footman came to the parlor door. She saw Damien standing in the shadows just behind him.

"Fetch Sarah down."

Marie turned away from Wheat's smile of triumph, from Little George's delight, and walked once more to the window. The little dog statue that Theodore had loved stood there. She picked it up, turning it over in her hands, running her fingers along its glossy edges. In silence they all waited until a few minutes later Sarah appeared in the doorway, carrying Théo. Marie put down the statuette and came forward to take him, shushing him softly as he fussed at being moved.

"Sarah, this gentleman has offered to purchase your freedom."

The girl looked not at Wheat, but at Little George. She ran two steps toward him, then stopped and turned. "M-may I take my other dress, Madame?"

"Yes, yes. Go and fetch your things." Marie watched the girl go, then turned to Mr. Wheat. "If you will wait here I will draw up a bill of sale."

Wheat's lip curled downward but Little George quickly said, "Yes, thank you, Madame." He met his friend's gaze and added, "She will need it to prove she is free."

The sailor's contempt changed to uncertainty, which afforded Marie some small satisfaction as she left them and went to her study. Mr. Wheat seemed not to understand completely the matters in which he was meddling. She wondered if he had agreed to house the girl, and how much of the gold he had brought for her price had come from his own pocket.

She set Théo in his downstairs cradle while she finished writing out the bill. She would have to ask Lucinde to care for him until something else could be arranged.

Suddenly weary beyond measure, she set down her pen and dropped her face into her hands, assaulted by conflicting feelings. She would miss Sarah, not only for her usefulness but because she had been a good nurse to Théo and a loyal servant, really. She was angry at losing her, yet she found she was also glad for Sarah's sake. The girl would now be free to make her own life and her own family.

She felt as if she were letting her slaves go one by one, setting them adrift like leaves on the river, seeing others fly with the wind and not having the heart to try to keep them. It was frightening; it made her feel helpless, yet she knew beyond doubt now that she wanted to be free of slavery. Perhaps the only way that could occur was through her own financial ruin.

She looked up at Theodore's portrait, feeling he would disapprove, that he would want her to fight to keep what she owned. Doubtless he would have done so. He was not here, however. This was her problem, and she must resolve it in her own way. All she truly cared about was that her son would have a home.

She went to the cradle and picked Théo up, hugging him tightly. He was the most important thing in her life, now—not cotton, not profit—just Théo. She would live for him, as she had pledged to do in her grief a year ago. She would hold on to what she could for him, but not through the possession of slaves. His life would be free of that stain.

Anxious now to release Sarah, she caught up the bill of sale and hastened back to the parlor. Mr. Wheat was there, looking up at her portrait above the mantel. Sarah and George stood a little apart and had obviously been talking, but fell silent as Marie came in.

She held out the bill to Mr. Wheat, who accepted it, read it over, then handed it to Little George. He then placed the empty purse in her hand, glancing toward the scatter of coin.

"You have chosen wisely, ma'am. We could have taken her without paying you a cent."

Marie held down a flash of anger, kept her voice cool and level. "Do you think you would have done so without a fight?"

His eyes met hers—cold, blue eyes, intense with thoughts she could not read. "You may have more of a fight on your hands than you realize."

Marie drew a breath. "What do you mean?"

He paused as if debating what to say, and she saw his expression soften slightly. When he did speak his words were measured. "I know you are not loyal to the Union, ma'am, and I am not the only one who knows it."

He held her gaze briefly, as if to emphasize the few words he had given her. She was chilled by them and at the same time wanted more, but knew that he had said all he would.

He signaled to Little George that they should leave. Sarah came shyly toward Marie, looking down at Théo with eyes full of fondness.

"Good-bye, Monsieur Théo. Good-bye, Madame—and thank you."

"Good-bye. You will soon have bébés of your own to care for."

Sarah looked up at her, a smile fleeting across her face before she turned to leave with the two men. Marie remained in the parlor, watching them go. A shaft of moonlight spilled into the hall as they went out the front door.

"Bon chance," she called softly just before Zeb shut the door behind them, bolting out the moon.

For a moment she stood still, listening to footsteps leaving the gallery and going down the drive, indiscernible voices fading into the night. When all was silent, she stepped out into the hall.

Lucinde had come down and stood near Damien. Marie beckoned to her and handed Théo into her arms.

"Take him back to bed, please. I must ask you to help me with him for now."

"Of course, Madame. I cared for his maman, I will care for little Monsieur also."

The gentleness in her voice made Marie's throat tighten with gratitude. She looked at her old nurse, the slave who had been hers longer than any other, and spoke in a voice that sounded very small to her. "I hope you will not leave me, Lucinde. I will try to find a way to pay you."

The soft, dark eyes met hers, the ghostly smile on her lips the same that Marie remembered from earliest childhood. "Where would I go, cher?"

Turning, Lucinde carried Théo away, murmuring to him as she went upstairs. The other servants in the hall looked toward Marie and she nodded dismissal, then slowly returned to the parlor. Kneeling on the floor beside the table, she scooped the coins back into the purse, picking up one or two that had fallen to the carpet. She counted them, finding the sum exactly what Mr. Wheat had claimed. Fingering the last few coins before dropping them into the purse, she was conscious of how much they meant to her, and also of how little they would do toward the larger problem of retaining her property. She rose and carried the purse to her library to put it away, wondering what Mr. Wheat's warning could mean. The thought of Dr. Montreuil's plantation, burned to the ground by the Yankees, made her pause before opening the desk. Instead she clutched the purse to her, and finding her knees weak she sank into the chair, listening to the ticking of the hall clock in the silent house, wondering what the dawn would bring.

Just before daylight, Jamie stood holding Cocoa's reins as the flatboat they were on made its way across the Mississippi, crossing at a bend between the mouth of the Red and Bayou Sara that was out of view of the Yankee boats at either place. With him were a dozen of his men, each with an artillery horse under saddle. When Major Semmes had asked for a volunteer to lead a scouting party across the river, Jamie had leapt at the chance. His task was to find a spot on the east bank where a battery might be placed to harass the enemy. His personal goal was, if possible, to get up to Belle View.

The closer Taylor's army had come to the big river, the more Jamie's thoughts had turned to Mrs. Hawkland. He had reached a decision last night, after the fight at Yellow Bayou which was probably the last of the campaign. Despite this brisk turn-up, the Yankee army had succeeded in crossing the Atchafalaya and getting to their transports on the Mississippi. Even now they were steaming away—some down to New Orleans, some up to Vicksburg to rejoin Grant. It was over.

Sitting up, sleepless, tending his section's sole campfire, Jamie had realized he must try to see Mrs. Hawkland once more. He was heartsick, still, from the loss of so many friends and comrades, and had been thinking of Cornay and of his wife and children, now without their father. He knew that he could be killed as easily and unexpectedly as Cornay had been, and he wanted to see his child once before that might happen. He had not the least idea what he would say to Mrs. Hawkland. He only hoped he could convince her fancy butler to let him in the door.

The boat reached the eastern bank and entered a little cove, where it scraped on a sandy landing below the bluffs. Jamie glanced up at them, wondering what was the fastest way up there. He might have to go all the way to the road through the woods. He hoped not.

"We will look for you at dusk," the corporal commanding the flatboat told him. "You remember the signal?"

"Yes. Thank you."

Jamie led Cocoa off the boat and waited until all his men were landed, then mounted and rode into the woods just as the sun was rising. He had less than a day. He would make the best use of it he could.

Marie sat in the music room, where she had taken to having her breakfast. The dining room was too large for her alone, and she still could not enter the parlor without a pang of sadness. She had caused the sofa in this room to be moved near the window, and sat sipping her coffee, gazing out at the Yankee boats on the river. There were quite a few of them today, though not so many as yesterday, when boat after boat had steamed out of the Old River and gone its way up or down. They had been steamboats, filled with soldiers. Whatever the Yankees had been doing in the Red River, they had finished and were now leaving.

She had heard vague reports—stories of atrocities—which she hoped were not true. She had grown accustomed to the idea that her cotton might be seized at any moment. She could survive that; she had more cotton planted and life would go on, though not in the

same way it had done. Almost a hundred of her slaves had run, now—
a dozen or so each night for the past week. Yesterday about fifty had
gone to the river and tried to flag down the army boats, begging to be
taken aboard. The boats had ignored them. Some had returned, the
overseers and drivers had retrieved others, but a number had fled
down the river. Marie knew that more would run. She wondered how
soon it would be before she had no field hands left. She had contemplated appealing to them, even offering them a share of the profits
from this year's crops if they would stay through the harvest. In the
end that was probably what she would be forced to do, if she was to
save any part of her holdings.

She got up and walked to the window. The dress she wore was a
traveling dress, the one she had worn on the steamboat to Shreveport,
and had dyed for mourning when she came home. She had put it on
thinking she would travel again today—to Killarney and the Creole
cottage there, which perhaps would be safer than Rosehall, though
she knew now there was really nowhere absolutely safe. Sighing, she
put her hand into the pocket of the skirt, and felt something there.

She drew out her hand and gazed at the little black bundle in her
palm. It took her a moment to realize what it was—the gris-gris that
Lucinde had pressed upon her that day, more than a year ago, when
she and Theodore had left here together. It had been dyed along with
the dress. She touched it with a fingertip, smiling sadly.

Lucinde came in carrying Théo, dressed and tidied after his morning feeding. He let out a chirp when he saw his mother. Marie sat
down again and held out her arms. Lucinde bent to give him to her,
and as she stood up Marie saw her glance toward the window.

"Madame!"

Lucinde turned a face of terror toward her. The next moment a
deep boom sounded, echoing on the river, followed by a crash nearer
by. Marie jumped up and went to the window.

One of the boats had moved out from the shore and turned to go
up the river. It was the very large boat, the one with two rows of guns,
and they were all protruding from their ports. Even as she looked,
several more fired, puffs of smoke billowing out from the boat.

Something slammed into a column outside the window where
they were standing, causing a shower of shattered plaster and brick
to rattle down on the gallery. Théo began to cry. Marie cast one glance
at Lucinde, then they both ran from the room, toward the back of the
house.

More cannons fired. Marie heard a ripping crash from the old oak out front as she hurried across the hall. The chandeliers rattled as something thumped through the outer wall and bounced along the floor upstairs. Glancing apprehensively at the ceiling, she ran to the rear doors, intending to get Théo out of the house, into the woods. She paused and looked back as a rising shriek drew her eyes toward the front of the house. The next moment the rose window shattered, hurtling colored glass throughout the hall.

Jamie urged Cocoa to a gallop the moment the gunfire began. He had been leading his scout up the bluffs, staying within the woods just east of the road, but now he broke out of them onto the better footing. Cocoa's hooves scraped at the steep road and she slowed, though she gave him her best. At the top of the bluff he reined in and signaled to his men to stay below, out of sight. His position was exposed, the woods giving way almost immediately to cane fields. The height of the bluff and the lack of foliage afforded him an excellent view of the land. Though he could not see the river he saw cannon smoke rising upstream, and judged it to be near the mouth of the Red. With a sinking horror he realized that the Yankee gunboats—some of them the very boats he had recently fired upon—were shelling Rosehall.

"Stay here!" he shouted to his men, and whistled Cocoa up to a gallop. The men would be all right where they were. If he didn't come back, they would know to return to the river at dusk.

Jamie rode up the river road, toward the noise of the shelling. Reason had not completely left him for he knew he was being reckless and stupid, but he did not care. Time seemed to pass too slowly and too quickly at once. He could not go fast enough, seemed hardly to be moving at all, and every second more guns hurled their shells at the house.

Nat stood watching the fleet pound away at the graceful mansion east of the river. The *Cricket* would be one of the last vessels to get underway, which gave him leisure to observe the bombardment and to wonder whether Mrs. Hawkland had escaped. He found he didn't much care; he had given her warning, which perhaps was more than she deserved. She was no longer his concern.

He turned away from the destruction being wrought by the fleet's guns, wrinkling his nose at the smell of powder that drifted to him on the morning breeze, and sat on the pilot house bench. Taking out his pocket notebook and pencil, he began to compose a letter he should have written long ago.

"Dear Father," he wrote, "I am being sent to Cincinnati on recuperative leave for a wound to the rib which I received during an attack on our boat in the Red River. Do not frighten Mother with this news. I am all right, only a little sore and temporarily limited in my ability to move."

He paused, chewing on the end of his pencil as he tried to suppress the anger that was rising in him. For himself he cared little whether his father ever forgave him, but for the sake of others—his mother, Renata, Adams and his Sarah—he had to try to make amends. For Charlie's sake, too. Whatever their differences, his father and Charlie had loved each other, even as did he and Quincy. Sometimes such love never found its way into words, but it was there nonetheless. He bent to write again.

"I believe I understand a little better now your reasons for not wishing your sons to serve in the Navy. I would like to talk more of this with you when I am home. I do intend to serve out the war, after which I hope to be at liberty to make myself useful in the shipyard. I look forward to discussing with you the possibility of my taking a position there, understanding that it may not be the one you were so kind as to offer me last year."

Nat read over the words, feeling a weight lift from him. He hoped, when his father read them, he would feel the same. Nat would not rule out piloting altogether, but he had made his point in that respect, and now it was time to think of those with whom he hoped to share his future.

A bell rang, demanding his attention. Putting the notebook away, he stood and went to the wheel, ready to pilot the *Cricket* away from the Red River, where he hoped she would never return.

By the time Jamie got near Rosehall, Cocoa was almost winded and he let her drop to a trot for a short rest. The bombardment had ceased; the boats were now proceeding up the river, all but one that looked as though it was anchored and had no intention of leaving. He would have to take his chances with that one. At least it wasn't firing.

Jamie looked toward the house, and his gut lurched. The walls had been struck in dozens of places. Some gunner had found the big stained glass window too tempting a target; it, along with every other window he could see, was smashed. A huge gap was torn out of the upper balcony, and some of the upper windows were scorched as if there had been a fire. He saw no flames now, though.

He reached the end of the cotton fields and turned off the road into the woodlands that bordered Rosehall's grounds. Riding within the meager screen of pecan trees, he kept a wary eye on the river but saw no activity from the boat. He asked Cocoa to run again and she responded as best she could; he knew she sensed his urgency. When he reached the top of the drive he flung himself from the saddle and left her to catch her breath, running to the house and up steps covered in rubble. A large chunk of one wall had been shot away, enough to make him worry about whether the structure would hold up. One of the great pillars was nearly shot through, the bricks it had been made of—tiny triangular bricks that would fit in his palm—scattered over the porch and steps. Reaching the front doors—one of which was in splinters, the other hanging crazily from its lower hinge—he hesitated, then stepped in.

Glass crunched beneath his boots—bits of red, blue, green, and white—glinting in the light that came through the doors and broken windows as well as a couple of good-sized holes in the wall. He peered into the rooms to his right and left, but saw only broken furniture and more glass. Cautiously moving forward, he was brought up by the soft double knock of a shotgun hammer being pulled back.

He froze, then slowly raised his hands into the air. A large negro stood just within a doorway to his right, glaring at Jamie with the barrel aimed at his chest.

Jamie's breath came short and ragged. "Is she all right?"

The negro frowned. Jamie swallowed.

"Mrs. Hawkland. Is she all right?"

"C'est bien, George," said a woman's voice.

The slave raised his gun and turned toward the room. Jamie lowered his hands, breathing relief. He looked past the gunman and saw Mrs. Hawkland standing in her library, looking faintly surprised.

"What are you doing here?" she said.

Jamie swallowed. "I wanted to—to see you."

A slight frown creased her brow, then she looked at the negro. "George, that box is to go in the wagon. Would you take it outside, please?"

George shot Jamie a mistrustful glance, then stepped into the room. He went to the desk and leaned his shotgun against it, hefted a large crate of books and papers onto one shoulder, then picked up the gun and went out, glaring at Jamie as he passed him on his way to the back of the house.

"Come in," Mrs. Hawkland said.

Jamie entered the room, which looked less disturbed than the rest of the house, almost normal except for the papers scattered on the desk and an empty glass-fronted gun cabinet whose doors hung open. Mrs. Hawkland stood watching him. He could not think what to say, and stared stupidly at a smear of plaster dust on her black skirt. She glanced down and brushed at it with a hand, then favored him with a tiny smile.

"Forgive me for not offering you coffee. My cook is not at hand."

Jamie gave a nervous laugh at the absurdity of it. Her smile faded.

"Did you come with the boats?"

Jamie glanced in the direction of the river. "No! No, I—I came to find a place from which to fire on them, actually."

"Oh! Well, you have permission to use any place on my property that strikes your fancy."

Jamie laughed again, and this time she joined him. Glancing down at her hands, she folded them before her.

"I believe I owe you an apology," she said softly.

"Oh, no—I said such an awful thing—"

"I pushed you to it. I hope you will forgive me."

Jamie stared at her, unable to form a sentence, astonished that she cared at all for his forgiveness. Maybe she didn't and was just being polite. Even that surprised him—that she thought he was worth being polite to.

His gaze traveled over her, noting that the fabric of her dress was a little worn. The last time he had seen her she had been heavily pregnant. Now she was slender again, which brought disturbing memories to mind. She was as beautiful as ever, though her face was pale and showed strain just now. He looked away, trying to straighten out his thoughts.

"I-I just wanted to find out . . ."

"Whether it is a boy or a girl?"

Jamie inhaled sharply. She looked amused; she was laughing at him. He should not have come.

Mrs. Hawkland went to the back of the room, where there stood a cradle that Jamie had not noticed before. He watched her reach into it and pick up a baby dressed in a linen shirt. She came toward Jamie, smiling, and his heart felt like it was trying to turn somersaults. Dark, drowsy eyes peered up at him, vaguely curious.

"Would you like to hold him?"

Jamie tore his gaze away from the baby long enough to nod to her. She moved closer; he could smell her as he carefully accepted the child, leaning its head along his upper arm.

"I see you know how to hold a baby."

Jamie found his voice. "I have a little brother. Gabe." He stared at his son, his heart feeling ready to burst with amazement. The boy looked back at him sleepily.

"What is his name?"

"Théo." She stepped closer and tickled the baby's nose with a fingertip, making him wrinkle it. "Théodore le Normand Étienne Jacques Paul Hawkland."

Jamie looked sharply up at her. "Jacques?"

She met his gaze, then glanced down at the child. "Oui, Jacques."

Jamie drew a slow breath. "You must know a lot of people named Jacques."

"I do. There are several in my family. But I would not care to name my son for them." She glanced up at him again, smiling a little, and he felt his throat tighten.

"Thank you," he whispered.

Her smile grew. Jamie read possibilities in her eyes that he had not dared to dream of. A buried longing woke and flamed into desire. He tried to choke it down but could not. She seemed to sense it and drew back a little, then stepped forward to kiss his cheek. Without thought his hand went to her shoulder and his lips found hers. All his bound up feelings poured out; his free arm embraced her and he felt hers slide around him. Between them their child let out a small, questioning squawk. It broke the moment and she pulled back, blushing prettily, leaning forward to soothe Théo.

Jamie took a shaky breath. "When this war is over I will come back."

"I may not be here, cher," she said gently.

"Oh." He swallowed the knot that was forming in his throat. "Ma'am, I know we are from different worlds—"

"Not so very different anymore." She gave a little laugh, made a hopeless gesture with her hand. "It is likely I will lose some of my land. Perhaps all. The house is ruined, of course. I have another at Killarney Plantation, but I think that will not be safe for much longer either."

"I am sorry," he said. Her losses were not his fault, but he wished he could somehow have prevented them.

She shrugged, and for a moment looked as though she might crumble. Jamie had a sudden sense that a great weight was pressing on her slender shoulders, but she threw them back and raised her head, smiling defiantly.

"C'est la guerre."

She went to the desk, and while she opened it Jamie looked down into his son's eyes. Dark, like Emma's, and his hair curled like hers, though it was a little lighter and redder. He felt a big, stupid smile blooming on his face. Théo smiled back.

Mrs. Hawkland returned with a pencil and a piece of paper. She sat on the sofa and, using the table before it for a desk, scribbled on the page. "I have a house in New Orleans. I will keep it as long as I can. You may look for me there, if you do not find me here." She tore the top half off the paper and handed it to Jamie.

He glanced at the address. "Thank you."

She stood up and held out her hands for Théo, and Jamie gave him up. Settling him on one hip, she gestured toward the other half of the paper. "Let me know where to write to you, in case I must sell the house."

Jamie sat down and wrote out "James Russell, Russell's Ranch, San Antonio, Texas." He handed it to her. She looked at it, then tucked it into the pocket of her dress.

"Thank you, Jacques," she said, a glint of mischief in her eyes.

"Thank you . . ."

"Marie."

He smiled, looking from her to Théo. It hurt to feel as much hope as he did, knowing it might all be destroyed tomorrow. He would not have traded it, though. Not for anything.

Epilogue

Sunday, May 29, 1864
Alexandria, Louisiana

Dear Gabe,

Here I am at last wishing you a belated Happy Birthday and many happy returns of the day. This is the first chance I have had to write although you have been very much in my thoughts. We have been a little busy here and in consequence I have only just today received your letter of March 20th.

You ask if I would get you a place in my section if you were to join up. Gabe, I will tell you honestly that is the last thing I would wish to do. I have no doubt you could deceive the recruiting board as regards your age but leaving aside the dishonesty it would be a wasted effort. This war can now have only one conclusion, one not favorable to us. There are simply too many of them and we cannot beat them. We could not do it even if you and every boy of fifteen or even younger joined the cause. I have seen a great general and brilliant commander whip a Yankee army three times the size of his own, but he could not destroy them. They will overwhelm us. It is only a matter of time.

I know you are eager to contribute and maybe working on the ranch is a dull life right now, but I must tell you, Gabe, sometimes the only hope I have had is when I remembered that you, at least, will survive this war, even if all the rest of us fall. I will see it through to the end because that is my sworn duty, but I would not have you risk your life for no good purpose.

You will make your mark. There is time and enough for you to do so. The ranch will give you better chances at it than soldiering in this war ever will. That is not what you wished to hear from me but I can do no less than to give you the truth of my heart.

Please give my love to Momma, Poppa, and Emma. I think about all of you every day. If I have learned nothing else from soldiering, I have learned that nothing is more important than family.

Your loving brother,

Jamie

Author's Note

While this novel is based upon actual events, it is a work of fiction. Any inaccuracies or errors are solely mine. In some cases I have given to fictional characters the actions and positions held by real people. For example, Jamie Russell commands a section in the Valverde Battery, a real unit with a proud history. All the men in his imaginary section are fictional. In actuality the third section commander of the battery was Lieutenant William Smith.

Fictional characters in this novel include the Russell family (Jamie, Emma, Momma, Poppa, Gabe, Matthew, and Daniel), the Wheat family (Nat, Quincy, Mama, Nathaniel Wheat, Sr., and Uncle Charlie), Theodore and Marie Hawkland, Théo Hawkland, Lucinde, Damien, Sarah, George Adams, Victor, Alphonse, Shelton, all the Hawklands' slaves and overseers, Renata Keller and her family, Albert Lawford, May Asterly, Rupert, Daisy, and various minor characters.

Many characters, major and minor, represented in this book are real people. For any errors I may have made with respect to them, I humbly apologize. This work is intended as a tribute to their memory and to their gallantry.

With the exception of the shelling of Rosehall, all of the military actions depicted in *Red River* took place. While the Hawklands and Rosehall are fictional, the plantations of Belle View, Panola, Loch Lomond, Killarney, and Angola were real. This area, the confluence of the Mississippi and Red Rivers, was an important location throughout the war, particularly for Confederate communications, transportation, and trade. Its dark and violent history was reflected in the continuance of forced labor at Angola for many decades after the war as the land became the infamous Angola Prison, which is now the Louisiana State Penitentiary.

The Red River Campaign was a near-disaster for Federal forces, who never again attempted to take control of the waterway. The defense of Louisiana was a triumph against odds for Major-General

Richard Taylor, but the victory was hollow, as the Federal army wrought destruction all along their retreat in what became a rehearsal for General Sherman's devastating march across Georgia.

For more information about Civil War events west of the Mississippi, please visit *www.pgnagle.com.*

Suggested Reading

This short bibliography represents a selection of references that the author recommends to readers wishing to learn more about the Civil War in Louisiana.

Ayres, Thomas. *Dark and Bloody Ground: The Battle of Mansfield and the Forgotten Civil War in Louisiana*. Dallas: Taylor Trade Publishing, 2001.

Johnson, Ludwell H. *Red River Campaign: Politics and Cotton in the Civil War*. Kent, Ohio: Kent State University Press, 1993.

Josephy, Alvin M., Jr. *The Civil War in the American West*. New York: Alfred A. Knopf, 1991.

Mahan, A. T. *The Gulf and Inland Waters*. New York: Charles Scribner's Sons, 1881–1883 (facsimile edition, The Archive Society, 1992).

Raphael, Morris. *Battle in the Bayou Country*. Detroit: Harlo Press, 1975.

Taylor, Richard. *Deconstruction and Reconstruction: Personal Experiences of the Late War*. Nashville: J. S. Sanders and Company, 1998 (first edition published 1879).

Winters, John D. *The Civil War in Louisiana*. Baton Rouge: Louisiana State University Press, 1963.

About the Author

A native and lifelong resident of New Mexico, P. G. Nagle has a special love of the outdoors, particularly New Mexico's wilds, where many of her stories are born. Her historical novel, *Glorieta Pass*, and its sequel, *The Guns of Valverde*, are set during the New Mexico Campaign of the Civil War. The continued career of the Confederate Army of New Mexico is featured in *Galveston* and *Red River*.

Nagle's work has appeared in *The Magazine of Fantasy & Science Fiction* and in several anthologies, including collections honoring New Mexico writers Jack Williamson, who lives in Portales, New Mexico, and the late Roger Zelazny, who lived in Santa Fe. Her short story "Coyote Ugly" was honored as a finalist for the Theodore Sturgeon Award.